*****

Into the Stars

Book One of the Rise of the Republic Series

By
James Rosone

****

Illustration © Tom Edwards
Tom EdwardsDesign.com

Published in conjunction with Front Line Publishing, Inc.

Manuscript Copyright Notice

ISBN: 978-1-957634-04-3
Sun City Center, Florida, USA
Library of Congress Control Number: 2022902555

Table of Contents

Prologue

2050 A.D.

Following the end of World War III, most of the world lay in ruins. Nearly two billion people had died either in the conflict or as a result of the famine and global depression that had ensued in its wake.

With most of Asia and North America destroyed and their people starving, new governments came to power. The Asian Alliance took hold of what was left of Greater China, India, Japan, the Koreas, and the rest of Southeast Asia. The United States, Canada, Mexico, Central America, and the Caribbean formed the Republic. When the European Union merged with the Russian Federation to form the Greater European Union or GEU, the United Kingdom broke ranks and instead joined the Republic.

The Middle East became part of the GEU, making it the strongest trading and military bloc following the war. The African Union came to power shortly thereafter, aligning themselves with the Asian Alliance.

Sensing a potential new Cold War emerging, the political leaders agreed to a treaty aimed at uniting humanity with the shared goal of forming a colony on Mars. This treaty, which would bind all nations together to share technology, resources, and territory in space, became known as the Space Exploration Treaty or SET. It was the first significant piece of global law written to govern the conduct of humans in space, and it led to a new reign of global peace.

Chapter One
A New Era

2075 A.D.
Mars Orbital Station

Commander Miles Hunt turned his head slightly toward Dr. Katherine Johnson. "If this works, Doctor, it'll change the power dynamics of Sol."

Dr. Johnson smiled as she stared at the monitor, eyes darting from one system to another. "If this works, Commander, it'll change the future of mankind. It will open up the entire galaxy to us."

Hunt smiled at the implication but didn't say anything further. Like everyone else, he was a spectator right now. Whatever happened next, it was out of his hands.

"Aries Four, ready to begin," crackled a voice over the secured coms network. A video image of the synthetic humanoid who'd be flying the craft was displayed on one of the monitors. Commander Hunt noted again how realistic the features were on this advanced robot. With the exception of its facial features, which were devoid of the emotions that would be etched on a human face, one would never be able to tell the robot wasn't made of flesh and bone.

The tension in the room was thick. Everyone was on edge, unsure whether this fourth test would be successful. The mission control operator turned to look at Dr. Johnson as if asking for permission. She nodded.

Leaning in next to Commander Hunt, Vice Admiral Chester Bailey whispered, "If this test fails, the Senate may pull the plug on further funding. You're confident it'll work?"

Hunt turned his face slightly toward the admiral, who was the program manager for the entire Faster-Than-Light Program. He whispered back, "It won't fail, sir. It worked when we tested the unmanned drone a month ago. It'll work now."

Despite the previous success, Hunt did feel anxious. A lot was riding on this test. While Vice Admiral Bailey was the overall program manager, Hunt had been the project lead at DARPA for the FTL program out of the Mars facility. He'd spent the better part of six years on this project, and he'd fought tooth and nail to get it the funding it needed.

"It had better work," Bailey retorted in a quiet but stinging voice. "My ass is on the line." The vice admiral resumed his gaze at the monitors.

"Aries Four, Mission Control. You are a go for the mission. Good luck."

The brass from Space Command and several crucial senators from the Appropriations Committee stood there like everyone else, watching the video feed of the test craft. Commander Hunt could hear some hushed whispers among the crowd; some people expressed skepticism, some optimism. All of them were anxious to see if it would really work. Decades of research and more than four trillion dollars had been spent on the Aries project. After three spectacular failures, the project was running on borrowed time.

The radio crackled to life again. "Engines activated. Moving to test position now."

The first test of the Alcubierre drive had been conducted fifteen years ago, and it had ended when the ship and the pilot had blown up just as the warp bubble had begun to generate. No one had been sure why the ship had exploded or what had gone wrong. A year later, scientists had determined that the craft had failed to generate an energy-density field lower than that of the vacuum needed for the warp bubble to work—that was also the last human-operated test.

In the second test, six years later, Aries Two had successfully created the warp bubble but had detonated fractions of a second before it should have jumped. After years of studying the failed experiment, scientists still couldn't fully determine what had happened. Despite the failure, the test had proven that a warp bubble could be created, and the program was allowed to continue.

The third test, just three years ago, initially appeared to be a wild success—that was, until Aries Three dropped out of its warp bubble. It summarily blew up moments later, when the release of forward-facing particles destroyed the observation ship and equipment nearby and the mass of particles in its wake caught up to the craft, washing over it like a crashing wave and utterly destroying it. Fortunately, that had proved to be an easy problem to solve.

"Aries Four has now reached the test position. Running through the final system checks now," announced the synthetic humanoid test pilot, his voice devoid of emotion. "I'm activating the Alcubierre drive."

A moment later, the emotionless creature stated, "Engaging the Alcubierre drive now."

The group of scientists, politicians, and military leaders observed with keen eyes as Aries Four generated its warp bubble. For a moment, it looked like a bluish sparkly distortion of color against the blackness of space around it. Then it disappeared.

Moments later, the ship reappeared at its destination, near Venus. They'd chosen that location in case there was an accident, since there wasn't anything vital nearby that could get damaged if the ship blew up.

The entire room held their breath, waiting to see if Dr. Katherine Johnson and her team had finally solved the last technical challenge to making FTL travel a reality.

This is all just a dog and pony show, Commander Hunt reminded himself. What he knew that few in the room were aware of was that Dr. Johnson had successfully tested the FTL drive on an unmanned ship a month ago. This test was really just to ensure additional funding.

Time seemed to pause as they awaited confirmation from the observation crew on the other end that the ship had arrived and this new technology officially worked. A few seconds went by, then a minute, and still nothing. The short time delay in the video feed and communications caused everyone to keep their fingers crossed. Then, after a couple of additional messages passed between the Mars Orbital Station and the observers on the other end, the radio from the test craft crackled to life.

"This is Aries Four. All systems are still green. I'm showing no red lights and the ship detects no problems. Everything seems to be operating within normal parameters," announced the synthetic humanoid pilot.

The room broke out in cheers. People hugged each other and exchanged high fives and jovial handshakes. Mankind had just entered a new era—the era of deep space travel.

Admiral Bailey shook Commander Hunt's hand and drew him in closer so he could speak without the others hearing. "You did it, Miles," he said. "I'm proud of you. I won't forget this."

****

From *Reuters*:

> After twenty years of research and trillions of dollars invested, Dr. Katherine Johnson's team of researchers successfully tested the Alcubierre drive today. The test craft,

Aries Four, traveled from the Mars orbital research station to a point in open space near Venus, 108.2 million kilometers away. It took the test craft a mere four minutes to cover that distance.

The successful test of the faster-than-light drive, or FTL, means that humanity will now be able to explore deep space and beyond our solar system for the first time. Already, numerous governments are entering formal talks about assembling exploration teams to travel to Alpha Centauri and many other star systems thought to contain habitable planets similar to Earth.

From *The BBC Online*:

The Greater European Union has officially approved the technology transfer of the recently invented neurolink implant to the Republic in exchange for the Alcubierre drive technology. The President of the Republic said in a televised interview this morning that his country intends to honor the Space Exploration Treaty obligations. He also stated that the Republic will make the FTL technology available to those nations that are signatories to the treaty and work to ensure humanity shares in this success.

The head of the Asian Alliance has likewise announced that they would share their recent breakthrough technology in inertial dampening and artificial gravity, discoveries made by using the Chengdu Super AI last year. Many scientists and engineers believe these technologies are just as critical as FTL to future space travel and humanity's expansion into the stars.

Some analysts remain concerned about a potential new Cold War in space. However, the consensus is that their concerns have been alleviated by the willingness of the world governments to share this technology with each other. As it stands today, humanity now enters a brave new frontier of space exploration, united together in their quest to colonize the stars.

Chapter Two
Piracy Problems

CMS *Dolly*
Mars Belt Sector

The M-337 mining drone stabilized its position near the giant asteroid, releasing a couple of short puffs of gas. As the drone completed a final adjustment, the operator on the ship activated its cutting laser one last time, slicing into the chunk of ice to cut it free from the floating rock.

"Careful, Hank. That's a big piece of ice," Joshee said.

Is it just me, or does his Indian accent come out more when he's stressed? Hank asked himself.

He kept his eyes on the monitor. "Get the grappler ready," he ordered. "I've almost got it free." A bead of sweat ran down the side of his face. Hank's left hand moved up to brush the perspiration away, only to slap the face shield of his helmet.

Joshee snickered. "Forgot to put your do-rag on?" he asked jokingly.

Hank shook his head in frustration. "Yeah. I guess I was in too much of a hurry to get suited up."

"You know, maybe it's time to invest in a newer ship that doesn't require us to be in these damn EVA suits when we mine," Joshee suggested.

Hank ignored the comment. "The ice is free, Joshee. Activate the grappler and let's get that piece pulled into the hauler."

"Firing…good hit. Retracting the cable now," Joshee confirmed. Then he proceeded to give instructions to their synthetic humanoid worker. "Lola, when the ice reaches the loader, size it down with the cutter so it'll fit in the hauler. Then I need you to bring it back to the ship so it can be unloaded. Repeat the process until you've got that entire ice block on the ship."

"Yes, Grand Lord Exalted," the humanoid replied in its emotionless tone.

"Holy crap, Joshee. You can't keep having Lola calling you that. It's ridiculous," Hank chided.

Joshee let out a guttural laugh. "Oh, fine, party pooper. I'll change it when we're done. I just wanted to see what you'd say to my new title."

Hank just snorted.

"How long do you think it'll take her to cut that block down and start bringing it back?" Joshee asked.

"Long enough for you to get those other blocks moved into the refiner. Where is Jorge? He's falling behind," Hank asked, annoyed.

Joshee floated across the cargo hold past the open bay doors to the far side of the room. His hands grabbed for the pull bars near the large refiner. "He said something about needing an urgent bio break. Something about my cooking didn't sit well with him," Joshee explained. "I'll get the next set of blocks going until he gets back. Then we can go in and grab some food ourselves."

Hank chuckled. "I like your cooking, Joshee, but we should let our actual cook do the cooking when we're in the Belt. Sometimes your stuff is a bit spicy."

"You all said you wanted it hot."

"Hot, yes—not Indian hot," Hank countered. "There's a distinct difference."

Joshee used one of the mechanical arms in the bay to grab one of the one-square-meter blocks of ice Lola had brought in earlier in the day. The mechanical arm gripped the block and placed it in one of the large vats anchored along the inner wall of the cargo hold. Each of the six tanks could hold roughly thirty square meters of ice. Over the next few hours, the ice would be superheated and melted down. During that process, the water would be stripped of any minerals of value such as strontium clathrates or other essential isotopes. The remaining liquid would be loaded into storage vats until they returned to the Mars Orbital Station, better known as MOS—at least until BlueOrigin finished their processing facility located halfway between the MOS and the Belt.

It was a bit of a long and tedious process, but ice mining was a very lucrative business. Not a lot of people liked this type of mining, but the ones that went into it typically did well, so long as they were able to find a steady source of ice.

"Come on, Hank. Let's go eat." Joshee motioned for them to head back into the pressurized section of the ship.

Hank nodded. "Let me tell the drone to go find the next chunk of ice for us. That way, it'll be ready for us when we get back from our break."

Joshee tipped his head in agreement and turned around to make his way toward the airlock at the other end of the cavernous cargo bay. It was the downside to using the older ship—to operate the control arm, the hauler, or the mining drone, they needed to use the workstations in the cargo hold. The internal part of the ship wasn't very big. Space was limited, and they didn't have a separate workstation with the same functions as the ones in the much larger cargo hold.

The ship felt much larger than it was when the bay was sealed and pressurized, but when they had equipment outside the ship, they almost always left the bay doors open. It took a while to pressurize and depressurize the cavernous room, so they only did it when they were going to move to a new location.

When he was done with the drone, Hank turned to follow his friend Joshee. The guy had already reached the airlock and was waiting for him. He had a look on his face like he was about to tell him again that this ship was a hunk of junk and that they should upgrade to a newer ship, but he held his tongue this time.

Maybe he's right, Hank thought.

"What do you think of the new kid?" Joshee asked as they both floated into the airlock.

Joshee closed the door behind Hank and sealed it while Hank worked to repressurize the compartment they were in so they could gain entry to the rest of the ship.

"He's green, but I think we can teach him to be a good space miner," Hank muttered as he tapped on a couple of keys. There was a loud hissing noise as the compartment flooded with oxygen.

The light near the door changed from red to green, and Hank pulled up on the lever, opening the entrance to the corridor that led them further into the ship. The two of them used the pull bars interspersed throughout the hallway to pull and push themselves forward as they traversed their way through the ship. Eventually, they made their way to the cantina, where their cook, Ivan, had just finished preparing some food for the crew of seven.

The cantina also functioned as their dayroom and locker room. Along one of the walls, the crew had a wall locker, where their EVA suits were stored. They also had a TV and a couple of computer terminals. With no gravity on the ship, there wasn't a need for tables and chairs. People just floated around as they ate their food, watched TV, or played a video game.

The radio communicator attached to Hank's sweater chirped. "Hank, it's Eric. Can you ask Ivan if he'd bring me some food from the cantina?"

Hank tapped the sensor on his communicator. "I just got to the cantina, Eric. I'll bring it up myself once I've eaten. Give me fifteen minutes," Hank replied.

Ivan handed Hank a prepared container of food to eat. "Any word on when we'll be headed back to the MOS?" the cook asked. "We're starting to run a little low on consumables."

Hank's left eyebrow rose. "Really? We've only been gone for five weeks."

Ivan shook his head. "Hey, it took us two weeks to get here," he countered. "It'll take us at least two weeks to get home. I've only got roughly four weeks' worth of food."

"Then we've got enough for at least two more weeks of mining," Hank insisted.

"Did you guys find another good chunk today?" Ivan asked.

Joshee nodded. "We sure did. Hank here found two large chunks. We're nearly done with the first one. Lola is cutting up the second one and bringing it back."

"Sweet. Looks like this should be a good payday, then," Ivan commented.

"It should be indeed. Pack up a container for Eric, will you? I'll take it up to him in a few minutes," Hank directed.

"Sure thing," Ivan replied.

Hank ate his meal hastily. Just as he was getting ready to bring food to Eric on the bridge, his communicator chirped. "Hank! I'm showing a contact heading toward us!"

Hank shook his head. "Hey, calm down, Eric. This is nothing to be worried about. Look at the display and tell me what kind of contact it is."

Hank floated out of the cantina and toward the bridge as he waited for Eric to reply. This was Eric's first time alone on the bridge monitoring the area, and his inexperience was showing. Hank's wife had twisted his arm to get Hank to hire him—the kid was related to a friend of hers and in need of a job. Bridge duty was the safest job he could think of until they got him trained up in space mining.

"Um, I…I don't know," Eric stammered before adding, "It doesn't have one of those transponder thingies on it you told me to look for. It just showed up on the radar screen and looks to be heading toward us."

"What do you mean it doesn't have a transponder code? All ships have a transponder code. It's how we tell what kind of ship they are and who they belong to."

"I'm telling you, Hank, it doesn't have a transponder code," retorted the young man, annoyed that Hank didn't believe him.

Hank shook his head angrily. "I'm almost there. This had better not be a joke, Eric, or I'm going to be pissed. I've got better things to be doing."

Hank grabbed at the bars spaced throughout the corridors, pulling himself as he floated through the vessel. After making his way from the midsection of the ship, he finally arrived at the ladder section that would take him up to the bridge.

For a ship's nerve center, the bridge wasn't anything fancy to look at. It had chairs for the pilot and copilot, another for the radar and communications officer and that was it. Just behind the bridge was a room with additional chairs for the rest of the crew when the ship was in transit. Unlike on a warship, the bridge was ringed with windows, allowing them to see out.

Maneuvering over to the radar screen, Hank motioned for the kid to move so he could take a seat. He hurriedly scanned the monitor; the radar was making sweeps of the area around them, and sure enough, the ship Eric had found didn't have a transponder code.

What the hell? Hank asked himself. Every ship he'd seen had a transponder. The unique ship code identified which country the ship was from and what type it was.

"See? I told you it didn't have any identification," Eric said, feeling vindicated.

"Yeah, yeah."

Hank reached over for the headset and put it on. "Unidentified ship, this is the Republic mining ship *Dolly*. Please identify yourself."

A moment went by without any response to his hails. Hank changed to a wideband network, hoping that if his message was transmitted across more frequencies, these guys might hear him.

Maybe they're operating on a different channel than us…

Hank tried hailing them again. They were now approaching 230 kilometers and still closing on their position.

"See if you can use the camera, Hank," the kid offered.

Damn. Why didn't I think of that?

Panning the lens toward the ship, Hank zoomed in as much as the camera would allow. When he saw it, his heart skipped a beat. A sense of panic washed over him.

That's no friendly ship, he realized.

Hank reached for the handset that would connect him to the ship's onboard speaker system. "This is the captain. We've got a possible pirate ship heading in our direction," he announced. "I need everyone to secure what you're doing. Close the outer cargo hold immediately. I'm initiating an engine restart. Once we can get going, we're moving." They'd come back for the hauler and the mining drone if they managed to get away.

Pushing himself out of the radar/coms chair, Hank grabbed at the pull bars and moved about the bridge until he was able to spin himself into the pilot seat. Once seated, he proceeded to strap himself in as he started spinning up the engines.

The readout on the monitor told him he'd have his maneuvering thrusters ready in sixty seconds. It'd take another three minutes to get the main engines ready to engage.

Joshee joined him on the bridge along with Ivan, their cook. Ivan had spent a handful of years in the Republic Navy, and he operated their lone self-defense weapon. Joshee and Ivan took one look at the camera and the radar screen and clearly knew they were in trouble because they went speeding into action.

Hank turned to Joshee. "Get on the radio and send a distress message to any Republic ships in the area," he directed. "Make sure the MOS knows we're in trouble and send them our exact location."

"Everyone, get your helmets back on and hook your EVA suits up," Ivan said. "This could turn ugly, guys." He swiftly followed his own orders, reattaching his helmet and fastening the life support hose to his suit.

"Get that gun spun up and ready, Ivan," Hank exclaimed. "I'm about to initiate our engines and get us out of this place." As he spoke, he began using the maneuvering thrusters.

In another minute, the engines would be spun up and ready. Once they got out of the Belt, he'd run the engines up to full speed and try to outrun these guys.

"On it, boss."

Ivan flicked a couple of switches, activating their lone self-defense weapon. It was a single-barreled 20mm autocannon. At Ivan's behest, Hank had installed the autocannon a few years ago, on the off chance they encountered a pirate. They'd mounted it on top of the ship, near the crew compartment behind the bridge. That way, Ivan could quickly reload the magazine when it ran out of ammo.

The next sixty seconds went by in a blur as everyone performed their individual duties. They'd run through a few drills like this in the past. Judging by how long it was taking them to complete a few of their tasks, they probably needed to practice more often.

"They still aren't responding to our hails," Joshee said to Hank.

Now that they'd cleared a couple of the large asteroids, Hank gave the ship a bit more speed. However, they still had a few dozen more to get around before he could really open up the engines.

"Should I fire a warning shot?" Ivan asked.

"Everyone, seal your EVA suits up, get your helmets on, and strap in. We're going to make a run for it!" shouted Hank over the loudspeaker.

"Hey! Should I shoot, Hank?" Ivan asked again, louder this time.

"Yes. Fire a shot across its bow and see if that wakes them up," Hank responded hurriedly. He was busily steering them around another floating rock.

A second later, Ivan fired off two rounds. The 20mm slugs zipped right in front of the approaching vessel. They missed, but that was the intent—to let the other ship know they could defend themselves and hope it didn't come down to that.

Suddenly, the radio crackled, and a voice with a distinctly Irish accent spoke. "This is Captain Liam of the *Gaelic*. Stand down and prepare to be boarded. If you cooperate, no one will get hurt. If you fire on us again, we will return fire."

The individuals on the bridge all looked nervously at each other.

"Who the hell is that?" Joshee asked. "I've never heard of a Captain Liam or the *Gaelic*."

"Hang on, guys, I'm about to go full throttle on the thrusters," Hank announced. The ship swiftly picked up speed as he ramped up the power to the engines.

They were just opening up some distance between them and the pirate ship when Ivan shouted, "He's firing!"

The ship shook and rattled as it took a couple of hits. Alarm bells rang, and a series of red warning lights blinked on Hank's computer display.

"We've been hit. They're going after our engines!" Joshee yelled frantically.

"Return fire, Ivan. Try to take 'em out!" Hank bellowed. He tried to position one of the asteroids between them and the pirate ship. Chunks of rock broke off as a few of the railgun projectiles slammed into it instead of their ship.

Ivan depressed the trigger, firing half a dozen more slugs at the pirate ship. Hank knew he'd be aiming for the centerline of the vehicle in hopes of hitting something important. It was also easier to hit a larger target than a smaller one.

A couple of chunks of metal broke off from the pirate vessel. The ship executed evasive maneuvers to avoid the strings of slugs Hank's ship was sending their way. Ivan fired another dozen shots at the ship, and Hank hoped like hell that the pilot of the pirate ship would decide to break off its attack and go find someone else to prey on.

The pirate ship took a couple more hits. Ivan depressed the trigger to send another volley.

Click, click, click.

"I'm out of ammo. I've got to change out the magazine!" Ivan shouted as he unstrapped himself and floated out of his seat. He made his way over to the magrail's magazine, pulled the hundred-round magazine out and reached for a fresh one to attach in its place.

Joshee, who'd been watching the pirate ship, yelled, "Hurry up, Ivan! He's firing again. Brace for impact!"

Hank tried to turn the mining barge to the right with his emergency maneuver thrusters. He desperately tried to dodge the slugs being thrown at them as he applied power to their engines. This time, several objects ripped right through the hull of the mining vessel and into the crew compartment behind the bridge.

The bridge began a violent decompression. Air swirled out of the three-centimeter holes being punched through their home. As Hank turned to look back, geysers of frozen blood erupted from the puncture holes in several of his friends' environmental suits. The magrail projectiles tore right through their bodies like a hot knife through butter.

Seconds later, the bridge section around Hank sparked and flashed as more projectiles ripped through the area around him. One of the slugs tore through the side panel of the *Dolly* and severed his right arm and left leg as it continued through the ship. It took only a fraction of a second for Hank's suit to lose oxygen pressure. He died before his brain had a chance to register any pain.

With the crew dead and the ship disabled, the CMS *Dolly* went into a drift. Power on board the vessel flickered for a moment before it eventually turned off.

A short while later, a boarding crew took control of the ship. The pirates went to work stripping the ship of its cargo and anything else of value. Once they had taken what they wanted, they towed the vessel back to their lair using a tractor beam. They'd add it to the collection of ships they'd stolen, which they would either turn into pirate ships or use for scrap. With virtually no military or police force to monitor the Belt, piracy was becoming a booming industry.

****

Captain Liam Patrick looked at the list of what they'd just captured from the mining ship. There were a few tons of water and other refined isotopes and minerals. It didn't sound like much, but this haul would probably net them a good twenty or thirty million, plus an ice mining barge—something they didn't encounter often.

Turning to look at his first officer, Liam asked, "How bad is the damage?"

David shrugged his shoulders. "Could've been worse, Captain. If we keep running into armed mining barges, we may want to slap some armor plates on the *Gaelic*. Otherwise, one of these days, these miners are going to get lucky."

Liam let out a deep sigh. He hated this part of the job. Not the stealing—there was plenty of ore and ice out here in the Belt to make a person rich. He hated the killing. Most miners would give up their goods and fly away with their lives. Occasionally, like today, they'd run across a crew that opted to fight. It always ended the same way—with the mining crew dead and their families left to wonder what had happened.

This world we're building needs to atone for what we're doing to make it possible, Liam thought.

Chapter Three
A Secret Mission

Fifteen Years Later
2090

Hilton Moorea Lagoon Resort & Spa
Tahiti

"Hurry up, Miles. Our ride is here," Lilly said urgently as she waved him on. She was so excited she could barely contain herself.

"I just got our bag, I'm on my way," he replied as he pulled their suitcase behind him.

The air smelled fresh, with the scent of wildflowers wafting in from somewhere as the sliding glass doors opened. Miles quickly followed his wife out the door. The two of them were greeted by a man from the resort with a digital placard that had their names on it.

Miles called out to the man as he and Lilly walked toward him. The driver smiled warmly as he approached. He immediately took charge of their suitcase and placed it in the back of his vehicle as they climbed in.

Miles and his wife, Lilly, had just arrived at the Fa'a'ā International Airport in Tahiti. They were here to celebrate their thirtieth wedding anniversary and Miles's promotion and prestigious new command.

In a handful of months, he would take command of Space Command's newest warship, the first of an entirely new class of deep space vessels being built for the ever-growing space navy. There was a lot to celebrate, and no better place to do it than away from the hustle and bustle of life on a small Polynesian island in the middle of the Pacific Ocean.

They boarded the electric vehicle, and their driver whisked them away to the dock a few kilometers down the road. As they got out of the car, they were greeted with an incredible view of the island of Moorea and its iconic jungle-covered mountains.

Lilly squeezed him as their driver handed their suitcase off to the boat attendant. "It's beautiful, Miles. Thank you so much for insisting that we come here," she said with a warm smile, her skin glinting in the bright sun as sweat began to form.

"It sure beats staying in Florida. It's just so flat there."

Their guide told them to board the boat that would take them, along with three other couples, to the Hilton Moorea Lagoon Resort & Spa for a relaxing eight-day, seven-night stay. With their only two children now safely in college, they were finally empty nesters and could take a trip like this alone.

When they arrived at the dock to the hotel, they completed a quick check-in and were then led to their bungalow. Miles had booked one of the overwater suites with an incredible view, surrounded by azure waters as clear as could be. The attendant showed them around their room and pointed out some of its incredible amenities. The most impressive thing about the place was the view from its many windows.

Once the attendant left, Lilly gave Miles a mischievous smile as she reached into her purse and pulled out a small zippered container. "If you can believe it, my entire swimsuit fits in this little thing."

Miles felt his cheeks redden a little. She'd been teasing him for a week about this new bikini she'd bought. Despite his many attempts to get her to model it for him, she'd insisted it was a surprise for when they arrived in Tahiti.

Dropping what he was doing, Miles made his way toward his lovely bride of thirty years when his Space Command communicator chirped, letting him know someone was attempting to get in touch with him.

You've got to be kidding me...

His wife proceeded to take her blouse off. As he continued to move closer to her, the device chirped a second time. Lilly saw his hand moving toward it and scowled. "Don't even think of answering that."

She had a look on her face that said he was jeopardizing the opportunity of getting laid before their welcome dinner at the resort.

He glanced down at the communication device in his hand as she slipped her bra off next. "Don't do it," she echoed as she slipped out of her capri pants.

The device chirped a third time, this time louder and more urgently. He tapped the communicator's sensor as he lifted the device to his mouth. "Captain Hunt speaking. This had better be urgent!" he growled.

Lilly just shook her head in disappointment. "Wrong choice, Captain." She reached for her clothes and began putting her capris back on.

"Miles, it's Admiral Bailey. I know you're on your second honeymoon, and I wouldn't do this to you if it weren't important. But something's happened. I've dispatched a shuttle to the resort you're staying at. It'll be there in half an hour to pick you up."

Miles just stood there, unsure if he had heard right. Lilly was rather angrily rebuttoning her blouse. He could sense her disappointment at this intrusion.

"Admiral, you have no idea what you just interrupted. Please tell me this is a mistake," he pleaded.

Shortly after the successful test of the Alcubierre drive, Miles been assigned to Admiral Bailey as his chief of staff and had followed his rise as Bailey had taken over as Chief of Fleet Operations, the second-highest position in Space Command.

A momentary pause took place before the secured communication device chirped again. Miles heard a slight snicker on the other end and then a sigh. "I'm sorry, bud. I imagine I…never mind. I'm afraid there's something critical happening out on Mars. Admiral Sanchez just left my office and ordered me to send you there to retrieve the information—as the head of Space Command, I obviously have to follow his instructions. I wouldn't do this if it weren't important. I proposed someone else, but Admiral Sanchez asked for you personally to retrieve it and bring it back to Space Command. Once your shuttle arrives, it'll take you to the spaceport in Darwin. A transport shuttle will be waiting for you at the orbital station when you arrive."

Miles shook his head in disbelief and frustration; he couldn't believe his luck. During his last eight years at Space Command, Admiral Sanchez had taken a liking to him, and Miles had found himself doing more and more of these secretive missions when a discreet hand was needed by either Sanchez or Bailey.

Depressing the talk button, he responded, "I understand, sir. I'll be waiting for the shuttle."

"Tell Lilly it's my fault. I'm super sorry, Captain, but this is big. We'll make it up to you. Bailey out."

Lilly suddenly appeared a meter away from him, having silently walked up to him while he had his back turned to her as he finished up the call.

"Let me guess. You're leaving. An hour after we got here," Lilly said, disappointment and anger written on her face.

Miles was visibly upset as he replied, “I’ll make it up to you, darling.”

She snorted at the gesture. “Sure you will.” She turned to look out the window, then back at him. “Well, how much time did he say you had until the shuttle arrives?”

“Thirty minutes,” he replied, a glimmer of hope in his eyes.

“Well, then, I guess we don’t have much time, do we, sailor?” A mischievous smirk spread on her face as she began to tear her clothes off again.

****

Three Days Later
Mars Orbital Station

Standing in front of the floor-to-ceiling window, Captain Miles Hunt looked at the Jonathan Kim Military Shipyard, named after the Navy SEAL turned astronaut who’d first stepped foot on Mars. The shipyard was abuzz with activity. Captain Hunt could see four new patrol ships and six frigates under construction. With the increase in pirate activity in the Belt, he suspected these new ships would be busy policing the area.

As the crawler continued its snaking descent down the stalk, he saw the far side of the shipyard before it moved out of view. There were hundreds of drones and humanoid workers expanding the construction facility. Five new construction bays were nearly done.

Looking more closely at the frigate nearest him, Hunt saw dozens of human-looking figures crawling over the outside skin of the ship. A group of them appeared to be attaching a refractive armor panel to the starboard side of the vessel. These panels would help to deflect enemy lasers by modifying the radio frequencies through the armor plates, thereby defraying the potency of the laser. It was a relatively new technology he was only just learning about.

The humanoid synthetics were meticulous machines that worked relentlessly. They were the worker bees of the late twenty-first century. Not being constrained by a need to breathe, the synthetics were the ultimate space workers. They could labor for days on end in the vacuum of space without needing to stop for food, water, bio breaks, or any other function a human would need. They were only limited by how long their batteries could last. Most synthetics could run on a standard charge for seven days. The heavy-duty spacers had an extended battery that allowed them to function for ten days. They made power cells that lasted for months, but humanoids were not permitted to have them—not after the last Great War in the 2040s.

Hunt shook his head at the miracle of modern technology, then turned his attention back to the planet below as they continued their transit to the surface. The crawler advanced at a good clip, rotating as it went. The spinning created just enough artificial gravity that Hunt felt like he was back on Earth. The private sector was still trying to miniaturize the artificial gravity technology so it could be used on more than a large orbital station or starship. They had partially solved that problem for space vessels with enough power to produce the gravity well, but they were still a little ways off from integrating that technology into all spacefaring ships.

In the meantime, DARPA had come up with something unique that appeared to alleviate part of the problem. They wrapped the bottoms of shoes and boots with a substance very similar to the membrane found on the feet of geckos, which essentially allowed a person to walk on the floor of a structure in zero g without floating away. Of course, someone could still push off and float through a ship if they wanted to, but this gave the person the ability to walk and function in an almost normal fashion. Couple that with the slight rotation of a ship during travel, and the sensation of artificial gravity was enough that it almost felt like he was back on Earth.

Hunt figured they'd miniaturize the AG technology to fit on every spacefaring vessel at some point. In the meantime, they had some of the best AI supercomputers working on the problem. But that wasn't why Captain Hunt had been sent to Mars. He'd been summoned by Space Command to head there for a secret mission—one so important that they had sent a shuttle all the way to Tahiti to pick him up, which meant it must be pretty earth-shattering.

The trip down the stalk to the surface would take most of the day—not that Miles cared. He was enjoying the view and wanted the time to think. Now that the crawler was facing away from the activities of the shipyard and the station above, Hunt walked over to one of the seats that looked out at the expansive view of Mars, daydreaming about the ship he would soon take command of.

His ship, the *O*, was still in the final phases of construction at the Elon Musk shipyard above Earth. It was the first of its class, a battlecruiser—a real brute of a ship made for deep space exploration and combat should the need arise. Constrained by the Space Exploration Treaty or SET, the battlecruiser could only be so big, so Space Command had fitted her to the gills with as much firepower and technological capabilities as they could.

Unlike the *Voyager*, a deep space explorer and troopship, the *Rook* would be equipped with a quantum computer and its own super AI. While the *Voyager* was built to carry a battalion of RASs or Republic Army soldiers with her, the *Rook* was packed with weapons and sophisticated electronic warfare equipment.

Opening his datapad, Hunt examined the image of the *Rook*'s exterior for what must have been the hundredth time. It was impressive. Despite its sleek matte black exterior, it was a squat-looking ship. The front section of the *Rook* held three turrets, each of which had two twenty-four-inch magnetic railguns. Its real power, though, was in its two phased-array laser banks. They were positioned near the bottom front section of the ship. For additional firepower, the ship was equipped with a series of antiship missile pods. The *Rook* was formidable, to say the least, and he was greatly looking forward to taking command.

Closing the datapad, Hunt placed it on his lap and closed his eyes. He took a couple of deep breaths in and slowly let them out. He tried to clear his mind and not focus on the *Rook* or his wife—they weren't his mission right now. He'd been sent to Mars for a specific reason. He needed to empty his head of everything else and focus on why he'd been sent here.

Opening his eyes, Hunt looked at the surface of Mars. In the distance, he saw some of the mountain ranges as well as the Valles Marineris, a system of canyons that ran along the Martian surface east of the Tharsis region. At more than four thousand kilometers in length, one hundred ninety kilometers wide, and up to seven thousand meters deep in certain parts, it was a mammoth geological feature, visible even from space.

There was a lot of talk about sealing the entire valley up and turning it into a massive habitable space. Several proposals even included the creation of lakes and rivers and an enormous effort to create a sprawling colony out of it. Hunt suspected that it would take decades if not a century to complete.

This was Hunt's third trip to the red planet in fifteen years. It never ceased to amaze him how fast the colony had grown since the discovery of faster-than-light travel. The volume of resources being sent from Earth to Mars had made it all possible. Of course, an army of three hundred thousand synthetics, working round the clock for a couple of decades, didn't hurt either.

Thinking back on it, Captain Hunt realized it had already been sixty-three years since humans had landed on the fourth planet from the sun and forever changed it. The northern polar cap was now dotted with skyscrapers made of steel and composite materials manufactured on Mars by thousands of 3-D printers. With more habitats coming online each month, the number of people immigrating to Mars from Earth continued to grow at an astonishing rate. Even with the synthetics, there was a constant demand for workers and technicians. Botanists, horticulturists, and farmers were in high demand as it became a critical priority for the colony to become not only self-sufficient but also able to grow surplus food stocks for Earth.

In the nearby asteroid belts, the mining corporation Deep Space Industries had grown significantly. The sheer volume of resources, precious metals, and rare materials being found in the Belt was an economic bonanza. Companies like BlueOrigin had started building a massive new station between Mars, Earth, and the deep space mining operations to act as a processing and distribution system. True to the company's roots, Amazon had also come to space.

Resources from the Belt would be refined at the station and then sold to parties on Earth, the moon, or Mars. It was a big business, and a very lucrative one if you were willing to brave the rigors of space on your own. Many an entrepreneur had tried and failed, yet many more continued to strike it rich in the Belt.

Returning his attention to the surface, Captain Hunt saw the eight large terraforming towers doing their part to slowly change the atmosphere of the planet. Even from this high up, he could easily spot them. He snickered to himself at the thought of one day turning this place into a habitable green space like Earth.

Whatever pleases the masses, I suppose...

An attendant made her way over to him, breaking his train of thought. "Excuse me, sir. Would you care for anything to eat or drink?" The woman was polite, beautiful, and attentive to the passengers on the business-class deck of the crawler.

I really wish Lilly could have come with me, he thought. Then they could have at least enjoyed part of their second honeymoon.

He smiled. "Yes. I'd like a whiskey, and I'll have the herb-crusted cod with wild rice."

"Excellent choice. I'll put your order in right away. Do you want to eat your dinner here, or should I have it sent to your stateroom?"

"I'll eat it here. It's a beautiful view."

She nodded and then walked over to the next passenger sitting a couple of seats over to take her order.

Activating his tablet, Hunt synced it to the crawler's Wi-Fi. As his tablet connected to the server, a wave of messages and emails flooded in. Some were marked urgent, others routine.

Activation code Sierra, Kilo, Yankee, November, Echo, Tango, five-niner, Hunt said internally to himself. A second later, the personal assistant that was embedded in his cybernetic implant activated and synced itself with the crawler's Wi-Fi and server, downloading the same messages and information as his tablet had.

Skynet, develop a response to the routine messages, answering their questions. Open first urgent message now, Hunt thought.

It had been four years since he'd received one of the neurolink implants, or NLs as people called them. He still hadn't fully gotten used to it. For one, it felt strange having an implant inside your brain, and it was still odd having an AI talking to him in his head and handling nearly all the mundane tasks he used to do himself. It was convenient as hell, but it always felt weird that an AI seemed to understand his intentions and responses to nearly any email or message he'd want to reply to. He'd named his PA Skynet because it was always interrupting his train of thought with a message or question when he was in the middle of doing something. The AI had gotten better after the first six months, but he still liked to call it Skynet out of spite. When he'd been promoted to captain, the neurolink had been a necessity. For the time being, it was a technology used only by the senior ranks of Space Command and Special Forces, but he suspected it would be implemented across the rest of the force and in the civilian world at some point.

Open the first urgent message, he thought.

First urgent message, the silent voice replied in his head.

Captain Miles Hunt,

You are to proceed to sector five, where you will receive a classified brief from Commander Niles and Dr. Johnson from DARPA. You must safeguard what you are about to be told and bring that data back to Space Command immediately.

Following your brief, the RNS Victory *will return you to Earth. Do not discuss the information with anyone.*

End of message.

Signed,

Admiral Sanchez

Commander, US Space Command

Hunt shook his head. *So this is why I was urgently dispatched to Mars*, he thought. Lilly would kill him if she knew that he was missing their thirtieth wedding anniversary just for another cloak-and-dagger courier mission.

Just then, the stewardess brought him his dinner and a refill of whiskey. Before she had a chance to leave, Hunt got her attention. "Excuse me, ma'am. How long until we arrive on the surface?"

"Five hours," she replied with a smile. "Do you need anything else?"

"No, I'm great. Thanks," he replied.

As she left, Hunt thought more about the message. He wondered what was so important that it required him to travel here in person to retrieve it.

When he had finished his meal and his second whiskey, he made his way over to his sleeping quarters to catch a few hours' rest. He set an alarm on his neurolink for an hour before arrival so he could focus on sleeping. Something told him he wouldn't be getting much rest once he was on the ground.

The crawlers on the space elevators, or beanstalks as they were called, had multiple levels. There were three coach levels, one business-class level, and four warehouse levels. The warehouse decks were the ones used to transport goods from the orbital station above, and minerals and resources from the surface back to space.

The space elevators were incredibly complex logistical systems that had taken more than a decade to construct. The massive crawlers would move in a circular crawling motion, either up or down the twists in the beanstalk linking the planet's surface with the orbital station above. It was an incredibly efficient way to move people and resources between the surface and space. Once built, they had led to the rapid expansion of the colonies on the moon, Mars, and soon Venus and several moons around Jupiter.

After lying down, Hunt fell into a deep sleep, which was inevitably interrupted by a loud ding in his head that got louder and more annoying until he was awake enough to tell it to turn off.

Good morning, Captain Hunt, his PA announced in his mind. *We will be landing on the surface in one hour. Please begin to collect and secure your belongings. If you would like to be served breakfast, please head over to the bar in the center of the crawler.*

Hunt yawned and brushed off the blanket as he placed his feet on the floor and slid them into his boots. After he fastened them, he put on his military jacket. Grabbing his tablet, he made his way over to the bar to grab a quick breakfast.

A few dozen other travelers had beaten him there, grabbing some of the better seats near the windows. Most were eating breakfast and making small talk with each other. He found a spot where he was mostly alone and sat down to eat.

Forty-one minutes later, the crawler touched down on the surface and connected itself to the ground port. The passengers began lining up near the exits as they waited for the two parts to seal and pressurize.

A moment later, a green light above the doors turned on, and they opened up. Captain Hunt heard a slight hissing sound and then the passengers began to disembark.

As he walked off the crawler and into the hallway that led to the immigration control booth, Hunt pulled out his military ID and his orders. The civilian passengers around him pulled out their passports and their authorization documentation for the inspectors.

While the colonies on Mars were growing, the governments that serviced the various habitats tightly controlled the number of people who could immigrate to the planet or visit it as tourists. Growing food and developing the local economy and lodging on the planet was a top priority, and it just wouldn't be possible to accomplish that if the floodgates were opened wide to any and all new immigrants. Everything on the planet was structured to make sure the highly regulated resources could sustain the residents who'd already populated Mars.

It was nearly impossible to enter Mars illegally, but that didn't mean people didn't try from time to time. There were also occasional problems with illegal contraband brought from Earth, like narcotics that couldn't be grown or cooked on the red planet.

A working dog made its way through the passengers, sniffing them and their bags. Its handler stood not too far away, allowing the canine to do its job.

Captain Hunt advanced steadily until he stood in front of one of the immigration booths. The man standing behind the counter saw his uniform. "Good morning, Captain, may I see your ID and orders?" he asked. He had a pleasant but stern look on his face as he eyed him suspiciously.

Hunt handed him the documents and waited. The agent scanned his ID and quickly read his orders. A moment later, his demeanor changed, and he gave everything back to Hunt. "Please enjoy your stay, Captain. Next person."

Hunt got out of the way as the next traveler presented their documentation for inspection. He made his way into the promenade beyond immigration control, where there was a massive sixty-meter-tall open-air causeway of bars, restaurants, hotels, and shops all lit up with neon lights and decorations. It was a symphony of artistically designed sights and sounds that greeted everyone when they entered the promenade. This part of the colony mainly catered to the tourists who flocked to Mars just for the experience of being on another planet.

Along the metal walkway, planters one meter tall by two meters wide were spaced every fifteen meters. Inside the planters, tall trees, underbrush, and flowers grew. Some of the buildings even had decorative hanging plants or vines that crawled up the sides of the structures, adding a charming ambience to the area. To the more discerning eye, they represented a significant part of the oxygen system for the biosphere, scrubbing carbon while enhancing the oxygenation of the colony.

Captain Hunt made his way through the crowds of people and synthetics, eventually reaching the first entry control point that led to the government and military district, away from the colony. After presenting his ID and orders again, Hunt was allowed to pass into the restricted area.

Once he was through the checkpoint, he made his way over to one of the hyperloop boarding stations and waited for the vehicle to arrive. About a dozen other military members joined him. Judging by the patches on their uniforms, they were stationed on the planet.

When the vehicle arrived, the doors opened, and two dozen passengers got out. Hunt and the others got on and strapped themselves in.

One of the military members must have noticed his anxious look as he fixed his own straps.

"Just in from Earth, sir?" he asked.

"Yeah," Hunt replied.

The man smiled. "I take it you don't like these things?" he said as he snugged his own straps tight.

Hunt shrugged. "I like them better on Mars than Earth, that's for sure."

"Attention, passengers. We will be leaving shortly," a voice announced over an intercom. "Please ensure you are firmly strapped in."

Moments later, the cabin doors closed, and the vehicle began to levitate above the track as it progressed into the cylindrical tube at the end of the bay. Captain Hunt heard a couple of clicks and then a soft hissing noise—the tube was being cleared of oxygen and any other gases that might cause friction.

Once the passenger compartment was ready to depart, it shot through the see-through cylindrical tube like a bullet, picking up speed until it reached a little more than fourteen hundred kilometers per hour. They traveled along the surface of the planet until they entered the side of a low-lying mountain range at the edge of the polar cap several hundred miles away. The area around the mountain was a densely built-up military base, which was part of the Jonathan Kim Military Complex, with the military base in orbit above.

Surrounding the perimeter of the facility was a nine-meter wall with guard towers positioned every few kilometers, built to shield the facility against the harsh winds and dust storms more than anything else. Captain Hunt could also see the planetary defensive weapon turrets interspersed throughout the base and the top of the mountain range. The weapons consisted of large ground-based laser weapons and magnetic railguns, primarily designed to intercept meteors or debris that might endanger the civilian colonies and to defend them from an orbital threat. Planetary defensive weapon systems were still relatively untested.

As the hyperloop vehicle neared the sprawling base, it slowed down immensely. It went into part of the mountain as it snaked its way into the military base, eventually pulling up to a station platform where a small crowd of people were waiting to board.

As Hunt disembarked from the cabin, he saw his long-time friend and Academy classmate Commander John Niles standing there, waiting to greet him, with a couple of RA soldiers accompanying him. The soldiers weren't tricked out in their exoskeleton combat suits, but they were carrying sidearms.

Commander Niles extended his hand. "Miles, it's good to see you again. I understand this mission took you away from celebrating your thirtieth wedding anniversary?"

Hunt grimaced at the mention of it. "It sure did, John. Lilly wasn't too happy about it. But here I am."

John nodded. "The sacrifices our wives make when they marry a man in uniform."

The two of them laughed and then started walking toward the DARPA facility, their security minders falling in behind them.

"So, what's up with the increased security?" Hunt pressed. "Aren't we secure on the base?"

"We are, but these guys and the rest of their squad are going to be accompanying you until you reach Space Command back on Earth. Once you get briefed, you'll understand why."

Nodding, Hunt shifted topics until they were in the SCIF, or secured compartmented information facility. "How're Linda and the kids liking Mars?" he asked.

John snickered. "The kids love it. They're calling themselves Martians now. Linda, on the other hand, she misses her social circle from back home."

"My kids did the same thing. They liked the idea of calling themselves Martians," Hunt replied with a chuckle. "I'll tell you, John, I'm frankly impressed with how quickly the place has grown. When our family was here more than a decade ago, this was barely a colony; now we have almost two million people living out here."

"FTL travel, my friend. It's made the growth and expansion of the colony possible. Add in the new mining colony Deep Space Industries finished building a few years back, and this place is crawling with new arrivals. Wait till BlueOrigin gets their new station built. I hear that thing is going to house some nine thousand permanent residents."

"Amazing, John," Hunt replied, shaking his head slightly. "We live in an incredible time. Oh, before I forget to ask—what's this I hear about piracy becoming an issue out here? I thought that had been largely tamped down a few years ago."

Space piracy was a growing problem. Organized criminal elements would jump some of the smaller mining vessels in the Belt, transports ferrying new immigrants to Mars or resources transiting between the colony, Mars, and Earth. The three major powers on Earth had done a poor job of stamping it out. The governing bodies had pledged to construct military frigates and patrol ships to hunt the pirates down and police the main transit routes better, but it was going to take some time. The value of the resources being mined in the Belt was considerable. A single mining ship could be carrying a billion dollars or more in minerals, making them tempting targets for those with no scruples.

"You saw those new frigates being built in the shipyard, didn't you?" asked John. "They're slated to be completed in a few months. Once they're done, another three will start construction. I suspect we'll only have to deal with the pirates for a little while longer."

Ten minutes later, they made their way into the DARPA facility, which was a controlled SCIF. This was the same facility Hunt had worked in when they were developing the FTL drive. The government found that some of their best R&D efforts were happening on Mars, away from prying eyes and all the distractions on Earth. Some experiments were also best done on a desolate planet or in deep space, for safety reasons.

Making their way through the facility, the two of them found their way down one of the hallways while the security guards waited outside. Eventually, they made it to the secured lab where Dr. Johnson and her team worked.

Dr. Katherine Johnson was originally from Houston, Texas. Her great-great-grandmother and namesake was the famed Katherine Johnson of NASA, the African American woman who had helped to land the first humans on the moon. She was far and away one of the most brilliant scientists and inventors of the twenty-first century.

Katherine had led the way in advancing Mexican theoretical physicist Miguel Alcubierre's theory of warp drive or faster-than-light travel, which he had first proposed in 1994, some ninety-six years ago. When she'd solved Alcubierre's theoretical problem with the help of a quantum computing AI, she was appointed to be the head of all Space Command R&D efforts at DARPA. The facility also oversaw a small section of the military known as the National Reconnaissance Office. The NRO was an old agency with a long and secretive history. In the last twenty years, they had been tasked with an important new mission: exploring nearby star systems in hopes of finding a suitable planet the Republic could look to colonize.

Although Katherine had solved the initial FTL problem, she had three teams working independently of each other to find ways to advance FTL travel speeds. Space was a big place. If humans were going to explore and colonize other star systems, they needed to develop a means of reaching these faraway places. Right now, at the current FTL speed, it took fifteen days to travel one light-year.

When John reached the sealed door leading to Dr. Johnson's work area, he entered a randomized code and looked at the iris scanner. Moments later, the door beeped as it unsealed.

Hunt smiled when he saw Katherine. She was looking at something with an intensity few understood but every scientist envied.

Looking up at the new arrivals, Dr. Johnson smiled and immediately got up and walked toward Hunt. Of course, they hadn't worked together in more than a decade, but the two of them had become good friends during the eight or so years they'd worked together on Mars, which had cemented a solid working relationship.

"Miles, it's good to see you again," she said warmly. "I'm so sorry we had to drag you away from your vacation. I hope Lilly wasn't too mad at me. There isn't anyone I trust more with what we found than you. That's why I asked Admiral Sanchez to send you specifically."

Hunt smiled as he sighed. "I understand, Katherine, and I'm happy to oblige. I can't say the same for Lilly, though."

Katherine knew his wife. She probably felt bad about dragging him away from his long-planned second honeymoon. She'd been the one who'd told Hunt he should take Lilly to Bora Bora for the milestone wedding anniversary.

"Well, I hope your trip was pleasant," she said apologetically.

"It's a lot better with FTL than the old-fashioned way," he responded. "So, what's so important I was sent out here to see you in person and report back to Space Command as opposed to you traveling to Earth?"

She motioned for him and Commander John Niles to follow her, then opened a folder on her computer and moved a file to the holographic interface. Two things appeared. The first was a system he wasn't familiar with, and the second was a planet. Next to them was a floating box of text that contained data on the system and the planet that continued moving in a slow rotating circle in front of them.

"A week ago, we received a message from one of our NRO probes when it returned back to Sol. Let's just say it delivered some unique information. This is 42 Rhea, a star system twelve light-years from Earth. It has three suns. The first is a K-type main star known as Rhea A, and two smaller brown dwarf stars, Rhea Ba and Bb, revolve around it roughly 1,460 AU away. However, Rhea also has a planet orbiting it that we've been trying to get data on for the last several decades," she said excitedly as she brought up more images and data points the probe had brought back for them.

Hunt lifted an eyebrow. "NRO, really? OK. I'm curious, and you obviously have me here. So what was so important that Admiral Sanchez had me sent to personally retrieve it?"

She zoomed in on the holograph image of a planet. "This—this is Rhea Ab. It's a planet with a mass of 1.05 times that of Earth. Meaning the gravity on the planet is roughly five percent more powerful than on Earth, but not enough to really affect humans or cause us many problems. More than that, Hunt—the probe has determined that this planet can sustain human life."

Hunt let out a soft whistle. "You said it could sustain human life? What's its atmosphere made of?"

She clicked on a data tab that opened up next to the image of the floating planet: 78.09 percent nitrogen, 20.95 percent oxygen, 0.93 percent argon, 0.04 percent carbon dioxide. As Hunt read it, his mind raced. It was practically an exact copy of Earth.

Katherine studied his facial expressions. "My thoughts exactly, Miles," she commented. "It's a replica of Earth. Believe it or not, it takes fifty-two years to circle its star, so we estimate its four seasons to be rather long. The planet also has two moons."

"Wow. What's the length of a day?" Hunt asked, his interest now piqued.

"Roughly thirty-two hours, by our standards."

"Great, just what we needed, John. An extra eight hours to each day," Hunt joked, elbowing his friend, who laughed as well.

"Hey. Get serious here, Miles. This is a huge discovery. Not only is Rhea Ab able to support and sustain human life, it has a smaller sister planet less than two astronomical units away that can also support and sustain human life. This is perhaps the biggest discovery of the twenty-first century—these planets could very well *have* life on them."

"How much more data was the probe able to collect before it returned home?" Hunt inquired.

She picked up her tablet and thumbed through a couple more folders. "Here," she said when she found what she was looking for. "The probe stayed in the system for a month before it returned home. Mind you, this was with our first-generation FTL drive, so it took four months to travel one light-year. That means the probe spent a total of eight years in transit and two years collecting data.

"The probe was able to collect atmospheric samples of both planets and carry out dozens of lidar and radar scans of the planets and moons nearby. It collected an immense amount of data. But what really caught our eye was this."

She pointed to one part of Rhea Ab and zoomed in on that area of the planet. It was a densely covered jungle area that edged up against a large outcropping of rock along a small mountain ridge. Captain Hunt felt a sense of awe at seeing plants on another planet. Zooming in further, they were able to spot several openings in the rock.

"What the hell is that?" Hunt said as he touched a spot on the holographic image floating in front of him.

"*That* is why you've flown out here in person," Katherine replied. "That's not a natural entrance in that mountain. As you can see from this image here, that looks to be a mining cart. Over here is probably a mining tool, and that right there—well, those are entrances into the mountainside that look to be about three meters tall and at least two and half meters wide. Two of them, in fact. One here, and one here.

"*That*, my friend, is proof that either there is intelligent life on the planet or there used to be," she asserted with pride. She was practically giddy with this discovery.

"Did the probe find any cities or signs of life on the planet, any electronic emissions of any sort?" asked Hunt, his heart racing a bit at the implications of what they had just found.

She shook her head disappointedly. "Unfortunately, no. That's not to say there isn't life down there. The probe just wasn't able to find it. Mind you, the probe was only able to scan a small segment of the planet's surface. Frankly, we got lucky finding what we did, Miles. We've obviously dispatched more probes to the system to carry out a host of additional scans and tests, but even with the second-generation FTL drives, it's still going to take time to get there, so we won't have any new data for a while."

Hunt paused for a moment and read the data on the planet. He'd spent the better part of two years preparing to be a part of the Alpha Centauri expedition, reading every tidbit of information they had collected on that system and its two planets that they were going to land on and colonize. His mind was comparing what he knew about those planets to what he was reading on this one.

A couple of minutes went by with no one saying anything. Finally, he came to the same conclusion they had—this was a more significant find than Alpha Centauri. Turning to look at Dr. Johnson and Commander Niles, he asked, "Who else knows about this discovery?"

The two of them shared a look and smiled. "No one yet, Miles," Katherine replied. "Not even the rest of our research staff. Aside from a few folks in the NRO office down the hall, no one at the lab knows what we discovered. That's why we didn't transmit this via normal channels, and we told Admiral Sanchez he had to dispatch a trusted person to take possession of this information immediately. We couldn't take the risk of it being intercepted. It's too valuable."

Ever since FTL travel had been made possible, the three major world powers had been sending hundreds of FTL-equipped drone ships and probes into deep space in all directions. The drone ships would warp into a known solar system, perform a series of scans of the system, and then send a communication probe back to Sol with the newly acquired information. Most of the focus had been on Alpha Centauri. Still, the Republic had been secretly exploring other regions of space, which had apparently yielded this new discovery.

John used his hand to brush away the holograph images so he could look his friend in the eye. "This is a huge breakthrough, Miles. Everyone and their brother is going to want to send a ship there. If it truly pans out, then we could see the largest emigration of humans in history to this new Earth."

Hunt was already trying to figure out how they'd hide this information from the other members of the SET. More importantly, his mind was racing with how they'd be able to lay claim to these two new planets. After a moment, he offered, "If we can keep this a secret long enough and settle it first after SET expires, then the Republic can legally lay claim to it and not have to share it with the other powers."

Katherine nodded. "Pretty much. Which is why this needs to go directly to Admiral Sanchez. They'll need to decide if we're going to continue with the Centaurus mission or not."

Hunt ran his left hand through his hair. "What about Alpha Centauri?" he asked bluntly. "That mission's been in the planning for two decades. The *Voyager* and my own ship, the *Rook*, were specifically built for that expedition. What happens now?"

"That's a political and military question beyond my scope."

He turned to look at his friend. "What are your thoughts, John?"

"Between the three of us, I'd say scrap the AC expedition," Katherine proposed, jumping in before John could speak. "The Europeans and Asians are going to settle there. I say we let them. Let them claim those planets for themselves, and we focus on the Rhea system."

Hmm... "You guys really think my mission to Alpha Centauri shouldn't happen?"

John shrugged. "Miles, that's not for me to say. But I suspect Space Command is going to want you to head here instead. This planet is about as close to Earth as we're going to find. It's probably rich in minerals and resources too. It'll be my recommendation that we send your expedition here instead of Alpha Centauri. If it turns out the way I think it will, we may have found a second home world."

Hunt could tell Katherine and his friend John were pretty excited about this discovery. Heck, he was too. He just wasn't sure it was worth giving up the other mission over.

"So are we going to keep calling this new planet Rhea Ab, or have you guys come up with something clever?" Hunt inquired. Knowing her, he suspected Katherine had already named it.

John and Katherine looked at each other for a moment. "Technically, it's called Rhea Ab. But we're calling it New Eden," she replied with a smile on her face.

Hunt chuckled at the name. "I'm not sure I'm the arbiter of planet naming, but I like it, Katherine. We'll see what Space Command ultimately calls it." Hunt paused for a moment as his mind raced with questions. "Why don't we take the rest of today and you brief me on what else you've discovered on this planet? Tell me about the solar system and the area around it as well. *If* we're going to scrub our mission to Alpha Centauri, then we're going to need more data than what you've just shared with me. This mission's been in the planning process for more than two decades. The *Voyager* and my own ship were built around the FTL drive specifically for the AC mission. If that's going to change, then there needs to be a major reason to scrub the current mission as opposed to waiting until our next *Hyperion*-class ship is built."

"That's like two years away. If we wait that long, I can guarantee the other powers will find out about this planet," said Katherine, urgency in her voice. "They'll either change course from Alpha Centauri or send their own explorers. We need to grab this planet as quickly as we can, Miles—plant our flag and claim it. Remember, the agreement signed by everyone twenty years ago was that Alpha Centauri would be a shared world. All others were first come, first serve. This is important, Miles. You need to convey that to Space Command."

"I will, Katherine, but you are coming with me," Hunt countered. "They'll want to speak with you as well."

Chapter Four
Ballad of the Infantry

Earth
Fort Benning, Georgia
Delta School—Republic Army Special Forces

Master Sergeant Brian Royce, the senior Delta instructor for Training Class 48573, stood looking at the recruits. Sweat poured off their faces from the physical exertion he'd just put them through. He was pushing them hard, watching to see if any of them would break down or quit. If that happened, he'd wash them out of the program. They'd be reassigned to a regular line unit in a RAS battalion.

As soon as the recruits finished hydrating themselves, Royce shouted loudly to get their attention. "Listen up, maggots! If you thought the last PT session was tough, you now have exactly sixty minutes to complete the ten-kilometer run with full packs. Now grab your gear and get moving!"

The group of trainees grabbed their rucks, personal weapons, and other gear and started running. In seconds, the entire group was running in an all-out sprint. Their bodies were being pressed hard, testing the limits of their biomechanical implants, stimulants, and neural implants. The recruits needed to grasp that their enhanced bodies were stronger; they could move faster and run longer than they were used to.

The Delta instructors ran alongside the young men and women, yelling and encouraging them the entire way. When a recruit appeared to be falling out of step, one of the instructors would either run next to them to help them push through it or yell at them through their neurolink to keep pushing beyond what they thought was possible. This final phase of the physical indoctrination training was the toughest. The recruits' minds had to adapt to a new reality—they were capable of far more than their pre–Special Forces bodies had been able to accomplish.

While genetically modified humans made up the bulk of the Asian Alliance's force, the Republic focused on enhancing their soldiers with physical modifications. They used a particular type of medical nanite that reinforced a person's bones, making them nearly ten times stronger than the average person's. They also used specially modified hormone supplements that gave the soldiers enhanced muscle strength without making them look like bodybuilders. But most importantly, they raised a soldier's overall physical endurance capability. Soldiers were also given a neural implant that not only enhanced all of their physical senses but also allowed them to retain and recall enormous amounts of information. Lastly, their blood was improved with the help of nanite technology so that it could carry and store more oxygen. This gave them the ability to run faster and longer and to hold their breath for incredible lengths of time. This was all done to allow them to operate in a zero g environment longer and more effectively than a standard human or even a genetically modified one could.

The challenge with all these enhancements was convincing the mind it could do something that had been out of reach for the person's entire life. A flea can naturally jump an astonishing seven inches, but if you put a flea in a container with a lid on it, it'll jump and hit the top. In time, its mind will automatically adjust its jump to match its imposed limits, continuing to jump lower even when the lid had been removed. With an augmented soldier, a similar situation occurred—their brains knew their bodies' old boundaries and would try to shut them down as a protective measure. That was why the first phase of Delta training was the longest and toughest to get through. It took many months of retraining the brain to realize the body could do far more than it used to.

Once these recruits graduated the basic course, they'd be sent to the John Glenn Orbital Station for zero g training before transiting to the moon and then Mars for more training. In all, it typically took a soldier two years to become a fully certified and deployable Delta member.

****

Later that afternoon, after running the recruits ragged through the rough terrain of Fort Benning, Master Sergeant Brian Royce walked into the staff-only training room, covered in sweat and dirt. He was about to make his way over to the locker room to shower up when Lieutenant Karen Disher stopped him.

As she stood there in her pressed uniform, Lieutenant Disher shot him a look of disdain. "Sergeant, come here for a second," she said, and then she walked briskly back into her office.

Royce bristled at the sound of the lieutenant's voice. He generally got on well with just about everyone, but he really hated working with her. The way she demeaned the sergeants, particularly the male sergeants, really grated on him. She was one of those Academy graduates with a chip on their shoulder. It seemed like she felt she had something to prove—but in Royce's mind, she was a fully qualified operator, an elite soldier who had nothing to prove to anyone.

Royce stepped into her office and came to attention, waiting for her to put him at ease. Instead, she kept him standing there at attention while she eyed him suspiciously.

"So, Sergeant, you want out of my training unit, do you?" Disher asked icily, her eyebrow raised as if she was surprised one of her senior NCOs didn't want to keep working for her.

Royce didn't say anything at first. He didn't want to give her any more excuses to make his life and the lives of his trainees and fellow sergeants any more tedious than they already were.

She grunted at his nonresponse. "Well, apparently you got your wish, Sergeant," Lieutenant Disher announced, voice dripping in venom. "You're being transferred to the Bravo Company, 2nd Battalion. They're being attached to a RAS battalion, the 32nd, to be exact. I don't know how you did it or what kind of favors you had to pull, but you're out of here. You are to report to your new unit in forty-eight hours. Now pack your gear and get out of here. Dismissed."

As he turned to leave the room, Royce smiled with satisfaction. He'd have to buy a beer for his old Delta buddy who'd been able to get him assigned to a deploying unit. It was a tough assignment to get—a lot of people wanted to be a part of the expedition heading to a new world.

It was also a long assignment. The battalion was being told to expect a three- or possibly four-year deployment. That was a long time to be away from family. It made sense that most of the soldiers and sailors being assigned to this expedition were ones without spouses or children, and it was strictly voluntary.

While there was a lot of excitement about this mission, there was also a lot of consternation about what might happen if the Republic didn't extend the Space Exploration Treaty. The Greater European Union and the Asian Alliance had been grumbling about the Republic's apparent lack of interest in renewing it and how this could end up leading to a new Cold War of sorts in Sol. Most of the Special Forces community and the Republic Army units felt the real danger and coming action would be between the three major powers. Fighting would almost certainly occur over the resources of the moon, Mars, Venus, the Belt, and the other moons and planetoids around Jupiter and Saturn if the SET expired.

Royce didn't care about any of that. He wanted a chance to start over—a chance to be a leader again and have his own platoon. This last stint in a training battalion had been brutal. Still, he was glad he'd been given a second chance after how thoroughly he'd messed things up at his last assignment.

During his previous mission on Mars, he'd been assigned to Joint Special Operations Command, or JSOC. His platoon had been loaned out to one of the three-letter agencies to do some secret squirrel stuff when things had gone terribly wrong. They had been collecting intelligence on an Asian Alliance installation on the Martian surface when one of his Deltas had accidentally bumped into a guard patrol near the facility they were surveying. Unfortunately, shots were exchanged. When one of his guys had been hit by the startled guards, a handful of his Deltas had opened fire on them.

The attack on the guards had resulted in a quick reaction force being sent after Royce and his men. It had taken them half a day to extricate themselves from the situation, dodging patrols and search parties. Sadly, three of his guys had been killed, and it had caused quite an international incident.

Royce's penance for his part was to disappear from space operations for a little while. He'd been assigned a training post back on Earth, and the gig had been hard. He'd spent the last fifteen years operating on the edges of space, hunting pirates on the frontier and safeguarding the expansion of the Republic into the stars. The idea of traveling to Alpha Centauri and the possibility of encountering real, honest-to-goodness alien life was exciting. It was an opportunity he couldn't pass up, even if it meant he might never see Earth again.

Chapter Five
Power Problems

Earth's Orbit
John Glenn Orbital Station
RNS *Voyager*

"What the hell is wrong now?" barked the engineering officer as another alarm bell sounded on their console.

"We're getting an error message on reactor four. The power's not transferring to the forward magrail batteries. Switching to manual override," replied one of the weapon petty officers in frustration.

"What seems to be the problem, Morgan?" asked Rear Admiral Abigail Halsey as she walked over to him.

Looking up, Commander Aimes Morgan just grunted. He didn't want to be bogged down answering questions from the admiral right now. He just wanted the damn ship to work the way it was supposed to.

"It would appear BlueOrigin still hasn't found that bug in the power relay junction box connecting reactor four to the forward magrail turrets. It's been plaguing us for months," he finally replied after relaying a message to someone down in the engineering room.

"Is this something that's going to delay the mission?" pressed Admiral Halsey.

I swear to God if she asks me about the mission one more time, I'm going to lose it, thought Morgan.

He paused what he was doing and took a deep breath, allowing himself to calm down before answering. "I don't think so, ma'am. We've still got four months before the ship leaves. But I'd like to have BlueOrigin come back and figure out why we're still having the same problem they told us they'd already corrected. It's not fixed, and my teams have spent weeks trying to rectify it."

Admiral Halsey chuckled softly so only the two of them could hear, then leaned in closer. "Smile, Morgan. You and your team are doing a great job. This is a brand-new ship. We're bound to have some problems. You all have done a great job thus far. You just keep telling me what support you need to get this ship ready and leave the details of making it happen to me, OK?"

"You're right, Admiral," Morgan said, letting out a deep sigh. "I think we're all under a lot of pressure to get the ship ready. We still need to run her through her paces before we even think about deploying. We have to make sure the FTL and propulsion systems are working so we can test the weapons."

"I know, Commander," she answered with a nod. "We'll do it. Just stay focused on your task and let me know what kind of help you need. I have the full weight of Space Command behind me to make sure we have all we need to make this mission a success."

Morgan turned to head down to Engineering, leaving Admiral Halsey on the bridge with a handful of workers finishing a few minor touches to things.

****

Admiral Abigail Halsey walked down the hallway to check on the forward gun battery. She wanted to inspect the turret herself and see how things were on that end. After a minute, she came to the elevator that would take her to the next part of the ship she needed to inspect.

The *Voyager* was a big ship. It was fifteen hundred meters long, one hundred and thirty meters wide, and one hundred and twenty meters tall. It had twelve decks connecting the various parts of the ship and the honeycomb network of rooms and workstations on board. The ship had a crew of four hundred and twenty souls along with five hundred and eighty Republic Army soldiers, or RASs, that would be tagging along with them.

Intermixed with the crew were twenty-two personnel solely dedicated to growing and maintaining their food supply. Aside from the crew quarters, the grow habitats took up the largest part of the ship. Using genetically modified seeds and twenty-four-seven UV lighting, they could grow fruits and vegetables rapidly. They also had a small section for egg-laying hens to add poultry into their diet. Having an ability to grow and maintain their own food supply was critical for a mission like this. They were expecting to be underway for two years or more, and a ship could only bring along so much freeze-dried food stock.

Stepping into the elevator, Admiral Halsey hit the button for deck two and waited for the door to close. Moments later, the metal box moved gently to the next floor, the transition so soft and smooth she barely knew it had traversed at all.

When the door opened, she walked into the hallway and was greeted by half a dozen humanoid workers, or synthetics, running bundles of electrical wiring in the ceiling and along the sides of the wall. She stopped and watched them for a moment. It always amazed her how much electrical wiring and plumbing moved through the walls and ceiling of a starship. Like an underwater submarine, space was limited, which meant they had to maximize every little nook and cranny they had.

Looking above her, Halsey saw the EM shielding and smiled. That was incredibly important for a starship. Aside from the potential for radiation from the sun and various stars, they also had to worry about solar flares that emitted electromagnetic pulses. If their ship wasn't adequately shielded against EMPs, it could run adrift if its electrical systems were ever fried. Every wire and electrical system was heavily shielded for this very reason.

Meanwhile, the Synths briefly acknowledged her presence but otherwise continued to perform their duties. They didn't crack jokes with each other or talk about a sports team. They just went about their assigned tasks and worked relentlessly.

Walking past the Synths, Admiral Halsey made her way further down the ship toward the forward section and the gun turrets. As she advanced toward the door, the sensor above the entrance recognized her access code and the door retracted into the wall.

Upon entering, Halsey observed two civilian engineers providing instruction to a handful of petty officers, junior sailors, and a couple of Synths on something pertaining to the weapon systems. This group of ship personnel had a dark red stripe that ran at a ninety-degree angle across their light gray blouse or coveralls, indicating they were part of the ship's weapon department. Like the old seafaring aircraft carriers on Earth, the starships also made use of color-coded shirts to designate who worked in each department.

The instructor bellowed, "Each main gun magazine can hold ten twenty-four-inch shells. That means you'll need to be ready to swap out the empty one for a full one in under ten seconds. If the ship ever gets into a fight, you're going to need to keep the guns firing for as long as needed. Now, when you've burned through seventy percent of the loaded magazines, it'll automatically send a message to the weapon storage locker deck below to start fabricating new projectiles. Just make sure the empty magazines are moved over there when they've been expended." The instructor pointed to a spot on the other side of the room.

"The group below will pull them down. They'll reload 'em and move 'em into position over here," the man instructed as he pointed to a different position closer to the base of the turret.

"What do we do if the guns run out of ammo?" asked one of the junior gunner mates. The kid looked barely old enough to be in uniform.

The instructor smiled as he replied with his thick Southern accent. "Well, if that happens—Spaceman Third Class, is it?—then it's probably time to make peace with your maker. 'Cause these guns shouldn't run out of ammo. Not with the fabricators below. They can 3-D print off new projectiles as fast as we can shoot 'em, so if we run out, it means either we've run out of materials for the printers, or something else has happened."

Suddenly noticing her, the senior enlisted man for the crew, Master Chief Petty Officer Ian Riggs, called the room to attention. Halsey held her hands up, telling them to resume what they were doing.

Master Chief Ian Riggs walked over to her. "Checking in on us, Admiral?" the man asked with a grin.

"Oh, you know me, Riggs. I like to see how things are doing. Are they going to be ready for their shakedown cruise in a month?"

"Yes, Admiral. Everyone is getting familiarized with the systems," Master Chief Riggs replied. "Aside from the laser banks and the missile batteries, this is probably our most complex weapon system."

"True. It's also one of our most important. These railguns are packing some of our heaviest combat power," Halsey said proudly.

Riggs chuckled. "It sure is, ma'am. A twenty-four-inch armor-piercing warhead will certainly put a dent in your ship."

"Don't forget the two thousand pounds of high explosives inside," she said with a wink. "That'll tear a ship apart."

Changing subjects, Riggs asked, "Have you been to Engineering yet? We're still having problems with the power relay or something. We're supposed to have two dedicated reactors for the weapon systems, but they keep shorting somewhere along the way. Best I've been able to get out of them is there's some sort of problem with the power coupling array somewhere midship between them and us."

Sighing audibly, she replied, "Yeah, I know about the problem, Riggs. Commander Morgan is crapping puppies over it. I was going to stop in Engineering next and see what I can find out."

"If we get held up on one thing, Admiral, it'll be engineering. All the other ship systems work and are ready to be tested."

She placed a hand on the man's shoulder. "Thanks for staying on these guys, Chief. You got your hands full getting them ready for this trip. How are they holding up? You know, knowing this is going to be a really long deployment?"

Riggs motioned for her to follow him outside the turret room. "Admiral, most of them are excited," he began. "The thought of exploring a new world and potentially discovering new life is thrilling. But some are really anxious. They aren't sure they're ready to leave Earth and everything we've known behind for such a long cruise into the unknown."

Seeing the concern on the chief's face, Halsey asked, "Do you think we need to reassign some folks?"

Riggs shifted on his feet for a moment. "I—maybe. I'd like to talk to them privately and make that assessment personally. I'll make sure they know if they want out of the expedition, it won't hurt their careers or promotional opportunities. But if they stay, they need to accept that in a few months, we may be gone from Sol for a very long time."

"It's a tough decision, Chief. That's why everyone on this mission has to be a volunteer. There's a chance we could come back to Sol in a few years. But beyond establishing a colony on Alpha Centauri, our mission is to begin exploring deep space," she replied softly yet confidently.

Admiral Halsey was excited to lead this expedition, even if it meant this would be as high as she'd rise in Space Command. It was a chance to lead humanity into the stars, something she couldn't pass up. She could have requested a captain be assigned to handle the ship while she managed the squadron they were deploying with, but she really wanted to command again. Rank had its privileges, and she intended to leverage that for all it was worth when they left Sol.

"Walk with me to Engineering, Chief," she said and turned to head down the hallway to the next set of elevators.

Chief Riggs nodded and followed her. "Admiral, if you don't mind me asking, why are we bringing a battalion of Republic Army soldiers with us on a mission like this?"

She snorted. "I asked that myself, Chief. Command said we needed to have a RA presence with us for the expedition—oh, and it's not just a battalion of RASs, it's a company of Deltas augmenting them as well."

Riggs shook his head at the mention of Special Forces. He seemed to be a bit uncomfortable with their involvement.

"I'll get briefed more on why they're coming as we get closer to leaving, but my gut says it has something to do with establishing the colony on Alpha Centauri. Remember, the GEU and Asian Alliance are going to set up colonies of their own. Plus, if we do find life and it's not friendly, I suspect having a battalion of Republican Army soldiers along for the ride won't be a bad idea."

"Makes sense," Riggs replied. "It's just a lot of extra bodies on a tight ship as it is."

"We'll make it work," Halsey replied. She brushed her hand along the side of the hallway as they approached the elevator. "This ship is enormous, Chief—the biggest we've ever built. We'll have plenty of room for a battalion of soldiers."

Riggs depressed the elevator button, and a moment later, the door opened. The two of them walked in, and he hit the button that would take them to the engineering deck. In seconds, the elevator moved down a couple of decks and then sideways as it moved through the center of the ship to Engineering.

When the door opened, the two of them got out and made their way over to the large room that housed the ship's engineering section. When they got close to the doors, the sensor detected her rank and access code and opened up.

As they walked in, Admiral Halsey saw one of the BlueOrigin contractors talking to a group of petty officers assigned to Engineering. She and Riggs stood in the rear of the room and silently observed for a moment. Unlike the weapon crewmen's red stripes on their gray uniforms, the engineering crew members had a yellow line on their blouses or coveralls. If someone was an officer or NCO, then they had a gold line above or below their department's colored line.

The BlueOrigin engineer leading the training thundered, "You must maintain at least a thirty percent charge on capacitors one and two. The ship's weapon systems are pigs when it comes to power. That means in a long, drawn-out fight, the higher-ups on the bridge may call down requesting you transfer power from reactors one and two to three and four, which run the magrails and the pulse beams. You can do that, but you can't allow the stored battery power on capacitors one and two to fall below twenty percent. Can anyone tell me why, and more importantly, why you don't want to override that safety feature?"

A couple of hands went up, and the contractor pointed to a young woman who looked super eager to answer his question.

"The ship needs power," she blurted out. "Power for the life support functions and power for the engines to maneuver. If the weapon systems suck us dry, we could end up jeopardizing the entire ship."

"Correct. That's why the ship has four fusion reactors. One dedicated to handling propulsion and the FTL drive, one to control the life support needs of the ship and the artificial gravity system, and two for the weapons platforms.

"If and when the ship comes under attack, chances are the two reactors dedicated to the weapon systems may not be able to recharge the capacitors fast enough if the ship is in a long, sustained battle using its pulse beam and magrail weapons at the same time. That means the folks on the bridge are going to want you to divert power to the weapon systems. As the engineering staff, you need to understand what the reactor limits are. Do what you can to help the fight, but make sure you don't jeopardize the ship in the process. Does everyone understand?" asked the contractor.

Everyone nodded; his warning and instruction appeared to have sunk in. Next, he dismissed them back to their department chiefs so they could continue with the rest of their duties.

Admiral Halsey liked listening to Adrian Rogers. He was one of the lead engineers and contractors for BlueOrigin. She thought Adrian was far and away the most intelligent man they had working on this project. He was extremely detail-oriented, but more than that, he had a way of distilling a super-complex problem down to simple terms even the average person could understand.

She waved to get his attention. *Let me hand these guys off to my assistant, and I'll be right there*, his neurolink said to her own. She nodded and waited near the door.

She was still getting used to using the neurolink for anything more than administrative purposes. She never liked trying to communicate through it. She loved being old-fashioned—using her own voice. But she had to admit, the personal assistant aspect of it was terrific. Not having to wade through hundreds of emails and other mundane tasks had freed her up to handle many more pressing matters. She just had to remember to double-check those email responses from time to time.

A couple of minutes went by before Adrian walked over to her and Chief Riggs. "Admiral, Chief, how are you both doing this lovely day? What can I do for you that'll make things even better?"

Admiral Halsey smiled at his way with words. "Adrian, it's good to see you again as well. I'm glad to see they still let you teach. With that said, there's a problem I need to go over with you. As I'm sure you know, we continue to have a power short. It seems to be happening somewhere midship. The guys up in the weapon section tell me they're still experiencing a short when they start to draw power for the magrails or the laser banks. Have you guys figured out what the problem is, or where it is? This is a serious issue that has to get resolved."

He sighed. "It's complicated, Admiral. Chief Riggs and Commander Morgan have told me about it a few times, and we've been running a lot of tests to figure it out, but we're talking about *hundreds* of kilometers of cabling to check. I think we've at least narrowed down what section of the ship it's happening in. Now we just need to figure out what junction line and box is the problem. I'm confident we'll have it sorted in a few more days, a week tops." Adrian sounded cautiously optimistic; his warm, inviting smile often defused a lot of problems with clients.

Halsey nodded but wanted to make sure he knew he was on a short leash. She still hadn't OK'd the completion of the ship, which meant the company hadn't received their final completion payment or bonus. "OK, Adrian. Stay on it. We start the shakedown cruise in four weeks, so you don't have much time to fix it before we leave the shipyard."

Adrian flashed those beautiful pearly white teeth of his. "We're on it, Admiral," he responded. "We'll get it taken care of. I won't let you or Space Command down. Now, if you don't have anything else, I need to get back to work on this very issue."

She didn't, so they parted ways, and she and Chief Riggs headed down to the flight deck to check on things there. Flight operations for

Voyager were positioned on the bottom deck of the ship. There were two rearward hangar entrances where shuttles and landing craft could land. For takeoff operations, the shuttles would depart via one of the forward-facing launch tubes. Along the entire length of the hangar bay on both the right and left sides of the ship were the orbital assault craft that belonged to the RA. When they needed to drop the grunts, they'd pile into one of the landing craft for the ride to the surface. Once the landers were loaded with their human cargo, an armored shield would lift up, exposing the drop ships. An arm would extend the small vessel beyond the side of the ship and then release them. The flight crew on the craft would take over and fly the grunts to the surface. Once they had dropped off their human cargo, they'd return to the ship and reattach themselves to the same drop arm. The arm would then retract them to the side of the hangar and reconnect them to the *Voyager* to pick up the next load of grunts.

The *Voyager* had a total of twenty-four orbital drop craft for the infantry. They also had six utility drop craft, which would land the RAS's drone tanks and mechanized combat suits, or Mechs as they were called. The Mechs were the newest infantry weapon—a 3.5-meter-tall bipedal armored killing machine operated by a single soldier. They were heavily armored and packed a .50-caliber magrail and 20mm smart munition launcher on both arms. They were the Army's heavy weapon option for ground operations.

When Halsey and Riggs entered the hangar bay, they saw several shuttles present. A few dozen synthetics were unloading them, bringing on more supplies for their maiden voyage. On the far side of the hangar was a group of mechanics working on one of the Army's new drone tanks while a couple more were doing some maintenance on one of the Mechs.

Admiral Halsey stood in front of one of the mechanical killing machines. "You have to admit, Chief, if you saw one of these things moving toward your position, it might cause you to run or give up," she said with a bit of a chuckle.

"I'd be more concerned with the tank. Those squat little things pack a hell of a punch and are hard as hell to take out."

She grunted at the response. "Let's hope we never have to use these weapons of war, Chief."

Looking at his watch, Riggs said, "You know, it's getting close to lunch. You want to head up to the mess deck before it gets busy?"

She nodded. "Sure, Chief. It looks like they have things under control down here. Lead the way."

Ten minutes later, the two of them arrived at the mess hall. The view from there was actually quite beautiful. The floor-to-ceiling windows provided a unique experience to those dining there, provided the blast doors weren't closed. When they entered the massive dining facility, they both walked over to the beverage section, where some fresh coffee had been brewing. They grabbed a cup of joe and some lunch and then made their way over to a table next to the window. Since they were the only ones in the room, they had their pick of the seating arrangements. Lunch didn't officially start for another five minutes, but rank did have its privileges.

Taking a sip of his coffee, Chief Riggs inquired, "Admiral, is *Columbus* still coming with us?"

She shrugged. "That's what I've been told."

"I still don't understand the technology involved in that thing. How the hell is it supposed to generate a space elevator and then act as the orbital anchor?"

"I'm no scientist or engineer, Chief, but this is what I was told during the brief about it a few months back. When a site has been identified, *Columbus* will unfold itself at the center of the ship and create a zero g platform. On the platform is one of these new super-advanced adaptive printers. You know, the 3-D printers."

"I know I'm old, ma'am, but I do know what a 3-D printer is," Riggs replied as he reached for his cup of joe again.

She blushed a bit. She hadn't meant to insult him. "Of course, Chief. As I was saying, this new printer apparently creates a molecularly perfect carbon nanotube cable. It's what they're looking at using in the armor of some of the new warships. Once they create the cable, it'll be slowly lowered with an anchor weight until it reaches the ground. Once it's anchored on the planet, they'll finalize the rest of the process, and we'll have a rudimentary elevator to bring cargo down to the surface."

"Huh. Sounds kind of crude and untested. I think I'll take a pass on the first trip down." Riggs downed the rest of his coffee and started on his sandwich next.

Halsey managed to stifle a laugh. "Yeah, I'm with you on that. I think I'll take a pass on the first few trips too. Still, I'm amazed at how much new tech has come out in the last ten years. I mean, who would have thought we'd have artificial gravity generators? I wish we had that technology when I first went into space forty years ago. I hated being stuck in zero g for months on end. The fact that I can sit here like this and enjoy a cup of coffee is incredible."

He nodded. "I've been in Space Command now for forty-eight years, ma'am. I wish we had half the stuff we have now when I first joined up. These kids don't know how good they have it these days," Riggs joked. He waved his hand in the direction of the crew that was now filtering in for lunch.

"So, changing subjects," Riggs continued, "what's going on with Europa? Is Space Command still moving forward with that colony? We're gonna need it for deep space operations."

She rolled her eyes at the question. "I have no idea, Chief. They were supposed to launch that colony group two years ago, and here they are, still in port." She waved her hand in the direction of the window, where the four ships that were supposed to bring the materials to get the space elevator and other essentials for the initial colony were still in orbit. "I agree, Riggs. We need that orbital station and colony going. It'll provide us a huge supply base for further deep space operations."

"You know how the Chinese are. They don't want us to have a base out there without them." Riggs replied with a chuckle. He and Halsey knew each other pretty well after forty-plus years in the fleet; while he might have been amused by her frustration, the two of them made a pretty good team.

With the advent of medical nanites some thirty years ago, scientists had been able to significantly slow down the aging process of the human body. It was thought that humans would now be able to live to the low hundreds in good health. It also meant people worked a lot longer. Instead of serving twenty or thirty years in the military to collect a pension, soldiers and sailors were now required to serve forty years before retiring. Considering people could comfortably live to be one hundred and twenty, or even one hundred and forty, many folks were staying in the military past the fifty-year mark before retiring and starting a second career.

After looking out the window for a moment, Halsey turned back to Riggs. "Between you and me, what are your thoughts on the Space Exploration Treaty? Is letting this thing lapse a good or bad thing?"

Riggs polished off the last of his sandwich. "Honestly, Admiral, I think some powerful corporations have made a case for why our country should withdraw. I understand their logic. They want to expand our footprint onto new planets and moons without having those communists in the Asian Alliance join us. You have to admit—they do tend to let us do all the hard work and then waltz right in and lay claim to their piece of the pie. You saw what happened in the Belt and on Io. We did all the work, and they got all the benefits."

Halsey drank the last of her coffee and finished her own sandwich. "I don't disagree with you, Chief, but to be honest, I'm glad we won't be here to deal with it. I have a feeling when the SET expires, we're going to see a clash over these moons and planets we haven't colonized yet."

Riggs's left eyebrow rose at the blunt assessment. "Let's hope not," he said soberly. "Weapon technology has come a long way since the last Great War. Nearly two billion people were killed in the 2040s. I'd hate to see what kind of war we could wage with the weapons of today."

The two of them talked for a bit longer before they continued to make their rounds touring the ship. The rest of the crews and the soldiers would start to arrive in another week.

Chapter Six
Decisions

Titusville, Florida
Kennedy Space Center
Republic Space Command HQ

Vice Admiral Chester Bailey drummed his fingers on the table in front of him. The presentation was over, and he watched as Captain Miles Hunt and Dr. Katherine Johnson took their seats opposite him.

Admiral Bailey liked Captain Hunt. He'd been an exceptional chief of staff; over the fifteen years they'd worked together, Bailey had even come to regard Hunt as a friend. When it had come time to select a captain for Space Command's newest warship, Bailey had rewarded Hunt with the command of the *Rook*—the most powerful deep space warship ever built. It wasn't a hard decision. Bailey was grooming Hunt to become an admiral one day, part of the little empire he was building.

However, in that moment, Admiral Bailey felt blindsided by the information his protégé and Dr. Johnson had just presented. This secret mission Admiral Sanchez had sent him on threatened to derail decades of planning—planning he had spent the better part of the last ten years working on. Bailey looked around the room at the others. He could tell they were just as surprised—everyone except Admiral Sanchez. That old goat had probably had an idea of what they'd found days before it had been revealed to them in this room.

When Hunt and Dr. Johnson took their seats, Bailey felt like he should say something before anyone else had a chance, gauge the room's response to see how this news might change things.

"This is incredible news, Dr. Johnson, and thank you, Captain Hunt, for safeguarding it," Bailey began. "However, I don't believe this should change our current plans." Dr. Johnson was clearly bristling at his remarks; she looked like she wanted to challenge his assessment. Captain Hunt, for his part, kept a stoic face, shielding his thoughts on the matter.

General Pilsner raised an eyebrow, but the Republic Army Commander was keeping his powder dry to see which way the wind would blow before he weighed in. Admiral Bailey watched Admiral Sanchez and President Roberts's faces for any cues. They were the ones who'd ultimately decide what would happen.

The President bit first. "How do you figure, Admiral? This is an incredible discovery. Surely you see that. Why wouldn't we want to change our plans and move to lay claim to this planet?"

Sticking his chin out a bit as he prepared his response, Admiral Bailey calmly explained, "Mr. President, if we deviate from the current Alpha Centauri expedition, the Asian Alliance and Europeans will not be pleased. They'll swiftly piece together that we found something—something of high enough value that we'd be willing to give up a joint colony. Worse, it'll kill any chance of us renewing our commitment to the SET.

"What's more, we'll lose out on any opportunities that may await us from this joint expedition. The Centaurus constellation is going to be a key launchpad to our further expansion and colonization of other worlds. If we deviate from our current plan, we'll have lost out on that opportunity—possibly forever."

President Roberts shook his head. "The SET expires in a matter of months if we do not recommit to it, and right now, there's not an appetite within the government to renew it," he countered. "Folks want to expand into space without having to partner with the Asian Alliance or the GEU. This is an opportunity for us to legally lay claim to an Earth-like planet that is only five percent larger than Earth. Do you realize the economic and colonization opportunities that would create for us?" He shook his head dismissively, adding, "I'm not sure we can pass on something like this, Admiral, nor do I think we should have to share it with the other alliances."

"Even if it means we sacrifice the SET?" Bailey asked pointedly. "It's kept the peace for all these years. We're stronger together as a race than fractured."

Admiral Jose Sanchez raised a hand. "If I may, Mr. President. Admiral Bailey brings up good points about the Centaurus constellation and the SET. If we leave the expedition, then we'll lose out on any future exploration and expansion possibilities in that region of space. We'll have ceded all future colonization of the region to the GEU and the Asian Alliance. We could also end up in a situation where they opt to renew the SET without us. That would be an even bigger problem for us strategically." Something about Sanchez's tone suggested he didn't really believe what he had just said but had said it more for show.

Admiral Sanchez was the overall Fleet Commander for Space Command, an extremely powerful position given that all Republic forces fell under his command and control. He was also starting to get up there in age, so there was a lot of speculation on who might take his place.

Chiming into the discussion for the first time, General John Pilsner asked, "What if our ship had a mechanical failure and was unable to make the journey?"

Admiral Bailey turned to scowl at the ground pounder. "Not possible. Even if we did have a problem, they'd just postpone the trip to wait for us if that was the issue."

"We could put together a second mission," Dr. Johnson offered. "Let the group heading to the Centaurus constellation go ahead, but send a second mission to this new planet."

Everyone glared at her. She was here to brief them on what her team had found, not set policy. She'd spoken out of turn, but she had a point.

"Is that possible?" asked the President, looking at Admiral Sanchez for confirmation. Roberts was in a tight reelection race; if he could somehow manage to appease all sides on this, he probably would.

Admiral Sanchez sat back in his chair and looked at the ceiling for a moment. Bailey figured he was using the neurolink to bring up an inventory of ships either in service or soon to be in service to see what they had available.

Sanchez returned his gaze to the President. He said, "It is—but only if we scrub a couple of other missions."

"You're not serious about scrubbing Venus or Europa, are you?" Admiral Bailey blurted out. He was barely able to contain himself at the thought of eliminating those essential missions.

Holding a hand out to silence his second-in-command, Sanchez continued, "We're supposed to launch the Europa mission in a couple of months and Venus a few months after that. I propose we use those ships for the expedition to Alpha, and we use the *Voyager* and *Rook* for this new mission."

Bailey shook his head in frustration. "As much as I'd like this idea to work, it won't," he insisted. "Those ships aren't fitted with the FTL drives yet. We're still close to a year away from having them ready."

"What?" Sanchez snapped, clearly surprised by this sudden announcement. "I thought we had retrofitted them already."

"They're being retrofitted right now," Bailey went on to explain, "but we hadn't anticipated them being needed for the Centaurus expedition, so that hadn't been a priority." He paused for a moment and sighed. "Mr. President, we're incredibly short on FTL-equipped freighters and transports right now. Our shipbuilding emphasis was on establishing a military force able to defend our colonies and Sol. We're still a few years away from having a small fleet of FTL-equipped transports and freighters, so we're limited in what we can do right now."

Admiral Bailey was still annoyed that his proposal to build heavy transport ships for deep space fleet operations had been overruled in favor of warships. He had argued that without a transport fleet, the warships would have a hard time staying supplied, and it would slow down the shipyard's ability to keep up with the grueling production demands. He was now being proven right.

Having heard the various pros and cons, President Roberts leaned forward. "History may judge me poorly for making this decision, but I'm the President, and it's my call. We're going to cancel our participation in the expedition to Alpha Centauri and move forward with sending an expedition to this new planet Dr. Johnson's team has discovered. The fact that there are signs of intelligent life on that planet only reinforces my decision."

Admiral Bailey quickly pounced. "Mr. President, we have to think about the balance of power in Sol and beyond," he insisted, making an impassioned plea. "We shouldn't throw away the SET or the opportunity of the Centaurus constellation. We can do both missions if you give us some time."

"Enough, Bailey!" Sanchez interjected angrily. "You may be in charge of fleet operations, but I'm still in charge of Space Command. If the President wants us to scrub the Centaurus expedition in favor of this new discovery, then that's what we'll do."

Admiral Bailey didn't say anything further. He did his best to control his temper and emotions. *So much for renewing the SET*, he thought. *The bastard never did like that agreement.* He hoped that their leaving wouldn't spawn a new arms race or worse, another war.

"Then it's settled," declared President Roberts. "Admiral Sanchez, please inform the SET members that we are canceling our participation in the upcoming expedition. Tell them we're running into some technical challenges with the *Voyager*, and as such, we're not going to be able to deploy with them. Wish them the best of luck and tell them we stand ready to help them further down the road should they need it. In the meantime, let's put together a first contact diplomatic mission to head to this new system." He spent a few more minutes issuing some additional orders before concluding the meeting.

As Captain Hunt stood, he saw Admiral Sanchez give Dr. Johnson a brief nod and smile. *Why do I have a feeling this entire discussion was a setup?* he asked himself.

Chapter Seven
Almost Human

Alamogordo, New Mexico
Walburg Technologies

Dr. Alan Walburg looked at a string of code, examining it for what might have been the hundredth time. *It just might work...*

Fifty years ago, when Alan was a robotics engineering student at the University of South Florida in Tampa, he'd had a vision. Maybe it was the psychedelic drugs he had tried at a frat party the night before, but he'd had a dream of what the future would hold. Robots and humans worked together for the good of the world; it was utopia.

Then he had been drafted, like nearly everyone under the age of forty when World War III had broken out between the United States and China. Being a PhD student in robotics, Alan had caught the attention of some folks at DARPA and had immediately been selected to be a part of the Department of Defense's revolutionary new surrogate program.

DARPA had been collaborating with Boston Dynamics for decades to create a fully immersive unmanned humanoid combat drone. The humanoid could be operated by a human operator, called a surrogate, from a remote location or set to function autonomously through a complex AI.

When this new technology was unleashed on the battlefield, the result was… horrific. Man's killing of his fellow man had now become so detached that governments had humanoids to do the fighting for them. That was, until the fighting spread and consumed the whole world.

When the war ended eight years later, many nations lay in complete ruin. Between the war and the famine and economic collapse that followed in its wake, twenty percent of the global population, a total of 1.8 billion people, were dead.

Alan had somehow survived the slaughter. Most of his friends hadn't. In the aftermath of the war, many Republic cities were in ruins. There was a critical shortage of skilled labor and able-bodied people needed to rebuild the nation and the world.

A short while after Alan had left the military, he climbed to the top of the Sandia Mountains in New Mexico one weekend. While camping at the summit, he remembered the dream he had had at USF before the war.

It was at that moment, with all the destruction the war had wrought, that he saw an opportunity to help his country. Alan moved to Alamogordo, New Mexico, and established Walburg Technologies; then he went to work developing the first-ever synthetic humanoid civilian worker. Unlike the military versions of similar design, his looked uniquely human. The only significant difference he incorporated into them was their eyes. While they otherwise looked human, they had a yellow circle around the iris, which helped to delineate them as synthetics. At first, he only made one copy, a man that looked to be in his late twenties or early thirties. Later, he would go on to develop seven more versions: three more in the likeness of men and four resembling women.

While the military had created humanoid surrogates to use as combat soldiers, Alan had finally figured out how to code and create a fully functional synthetic humanoid worker that could function and act just like a human, not a surrogate operated by a human. The first prototype he built was a construction worker. The Synth, as he called it, was programmed with all the pertinent knowledge needed to produce nearly any structure it was instructed to build. It understood plumbing, electrical, carpentry, electronics, cement working, and bricklaying.

When he debuted his new humanoid worker to the world, it took off. In his first month, Alan had orders for more than two thousand units for a construction firm in Chicago, three thousand units for a firm in California, and two thousand units for a firm in Florida.

What really astonished the country and the world was that Alan's entire factory had been built by his own humanoid workers. Then his synthetics began self-replicating: working twenty-four hours a day, seven days a week, his robotic army was cranking out human worker replacements at an astonishing rate.

Soon, he coded his synthetic humanoids to do more than just build buildings. He began to code them to cook, to clean, to handle all sorts of routine daily tasks in addition to the more dangerous and difficult work humans used to do. Within ten years, nearly every business in the Republic had at least one synthetic.

By the mid-2060s, synthetics were working the farm fields of the Midwest and California, cultivating more food than the country could possibly use. When Alan had received permission to export his humanoid helpers, Walburg Technologies became the most valuable firm in the world.

During a meeting with NASA, BlueOrigin, and SpaceX, which later became Musk Industries, Alan proposed using the synthetics in space. That's when the whole idea of landing a man on Mars and establishing a colony on the moon really went into high gear.

With several thousand of Alan's synthetic workers, Musk Industries completed the space elevator near Walburg Technologies' main factory in New Mexico in 2064, which paved the way for not only near-earth mining of asteroids but also deep space travel and the colonization of the moon and Mars.

Just two years after the space elevator's completion, BlueOrigin completed the first shipyard in high orbit with the assistance of more than three thousand humanoid workers. The Synths began building a fleet of ships that would help to colonize the moon and beyond, and as they say, the rest was history.

Alan looked again at the newest piece of code; he was onto something. If he pursued this much further, he'd probably solve the problem. That was the benefit of living longer—he had retained such a wealth of information he could draw on. The question Alan was struggling with was a moral question he wasn't sure he had the authority to answer. He had seen how autonomous humanoid combat drones had been unleashed in Beijing, and later Los Angeles, and it was something he never wanted to happen again. He was still haunted by the nightmares of the last war. But he was playing God with this new code, and he wasn't sure what its unintended consequences might be.

Alan had been the godfather of the synthetic humanoids that had revolutionized the world, but his latest project, fully autonomous artificial intelligence—not just AIs, but fully living AIs—presented new ethical and moral questions. These synthetics would be, for all intents and purposes, fully conscious, fully independent and able to think beyond their programming. They would be able to choose their own responses to questions, commands, situations, and anything else they encountered.

How would the synthetics respond if they were suddenly conscious? How would they integrate into a society that, for better or worse, had used them as little more than slaves or serfs? What would they think of their former masters—a race of people who had tried on countless occasions to wipe each other out? What if he gave his creation this fantastic gift, the gift of free thought and will, and they suddenly turned on their human masters?

No. He couldn't risk it. Not yet. He needed to code in more safeguards. That would take time, but if he was going to one day give his creations the gift of life, he needed to make sure he didn't doom his own species in the process.

Chapter Eight
Nefarious Intentions

John Glenn Orbital Station
RNS *Voyager*

Shimada Zengo pushed his toolbox ahead of him as he moved through the crawlspace between the reactor room and the engineering control room. It was a tight fit. If he had been even the slightest bit claustrophobic, this would not have been the job for him, but Shimada held no such fears.

He stopped crawling and rolled over onto his back, reaching for the first power junction box. Luckily for him, these crawlspaces were well lit. The ceiling had soft white backlighting while the walls and floor were painted a light cream color, which amplified the light provided in the tight space. This was an intentional design feature meant to help maintenance people like himself see what they were doing.

Shimada opened his toolbox and went to work. The first thing he did was to remove the top tray containing most of his tools. Then he took the remainder of the tools out, placing them on the floor next to him. He gently inserted a flathead screwdriver between the inside wall of the toolbox and the base of it until he was sure it was fitted tightly, then pried at it until he felt the false bottom open up. Pulling the six ounces of C-4 explosives out, he used a Phillips head screwdriver to open up the junction box he'd been sent to test. He took the C-4 and packed it in tight around the wires and cabling he was there to inspect, then made sure the timer was seated correctly and set the detonator, programming it for twenty-eight hours from now.

With his immediate task completed, he used one of his diagnostic tools to test the power relay box and the cables feeding into it. Sure enough, everything tested fine. The short that was taking place between the engineering room and the weapon systems in the forward section of the ship wasn't originating here. With the test done and his sabotage mission complete, he packed up his tools and prepared to move further down the crawlspace to the next junction box.

For the next six hours, Shimada would crawl through more than a mile of crawlspaces. He, along with a dozen other technicians, tested one junction box and power relay after another as their company, BlueOrigin, continued to search for the source of the short in the power supply. Since the ship was no longer participating in the Alpha Centauri mission, they had a bit more time to find the problem.

When Shimada finally crawled out of the last crawlspace he needed to check, he heard from two of the other technicians that one of their colleagues believed they had found the problem. It was a couple of decks above where he and his friends had been checking. The BlueOrigin folks were glad they had found the source of the problem that had been plaguing them for months. It had also held up their completion bonus, which they were all eager to receive.

With their work for the day complete, the group of contractors left the ship and returned to the orbital station. A couple of hours later, Shimada left for his scheduled leave. He was taking a week off work to soak up some sun on the Florida coast. What few people knew was that Shimada would be using that time to slip out of the country and eventually arrive in Japan, to a secret hero's welcome by the intelligence service of the Asian Alliance.

****

Admiral Abigail Halsey had just sat down in her office outside the bridge when she felt the ship vibrate. Then an alarm blared through the ship's speakers.

"Damage control parties, please report to deck five, Engineering. Medical personnel, please report to deck five, Engineering."

Admiral, please report to the bridge, her neurolink announced.

Halsey stood up and sprinted out of her office. She turned down one hallway and was running onto the bridge when she observed a lot of commotion taking place.

"What the hell happened?" she barked to no one in particular.

The lead engineering rep assigned to the bridge spoke first. "Admiral, there was an explosion in Engineering. We're trying to figure out what happened and how many people have been hurt."

Moments later, the lights flickered off briefly before the backup generators kicked in. A second explosion rocked the ship, this one much larger than the first. More alarms blared, and additional red and yellow lights flickered on the damage control board.

Depressurization alert, depressurization alert...

"Commander Morgan!" shouted someone trying to get his attention.

Morgan rushed over. "What is it, Lieutenant?"

"Sir, that secondary explosion was a depressurization event," she explained. "It looks like the fire in the reactor room reached critical mass, and the emergency system took over and depressurized the entire compartment. The fire in the reactor room appears to be out."

Taking charge of the situation, Commander Morgan barked out orders to get more damage control teams over to Engineering. They needed to contain the fire and put it out before it had a chance to spread. If the computer had determined the best course of action to put the fire out was to vent its oxygen, then it'd do the same with the rest of Engineering if they didn't get it contained.

Five tense minutes went by as the damage control crew below decks worked feverishly to gain control of the situation. Finally, word was sent to the bridge that the fires had been put out. It took the damage control teams another ten minutes to get the injured crewmen moved to sickbay and eventually start assessing the damage to the ship.

When Admiral Halsey and Commander Morgan approached the rear of the ship to evaluate things themselves, they saw a lot of flash damage on the walls and ceiling of the corridors. The floor was covered with the chemical powder that had been used to put out the electrical fire.

Several crew members stood aside as the two of them approached. As they walked into Engineering, the first sight that greeted them was a gaping hole in the ceiling leading toward the reactor room.

"It's sealed off, Commander," one of the damage control crewmen said.

"How soon can we get the reactor room pressurized?" Morgan asked. Halsey knew he wanted to assess how severely damaged the reactors were.

The damage control crewman shrugged. "Maybe an hour, sir. We need to run some diagnostics first to check for radiation leaks. If any of the reactors are damaged or venting radiation, then we'll want to keep them venting into space and not onto the ship."

Morgan nodded, then ordered them to get on it.

****

The Following Day

As Commander Morgan briefed Admiral Abigail Halsey on how the fire had started and what kind of damage had been done, she shot Master Chief Riggs a look of concern.

"Commander, you're saying someone sabotaged our ship?" she asked skeptically.

Commander Morgan solemnly looked each person in the eye before he nodded. "Unfortunately, yes, Admiral. There isn't any other explanation. When we looked at where the fire originated, we saw blast damage. We ran the debris through chemical analysis, and that's when it came up as C-4. There's no doubt that this was deliberate."

"This is outrageous. Who the hell would have sabotaged the ship like this?" bellowed one of the officers.

"My money says it's the Asian Alliance," Master Chief Riggs said under his breath.

The head of security heard him. "I think the chief is right."

Crinkling her eyebrows, Halsey clarified, "I'm sorry, what did you say, Chief? I think the rest of us missed that."

Feeling his cheeks redden, he replied, "My apologies, Admiral. I said I believe the Asian Alliance may have been behind this. We all know they're not happy with us for not renewing the SET. Maybe they didn't want us to have the most powerful warship in Sol when their expedition leaves in a week."

She shook her head in disappointment. "Until we know for certain who did this, let's not start leveling accusations, shall we?"

Turning to look at Commander Morgan, she asked, "How long will the repairs take, and are the reactors still functional?"

Looking at the see-through tablet, Morgan used his finger to move through a couple of pages of text only he could see before he replied, "The reactors are OK. No radiation leaks or problems in that regard. So we got lucky there. Unfortunately, the blast caused considerable damage to the inertia dampener. We can't leave port until we get that repaired. The best guess is it'll take us at least a month. Then we'll have to test it to make sure it's properly integrated with the ship."

"Can't we just fabricate the new parts and continue our shakedown cruise?" asked one of the other section chiefs.

"No. We could end up killing the crew if we did that," Morgan replied angrily. "You have to understand—if we're moving at full speed without it, then the human body is going to experience a lot of g-forces. If we make a maneuvering turn at full speed, the crew could be hit with sixteen g's or more. It'd crush you. I'm sorry, Admiral—without the internal dampeners, we're stuck in port for the time being."

Halsey sighed, mostly to herself. They were supposed to head out in a day to begin their shakedown cruise. "Let me report to Space Command what's happened and how long it'll take us to get the ship repaired."

The section chiefs all got up and filtered out of her office to head back to their areas of the ship. Whether they left in a couple of months or next week, they still had a lot to get done.

When everyone had left, an ensign poked her head in. "Excuse me, Admiral, a captain from Space Command just arrived. He said he needs to speak to you in private. Shall I send him in?"

Space Command...why would they be sending someone here? she wondered. She was just about to brief them via the holograph.

She stood up behind her desk. "Yes. Please send them in."

Halsey walked around her desk and made her way toward the door to her office. When a familiar face walked in, she smiled. "Miles, it's damn good to see you. They said someone from Space Command was here to see me, but I didn't realize you were still there. What do they have you doing these days?"

She walked up to him and gave him a brief hug. Miles Hunt had been the executive officer on her first space command, a research mission to Jupiter, and then they'd been on assignment on Mars together.

"It's good to see you, Admiral. Congratulations on the promotion, by the way. I'm sorry I wasn't able to attend the official ceremony."

She blushed at the compliment. "It's OK. I wasn't able to make it to your pinning on captain either. I believe I was commanding a ship out in the Belt at the time. How are you? What brings you up here?"

She gestured to a set of couches on the far side of her office, angled just right to allow those sitting in them to have a great view outside the ship when the blast doors were open, like they were right now.

Pulling out one of the new see-through digital notepads, Hunt pulled up a document that required an official biometric signature. "Before I discuss why I'm here, Admiral, or tell you anything further, I need to read you onto a Special Access Program. You can read over the NDA if you'd like, but I need your thumbprint and iris image to unlock the orders and tell you why I'm here," he said, very businesslike as he handed her the notepad.

She lifted an eyebrow. "All cloak-and-dagger, are you, Miles? Let me see what I'm signing myself up for."

Halsey took the tablet from him and read the essential information—nothing too revealing. She had a feeling that once she was officially read in, she'd know more than she wanted to.

Looking up at Hunt, she said, "I suppose I don't have much of choice, do I?"

He took a deep breath before he answered. "We always have a choice, Admiral. We just may not like the consequences. That said, I was told by Admiral Sanchez that if you don't sign for the orders, you'll be replaced as the commander of the *Voyager*." Hunt held a hand up to stall her from launching a protest. "Abigail, I can assure you, you're going to be very pleased with what you're about to read."

Snorting at the threat, Halsey bristled a little bit. Command of the *Voyager* and the four other ships that would be accompanying her was the chance of a lifetime. She was going to command the first Republic fleet to leave Sol and colonize a new world.

"If we weren't friends, Miles, I'd be mildly put off by what you just said. But I'm going to trust you and sign this."

She placed her thumb on the tablet, then held it up and looked at the camera, which snapped a picture of her iris and attached it to the report as well. When those two functions had been completed, the screen on the tablet materialized to show her a new set of orders and information. Hunt got up at this point and walked over to the window to look out at the other ships in port. It was going to take her a few minutes to read through everything.

Halsey rapidly read through the executive summary. Then she moved into the meat of the orders. She was appalled to learn from one of the reports that Space Command had known in advance that a plot had been underway to sabotage her ship, and even angrier when she learned that Space Command had allowed it to happen. That act of sabotage had cost the lives of three of her crew members. It was nothing short of an act of war.

Hmm...Chief Riggs was right. It was *the Asian Alliance.*

Just as she was about to demand that her friend explain why Space Command had allowed such a thing to happen on her ship, she saw it.

They *wanted* the *Voyager* disabled and unable to leave Sol—the attack gave them the justification to formally withdraw from the SET, and it gave them plausible deniability for what they were about to do next.

She paused her reading of the orders and stared at Hunt, who still had his back to her as he looked out the window. "NRO found another planet?"

Hunt turned and nodded. "It would appear so. They're calling it New Eden. According to the readings from the probe, it's practically a carbon copy of Earth. It's also only five percent larger than our own planet, if you can believe that."

She let out a soft whistle before he continued.

"There's more. What hasn't been talked about—and this stays between us, Admiral—is that it would appear we've found intelligent life on the planet. Or at least remnants of it."

Halsey paused for a moment and looked up at him. "And no one else knows about this discovery?" she inquired, excitement and zeal in her voice.

Hunt sat back down, a smile on his face. "As of right now, no. The Asian Alliance just sent an FTL probe in that general direction, but we have no idea if it's headed to the same system or not. Right now, Space Command wants us to lay claim to the system before anyone else can investigate the signs of intelligent life they believe they've found."

"Why didn't we put together another expedition to explore this new system? They have to know we're never going to get another shot at having an outpost in the Centaurus constellation after backing out of the expedition as we did. We're going to be frozen out of future exploration in that part of space," she said, hoping like hell someone had made that same argument.

Leaning forward in his seat across from her, Hunt explained, "I was in the room when this was all discussed, and that argument was made by Admiral Bailey. He pushed to send you on the original expedition and put together a second for this new world. However, as you know, the President and Admiral Sanchez aren't exactly fans of the SET, and neither is most of the Senate. This discovery gave them a reason not to extend it and further tie our hands in the new system. When they discovered the Asian Alliance was planning an attack on your ship in response to our withdrawal from the mission—well, that was the icing on the cake they needed to sell the withdrawal from the treaty to the public, and the justification to lay claim to this new world on our own."

Admiral Halsey placed the tablet down on the coffee table between them and sat back in her chair. She looked up at the ceiling for a minute, deep in thought, before finally returning her gaze to him.

"You know, three people died from that act of sabotage."

Hunt grimaced and nodded, remaining silent for a moment. He finally responded, "It wasn't my call not to warn you, Admiral. I wish I had been allowed to, because I would have worked to make sure no one was near the area when the bomb went off."

"That's easier said than done. I had to make a tough call to the families of those we lost. That's not the kind of call you want to make, Miles. So, are there any further traitors within my ship, or was that it?"

Hunt felt the rebuke and heat in her words. It hurt him. He had always viewed her as a friend and mentor. He looked up at her, their eyes locking. "I'm sorry they put you in this situation, Abby. I really am. Right now, Command is not aware of any further saboteurs. Intelligence believes the Asian Alliance, and maybe the Europeans, wanted to freeze us out of future exploration on our own, at least for a little while.

"As you know, the SET treaty is going to expire in a month. Right now, no other spacefaring nation is as prepared for that inevitability as we are. The GEU has spent its entire focus on the Centaurus expedition. Only the Asian Alliance has built ships to challenge us here in Sol," Hunt said, laying out the situation for her as seen by Space Command.

"You really think we may fall back into a shooting war once the SET expires?" she asked nervously.

He shook his head side to side. "I don't think so. Neither does Space Command. They believe the Asians are going to make a concerted play for several of Jupiter's moons and those of Saturn. That'll position them for exploration outside Sol and give them some deep space supply depots, which may come in handy down the road. It's the same strategy we're moving forward with as well."

"All right. Well, since my mission is obviously going to change, how do you fit into this, Miles? Are you still coming with me?" she asked, her curiosity piqued.

Now it was his turn to smile. "Yes, I'll be coming with you. But not on the *Voyager*. I'll be taking command of the *Rook*. We'll be your primary escort ship for the expedition."

"The *Rook*? Really?" she asked, grinning. "I hadn't heard they'd assigned her a skipper yet. I thought Space Command was going to keep that ship here in Sol to keep the Asian Alliance in check."

The *Rook* was a battlecruiser, the first of a series of ships to be built in that class. Unlike the *Voyager*, the *Rook* had been made and designed for war. It was a third the size of the *Voyager* in length and tonnage but packed just as much firepower and had a much thicker armored hull.

"I thought so too. Right now, since it appears there may be some sentient life on New Eden, this is going to be a first contact diplomatic mission," Miles explained. "My ship is your muscle in case things go south. If they don't, then I'm to expand our footprint in the system and the nearby constellation to look for new worlds we can settle and any possible signs of life beyond what we've already seen on the planet. Since we're going to be alone on New Eden, Space Command wants us to be able to defend ourselves while we get a more permanent outpost established and additional ships deployed to the region, provided we're given a warm welcome by whoever's currently there."

Looking down at the tablet, Halsey found the distance to New Eden: twelve light-years away. It would take six months to arrive there with current FTL travel, and it was two months further away than Alpha Centauri.

"So when do we leave?" she asked coyly.

Miles smiled. "As soon as your ship is repaired."

Chapter Nine
Lunar Assault

Lunar Orbit – Training Range X-Ray
Bravo Company, 2nd Delta Battalion
1st Special Forces Group

Standing on the flight deck of the RNS *Voyager*, Master Sergeant Brian Royce looked at the soldiers in his platoon. Half of them were green cherries, fresh from the schoolhouse. Hell, he remembered training them at Fort Benning. Now, they were preparing for their last training exercise before they shipped out.

One of the squad leaders walked up to him. "Master Sergeant, the men are ready."

Royce looked at Staff Sergeant Perry. "All right, tell 'em to load up. Oh, and Perry—keep an eye on those new M90s. This is the first time we'll be using them in a live-fire exercise."

The M90 was the newest Special Forces weapon. It was a squad automatic weapon, or SAW. Instead of shooting projectiles like a railgun or a propellant-powered projectile like the older military weapons, the M90 was a blaster. It fired electrically charged blaster bolts at an incredible rate of speed. Each squad had a single soldier equipped with the rifle. If the Deltas liked using them and they proved to be effective, then Big Army would look to integrate them into all the Republic Army battalions to beef up the firepower of the ground forces.

Perry nodded and turned around to order his squad to load up. Once his squad started heading toward the Osprey, the rest of the platoon followed suit.

"Master Sergeant, I'm going to ride with Third and Fourth Squad," called out Lieutenant Crocker.

"Sounds good, LT. See you down on the surface," Master Sergeant Royce replied before following the last of the soldiers into the back of the Osprey.

Once he climbed in, the crew chief closed the door, allowing it to seal and pressurize the cabin. Sitting on the last seat next to the door, Royce attached the five-point harness to himself, pulling it tight, then looked at the others. They all appeared to be fastened in and ready.

A couple of minutes later, the Osprey started to get in position. It was being moved into one of the launch tubes near the front of the hangar deck and the ship. This process didn't take too long, especially since the ship had been positioned near the launch tubes before being loaded with its human cargo.

As the ship was moved into place, Royce heard a series of clicking noises. Then the Osprey levitated inside the magnetic launch tube as it prepared to be shot out of the mothership.

"Prepare to launch," came a voice inside their helmets from the pilot.

Master Sergeant Brian Royce craned his neck to the left and looked at the row of troopers. The tension inside the troop compartment was almost palpable. He fixed each trooper with his eyes and gave them a short nod, and they did the same, letting him know they were ready.

The lights inside the ship suddenly turned from an ambient white to a soft blue as the ship jerked.

"Launching!" announced the pilot, excitement in his voice.

Royce heard a loud swooshing noise as the shuttle was forcefully pushed out of the magnetic launch tube. The lights illuminating the runway whipped past them at an alarming rate. Seconds later, they were shot out of the *Voyager* and into the darkness of space. The artificial gravity of the mothership was gone in an instant, and the Deltas felt the weightlessness of zero g return. The pilots applied more power to the thrusters, angling the Osprey toward the lunar surface.

The tight turn and the increase in speed meant their bodies were now being slammed with seven g-forces. A few of the soldiers grunted audibly at the increased pressure on their bodies. Their mechanical combat suits kicked in, applying pressure to their legs and waist, pushing more blood up to their heart and their heads to keep them from passing out.

"Hang on, guys. We're seven minutes out from the DZ. I'm going to angle us into a couple of canyons and craters to evade the base's radar systems," the pilot informed them.

The Osprey angled steeper for the lunar surface as it picked up in speed. The g-force monitor in the soldiers' HUD was now showing nine g's. A few jarring minutes later, the Osprey pulled up hard, leveling them out just a few meters above the surface. Then it popped up briefly before it dove down into a large crater. The ship did this a few more times as the pilot deftly maneuvered them, staying close to the surface. This type of nap-of-the-ground flying was what pilots lived for. It also caused some soldiers to vomit in their helmets if they weren't prepared.

"Five minutes!" barked the pilot, tension and stress in his voice.

Royce used his neurolink to communicate with his platoon. *Listen up, Deltas. The opposition for this training mission may be synthetics, but they've been programmed to fight and defend this position hard. They'll be using blasters set to stun, so if you get hit, it's going to hurt like hell, but it won't kill you. This is about as real a scenario as we're going to get. Don't think of these defenders as Synths. Think of them as the Asian Alliance or some alien race.*

Sensing their excitement rising in anticipation of what was about to happen, Royce reiterated their primary objectives.

The RASs will be hitting Objective Yellow twenty mikes after we drop. That means we'll have minimal time to disable the point defense weapons. If we fail, their landing craft won't make it to the surface. Once we take those guns out, we need to storm the command center below the surface next. Hooah!

Hooah, came the reply from his troopers.

He continued, *I want First Squad to lay down suppressive fire while Second Squad bounds forward. The lieutenant and Third and Fourth Squads are on the other bird. They'll flank to the left and right.*

Staff Sergeant Perry will be in command of First and Second Squads once the action starts. I'll be with Third Squad while the LT is with Fourth Squad.

Remember, use your magrails for the assault. When we reach the structure, switch to blasters. If I see one of you guys fire a magrail inside the facility, I'll have you pulling guard duty in the Belt for the next year! Understood?

Hooah! came the reply.

"Three minutes!" shouted the pilot in their helmets.

The Osprey darted from one side to the other as the pilot did his best to evade simulated enemy ground fire from the surface. This would be their last real training exercise before the *Voyager* left for a completely new planet. Royce wanted to make the most of this exercise for his men.

The Deltas carrying out this initial assault were coming in from a different angle than the regular Army grunts. Their objective was simple:

take out the lunar defenses and the command-and-control bunker so the main body of infantry soldiers could land and assault the base itself.

"Two minutes!"

Readying himself, Royce looked at his rifle, making sure he had it on the right settings. *Magrail…*

The M85 assault rifle was a real beauty. It was the standard infantry assault rifle of the regular Army and Special Forces. The rifle had three weapon capabilities built into a single frame. The first was the magnetic railgun, or magrail. It fired a standard 5.56mm projectile with a three-hundred-round magazine. The magazine had a nifty counter on either side that let the soldiers know how many rounds they had left—an important thing to know in a gunfight. They primarily used the magrail setting when they wanted to shoot at something over a great distance or needed to punch through heavy armor or another solid defense.

The rifle also incorporated a newly miniaturized laser blaster. This was a new weapon that hadn't been in military service for more than a few years when it had been integrated into this new assault rifle. The blaster had a powerpack that could provide two hundred shots before it needed to be swapped out with a new one, so it had some limitations. It also wasn't very effective beyond a thousand meters. The Deltas typically carried three magazines each for the blaster and the magrail.

To top it off as the ultimate infantry combat assault rifle, the new system integrated a third weapon that fired a 20mm high-explosive smart munition. It was kind of like the older M203 and M320 40mm grenade launcher on the infantry rifles the military had used in the past. The 20mm grenade gun used a six-round magazine. The AI targeting computer on the rifle could preprogram the smart munition to explode on impact or as an airburst over a cluster of enemy soldiers. It was a truly badass weapon and beloved by the infantry and Special Forces alike.

The M85 truly was the ultimate multipurpose rifle for both planetary and space operations. When it had come out five years ago, it had quickly become the primary weapon of the Republic Army and the Delta battalions.

The Osprey leveled out in one of the shallow trenches on the moon as it slowed down. Then the rear hatch opened up to the blackness of space, allowing the Deltas to see out. The light inside the shuttle had shifted from a soft blue to a dull red.

Unlatching himself from the seat, Royce felt his body start to float momentarily. He activated the magnets in his boots, which instantly attached themselves to the floor of the bay. He waved for the others to do the same.

Royce walked toward the rear of the ramp, the metallic clicking from his boots the only noise in the cargo bay. Moments later, the rest of the platoon did likewise. If they didn't use magnetized boots, they'd have a hard time trying to stay upright or move about in a coordinated manner in the cargo hold. The specially designed space boots allowed them to walk normally in zero g.

The crew chief for the Osprey stood near the ramp. When he saw they were lined up and ready, he sent a quick message to the pilots. The shuttle turned briefly and then rose in altitude. They were no longer skimming the surface. They'd risen just high enough to allow them to safely jump, given the speeds they were moving at.

Looking at his own map, Royce saw they were approaching the drop zone. He needed to get ready to go. Moving toward the edge of the ramp, he saw the lunar surface whipping past below them at a decent clip. Taking a deep breath, he took a couple of steps forward and jumped. His body, encased in his exoskeleton combat suit, began a rapid descent to the lunar surface not more than thirty meters from the ship.

In a matter of seconds, he was on the ground, landing in a controlled fall that would be impossible on Earth. His combat suit absorbed much of the impact. Once on the ground, he had his rifle at the low ready, barking out orders to his platoon to get a move on.

Looking toward where their objective was, he spotted a slight rise in the terrain, just like the recon photos had shown. He took off at a quick trot with his squads following behind him. It was hard to keep from bouncing on the lunar surface given the lower gravitational pull.

"Master Sergeant, I'm going to get our heavy weapons set up on that crest," called out Staff Sergeant Perry.

Royce turned to look at the crest he was pointing to and nodded. "Good call. Get it done, Staff Sergeant."

As Royce approached the rise in the terrain, his AI-assisted heads-up display, or HUD, began to compose a three-dimensional map and lay of the ground around and in front of him. It also populated with every person in his platoon. When he reached the rise in the terrain, he poked his head above it, allowing the HUD's sensors to locate their objective and the enemy soldiers defending it.

Moments later, dozens of red marks appeared on the map, letting him know where the enemy soldiers were in relation to him and his soldiers. Through his neurolink, he started passing out assignments to his squad leaders, making sure they knew where the enemy was and how they needed to carry out their assault.

Within a few minutes of landing on the surface, his four squads had reached their assault positions. Staff Sergeant Perry had their heavy weapons set up and sighted in on the base. The crews had just sent him a quick note letting him know the .50-caliber magrail guns and the 20mm pulse beam blasters were ready to open up when Royce or the lieutenant gave the order.

Royce looked over to where the lieutenant was. Through their neurolink, he said, *The platoon's ready, sir.*

Lieutenant Crocker, their platoon leader, was new to their platoon. He'd just transferred to their company a month ago, and this was his first live-fire training exercise with them.

Lead the way, Sergeant. Let's do this, Lieutenant Crocker replied, clearly excited and ready to start.

All squads—attack now! Royce shouted over the neurolink, giving them all a good kick in the butt to move.

The platoon's two heavy magrails and two heavy blaster guns opened up on the unsuspecting guard towers and perimeter of the base. The .50-caliber slugs tore right through the towers, ripping them to shreds. The blue flickers of light from the blasters hit the fortified bunkers and sentry positions with lightning speed and precision, blowing them to pieces. Royce had designed this part of the assault to be the distraction. The goal was to focus the enemy's attention on his heavy guns while his other two squads advanced on the flanks.

With the covering fire initiated, Second Squad charged forward, bounding from one covered position to another as they carried out a direct frontal assault. This was again part of the distraction. Racing from one covered position to another, firing as they went, Second Squad kept the defenders firmly focused on them. Meanwhile, Sergeant Royce moved with Third Squad on the left flank while Lieutenant Crocker advanced with Fourth Squad on the right.

They bounced ever so slightly on the surface as they ran, with Royce doing his best to keep up with his squad. The younger Deltas were fully exploiting their youth and the abilities of their exoskeleton combat suits. As they approached the enemy's exposed flank, Royce's HUD spotted a Synth defender in a bunker, turning to shoot at them with one of the heavy weapons.

Seeing the threat before anyone else, Royce raised his rifle to engage it. The HUD placed a targeting reticle over the Synth, waiting for Royce to pull the trigger. The enemy Synth must have spotted his targeting laser because it ducked, probably moving to another position somewhere along the trench line.

Royce kept his rifle pointed in that general direction, letting the targeting radar on the helmet work to locate the Synth when he inevitably popped up again. A couple of seconds later, he was rewarded with a target to shoot. The Synth had popped up twenty meters further away with that same heavy-caliber weapon. Just as it was gearing up to fire on his guys, Royce's targeting reticle turned green, letting him know his HUD had synced with his rifle and he had a lock. He squeezed the trigger a couple of times, sending several magrail projectiles at the Synth's position. Seconds later, it was ripped apart by his slugs.

Planting his foot on the porous lunar surface, Royce pushed off hard, using the reduced gravity to hurl himself forward at a quick pace, closing the distance to the enemy lines. His squadmates were running with their rifles raised, using the AI-assisted HUD to help them neutralize the defenders as quickly as they could be identified. In moments, the squad had overrun the enemy positions and were inside their perimeter.

One of his soldiers ran toward the base of the enormous orbital defensive weapon and attached two large high-explosive charges to the side of it. The man set a detonator on the devices and then ran to join his comrades further away as they focused on fighting the reinforcements that continued to arrive from the hidden parts of the base.

A Synth defender surprised Royce and a couple of his squadmates by suddenly popping out of a fighting hole covered in loose dust and gravel from the moon's surface. It managed to shoot two of his guys before they took it out. Royce scolded himself for letting two of his guys get taken out of the exercise like that.

I'll have to look back at the video and figure out who missed that defender...

The squad leader on the right flank sent him a quick NL message, letting him know they had attached their own explosives to the orbital gun and were ready to detonate. Royce sent a fast reply to do it, then told his own squad to blow their charges as well.

Moments later, there was a bright flash as the charges went off. In that instant, both the orbital defensive weapons for the base were taken offline. Once the flash subsided, Royce looked up just in time to see several dozen landing craft descending rapidly on the base from orbit, right on time.

When the first wave of two hundred Republic Army soldiers landed, the newly arrived infantry went to work capturing the parts of the base that were above ground. Royce's Delta platoon had moved in on the building that would lead them down to the subterranean levels of the facility, where the command-and-control bunker was located. As they prepared to breach, the second wave of infantry arrived, bringing with them several of their Mechs and a few tanks. The heavy weapons would make short work of the remaining enemy defenses.

Royce's team had lined themselves up against the side of the building they needed to get inside. Once Royce saw they were ready, he signaled for them to breach.

A bright flash erupted along the edges of the airlock door, and then a violent depressurization occurred as the door blew out into space along with a couple of Synths and other contents from the room. They shot the Synths that flew out of the room, making sure they were neutralized.

The group of Deltas waited just a moment for the depressurization to finish before they rushed into the building, clearing the room of possible holdouts. Synths didn't need oxygen to breathe, so there could still be a few defenders inside.

With their blasters at the ready, they ran into the room as best they could in the low-gravity environment of the lunar surface. No sooner had they rushed in than two Synth defenders opened fire on them with their blasters. One of Royce's guys got hit, his body shaking from the stun before he slumped to the ground. He was out for the remainder of the exercise.

While his squad got their charges ready on the next airlock door, Royce took a moment to look at the readout of his platoon. He saw he'd sustained nine casualties since the start of the assault. Other than the troops that were down, everyone else seemed fine. Their biomechanical suits were operating normally: oxygen levels were optimal, power packs and weapons were good. Everything appeared to be going according to the plan, minus the casualties.

"Stand by for breach!" barked one of the junior sergeants as he moved to the side of the wall.

The other soldiers in the squad moved to the side except one. He had his rifle aimed at the door, ready to shoot whoever was on the other side when the door was blown open.

"Breaching!" yelled the sergeant.

Boom.

The door blew backward into the room they were in. The Delta aiming at the door didn't quite get out of the way in time as the door flew off-angle and right at him. It slammed into his body and threw him backward several meters until he thudded against the opposite wall.

Slumping to the ground, the soldier started to panic as the front glass of his helmet cracked and started venting oxygen. He let out a sharp yelp as a piece of metal sliced through his EVA suit and into his left thigh. That rip in his suit also started venting oxygen on him, further adding to his horror.

Royce switched over to the man's suit and his vitals. He quickly saw the problem and moved over to check on him. Two of his soldiers tried to help the wounded guy, but Royce yelled, "Stand down!" He wanted the injured Delta to work on sealing the leaks himself.

The rest of the squad proceeded to clear the next level while Royce stayed near the wounded soldier as he applied a quick sealant to the crack on his visor. He then pulled the piece of metal out of his thigh with a yell. With the metal removed, the soldier slapped a patch on the puncture in his EVA suit. Once he'd stopped the oxygen bleed, his suit repressurized itself. The soldier then released an injection of biomedical nanites into his bloodstream to stop the bleeding in his leg.

Leaning down to the wounded Delta, Royce held out his hand and helped him up, pulling the man close to him so their face masks were right in front of each other. "I hope you understand why I had you fix yourself up, soldier," he said sternly.

The young trooper looked at him and nodded. "To prove that I could treat myself and the others could as well."

Royce nodded in satisfaction. "Exactly. We're not RA, we're Special Forces. That means unless you're really effed up, you need to be able to take care of yourself. In the vacuum of space, you have to make split-second decisions that'll save your life and the lives of those around you. There isn't any wiggle room out here. If you mess up, you could end up dead—or worse, your squad or platoon could end up dead. Is that understood?"

"Hooah, Sergeant," came the quick reply.

"Good. Now go catch up to your squad, and let's finish clearing this objective."

Two hours later, the Osprey that had brought them to the lunar surface settled on the ground, not far from their positions. Sergeant Royce yelled out for everyone to load up. It was time to head back to the *Voyager* and write up their after-action review of the exercise.

They had accomplished their objective, sustaining thirteen casualties out of forty-eight soldiers. Now it was time to evaluate what had happened and examine what had gone right, what had gone wrong, and what could have gone better.

You train as you fight, and you fight as you train, Royce said to himself. It was important to study everything about these training exercises, so when the real deal happened, they'd be ready, and it would be like second nature.

Walking into the *Voyager*'s medbay, Master Sergeant Royce made his way over to his injured trooper. "How's he looking, Doc?"

Looking up at him, the doc grunted. "He'll live. I just gave him another injection of nanites. It'll ensure he doesn't come down with an infection and finish healing up the wound."

"Didn't that first injection do that?" asked the young soldier with a curious look on his face.

The doctor snickered at the question. "No, son. The first injection kept you alive, soldier. The medical infusion in your EVA suit doesn't pack enough nanites to fix you up to one hundred percent. It's just supposed to get you back in the fight and keep you alive long enough to make it back to the ship or a hospital unit."

"You hear that, Hawkins? Don't go taking a chest full of bullets or shrapnel. This thing might not be able to bring you back from the dead," Royce joked good-naturedly with his trooper.

"Give it a few more years or a decade, Master Sergeant, and this stuff will be able to do a lot more than it already can. As it is, it's able to cure nearly any known ailment the human body faces, to include cancer. Hell, they say in time, this thing'll be able to keep you alive well into your two hundreds or more, if you can believe that," the doctor said before he moved on to another task.

"When you're done here, Hawkins, report back to your squad leader," Royce ordered. "I want you to review what happened and why you got injured. Let's make sure that doesn't happen again. Next time you may not be so lucky, OK?"

The young soldier nodded. Royce then left to go check on the rest of his platoon and see if the captain had any additional orders for them.

Walking up to the captain's office, Royce rapped his knuckles on the door frame. The captain looked up, then motioned for him to come in and take a seat. "I reviewed the video from the exercise and your notes. The platoon did well," he said. "Actually, the platoon did better than I thought they would. That objective had more than six hundred defenders. The battalion commander was impressed as well. Do *you* believe the platoon is ready should we have to execute a mission like this for real?"

Royce paused for a moment to consider his answer. "That's hard to say, sir. To be fair, an assault like this has never been done outside of a training scenario. I'd like to think we'd handle it fine—but until the enemy votes and the bullets fly, it's hard to know."

"I agree. Which is why we continue to train over and over again. I'm honestly not sure if the Europeans or the Asian Alliance practice this kind of stuff. But should hostilities break out after the SET ends, we'll be ready."

Royce nodded. "Sir, since the Alpha Centauri mission isn't happening, any word on where we may be going next?"

The captain looked up at him. "No idea. All I've been told is we'll be shipping out on the *Voyager* in a month. We'll receive our new orders and mission once we're on our way."

Chapter Ten
A Pirate's Life

Sol
The Belt

Captain Liam Patrick looked at his lead engineer, puzzled. "Are you saying you can't fix it?"

Sara narrowed her eyes a bit as she replied, "I didn't say that, Liam. I'm telling you that you need to stop shooting them up so bad. You can't keep bringing me ripped-apart mining ships and then expect me to put them back together for you. It doesn't work like that. I need spare parts, and I need the right type of equipment. Heck, I need a shipyard with the tools to get all this done."

Liam shook his head. "We will have all that, one day. Right now, we have to keep working toward our goal. To do that, we need money. Heck, I spent nearly all our cash on those 3-D printers you wanted and bought a new Synth to help you with the repairs. What more do you want?"

"I want a freaking station and a yard to work from," she replied hotly. "I want you to stop killing miners."

Liam's face turned beet red. He stood and walked over to the window and looked out at the little empire they had built these last ten years. It still ate him up to think about the lives lost to build what they were building.

As he stared at the jumble of ships and two small habitats on the side of a massive asteroid, Liam replied, "You know I don't like the killing any more than you. I only do it when there isn't any other choice."

Their ultimate dream sat out there, a few hundred kilometers away. Even now, Liam and Sara had crews working around the clock on hollowing out the enormous rock so they could build a base within it. Heck, that rock was practically a planetoid in its own right. They were still years away from that dream—having an outpost of their own, run by them and other people who wanted to be free of a world or colony controlled by the Earth-based governments. Over the years, they had bought a few small commercial cruise ships that had room to house a few hundred people and grow their own food. Those ships were the start of their new colony.

Sara walked up to Liam and placed her hand on his shoulder. "I know you don't like the killing any more than I do, but we have to find a way to build this world of ours more peacefully. We can't keep terrorizing the Belt like this."

He sighed. "When we bring this next haul in to sell, it'll give us a hundred million, I think," he explained softly. "What I need to know is what do you need to get that ice miner back operational? I want to add that ship to our mining operation. Water's an important resource we need out here. We need that ship, Sara. When we get this mining fleet going, we may finally be able to put an end to our piracy efforts and go legit."

Now it was Sara's turn to sigh. "I've made a list of parts we need. If you can get the items I've highlighted, that should be enough. I think it'll be close to forty or fifty million unless those bastards have raised their prices again. Oh, and I could really use a couple more Synths if possible. Engineers, ones that know how to repair and rebuild the shot-up ships you keep bringing me. We've got close to a dozen miners out there that need repairs. If we can get them all back up and running, then yeah, it should end our piracy days. But, Liam, even if it doesn't, there has to be a better way of doing this than killing people. These miners are like us, just trying to make a better life for themselves."

"You're right. We'll figure something out," he replied, running his right hand through his hair. "As to those engineering Synths, you know those models are expensive. Last I checked, they were close to forty million apiece."

"They are, but you can't keep buying those cheaper models for your base building and not give me any of the expensive ones to keep these ships up and running. I'm trying to maintain a fleet of seven miners with twelve people and one Synth. I need help if you want me to keep things going."

He shook his head. "Fine, I'll get you another one. No more, though. We have to get our base up and running. Once we have that, we'll have our home. We'll be able to build our society the way we want it."

****

Two days later, Liam was sitting in the captain's chair of the freighter *John Galt* as they neared the Mars Orbital Station. Buying the massive cargo hauler four years earlier had been one of the smartest moves he'd made. His little band of pirates had been ganking smaller mining ships and cargo vessels along the various trade routes for the better part of a decade—all part of their larger plan to acquire the resources they needed to build their own station and facility in the Belt.

The problem was, they couldn't just show up at the MOS with a stolen ship and expect not to get caught. For now, Liam kept his pirate fleet tucked away in the Belt, out of sight of prying eyes.

The *John Galt* handled all of their supply runs now. It had been an expensive purchase at the time, nearly two billion dollars. It was a brand-new ship, custom-built for them, equipped with its own inertial dampeners and artificial gravity. It was also FTL-capable and had a sizable cargo hold that could transport raw ore and refined water. His pirates had added a few aftermarket magrail turrets for defense as well. There were, after all, pirates running amok in the Belt.

The radio crackled to life. "This is Mars Orbital Station. Welcome back, *John Galt.* You are cleared to dock at Port Six Alpha. Stand by to receive docking tug and crew."

I love coming to MOS, Liam reflected. It was a chance to be around people again, an opportunity to learn what else was going on in the system. He'd also gain some intelligence on what ships and companies might be operating near the empire he'd built. Liam liked the space operations crew on the MOS too. They were a wealth of scuttlebutt, which, as a pirate, was invaluable when he needed to stay one step ahead of being caught. Of course, if they knew who he really was or how he continued to acquire his large mining loads, they'd probably blast him from space or have a Republic Army raiding party waiting for him at the docking port.

He depressed the talk button on the radio. "That's a good copy, MOS. Standing by to receive docking crew and tug."

Liam finished decelerating the ship until they came to a complete halt two hundred kilometers from the station. Now they'd sit tight and wait until a docking tug came out there. It'd dock with them first and offload a pilot who would steer them into the port. The tug would then use its tractor beam to tow them in at a controlled speed. Once they got near the docking berth, the pilot would use the maneuvering thrusters to connect them to the station. Then they'd all get off and wait for the ship to be inspected before they offloaded their cargo to be sold. Liam would go on a buying spree, picking up new equipment for their home away from home.

Half a day later, the tug finally reached them. Liam went down to the docking station to greet their pilot for the day.

"Hey, Captain Dasani. Back with another load to sell, I see," Mike Miller said as he climbed aboard the ship.

Liam smiled as he extended his hand to shake Mike's. The people on MOS knew him as Captain Tim Dasani, a successful mining company owner that operated deep in the Belt. "A guy's gotta pay the bills, right?" he said with a wink.

Mike snickered. "Shoot, you guys have to be making a killing. The price of water, iron, nickel, gold, and platinum keeps going up. It's a construction bonanza out here." The two of them walked through part of the ship on their way up to the bridge.

"So what's new on MOS?" inquired Liam.

Mike lifted an eyebrow as he settled into the helmsman's chair. "Seriously? Haven't you heard about all the pirate activity out there? I'm almost surprised you haven't had your own share of run-ins with them."

"Who says we haven't?" Liam countered.

Mike turned to look at him. "You have? You should file a report with the station. They've been trying to collect intelligence on them. There's even a twenty-five-million-dollar reward for their capture or death."

Liam laughed at the reward amount. "That isn't worth the risk if you ask me," he explained. "We make more than that in a week if we find the right rock to mine. Nah, I'll leave the pirate hunting to those who have nothing else to lose. Besides, we've equipped most of our ships with magrails, so I'm sure we'll be fine."

Mike radioed to the tug that he was ready. A few minutes went by, and then the tug activated its tractor beam and started pulling the ship forward at a slow, controlled rate.

Mike pointed to something on the far side of the accompanying shipyard. "You see those ships over there?"

Liam craned his neck around to get a glimpse of what Mike was pointing at. When he saw it, his heart skipped a beat.

"The Republic, GEU, and Asian Alliance are constructing two each. They're going to be a new frigate-class patrol boat. They plan on using them to help police the Belt and some of the major shipping routes against piracy."

"Whoa. They aren't messing around, are they?" Liam asked, trying to act surprised and happy at the news. Secretly, he was nervous. This would put a considerable dent in their operation. Building a colony out of an asteroid the size of Rhode Island took resources—a lot of resources and money. And over the last ten years, their money had mostly come from their piracy efforts. They might have to switch to earning money the hard way if this new police force of sorts was able to find and stop them.

Liam spent the rest of the day making small talk with Mike, doing his best to subtly milk him for information about the latest gossip on the MOS and the three governing alliances that ran the station. When their ship finally docked, a customs agent came aboard and did a quick inspection of them and their cargo. Once the inspector had completed his job, he signed off on their paperwork and cleared them.

The first thing Liam did was head over to the exchange market. He met up with his commodities rep and started looking over the price of the various resources currently in demand. The station would purchase anything you brought in, but some items were obviously worth more than others. Liam liked to do a quick check on things so he knew what to look for when he went back to the Belt.

"Water is still in high demand," commented his rep. "I see you have a large quantity of it this time."

Liam smiled. "Yeah, we managed to find a decent chunk of ice. We were able to refine some pretty good minerals from it as well. I also have four tons' worth of Erbium."

"Whoa. Did you say you hauled in four tons' worth of Erbium?" his rep asked in astonishment. "That stuff has gone up over eight hundred percent since your last visit. There's a huge demand for it right now with the construction of some new warships back at the John Glenn Station." The man was ecstatic; he got a half-percent cut of everything Liam brought in.

"So what does that come out to in dollars?" Liam asked, his hopes rising a bit at the thought of a windfall about to be bestowed upon them.

The man's fingers were already pecking away on the calculator, adding up how much his entire haul was worth. A smile crept across his face as he looked up at Liam. "Captain Dasani—you just brought in more money in this single load than you have in the last ten years. The load is worth eight billion when it's all said and done." The man let out a laugh of excitement when he realized how extensive his own cut would be. "Drinks are on you tonight, my friend. You're now the third-richest independent miner in the Belt."

Liam felt a sudden rush of excitement at the news. He'd thought his load might be worth a few hundred million—enough to buy most of the supplies they needed and still stash a bit away in the bank. But this—this was huge. He could buy Sara enough engineering Synths to get their motley collection of ships repaired and either put them to use mining in the Belt or resell them for a profit back here at the MOS.

Later that day, Liam made his way over to where a number of the shops on the station were set up. The promenade had a host of merchants selling just about anything he could need. For deep space miners like himself, it was an opportunity to stock up on some hard-to-find items or things they couldn't fabricate themselves.

Liam walked into the Walburg Industries store and made his way over to the back, where they had several Synths on display for prospective buyers to look at. One was labeled a domestic. This was the type of Synth you used to help with daily chores and household duties, to include assisting with children. Another was a builder Synth; these were the most popular. They were used in nearly all construction-type projects, programmed to build just about anything he could think of, and they knew how to do it, and do it well. There was a mining Synth. These were big in the Belt. They were experts in zero g mining operations and could operate in the vacuum of space for days. Then there were the engineer Synths. These were the most expensive ones—the ones that knew how to build ships, repair them, and perform complex tasks that required incredible computing power and knowledge. They were also the one type of Synth Sara had asked him to buy.

Liam knew they needed a few more of them, but they had been financially out of reach. They had one, but they needed a lot more to accomplish what they were trying to build. Looking at the price tag, he saw they had gone up too. They were now fifty million apiece. The builder Synths were thirty million, and the mining Synths were twenty million. None of them were cheap, but since his people knew how to employ them, they could earn their money back in a couple of years and then they were just profit machines.

"Checking out the latest Synths? You have any you want in particular?" asked the shop manager, eying Liam suspiciously like he was just another tire-kicker wanting to look but lacking the money to purchase one.

"I run a small outfit out in the Belt. But yeah, I'm looking to purchase a few Synths."

The merchant lifted an eyebrow. "A few, you say? How many and which kind are you looking for?" he asked skeptically.

"I'd like to purchase five of the engineer Synths, twenty mining Synths, and twenty-five builder Synths," Liam replied.

Before the man could open his mouth to shut his request down or say something snarky, Liam pulled out his smart wallet and showed him his account balance. The man's eyes went wide when he saw the amount, and then his entire demeanor changed.

Now sporting a warm smile, he said, "That's a hell of a small outfit you run. You know, I just so happen to have those Synths on hand. Let me draw up the paperwork, and we can get them delivered to your ship."

This ought to speed up the construction of our new outpost, Liam thought happily as he continued his shopping spree. *Now, if I could just find some additional weapons to purchase for our ships...*

Chapter Eleven
A New Adventure

John Glenn Orbital Station
RNS *Rook*

Miles Hunt stood there for a moment, holding his wife tight in his arms. A couple of tears ran down his cheeks as he fought to maintain control of his emotions. He could feel her heavy breaths as she too struggled to keep from becoming an emotional wreck.

Pulling away, he looked at her beautiful face. Those deep blue eyes that stared back at him were moist with tears as her mascara threatened to smear across her face. He used his thumb to wipe them away before they washed away her makeup.

"Two years, babe. I'll be back in two years," he said softly, trying to convince her it wasn't so bad. She leaned in and kissed him. He tasted the salt from her tears on the side of his lips. They held that kiss for a moment before pulling away.

"You better be back in two years, or I'm going to have to find someone younger. Someone who'll stay put with *his* wife," she joked as she wiped another tear away.

Stealing a look around the room, Hunt saw many of the other married crew members doing the same thing he was—saying goodbye to their loved ones for what would surely be a long and tough mission. This tour was different from previous deployments in the solar system. It was going to take them six months to travel to this new system; then they'd spend another ten months exploring the area before returning to Earth. Presumably, when they returned, either their ship would be reassigned to Sol, or they'd be escorting their families and thousands of colonists to the new world they had discovered.

Hunt looked at his wife one last time. He gave her a good long kiss and one final hug before he said goodbye. Without waiting for him to leave, she turned and walked away. Several other spouses did the same thing, heading out of the departure gate of the station. They'd start the daylong journey down the beanstalk back to Earth and the rest of their lives while their loved ones would travel on to discover a new planet and possible second home world for humanity.

Fixing his uniform blouse, Hunt turned on his heels and started walking toward the connecting gangway that would lead him back to his ship. As he advanced down the walkway, he couldn't shake the feeling that this deployment was different. It was more than just the discovery of a new planet. Something deep within him felt like this deployment was going to change humanity—hopefully for the better.

****

With the crew on board and the last of their supplies loaded up, the walkway connecting the *Rook* with the orbital station disconnected and retracted away from them. The docking clamps holding them in place separated next, allowing the ship to float freely in its berth. A small tug moved forward and pushed them out of their docking position so they could initiate their maneuvering thrusters. Once they had been pushed a sufficient distance from the station, the helmsman gently applied some power to the auxiliary thrusters while the main engines spun up their primary propulsion system.

This would be their first cruise with the new magnetoplasmadynamic or MPD thrusters. They would provide the *Rook* with a lot more speed for interplanetary travel and acceleration as a warship. The *Rook*, the *Voyager*, and the smaller supply ship, the RNS *Gables*, were the first ships to be equipped with the newer MPD thrusters. Up to this point, nearly all space vessels had been outfitted with either an EmDrive or an Ion thruster system for interplanetary travel. While those were effective, they didn't have the same speed and thrust the new system was capable of. The MPD thruster worked differently, using the Lorentz force—the force on a charged particle by an electromagnetic field—to generate substantial thrust, up to two hundred newtons. The fielding of this new propulsion system would ensure that the Republic would dominate interplanetary travel for several decades to come.

The new propulsion system was also revolutionary in that they had designed the new ships with forward-facing thrusters as well. In the past, a ship would have to turn around as it started its deceleration toward a station or planet. Now, by adding thrusters to the front of the ship, they could eliminate the need to turn around. Considering these were warships, the Republic Navy wanted to keep their heavily armored front and weapon systems pointed at the enemy at all times. It was a revolutionary design change that would have a profound impact on all future ship construction.

As the *Rook* put more distance between themselves and the station, the helmsman steadily applied more power to the MPD thrusters, and they headed further away from the station to take up a position near the *Voyager* and the *Gables*.

As the *Rook* approached the two ships, they decelerated using the forward-facing thrusters until they came to a halt next to the much-larger *Voyager* and the *Gables*. The *Gables* was about the same size as the *Voyager*, only it was unarmed, being a supply ship. Two thousand, four hundred and eighty-four sailors, six hundred and forty-two Republic Army soldiers, and two hundred synthetic humanoids were setting off to make history.

In a few hours, the public would be told about the discovery of the habitable planet in the Rhea system and the expedition that was being sent to settle it. This news, of course, would set off a firestorm of activity worldwide as excitement and anticipation of what would be discovered by both the expeditions to Alpha Centauri and New Eden would filter back to Earth.

Hunt looked at the ships floating in space before him and smiled. He felt incredibly honored to be joining this expedition.

Turning to his executive officer, Commander Asher Johnson, he said, "XO, bring up a screen showing the shipyard, will you?"

Nodding, Johnson ordered Lieutenant John Arnold, the operations officer, to put the shipyard up on one of the two main screens on the bridge. A moment later, the expansive shipyard popped up on screen. He asked them to zoom in a couple of times until they had a much better picture of the yard and the activity taking place.

Captain Hunt walked toward the screen in front of the bridge, then turned around so he could face his bridge crew. Pointing to the image of the mammoth hulls being worked on, he said, "Before we leave on this mission, I wanted to show you what's being built while we're away. These ten massive hulls you see under construction are the new *Ark*-class transport ships. These ships are going to be pivotal to the expansion of the human race into the stars."

He paused for a moment as he turned to look at them briefly. "Each one of these ships is going to be six kilometers in length. They'll be able to house thousands of passengers at a time. When we return to Sol in two years, these ships will be nearly halfway done. A decade from now, they'll ferry hundreds of thousands of people to this new system. What we do on this mission is going to change the course of humanity. The heavens are being opened up for mankind. Now it's time for us to step forward and seize it."

The bridge crew clapped as he finished his little speech, thrilled to be on this incredible adventure with him as their captain.

He held a hand up to quiet them down. "We are all making sacrifices to be on this mission. Some of us are married, some of us are parents with little ones and a spouse staying behind. My wife and I recently celebrated our thirty-first year of marriage, and I've got two kids of my own now entering the Academy. This is going to be a tough mission for most of us. But know this—we are creating a better future for our loved ones and our country. Your sacrifices are not being made in vain. They have a purpose, a meaning, and one day, historians will write about what we're doing today with fondness and gratitude." Having concluded his little speech, Captain Hunt walked over to his command chair and took a seat as the bridge crew nodded in agreement.

"Captain, we're receiving a message from the *Voyager*," announced Lieutenant Molly Branson, his communications officer.

Hunt smiled at the mention of the *Voyager*, knowing Admiral Halsey would want to make her own speech. "Send it to my station."

Hunt looked at the small screen before him and watched her message. She was sending over some last-minute adjustments to their jump route. He nodded to himself. With current technology, their FTL drive could only run for a week at a time before they'd need to drop out of warp and allow the capacitors a day to recharge before continuing on. The third-generation FTL drive was twice as fast as the second-gen, but it was an energy pig.

Knowing this trip was going to require a number of stops along the way, Space Command had planned on leveraging those stops to continue its mission, gathering data on the systems they needed along the pitstops. They had also developed a plan to establish a rudimentary communication line between the Rhea system and Sol. When the fleet dropped out of warp, the *Gables* would deploy a deep space telescope along with two FTL-equipped probes. They intended to string a line of communication buoys to allow them to move information between the Rhea system and Sol. With their third-gen FTL drive, they could cover two light-years in a month. It was believed they'd be able to cut that at least in half within a few more years, but not until they figured out how to create new reactors that could generate substantially more power than their current fusion ones.

A few minutes later, his communications officer announced, "Transmission coming in from the Admiral to the Fleet."

Time for her speech to the troops...

"Go ahead and pipe it into the rest of the ship," Hunt ordered. He wanted the rest of the crew to hear the message she was about to deliver.

"Attention. This is Admiral Abigail Halsey speaking. Today marks the first day our people will venture beyond our solar system," she began. "Our fleet was initially built to travel to Alpha Centauri and the Centaurus constellation. However, when our deep space probes explored the Rhea system, it carried out an extensive scan of a planet called Rhea Ab in that system. The planet, as it turns out, is a near clone of Earth. It has a breathable atmosphere and is only approximately five percent larger than Earth. This means its gravity is not that much more powerful than our own. It's an ideal planet for us to colonize. When this discovery was made, it was determined that we should forgo the Alpha Centauri expedition in favor of this mission."

Hunt saw broad smiles on the faces of his bridge crew and knew the rest of his team must be smiling as well. They had all been disappointed when word had come down that the Alpha mission was scrubbed. The senior leadership of their little fleet knew they had been given a better mission, but most of the crew did not. They knew only that they were heading to a new system, nothing more.

"There's something else I need to tell you. While we were unable to detect any electronic signatures or spot any life forms, our scientists did find evidence to suggest there may be life on the planet. As such, we have a small first contact diplomatic group that will be accompanying us on this trip.

"When we arrive in the system, the *Rook* will begin a more detailed survey of the system and the surrounding area while the *Voyager* will focus on looking for signs of life and, if we find any, make contact with them. We will also begin a survey to identify where to establish the colony and our first city on this new planet. The *Voyager* will stay in the system for fifteen months, gathering information and carrying out various geological studies. We'll then leave the colony and our Republic

Army battalion on the planet while we transit back to Earth to report our findings."

She continued, "If things go according to plan, we will see the largest migration of humans in history to our new home world, or we'll find an alien race and look to establish a peaceful coexistence. For the time being, I need everyone to focus on their tasks at hand. Train, study, and be ready for this new adventure when we arrive. Admiral Halsey out."

When her transmission ended, there was silence on the bridge for a moment. Most of the crew turned to look at Hunt. A few had big smiles on their faces. A few had questions; only one looked annoyed at the deception. Hunt felt he should handle that problem soon, so it wouldn't develop into something later.

Standing up, Hunt grabbed the handset that would allow him to speak to everyone on the ship. He cleared his throat. "This is the captain speaking. I know many of you have been surprised by the admiral's speech. Some may be happy; some may feel misled. I want to explain something to you. Rhea Ab, otherwise known as New Eden, is an opportunity for our country to start over on a new planet—one that hasn't had the environment destroyed or plundered by the titans of industry and war," he explained.

"Most of you know our home world, Earth, has taken an environmental beating, especially after the last Great War. The damage done from the multiyear-long nuclear war has brought our planet to the brink. New Eden offers humanity a chance to start over. This had to be kept a secret until the last minute. As most of you know, the Space Exploration Treaty expired earlier in the year. That means we'll be able to legally lay claim to New Eden as ours, just as the GEU and Asian Alliance will lay claim to the planets in the Centaurus system. Had we joined that expedition, our country would not have been able to put our stake on either of the two known planets in the system we're headed to. New Eden represents the best opportunity for our country and humanity to thrive and grow."

Hunt paused for a moment as the bridge crew waited to hear what he'd say next. "For the next six months, I want everyone to study every nugget of information the probes bring us. I especially want you guys to start studying the system: the moons, planets, suns, and everything else we have on record about where we're headed. Our focus isn't on the colony or the search for life on the surface, but on the exploration of the system. The probe says there is one more potentially habitable planet nearby. We need to determine if it can, in fact, sustain human life. We also need to look for signs of possible alien life on this other world and the moons as well. I want everyone to know that we can do this. I trust you implicitly with this task. Now, let's get back to work. We have a lot of information to analyze and absorb before we arrive."

Chapter Twelve
Killing Time

RNS *Voyager*
Troop Deck

The air smelled of dirt mixed with some sort of floral essence. The birds sang a soft melody in the trees above. A couple of parrots squawked, adding their own noise to the jungle. Master Sergeant Brian Royce moved slowly, deliberately, one foot in front of the other. From time to time he looked down to make sure he didn't inadvertently step on a tree branch or somehow miss a tripwire or landmine.

Trailing behind him were twelve Deltas, members of the second squad he was training with today. Each of his troopers had their weapons pointed outwards in forty-five-degree arcs as they scanned their sectors. Their heads-up displays showed them everything that was happening in their assigned field of fire. Suddenly, the point man twenty meters in front of Royce held his hand up. Everyone's senses kicked into overdrive at the signal that something was out of place. Then the Delta balled his hand, then opened it and lowered it, telling them they needed to go to the ground.

Using his NL, Royce asked, *What do you see, Price?*

I thought I spotted some movement, two hundred meters to our front, the point man replied, pointing his rifle.

Lying still, Royce continued to use his senses to discern what was happening around them. Then he heard something alarming, or rather he didn't hear something. The birds had stopped chirping. It had suddenly gotten quiet.

Everyone get ready, Royce said over the NL as he moved his rifle to point in front of where Corporal Price had his own rifle aimed. If they got hit, Price would need immediate covering fire to counter the ambush.

A fraction of a second later, Royce saw a dark object fly out of the forest in front of them, sailing directly for them. Price yelled, "Grenade!" Seconds later, it thudded to the ground several meters in front of Royce and blew up fractions of a second later, before he had a chance to move or get out of its shrapnel radius.

"Damn it!" Royce cursed loudly. His mind suddenly transported him out of the virtual reality training simulation. He flipped open the bed cover and sat up. His physical body was sweating from what it had just gone through. His pulse was up, as was his adrenaline.

"Sorry about that, Master Sergeant. Better luck next time," Lieutenant Crocker said as he offered him a glass of water.

Royce shrugged. "It happens. I'm eager to see how Sergeant Wagman does in my absence."

"That was the idea in taking you out. So far, he seems to be doing pretty well," the lieutenant commented as he looked at the video display of the fight.

"LT, thanks for getting us some more time in the sims," Royce said before he downed the rest of his water. "I know the RA guys have been using it a lot to practice their landing, but we also need more time in if we're to stay sharp."

In the troop decks of the *Voyager*, they had four training simulation rooms. Each room had thirty virtual reality training simulation pods or beds. They looked like those old tanning beds from earlier in the century. A soldier would lie on the bed while a technician attached all the bio feeds to the user. Once they were hooked up, they'd close their eyes, and then their mind would be transported into whatever simulation scenario had been loaded up. Most of the time, Captain Jayden Hopper, their company CO, had them practicing orbital insertions, small-unit patrols, or surveillance missions in preparation for their real mission on New Eden.

The lieutenant, for his part, was trying to get them as much time in the sims as he could. Lieutenant Crocker was a late addition to their platoon. They'd been down a lieutenant once the previous guy had gotten promoted and transferred to a different company—one that wasn't deploying with the RA for this mission. Fortunately for Royce, Lieutenant Crocker was a mustang—he'd previously been enlisted, a sergeant himself. He mostly stayed out of his platoon sergeant's way and let Royce run the platoon as he saw fit.

"Oh, hey, before I forget—the captain wants to see you up in his office," the LT said before taking another sip of his coffee. His eyes were still affixed to the monitor, watching how the squad handled the ambush he'd set for them.

"Ah, OK. Do I have time to hit the showers, or does he need me up there right now?" asked Royce as he cinched up his boots.

Turning to look at Royce, the LT took a sniff and made a sour face. "I'll tell him you're hitting the showers. You're not going to talk to him smelling like that. It's my job to protect the man, and make sure you NCOs don't get in trouble," he joked.

Royce laughed, then made his way up to the team room. He'd clean up in their own spaces.

While the Deltas waited for the *Voyager* to arrive in the Rhea system, they continued to train hard. For three months, there was little else to do than train, train, and train some more. It kept their minds busy and gave them less free time to get in trouble.

Once they arrived in the system, it'd be the responsibility of the four Delta platoons to scout the area for suitable landing zones and escort the first contact team if they found signs of life. They'd be the first humans to set foot on the new planet, and that excited the hell out of the men.

Accompanying them to the surface would be a group of scientists and a first contact team, who'd verify that the location they identified was suitable for a colony and screen for any signs of life. Once that had been determined, the battalion of Republic soldiers would land and expand the base perimeter. A couple of days later, the first batch of Synths would land and go to work building up the base.

When Master Sergeant Royce knocked on Captain Hopper's office door, he heard the man tell him to enter. Once inside, he saw the captain sitting at his chair, looking at a report and a holographic floating image of the planet they were heading toward.

"You wanted to see me, sir?"

The captain nodded. "I did. Take a seat. We need to talk."

Sitting down, Royce braced himself for whatever might be headed his way, not sure if this was a good or a bad talk.

Apparently, seeing the pensive look on his face, Captain Hopper said, "This is about New Eden, Royce. Nothing bad. As a matter of fact, I've chosen your platoon for a special mission."

A sense of relief washed over Royce. "Should the lieutenant be here?" he asked.

"No. I already briefed him earlier this morning. He knows what we're doing. He's going to start tweaking the training sims for you over the next few weeks to reflect your new mission. What I wanted to talk with you about is a sensitive mission that's been handed down to us."

Royce's interest was now piqued. He'd worked on a few sensitive missions during his career. His last mission on Mars, however, had broken down, and he'd ended up in a training mission assignment as a penance.

"What I'm about to show you is strictly confidential, Sergeant," the captain continued. "You don't talk about it with anyone else in the company, and certainly not anyone on the ship until we're cleared to. Is that understood?"

Royce nodded.

"One of the key reasons why we are heading to New Eden as opposed to the Alpha Centauri is this." The captain pulled up several images of a cave entrance and what appeared to be some mining equipment nearby. "When we first left Sol, the admiral mentioned the possibility of life on the planet. We're not sure how old this is, but it was clearly made by someone or something. It's the surest sign of intelligent life outside Sol that we've found, and it appears to be active. That mine looks like it's being regularly used. As you can see, there isn't any overgrowth around it. Space Command wants us to investigate the site and see what's there."

Royce held a hand up. "Captain, you're saying there really are little green men out there?" he asked sarcastically as he looked in awe at the still images.

The captain laughed. "Apparently. In any case, I've selected your platoon to have the honors of escorting our first contact team down there to check it out. Putting aside the debacle on Mars, which I don't think was your fault, you are the only Delta in the unit with any real experience doing reconnaissance missions deep behind enemy lines. This mission is a chance of a lifetime, Master Sergeant. But it's also a complete unknown. We don't know if these are friendly aliens or if they'll be hostile. What I do know is I'm jealous I can't go with you—but someone needs to stay with the rest of the company in case you do find aliens and they aren't friendly."

Royce shook his head in disbelief. "This is incredible, sir. I don't even know what to say. Is there anything specific you want me to have the platoon train up for in anticipation of this mission?" he asked. The gravity of the situation was fully sinking in.

Thinking for a moment, the captain finally replied, "Maybe do some additional training on clearing caves and tunnels. Throw in some protective detail training as well. If you look at the surrounding area, you can see it's pretty rugged and heavily forested. I'd work on doing some sim training in environments like that. We'll have a better idea of what the place looks like once we get in orbit and we can start sending some recon drones down."

Royce nodded. "Roger that, sir. I'll make sure we work this stuff into our training cycle. If I'm not mistaken, we still have a few months until we arrive."

****

RNS *Voyager*
Science Deck

Professor Audrey Lancaster gazed at the video monitor. She never got tired of seeing the swirling colors and the faint glimmers of stars zipping past the *Voyager* as it traveled inside the warp bubble. It was one of the most incredible things she'd ever seen. It almost reminded her of when she was a kid living in Wisconsin during the winter. As their minivan drove through snow at night, the vehicle's headlights would illuminate it, creating the illusion that they were flying through space. It was one of her favorite childhood memories.

Finally, prying her eyes away from the image, she returned her focus to the computer terminal, completely in awe of what she now had access to. *I wish I'd had this kind of raw computing power back at Harvard*, she thought wistfully. The way this program could crunch numbers was genuinely incredible.

For the past two weeks, Audrey had been working on the programming to solve a sociolinguistic problem that had been bothering her for decades. When Audrey was a graduate student, she had traveled to Iraq and Russia to study changes in the Chaldean language. She had done her dissertation on how the three mass waves of migration to Russia following the Treaty of Turkmenchay in 1828, World War I, and World War II had affected the Chaldean language. What she found most fascinating was how rapidly the English language had evolved when compared to a language with nearly six thousand years of history attached to it, even despite the major world events that impacted the Assyrian-Chaldean diaspora.

Two years ago, when Space Command had approached her about being a part of the group's first contact team, she had been ecstatic. It had meant she'd have to give up her tenured professorship at Harvard, but being one of the world's leading sociolinguistic specialists meant it shouldn't be hard to reobtain it when she returned from the expedition. She was only supposed to be gone for five years.

For Audrey, this was an incredible opportunity. If humans discovered sentient life on Alpha Centauri, they'd need a team of scientific experts to understand the alien language so they could effectively communicate. When the mission changed, she had begun to have second thoughts about going, but Dr. Katherine Johnson had intervened and had been able to get her read onto the real reason for the change in missions.

Seeing those images—images of what appeared to be a functional mine on an alien planet—had sealed the deal for her. She knew this expedition wasn't going to have a chance encounter with an alien race; they were actually going to be the ones to make the first contact. Audrey wanted to be a part of that, so she opted to stay on the mission.

Knowing she'd have six and a half months of travel time, Audrey brought some linguistic projects with her that she'd meant to get around to. With a lot of time on her hands and access to a quantum computer and a super AI for the first time, she would work on some of the toughest linguistic challenges she could find. When she returned to Earth in a few years, she'd have solved some of these lingering issues and further cemented her status as one of the world's leading researchers in her field.

As the computer plotted the changes from ancient Chaldean to the language it was today, she saw patterns emerge. As warring factions interacted, new technologies were introduced, people migrated to new regions, and plagues ravaged, the language morphed. The changes would become more pronounced over time. For posterity's sake, she began running these same calculations across all the different languages still in use on Earth, and the dead languages no longer spoken. The infographic the AI created was fascinating. Seeing the ebbs and flows of styles over time and then cross-referencing those changes with the transient nature of humans explained a lot. Couple that with the spread of diseases, plagues, and wars, and it was the most complete explanation to date of how a language would evolve over time.

After completing her PhD in sociolinguists, Audrey had become very interested in studying comparative linguistics, though she had never formally sought a degree in that field. She was the consummate academic, always learning anything to do with language and branching out into various areas within her field. Between her studies of syntax and morphology across many diverse languages and her understanding of how languages changed over time, she was hoping that they would have enough information in their computer models to be able to understand and dissect any new languages quickly. As the lead linguistic expert on the ship, it was going to be her job to decipher the alien language and develop a means to communicate with them. It was a big task, but one she relished.

****

Three Months Later
RNS *Voyager*

Admiral Abigail Halsey walked out of her office and onto the bridge. One of the crew members had sent her a message letting her know they were about to cross into the Rhea star system in ten minutes. She walked over to her chair in the center of the bridge and sat down, observing the others around her. Everyone was excited. After months of travel, they were about to enter the system New Eden was a part of.

The images of starlight whipping past them at high speeds intermixed with a multicolor aurora around the warp bubble, made for some stunning, almost hypnotic views. Halsey thought how easy it would be to just get lost staring at it for hours if she were to let her mind wander.

"Dropping out of warp in ten seconds," the navigation officer announced calmly.

The warning was echoed throughout the ship, letting everyone know to prepare. Even with the inertial dampeners, it was still a little bumpy when they came out of warp. Moments later, the *Voyager* and the two other ships she was traveling with made their grand entrance into the system.

As soon as they were out of the warp bubble, the crew went into action, just like they'd done in previous drills.

"Ops, I want a system-wide scan. Use our full spectrum of systems and send a message to the *Rook* that we'll hang back and protect the *Gables* until they clear us a path," Admiral Halsey ordered as she began the process of getting a picture of what they'd just jumped into.

After twenty-six FTL jumps, they practically had the procedures to follow when they dropped out of warp on autopilot, but this was their end destination. They weren't just passing through.

"Beginning system-wide scan now," called out Lieutenant Moore, her Ops officer.

The Operations or Ops section of the bridge consisted of five people on duty at all times. Three of them worked the active and passive scanner suite while the other two consisted of the senior enlisted on duty and the officer in charge of the department.

It would take some time for their electronic sweeps to return with some usable data. In the meantime, they'd hang back with the transports while they waited to see what all was in the system.

Looking at the monitor, Halsey saw the *Rook* starting to engage her main engines. In a way, Admiral Halsey was jealous of her friend Hunt, whose mission was to explore, protect, and fight if need be.

She turned to her chief science officer, telling him to have his department get ready to analyze the data that would start pouring in from the probes they were launching and the scans of the system. She wanted them to get to work on identifying the location Dr. Johnson's team had told her to investigate. If there was life down on that planet, then she wanted to find it.

****

RNS *Rook*

With the jump complete, Captain Hunt ordered the ship to secure from FTL and begin regular operations.

"All right, people, this is it," Hunt announced. "We're finally in the system. Ops, I want you guys to go ahead and raise our search radars and electronic antennas. I want full sweeps of the entire system. Start looking for any signs of ELINT or MASINT happening in the system. Pay special attention to New Eden and her moons. If someone or something is transmitting from the surface, then I want to know about it."

Tapping the sensor on his communicator, Hunt pinged his engineering section next. A moment later, his engineering chief pinged that he was ready to receive. "Commander Lyons, let's get the main engines up and running. I want us underway as soon as possible."

"On it, Captain. Give us five minutes to finish securing from FTL and transition to the MPD drives," his engineering chief replied.

Next, Hunt turned to his Ops section. "Lieutenant, start launching our satellites. I want one sent to each of the moons. Let's get a few of them in orbit around New Eden itself. We need to get a sense of what's down there and in the immediate area."

While Hunt waited for Engineering to tell him the engines were ready, the *Rook*'s active sensor systems blanketed the system, in search of whatever might be out there. Their incredible array of deployable antennas and radar systems were running at full power. It would now be a matter of waiting for the returns. Some of them might happen in a few minutes, while it would take hours, and in some cases days, for others to return to the ship and provide them with a better picture of the system.

Hunt's communicator chirped. "Bridge, Engineering."

"Engineering, this is the captain. Send it."

"Sir, MPD drive is warmed up and ready," Commander Lyons informed him.

"Excellent. We're going to start moving, so have your people ready. Bridge out."

Hunt turned to his helmsman. "Lieutenant Donaldson, bring us up to full speed. Let's set a course for New Eden. Navigation, let's get set up in a high orbit around the planet. I want to use our shipboard scanners to map out the situation on the ground."

Forty minutes went by as the ship moved deeper into the system. They were still six hours from the planet. In the meantime, they'd continue to collect information. As they neared New Eden, it started to show up on their forward cameras.

Hunt was just as eager as everyone else to see what this new planet looked like up close. He'd been waiting patiently for them to get nearer before he had them bring it up on the cameras. There wasn't a reason to bring it up if they were too far away to really take in any of its beauty, he reasoned, which was why he had held off.

After what felt like forever, his XO whispered in his ear, "Sir, we're in close enough to put New Eden up on the screen if you'd like."

Commander Asher Johnson was apparently eager to see the planet as well.

Nodding, Hunt turned to Ops. "Let's bring up the forward cameras. I'd like to see what New Eden looks like."

The rest of the bridge crew leaned forward in anticipation. Hunt made sure to have the image piped through to the rest of the monitors on the ship. He wanted the rest of the crew to share in the excitement of this new discovery.

A moment later, the smallish image of the planet appeared. Everyone stared at it for a moment, awestruck by what they saw. One of the Ops people zoomed in as far as the camera would go, then several people spontaneously said, "Ooh," in an awestruck voice.

The planet looked so similar to Earth, yet so uniquely different. Captain Hunt studied the bodies of water, clouds covering parts of the sky, various shades of blues, greens, browns, and other colors as this beautiful glass marble floated in front of them.

The planet also had three moons in various orbits around it. One of the moons looked like a small planet in its own right, with its own atmosphere and bodies of water and clouds.

Captain Hunt looked out at New Eden, which was in orbit around a single K-type dwarf star. The two smaller brown dwarf stars that orbited the main star gave off a beautiful display of color: one was mostly magenta while the other was emitting a greenish tint.

Stunning, thought Hunt.

Snapping himself out of his momentary trance, Hunt ordered the ship to approach the moons in orbit around the planet first as they neared the primary world. Once their scan was done, they'd settle into orbit around New Eden and begin a more thorough scan of the planet. Right now, Hunt needed to make sure there wasn't life or some other electronic signal on any of the moons that could pose a threat to their ship, or the *Voyager* and the *Gables*.

The next several days would prove to be busy. Batches of data continued to stream into the ship from the various scans, sensors, and satellites they had launched. When they had sufficiently verified that the fleet wouldn't be in any immediate danger if they approached the planet, Hunt would tell Admiral Halsey she could proceed with her mission.

Chapter Thirteen
Planet Fall

RNS *Voyager*
In Orbit—New Eden

The Deltas sat in the briefing room, waiting for the captain to provide them with their final brief before they headed down to the planet. In the four days since the fleet had settled in the orbit of New Eden, the scientific crew of the *Voyager* had been going over satellite data being fed into the computers along with data from the handful of drones they had dropped into the atmosphere of the planet. They were studying the topographical areas of the planet, trying to figure out where would be the best place to set down first. Knowing they needed to get the space elevator established at some point, they were exploring mainly locations around the planet's equator.

As the soldiers started getting antsy for the briefing to start, two scientists, along with Captain Hopper, walked into the room. Everyone jumped to attention and waited for him to tell them to take their seats.

When the trio had reached the front of the room, Captain Hopper sternly ordered, "Sit down, shut up and listen to the scientists' briefing on what's going to be happening."

For the next thirty minutes, they went over the assignments for First, Second, and Fourth Platoons' missions: where they'd be dropping, what they'd be doing, and how long they'd be on the ground. When the brief for the First, Second, and Fourth Platoons had finished, those soldiers left the room, leaving only the forty-two members of the Third Platoon, who were told to stay behind after the brief; they were doing something different.

If any of the units on the ground ran into trouble, a company of Republic Army soldiers was going to stay on QRF alert. If things somehow went to hell, the entire battalion would land and bring with them their heavy equipment and deal with it. No one expected any problems, but it was good to know they had help should they need it.

Captain Hopper, along with Lieutenant Crocker and Master Sergeant Royce, stayed in the room as they watched the other platoons filter out. They'd head to the flight bay and start getting their equipment ready.

Once they had cleared the room, two different scientists walked in, along with Admiral Halsey and her XO, Commander Erin Johnson. Everyone jumped to attention again when they saw the admiral walk in.

"Take your seats, everyone. This is going to be a long and interesting brief, so get comfortable," Admiral Halsey stated as she took the lead in briefing them.

The Deltas shared a few nervous glances. It was clear that they understood that if the admiral was briefing them, then this was going to be anything but routine. Something was up.

"Four months before we left on this journey, our scientists discovered something on this planet," Halsey began. "Much to our surprise, we identified verifiable signs of intelligent life. It may even be an advanced race. We're having a hard time determining what kind of communications systems they're using or finding their electronic signatures just yet, but we believe we know approximately where some of them currently are."

She paused for a moment for added effect. The operators shared nervous glances with each other as they waited for her to continue. "I'm going to show you something," she said.

Then a short video played, presumably from one of the drones they had just dropped into the planet a few days ago. It made a couple of passes over the mine and the surrounding area. Sadly, it had not been able to grab a lot of good video coverage due to some sort of electronic interference, but what it did show was a tall figure escorting what looked to be a few dozen smaller figures. They couldn't make out any precise details, but what the operators could see raised the hair on the back of their necks.

Clearing her throat as the grainy video ended, Halsey moved back to the center of the room. "Proof positive of alien life—this is why we scrubbed our mission to Alpha Centauri. This is also why we have a contingent of Special Forces on the *Voyager* and a Republic Army battalion. We have no idea if these beings are peaceful."

"Uh, Admiral"—one of the sergeants raised his hand—"is there any way of knowing how tall those aliens are, or maybe some additional details on them before we land dirtside?"

"We're working on that as we speak, Sergeant. We're running into some interference near the mountain, but hopefully one of our drones will gather some better images on its next pass of the area," she replied.

They were using some very high-altitude drones to map the planet, not the more precise ground surveillance drones the SF operators were used to working with.

Halsey took a deep breath before she continued. "I know we're short on information right now, and we're sending you to a planet full of unknowns and at least two alien races. But that's why we're sending you guys down to investigate and not the regular army. Your platoon's mission is going to focus on surveillance. We know there is life on the planet. So your job is to recon the surrounding area and get us in-person confirmation. Then our first contact team will attempt to make contact with the aliens and try to establish some sort of dialogue with them. Right now, we need intelligence. Survey the forest and do your best to see if there's a base camp they're operating out of."

She paused as she looked several of them in the eye, settling on Lieutenant Crocker and Master Sergeant Royce. "I know I'm asking you guys to carry out a dangerous and unknown mission. Your platoon has the most experience in this field, and I need my best people on this mission. When our first contact team feels they have enough information, a few soldiers from your platoon will escort our diplomat to try and speak with them. Under *no* circumstances are you to shoot at or attack them unless you have permission from me, or your lives are in immediate danger. I cannot stress enough how important it is that we do not come across as hostile in our first interactions with an unknown species. Is that understood, Deltas?"

The admiral left no doubt that if anyone on this mission deviated from the orders she'd given, it would not go over well for them or their career. The Deltas were awestruck by what they had just seen. They'd really done it; they had discovered alien life. Now it just remained to be seen if they had just found a new ally or a new enemy.

****

Admiral Halsey left the briefing room and made her way back to the bridge. She felt she had given the Deltas enough information to complete their objective without endangering themselves or her mission.

Since arriving in orbit, she'd had her operations section working overtime deploying drones and additional satellites to scan and scour every centimeter of this planet. The challenge they faced was the planet was just so damn big. At 1.05 times the size of Earth, it could end up taking months for their satellites to have even a working map of the entire planet, let alone any real detailed scans of it.

She kept telling herself that once her teams were on the ground, they'd have a better idea of the composition of the planet and what they were dealing with. She hoped like hell they were able to figure out who was mining that mountain. It was clearly an organized operation. What troubled her was the video they'd just acquired. Either they had stumbled upon two alien races, or something was off. But seeing the large creatures next to the group of smaller ones unnerved her. It was also causing her some angst that those smaller aliens looked an awful lot like humans.

Entering the bridge, Halsey made her way over to Ops to see if they had come up with anything new in the last few hours.

The bridge of the *Voyager* was actually laid out very similarly to how the older US warships' Combat Information Centers, or CICs, were. Sitting at the back of the bridge were the commander's and XO's chairs, along with that of the senior enlisted. To the right were the operations, communications, and engineering sections, and then to the left was navigation, helm, and weapons.

In front of everyone were four enormous digital monitors. They could be configured to display one large image of whatever the admiral wanted to see or they could be broken down to cover multiple sections or pieces of information. On the edges of the room, angled inward to give everyone, especially the admiral and XO, the best visual, were additional monitors. These would typically have the status of each department along with any damage report information should the need arise. In all, this room enabled the officers and senior enlisted that managed it to fully understand and process everything that was happening around them.

"Ops, have we spotted anything unusual around the landing sites? I want to make sure our people aren't landing in a hot zone once they get on the ground," Halsey asked as she stood looking at the various monitors and information feeds.

The chief petty officer who'd been coordinating the drone data looked up at her. "Not that we've detected thus far," he responded. "The drones just completed their fourth pass of the area an hour ago. We're still getting a lot of electronic interference, though. I'm not sure what the problem is. It could be something in the soil or the atmosphere that's interfering with our signals."

"Have we been able to carry out any geological surveys yet?" she asked next, hoping that might offer an explanation for why the coms with the drones were going haywire.

Taking his eyes off his station, the drone operator replied, "They've completed a pass using thermal imagining, infrared, lidar, and the good old-fashioned mark one eyeball. They look clean, deserted. But closer to the mountain, there's definitely something that's causing a lot of radio interference."

She nodded, realizing she couldn't do anything about the irregularities until they had teams on the ground. She thanked the crew for doing a good thorough job, then walked over to the chief petty officer overseeing the drones.

Halsey leaned down a bit. "How about the second site?" she asked in a hushed tone. The chief had been read onto what they were doing over there and was personally managing that drone's feed.

Motioning for her to lean in even a little closer, he answered, "I found something."

Halsey's eyes went wide. She walked around his station and knelt down next to him. "What do you mean?"

He brought up a file to show her. Halsey almost gasped when she saw it but caught herself in time.

"That's what I said. I was about to come to get you when you walked on the bridge. I think this changes things." He showed her more of the video. They'd finally gotten one of their surveillance drones the Deltas were used to using near the site.

Admiral Halsey's mouth fell agape a little as she watched what was being played for her. "They look human," she said in shock.

"That group does, yes. But look over here." The chief used the cursor to display an image of something entirely different.

Now her eyes went wide as saucers as her left hand moved up to her mouth. She suddenly became aware that others on the bridge might see her reaction. "Close your workstation up. Let's go to my office," she ordered as she got up.

As she headed to her office, she sent a message over to the head of her science department and Captain Hopper. His Delta team needed to see this before they went planetside. She also sent a message down to the flight deck and delayed the launch of the surface team for a few hours.

They needed to figure out what to do with the information they had just discovered before they started putting boots on the ground.

When it was just her and the chief petty officer who had been manning the drone alone in her office, she had him pull up the video image again.

"Where do you think they're going? Oh, and why haven't we found anything from our satellites yet?"

"The satellites are still carrying out their scans, so it's going to take time," the chief replied. "Plus, this entire area we're looking at is pretty heavily wooded. It's easy to hide things under the tree cover."

"Do you suppose those are prisoners?" she asked.

The chief looked at the images and then back at her. "I couldn't see any other conclusion. If you look at them, they look shabby and unkempt, and their clothes are torn. Those taller figures are holding objects, which you'd have to assume are weapons of some kind."

Ten minutes later, her chief science officer and Captain Hopper joined them in her office. She showed them the images of what they had just found.

"Whoa. What the hell are they?" asked Captain Hopper in surprise.

"Clearly an alien species, Captain," Dr. Milton said sarcastically.

"Yeah. Obviously, Doctor. But seeing them changes the equation of our ground operation a bit. Look at that." Hopper pointed to something the creature was holding in his hands. "That's clearly a weapon."

The Delta commander looked at the drone operator. "Is there any way to get us a closer image of that blue alien?"

Dr. Milton chimed in. "Let's look at those human-looking prisoners first."

Turning to look at the science officer, Hopper countered, "With all due respect, Doctor, you can look at them later. Right now, my team is getting ready to go dirtside. I need intel on those guards more than I do on the prisoners. They're a threat to us."

Interceding before the two alpha males got going, Halsey calmly said, "Dr. Milton, you and I can look at the prisoners in greater detail later. Let's focus on those guards for now."

"Let me move the drone to a different position so we can see the front of that guard better. He appears to be standing watch or something, so he'll be the easier one for us to look at," the drone operator said as he moved their eye in the sky around.

Looking at the alien guard, they could see its skin had a bluish tint, and it appeared to be reasonably muscular around the arms, shoulders, and chest. It was also wearing a uniform and had a few pieces of equipment visibly attached to it. It toyed with its weapon like it was bored. They couldn't make out a lot of details on its face, but they could tell it had long jet-black hair that appeared to be braided. It came down to around mid-back level.

The drone operator looked at Captain Hopper. "I'd have to get a lot closer to get you a better image of the face or more details, sir. Right now, I've stationed the drone thirty kilometers away and three thousand meters in altitude. I didn't want to get much closer for fear of being detected."

"Don't these drones employ stealth technology?" chided Dr. Milton, obviously disappointed that they couldn't get a better image of the beasts.

"They do," the drone operator countered, "but we don't know if they have the ability to detect our electronic signals, or how good their hearing or eyesight is. Our goal isn't to risk being seen right now."

"OK, I think we've seen enough for right now," Admiral Halsey announced. "Captain, when your soldiers get on the ground, I want them to start using their parabolic mics and video cameras to collect audio and video on both those guards and the human-looking prisoners. I want that data sent back to us so we can have the super AI start crunching it. If we can get a working understanding of their languages, then our first contact team will have a much better chance of succeeding."

The Delta commander smiled as he got up, his new marching orders in hand.

****

Standing back in the briefing room, Captain Hopper bellowed, "Listen up, Deltas! Our mission's changed a bit. We've just received new intelligence from one of our drones on the surface, and I have to say, I still don't fully know what to make of it. So as they say, Semper Gumby. Our new mission is still a recon mission, but now we're going to use our parabolic mics and cameras to grab as much audio and video of these unknowns as possible. The scientists on the ship here believe our super AI may be able to decipher their languages as we start to collect audio recordings of them interacting with each other. All of this will help our first contact team when it comes time, and us if things end up going south."

Hopper paused for a moment as he let his words sink in. "When we get down to the surface, I want everyone to deploy your surveillance kits and start gathering the data the admiral wants. When they believe they have a working understanding of the language, then Ambassador Nina Chapman and her assistant will look to make contact with the aliens. The rest of us will monitor and observe things to make sure it all goes smoothly.

"I'm now going to play some drone footage so you can see what these aliens look like. I don't want it to be a shock when we get down on the surface, and I want you all to know what we're up against."

Hopper showed the drone footage he'd seen in the admiral's office along with several close-up images of the two figures. It was pretty clear in the video that one of the figures looked amazingly like a human. The other figure, however, was anything but. The soldiers started commenting on what they looked like and how large they appeared to be. It kind of blew the myth of little green men out of the water.

Master Sergeant Brian Royce was just as shocked as everyone else by what they had just seen. Still looking at the freeze-frame of the big blue alien, he asked, "Aside from collecting audio and video on these two groups, are we going to seek out their base camp as well?"

Looking at his most experienced NCO, Captain Hopper took in a deep breath and let it out before he replied, "That's a good question, Master Sergeant. Right now, we're going to have Fourth Squad stay at the Osprey with our first contact team and a couple of scientists who are going to start collecting some soil and other samples. First and Second Squads will look to observe the aliens around the mine, and Third Squad will look for their camp or where they're bunking. Once the scientists and the first contact team feel they have enough information to approach the aliens, we'll have everyone stand by to support that operation."

Nodding in approval, Royce asked a follow-up question. "What's going to be the coms situation once we're on the ground?"

Lieutenant Crocker answered this one. "For the time being, we're going to use the neurolinks unless things go south—then voice and radios will be fine. Right now, we don't know if they have any sophisticated communications equipment on them, so we're not going to chance it with the radios. I talked with someone in the CIC about electronic signals down on the planet. What they told me is, as of right now, they aren't detecting anything on the spectrums we normally monitor or some of the lesser-known ones. That's not to say they aren't communicating with each other or even off-world. It just means as of right now we don't know if or how they're doing it. Determining that will also be part of our mission."

"Thank you, Lieutenant Crocker," Captain Hopper interjected. He then turned to Master Sergeant Royce. "Make sure one of the guys in Third Squad is packing our ELINT equipment. Once we locate the enemy camp, I'm going to need you to deploy it so we can try and see if they're operating on a different band or frequency. I highly doubt an operation like this is unable to communicate with the outside world."

Royce nodded his head and sent a quick NL message to one of the troopers to pack the specialized equipment.

The rest of the platoon talked for a bit longer about how they were going to insert into the area and where. While they had initially planned on inserting closer to the objective, the plan changed to drop them further away and not risk detection.

They settled on a new position, a clearing in the dense forest roughly ten kilometers from the objective. With their augmented bodies and exoskeleton combat suits, this should be a walk in the park.

Three scientists were also heading down to the surface with them—a biologist, a botanist, and geologist who'd gather samples from the drop site and begin running their initial tests. Accompanying the scientific team was the diplomatic team that would make contact with the aliens. Unfortunately for the Fourth Squad, they got stuck with babysitting duty at the landing zone with the civilians.

****

Five hours later, after swapping out some of their gear, they boarded up on the two Ospreys that would take them down to the planet. Unlike the Republic Army troopers, who had their own orbital landers, Special Forces tended to rely on specially rigged shuttlecraft called Ospreys for both orbital and atmospheric landings. It was a different kind of mission they carried out, and they had their own set of tools.

When the First and Second Squad were loaded up with Sergeant Royce and Captain Hopper, the crew chief closed the boarding door and sealed them in. The rest of the platoon was in the other Osprey with

Lieutenant Crocker. Minutes later, the pilot readied the craft to be shot out the launch tube. The docking clamps holding them in place released, and the craft levitated for the briefest of moments. Then the magnetic launch tube shot them down and out the tunnel like a bullet from a rifle.

In seconds, the Osprey was racing underneath the *Voyager* as they descended into the upper atmosphere of the planet. Once they were out of the ship, the sensation of floating in space suddenly returned. Their artificial gravity field was gone, and they were back in zero g.

The Osprey moved further from the *Voyager* and continued its descent to the planet below. During the initial dive into the atmosphere, it was a relatively smooth ride. Once they dipped lower into the atmosphere, the wind shear began to buffet the body of the craft. The standard fiery glow started to envelop the front and bottom of the Osprey's heat shield and would continue to do so until they broke into the upper atmosphere and were able to slow their descent.

Looking out the windows, the Deltas watched the colors change from the darkness of space interspersed with the stars, to the shades of clouds and the greens, browns, and blues of the ground below. Somewhere during their glimpses of the new world, the pilots changed their engines to atmospheric flight. The short stubby wings the Osprey had in space started extending from beneath it. Once they were fully extended, the tips of the wings bent up to provide more stability. In less than a minute, the Osprey had transitioned from a spacefaring craft to an atmospheric assault transport craft.

The pilots deftly worked the controls, slowing their flight and doing their best to keep them from crashing through one sound barrier after another. The last thing they wanted to do was announce their presence to whoever was down below with a sonic boom.

The ride to the surface lasted nearly an hour—longer than usual—because they wanted to arrive stealthily. Every so often, the crew chief would announce their current altitude and the time until they reached the objective.

When they got close to the landing zone, the rear hatch of the craft opened up, allowing the soldiers inside to catch their first real glimpses of the new planet. It was incredible seeing the new species of birds and flying animals soaring through the air. The pilots slowed down even more as they neared the landing zone. A drone had found a clearing big enough for them to vertically land both of the Ospreys. Moments later, the nose flared up as the pilot saw the spot and gently settled on the ground.

"Everyone out!" shouted Master Sergeant Royce, and the Deltas from First and Second Squad piled out.

One squad broke to the right of the Osprey and advanced outwards, establishing a twenty-five-meter perimeter around their ride. The two other teams on the second Osprey did the same as the pilots moved to shut down the engines. For the next five minutes, the platoon of soldiers sat tight in their perimeter, weapons at the ready as they took in all the sights and sounds around them. Meanwhile, their HUDs rapidly built a topographical picture of the immediate area, looking for possible threats.

Royce assumed a kneeling position. One of the first things he noticed was how tall the trees were. Some of them must have been upwards of two or even three hundred meters tall. Having been to the American redwood forests in California, Royce knew what tall trees looked like, but these were something completely different. Plus, their trunks were enormous at the base.

He craned his head to look up at the tree maybe thirty meters in front of him. It was massive. It had to be three or four times the size of the redwood trees he'd seen in California, but at the same time, these trees almost looked a bit like banyan trees with the way their canopies expanded outwards—parts of the branches extended out and down into the soil below.

Master Sergeant, let's go ahead and get the drones up. I want to get a lay of the land around here before we move out, Lieutenant Crocker said over the neurolink.

Using the same system, Royce directed his two drone operators to get the tools of their trade up and running.

A corporal pulled a rucksack off his back and unpacked several drones. Two of them would stay in orbit above the Ospreys, keeping an eye on them and the surrounding area. One drone was a bit larger and would act as their communications drone, relaying their coms to the Osprey, who'd transmit it to the *Voyager* in orbit. Lastly, the corporal popped out five smaller drones the size of golf balls. One would scout a few hundred meters ahead of them, looking for any possible threats, while two others would operate on their right and left flanks and a fourth would pull up their rear. The fifth drone would stay right over the top of them, providing the platoon with complete situational awareness of their surroundings.

The suite of drones would extend their eyes and ears beyond what the platoon of operators could do on their own and alert them to any impending danger that might be headed toward them. With their equipment deployed and now integrated into their HUDs, the AI built into the system would help them identify any threats as they moved along.

Master Sergeant Royce assigned the corporal and his second-in-command, Sergeant Wagman, to keep an eye on the drones and handle whatever they saw. Royce wanted to focus on leading the platoon. They were about to enter a new and dangerous part of their mission.

Royce felt he should say something before leading them down the rabbit hole. He linked into the platoon's NL channel. *Listen up, people. There's a lot of strange and interesting stuff to look at around here. I can almost guarantee we're going to see a lot more when we get into that forest and head toward the mines. I need you all to stay focused. Keep your heads on a swivel, but don't let all this stuff distract you. Remember, we have two alien races in our vicinity. We don't know if they're friendly or hostile, so stay frosty and ready for whatever may be headed toward us.*

Switching to a channel between just him, Crocker, and Hopper, he said, *Lieutenant, Captain, we're moving.*

Sounds good, Master Sergeant. Let's see how deep this rabbit hole goes, Captain Hopper replied.

Standing up ever so slowly, Royce kept his rifle at the low ready as he moved forward, into the strange-looking forest before him. As he glanced down at the ground, his eyes registered the dirt, some patches of grass that had found some light, and some odd-looking flowers and other plants and foliage he'd never seen before.

While they could breathe the air around them, they were keeping their exosuits sealed up for the time being. They needed to let the scientists run a spectral analysis of the airborne particulate matter to make sure there wasn't some unknown bug out there that could make them sick.

Royce brushed aside some shrubs and made his way deeper into the forest. It was much darker than he had first thought. Looking up, he saw two or more canopy layers, which might explain why it had gotten a lot darker the deeper they moved into the forest. As Royce walked on, he had a hard time keeping his eyes focused and alert. They wanted to wander and drift around, taking in the sights of this new world he found himself immersed in.

Ten minutes into their trek in the forest, Royce saw the oddest-looking creature. He wanted to say it looked like a deer, but it also looked like a horse, almost like a Minotaur. The beast had two small arms near its upper torso, like those of a monkey or even a human, but its head was shaped a lot more like that of a bear, with a medium-sized nose and mouth, as opposed to a long nose and face like a deer or horse. It was so crazy-looking, Royce had to send a message back to the rest of the platoon not to get stuck gawking at it. They had a mission to complete, and that meant they had to keep moving.

Picking up the pace of their march, mostly to keep from getting distracted, they eventually made it to the mining site. It looked to be approaching midday, though they didn't really have any hard data on what time it actually was on this planet. With three suns in the solar system and a few moons in orbit, their sense of time was completely thrown off.

Once they had reached the location of the mine, First Squad would take up a rearguard position and fan out. They would make sure no one came up behind them and keep their line of retreat to the Osprey open should they need it. Second Squad would take up a wide observation berth around the mine itself. Their goal was to see if anything showed up and observe any work being done at the mine. They'd also be in charge of collecting as much audio and video surveillance on the two alien races as they could so the *Voyager*'s computers could start to decipher their languages.

The final squad, Third Squad, was on standby. They'd be the ones to try and locate the alien base camp once they knew what direction the aliens had traveled in.

As the squads approached the mine, Fourth Squad sent a quick update, letting them know the scientists were already doing their thing. They'd continue to keep an eye on them and make sure nothing happened to their ride out of this strange new world.

Twenty minutes went by with the various squads getting moved into position. They made sure their camouflage system was turned on. This was a cool new feature that mimicked the user's surroundings, turning their exoskeleton suits into a twenty-second-century version of a ghillie suit. The discerning eye could still spot them, but at a passing glance, no casual observer would ever see them. Once everyone was in position, it was a waiting game.

An hour later, Sergeant Wagner got bored and decided to fiddle with one of the drones. He found the path that led away from the mine and down toward the house a little further back that they'd seen on the drone feed from the *Voyager*.

He sent a quick message to Royce and Crocker, letting them know he'd found it and asking if he could use the drone to follow the path and see where it went. The lieutenant wasn't too sure, but Royce convinced him it might be useful to know how many aliens were nearby. Besides, they needed to figure out where these aliens were staying, and following the trail for a while might just lead them to the camp.

With permission, Sergeant Wagner guided the drone further down the road while doing his best to keep it out of sight. Royce and Crocker watched with bated breath to see what it might uncover. After moving a kilometer down the path, they opted to find a spot to land the little drone and let it keep monitoring the trail while it recharged its solar pack.

As they sat there, killing time, Royce swatted at some unknown bug that jumped on his forearm. They'd been in their hide position for some three hours, and still nothing but these odd-looking bugs had explored the newest visitors to their planet.

Royce was getting bored, and boredom was dangerous. If he felt that way, he was sure his soldiers were on edge, and that wasn't good. Using the neurolink, he directed the squad leaders to start quizzing their squads on some infantry skills—effective ranges of some of their weapons, when and how to use certain weapons, etcetera—to keep their minds sharp while they waited for someone or something to show up at the mine.

Then he remembered the bug he'd swatted just a minute ago and looked down at it. It was just sitting there on the ground next to him, not moving. He wasn't sure what to make of it. It had purple stripes around its black-and-gray body, which he thought was pretty unique. It certainly wasn't like anything he'd seen on Earth. It almost reminded him of a grasshopper from back home. It was about the same size and had long legs like a grasshopper. Reaching down to pick up the critter, Royce held it a little closer to his visor for inspection. His body was encased in his armored exoskeleton combat suit, so he didn't feel threatened by it.

Its eyes stared right back at him. Then it opened its little mouth and spat some liquid right at him. Flinching, Royce tossed the little insect as he muttered a few curse words. Then he wiped away whatever spit the damn thing had plastered his visor with.

Just five minutes ago, Royce was going to ask if they could unseal their suits and try breathing in some fresh air. Now, he was glad he was still sealed up. For all he knew, that little bugger had just sprayed him with some neurotoxin or some other poison that was likely to kill him or give him a bad case of gut rot.

Lieutenant Aaron Crocker was propped up against a tree maybe ten or fifteen meters away, looking about as bored as Royce was. *Hey, LT. Why'd you switch over to being an officer?* Royce asked over a private NL channel.

I ask myself that question a lot. You know, prior to being an officer, I was a master sergeant in the regular Army. I had just finished my fifteen-year mark and knew if I didn't make a switch, I was going to be stuck as an E-8 for a very long time.

What did you do in the regular Army? Royce asked, his interest piqued now.

I was a supply clerk, if you can believe it. I wanted to cross-train into anything I could, but I was stuck, Crocker explained. *The only way I could get out of supply was to go officer. But being a senior NCO, there weren't many officer billets I could go into. My options were either supply, which I said hell no to, maintenance, which I thought was just as bad as supply, or Special Forces. They told me if I washed out of the program, I'd at least be sent to an infantry unit, which suited me fine. I mean, at this point, I could either stay an E-8 for another ten or more years or rise to be a captain or even major in that same time. It was a pretty easy decision. What about you, Brian? You thinking of making the switch? Oh, and just call me Aaron in private chat.*

OK, Aaron. No, I have no intention of being an officer. I like being an NCO. What I'd really like to do is get back into JSOC. I spent ten years in the Unit. I miss it.

I didn't know you were part of JSOC, Brian. What happened? Why are you in a regular SOF unit, then?

Ah, that's a long story best told over a beer or something strong, Royce replied. *Let's just say I had a mission that didn't go so well. It wasn't my fault or anything, but sometimes things happen that are out of your control. In my case, I had to leave the Unit for a little while. I was told after I completed my tour with First Group, I could apply to get my slot back. So, we'll see.*

I think I heard Hopper mention something to me about you having a background in some secret squirrel stuff. He said that was why the admiral had picked my platoon to lead this particular mission. You were some sort of SpecOps badass or something, Crocker joked.

Royce snickered to himself. *You remember hearing about some international incident on Mars with the Asian Alliance?*

I think so. Some black ops mission that went south. I think I remember hearing about it at the Officer Basic Course at Fort Bragg.

Yeah, that was my team. We were on loan to the Agency to carry out an infiltration mission to retrieve some intel from one of their sources. The only problem was the source was working at a facility that didn't exist, protected by a group called South Sword. Something went sideways, and we ended up getting detected. I guess you could say the rest was history, Royce explained.

Damn, Hopper wasn't joking. I heard you guys held your own against a force three times the size of yours and had to spend more than a day alone ducking and dodging enemy patrols six hours after your oxygen should have run out.

Yeah, something like that. Let's just say we found ourselves in a tough spot. In moments like that, you have to figure out how to survive, or you'll die, Royce said somberly.

How'd you guys survive beyond your oxygen limits?

You know we lost a few guys on that mission, right? asked Royce.

Yeah, I heard you lost three soldiers, but wouldn't their tanks have been depleted if their EVAs had been penetrated during the fight?

They were, so we couldn't scavenge much from them. We also killed seven South Sword soldiers, but we had the same problem.

So what did you do, then? Crocker asked.

Royce sighed briefly. *I had six guys still functioning, but a few had also been wounded, so they were already short on oxygen. What the reports omitted was that we also had eight prisoners. When I realized we'd need to E&E out to our alternate rendezvous point, I knew none of us would make it on the oxygen we had left, especially my wounded guys. Our lieutenant was killed, so the decision fell on me to get my remaining guys out alive and get our intel to our Agency handler. I had a make a tough call, but it was the right call if my men were to survive and complete the mission.*

You took the prisoners' tanks? Crocker asked. Even over the neurolink, it was apparent that his voice was rising in shock.

A moment passed before Royce responded, *I did. I swapped out their tanks with ours. We had 'em tied up, but I placed a knife nearby and told them by the time they eventually reached it and cut themselves loose, we should be far enough away they wouldn't be able to follow us. If they used the remaining oxygen from our tanks, they should be able to make it back to their base. If they chose to follow us, then they'd die.*

Damn, Brian. That was a tough choice. Did they follow you guys?

If they did, we didn't spot them. Twelve hours later, we made it to the rendezvous and got picked up, Royce explained. *Privately, they gave us a medal for our actions and then dispersed us out of the Unit and back to Special Forces. For the time being, travel was undesirable. We couldn't evade detection, not after what happened went public. That's how I ended up in a training battalion at Benning.*

Well, I'm sorry about how things shook out for you, Brian. But I'm sure glad we have you in our platoon and company. If things go to crap out here, your additional JSOC skills will come in handy, Crocker said.

It's OK. The training battalion wasn't too bad of a gig. Heck, a couple of our newest members were some of my recruits from a few years ago. Good people. I suppose we should get back to watching and waiting, Royce said, and they went back to listening to some of the idle chatter among the platoon.

****

The longer the soldiers sat there, the more anxious they got. They knew at least two alien species were down here, and they were pretty confident they should have seen them by now, but they hadn't, and the sun looked to be nearing its zenith.

Just as Royce was about to suggest to the LT that they start using the drones to snoop around the area more aggressively, maybe even follow the trails back to where they led, Sergeant Wagner sent him a message.

Master Sergeant, I got activity on the trail...holy crap, you aren't going to believe this, he said as he piped in the video feed to Royce's HUD.

Royce's eyes went wide as saucers. *Captain, Lieutenant, you're going to want to see this*, he said as he patched them in to the video feed of the drone.

There was some silence on the other end for a moment as the captain and lieutenant watched what Wagner and Royce were seeing. At first, no one was sure how to respond. This wasn't what they had seen on the drone footage on the *Voyager*. It was a lot more than a small gaggle of prisoners and a few guards.

That looks to be more than a hundred prisoners and at least two dozen guards, Lieutenant Crocker said over the NL.

Um...this is a lot bigger operation than we first thought, sir, Royce replied.

I'm going to let the admiral know what we found and see how she wants us to proceed. Any ideas or suggestions from either of you? Hopper asked.

Royce thought for a moment. *I think we move forward with the initial plan. We collect as much video and audio of these two groups as we can, and we go find the base or camp they're operating out of. Clearly, there's a relatively large contingent of them somewhere around here. The bigger question is, how are we going to approach them and where? Here at the mine, or at their camp?*

I agree with Sergeant Royce, sir, Lieutenant Crocker added.

OK, Master Sergeant, when the admiral gives the go-ahead to start searching for their base camp, you take Third Squad and find it, Captain Hopper ordered.

Sitting there watching the prisoners and guards, the Deltas couldn't help but notice how the smaller prisoners looked exactly like humans. It was one thing to see them on a drone video, but seeing them in person, just a hundred or so meters away, was completely different. There was virtually nothing distinguishing the prisoners from their platoonmates. The guards, on the other hand—well, they were a completely different story.

Those have to be the ugliest and scariest-looking things I've ever seen, commented Sergeant Wagner to Royce over the NL.

Stay frosty and out of sight, guys, we don't want a fight with them, Lieutenant Crocker said to the platoon.

The tension was palpable as they waited for word on what to do next. They had visions of snatching one or two of these aliens and bringing them back to the *Voyager* or a controlled place so Ambassador Chapman could speak with them. But with a gaggle of more than a hundred of them down there—well, that wasn't in the cards now.

What are those human-looking things doing? Captain Hopper asked.

It looks like they're filing into that mine, Royce replied.

As far as any of them could tell, the majority of the prisoners were issued a pickaxe tool or a shovel. Every fifth or six person carried a backpack instead, presumably to carry rocks out in. Once a prisoner had received whatever the guards gave them, they were motioned into the mine.

Not wanting to waste any time, Royce pulled his M85 up and aimed it at one of the guards. He made sure the safety was on and then turned on the video and the parabolic mic. Next, he synced it with the drone, providing overwatch for them. This would relay the images to the Osprey, which would beam it back to the *Voyager*.

Looking through the weapon's optical targeting scope, he got his first good look at this alien creature. It was wearing something that looked almost like a ball cap to keep the sun out of its eyes. It had a uniform on with a vest that had some equipment attached to it. It pretty much looked just like the image they had seen on the *Voyager*.

Once Royce had annotated the outerwear of the guard, he transitioned to the guard's physical features, mostly the face as that was the one feature they couldn't make out on the ship. He felt stupid calling all of these little details and items out, but he knew the intelligence weenies on the *Voyager* would look for all these minutiae.

He toggled a button on his targeting scope, which gave him the alien's height. The creature stood three meters tall. The beast's skin had a bluish tint to it and was covered in thinnish black hair on the exposed parts of its four arms.

From underneath the cap, Royce could see a lock of long black hair that flowed behind its body. It looked like it was braided, but Royce couldn't tell if there was anything interwoven in the braid. The creature's eyes were weird to look at, like cat's eyes, with the pupils running vertical, almost like slits. There was a third eye higher on the forehead, in between the other two. It had high cheekbones, and when it talked, you could see both top and bottom rows of teeth, all similar to canine teeth, which meant whatever type of alien life form they were, they most likely ate meat.

Just as Royce had finished videoing and describing the aliens, they received a message from the *Voyager*. The brass had finally made a decision. They gave them the go-ahead to pursue Royce's plan. They wanted him to take his squad and go search the alien camp and see what he could find and report back.

Finally, time to get moving, Royce thought.

Switching to the NL channel between himself and the captain, Royce said, *I'm going to take my squad and backtrace this trail and see where it leads. When we find their base camp, I'll get some surveillance drones up, and we'll get a better picture of what we're dealing with.*

That's a good copy, Master Sergeant. If you think you may run into some trouble or get spotted, try your best to withdraw as silently as possible, Captain Hopper instructed.

With their new orders in hand, Royce collected his squad. They withdrew from their current overwatch position and made their way as stealthily as possible to a position parallel to the trail down which they had seen the guards and prisoners travel earlier.

They moved through the underbrush slowly, cautiously since they didn't know what to expect. Everything inside this forest was new. New birds, new animals, new flowers and underbrush. It was all so foreign that it was taking an incredible amount of concentration to stay focused on the task at hand and not get distracted by it all.

After they crept through the woods for two hours, the trail they had been following veered off into what could only be described as a camp. From their current position, they couldn't make out all the details of it, but what they did see was a guard tower, a gate, and the outlines of a fence.

Continuing to use the neurolink, Royce sent a quick message. *Captain Hopper, we've found the encampment. I'm going to have my guys work the perimeter and try to get us a better visual of what we're dealing with. Stand by for a video link from our microdrones once we launch them.*

Royce motioned for Sergeant Wagner to take his fire team and move to one side of the camp while he took a team and checked the other side. Just before they moved out, he ordered one of the specialists to go ahead and launch one of their microdrones.

Seconds later, the drone flew across the perimeter wall and into the compound. Its microburst radar gave them a great display of what was beyond their line of sight and beyond the perimeter wall. Royce needed to know how big the camp was, and hopefully how many prisoners and guards were inside.

Once Sergeant Wagner and Royce's fire teams got set up in a good overwatch position not too far from each other, they settled in and examined the drone footage more closely, trying to figure out what else they should focus in on.

One of the first things they saw was a couple of guards overseeing a group of human-looking prisoners working on what appeared to be a foundry or smelting machine. It was unlike anything Royce had ever seen in pictures or history books, and nothing like what he thought a foundry should look like. He had envisioned a factory where large buckets of ore were dumped in and then melted down into a liquid form. Not this thing, apparently. It looked to be five meters in height, about the size of two Tesla Cybertrucks parked end to end. On what might have been the front side of this machine, a group of prisoners took bags of small chunks of rocks and dumped them into the device.

A different group of prisoners pushed a levitating cart that looked like a floating pallet jack, which had a series of empty rectangular molds on it, toward the other side of the machine. Royce wasn't sure what to make of it at first. Then they pushed the cart toward what seemed like a spigot. Another prisoner worked a lever on the machine, and out came glowing red-hot liquid that poured into the molds.

When the molds were full, the prisoner on top of the machine turned the spigot off. Another prisoner sprinkled dust on top of the liquid ore, and then the two of them pushed the floating pallet jack to another spot in the camp.

Interrupting his viewing, Captain Hopper asked over the NL, *What do you think they're doing with that stuff, Master Sergeant?*

Royce snorted. *If I had to guess, sir, they're refining whatever the prisoners are mining. It looks like they're building up a big pile of these blocks on the far side of the camp, near that other entrance that leads out to that open field.*

Sit tight and keep observing the camp, Hopper replied. *See if you can't use the drone to get us a better view of the buildings in the camp. Specifically, see if you can find a coms room or anything that might indicate this base is communicating with others on the planet or off-world. Hopper out.*

Royce passed along the instructions to Sergeant Wagner as he continued to observe the camp and started counting the guards he could see. So far, they'd counted fifty-two. Back at the mine, they had counted two dozen, so that pegged them as having seventy-six guards give or take. *That doesn't seem like a lot of guards for this many prisoners*, Royce thought. Next, he began counting the prisoners at the camp and the mine. They had a total of three hundred and forty-two prisoners.

One of the corporals crawled over to Royce. *Master Sergeant, I don't think these aliens are from here*, he said over the neurolink.

Royce's left eyebrow rose. *Explain.*

Sure thing, the corporal replied. He went on to describe how a foundry and smelter back home would work and how this large machine appeared to function as both. He added that the levitating pallet jack device was something similar to what he had used when he'd worked a summer loading transport crafts for UPS. The absence of a city on the planet meant all of these things had probably been brought here from somewhere else.

Looking at the young man, Royce calmly replied, *You're probably right, Corporal, but right now, I need you to crawl back to your position and keep observing. I know it's exciting to think about the possibility of more worlds populated by these aliens and stuff, but I need you to stay focused on what's in front of us, OK?*

Eh, yes, Master Sergeant. Sorry, that must have sounded stupid what I said, didn't it? the young man stammered.

Placing his hand on the younger man's shoulder, he replied, *It's OK, Corporal. We're all excited. We'll have plenty of time to talk about all this stuff once we're back on the* Voyager, *all right?*

Copy that, Master Sergeant, the corporal replied and crawled back to his position.

The kid had been so excited about this discovery that he had to tell someone, and Royce just happened to be the closest person.

Royce told Sergeant Wagner to steer one of the drones in the direction of a building he thought looked a little out of place. Sure enough, as the drone got closer, they spotted what looked like a directional antenna on top of it.

That must be the communication building.

As the drone approached, they saw several guards near it. One of the guards unsealed a door and started to walk in. As the door opened, Wagner made sure the drone was able to grab some video of the inside. They'd play the video back and analyze it frame by frame to see if they had gotten any images of possible electronic equipment inside.

Something wasn't adding up. The more Royce thought about that communication building, the more his spider senses were telling him they'd missed something.

Why didn't we detect any electronic transmissions or activity on the planet or during any of the drone or satellite overflights of this position? he wondered. The aliens could be using some sort of advanced communications equipment that couldn't be detected by their sensors—if that was the case, the fleet in orbit could be in trouble.

As Royce sat there trying to figure it all out, he got a radio transmission from the fleet above.

"This is Admiral Halsey. Master Sergeant Royce, we're seeing what you're seeing. The intelligence shop wants you to run a full spectral analysis of the camp like we talked about during the briefing. These guys have to be communicating somehow. We need you to try and find out what band they're operating on. Out."

And just like that, our electronic blackout has been broken, Royce thought. *Fleeters...*

"That's a good copy, *Voyager*. Stand by for data feeds," Sergeant Royce replied, trying to hide his frustration and contempt.

"Corporal Coy, set up your equipment and see what you can find," Royce said over their squad net. No sense in hiding their radio traffic if the *Voyager* was going to communicate directly with them. The truth was, the NLs were still kind of a pain in the butt to use. They sometimes transmitted random thoughts if the users weren't careful, which could be embarrassing.

Corporal Coy lay on the ground fifteen meters away. He pulled his patrol pack off his back and started grabbing pieces of equipment out of it. In a matter of minutes, his little suite of electronic wizardry was up and running.

He looked at Royce, letting him know he was ready to turn it on. Once he did, it would begin an intrusive sweep of the area, looking for any electronic transmissions, no matter how small. It'd scan the entire electronic spectrum and light their position up like a Christmas tree, which was why he looked for verification first.

Royce shrugged and then nodded. *If that's what the higher-ups want, then that's what they'll get.*

A couple of minutes went by before Corporal Coy said, "I found something, Master Sergeant. Take a look at this." Coy passed him a file with the electronic analysis in it over to the HUD built into his helmet.

Rolling over on his back, Royce sought to get a bit more comfortable on the ground. He opened the file and examined it on his HUD. *No wonder we didn't spot any signals. They're operating on an extremely high frequency—one we don't ever check*, he thought. They appeared to be transmitting whatever data they sent via a short microburst. *But why haven't they detected us?* he wondered.

They forwarded the data up to the *Voyager* and continued to observe the camp.

As Royce listened to the big blue aliens, he had to admit, he was having a hard time trying to distinguish their speech from other noises they appeared to be making. It was a lot of odd clicking, popping, and almost barking noises they made when they interacted with each other. The human-looking creatures spoke differently. They'd interact with the guards and sound pretty similar to them, but when they talked amongst themselves, they sounded almost...*human*. Royce couldn't quite place what they were speaking, but it seemed somewhat familiar. He was sure the super AI and the scientists on the *Voyager* were already hard at work trying to understand the language.

As Royce sat observing in silence, a slight crackle came over his earpiece as he received a transmission, their second direct electronic transmission since landing on the planet. "Master Sergeant Royce, this is Commander Johnson from the *Voyager*. The scientists are asking if you can have the rest of your squad focus their parabolic equipment on collecting speech from the human-looking prisoners. They're telling me if you can get us a few hours of conversation from them, the AI may be able to give us a translation of what they're saying."

The radio transmission ended, and Royce's anger rose again. He wasn't mad at the request—that part made sense. What angered him was that his squad was sitting a few hundred meters from this base camp, and no one knew if these aliens had the ability to electronically detect them and then eavesdrop on what was being said. The *Voyager* was supposed to transmit to the Osprey—then someone from the Fourth Squad babysitting the scientists would relay the message via their NLs so they'd avoid using their radios near the aliens.

Depressing the talk button, he replied, "That's a good copy. Out." He hated doing that, but he couldn't just ignore the *Voyager*'s XO either.

He passed the word along to the rest of his team, and before long, he had thirteen guys with their mics focusing only on collecting audio from the human-looking creatures.

Royce watched the prisoners again. Although they were a bit unkempt, it would have been difficult to distinguish them from any other human he'd met. Deep down, though, he knew there must be something different about them. It was a bit odd to think that there could be humans exactly like him living somewhere else in the galaxy.

Five hours passed with his squad observing what was going on in the camp. The entire time, they were feeding voice and video data to the *Voyager* in orbit above them. They'd collected hours' worth of data for the super AI to crunch. Eventually, they were directed to start doing the same thing with the bluish aliens.

While the Deltas carried out their observation roles at the alien base camp and at the mine, the two groups continued to collect information, hoping that at some point, their supercomputers would decipher the languages of these two groups. Once that happened, they'd try to make contact with them and hope for the best. The waiting, however, was killing them. The whole place around them was so strange, so different. If some critter was crawling on your armor, you didn't know if it was deadly. That was hard to deal with and also maintain noise discipline. Everyone wanted to talk and share what they were seeing.

Eventually, they'd been in their hide positions for so long that the sun had finally shifted in the sky enough that it looked like it was starting to get dark. The work gang of prisoners was now on their way back to the camp, presumably to eat and catch some sleep.

****

RNS *Voyager*
Science Deck

Professor Audrey Lancaster looked at the computer analysis of the language. She couldn't believe what she was seeing.

This has to be a mistake...

The Deltas on the surface had provided her with nearly twenty hours of conversation between the human-looking people, so it wasn't an error on their part. *It has to be a computer error*, she surmised as she ran a diagnostic on the program. When the system check came back as normal, she put the headphones back on and listened to the speech again.

This can't be right...

"You have a sour look on your face, Aubrey. Does that mean you found something, or was it my offer of a nightcap last night that offended you?" Dr. Milton joked, his British accent making his suggestion sound less crass than it otherwise might have.

She looked up in disgust. "No, Jonathan. It wasn't your inappropriate offer for a nightcap. I think I may have deciphered at least one of the languages being spoken."

Lifting an eyebrow, Dr. Milton walked a little closer to her, invading her personal space as he did. "Why is this not a good thing, Aubrey?" That irked her more.

My name is spelled with a d, *not a* b, *jerk*, she thought angrily.

"Because it doesn't make any sense," she shot back. "Here, look at this." She pointed to the language being spoken down on the planet, then cross-referenced it against a variant of the Chaldean language.

The British scientist crinkled his eyebrows. "Did you run a diagnostic of the system to make sure it wasn't computing an error?" he asked, skeptical of the results.

Audrey nodded. "I did. It's Chaldean. Or at least a variant of an older version of the language. There are no two ways about it. What I can't understand, though, is how could there be a group of humans on a planet twelve light-years away from Earth that speaks one of our oldest languages."

Dr. Milton opened his mouth to say something, then closed it as his mind began to wander. He eventually returned his gaze to her. "I don't know how this is possible, Aubrey. But right now, we have to work on the assumption that these human-looking aliens down there are, in fact, humans, or at least a close derivative of our own species." He paused for a second before adding, "The language piece puzzles me. That said, if we've managed to decipher their communications, then we need to integrate that into the universal language translator and update the ground force's systems with it. They'll need to use it to make contact with them. Do you want to pass this along to the admiral?" Dr. Milton asked with a crooked smile that said he was doing her a favor.

With a look of surprise on her face, she replied hesitantly, "Me? I would have thought you'd want to tell the admiral we deciphered this."

Dr. Jonathan Milton was, if nothing else, a pompous little man who loved to take credit for discoveries his subordinates had made. It surprised her that he would let her be the one to make this announcement.

He shrugged as if to say it wasn't that big of a deal.

"You're the linguistics specialist, Professor. It only seems right that you should make the announcement."

He winked at her. He'd probably continue his unwanted advances in earnest now, feeling that she owed him for allowing her to make this discovery.

"Very well, Jonathan, and thank you."

****

New Eden
Planetside

As the Deltas continued to collect information, the AI computer on the *Voyager* had finally made a breakthrough. A message was sent down to the ground units that the human-looking aliens were, in fact, speaking a variant of Chaldean.

Once the computer had pieced that much together, it began to sequence the rest of the words they were using and then analyze the contents of what the prisoners had been saying all day. With all that information, the AI was able to provide the Earthers a translation of what the prisoners were saying with better than ninety-seven percent accuracy, and the ability to communicate with them through the use of their universal translator.

Granted, they could now understand the prisoners, but what they were talking wasn't all that interesting. Their conversations were mostly about the work they were being ordered to do. Some of it was about food, some of it just generalized complaining.

The shipboard computer was having a harder time piecing together the spoken language of the bluish aliens. It was attempting to extrapolate, from what the human prisoners were saying in Chaldean, what they were saying in that clicking, almost barking language back to the bluish aliens. The AI was deciphering a few words here and there, but they needed more interactions between the prisoners and the aliens to make it work.

Looking at the clock his internal PA displayed for him, Royce saw they had been on the planet now for thirty-one hours. He was getting tired, and he knew his troopers were as well. He needed to start cycling them through some sleep. Royce broke the squad up into two groups: one on, one off. They'd take four-hour shifts and start getting some shut-eye. Once the darkness fully set in, they'd have thirteen hours until dawn. If they were going to make contact with these aliens, then it would happen sometime in the morning. He needed his guys rested before that happened.

Royce rolled over on his back and racked out a meter or so away from his coms specialist. The man was going to take the first four-hour watch while he slept, then Royce would stay awake the rest of the evening and into the morning. He had some administrative work he needed to assign his AI PA to handle for him, but other than that, he just wanted some sleep.

Before he tried to join dreamland, Royce studied the sky above him. He couldn't see anything. The double canopy cover of the forest blocked his view of the stars and the moons in orbit. He did hear a *lot* of strange-sounding critters and animals moving about. He just hoped none of them decided to make him or his men their dinner.

Master Sergeant Royce! Wake up! came an urgent tone through his neurolink. It was like something was buzzing inside his head. It pulled him violently out of his dream. Royce had forgotten that the neurolink had the ability to wake him, even out of deep sleep, if the proper command code was sent.

This is Master Sergeant Royce, I'm awake. Who is this, and what's going on? he managed to foggily say through the NL, not bothering to check who had sent the message.

This is Captain Hopper. The Voyager *was finally able to decipher what those big ugly aliens are saying. About an hour ago, the fleet detected a transmission from the base camp to a communications relay at the other end of the system. The message was then sent on to some other location outside the system. In light of that, Admiral Halsey has given us a FRAGO. She now wants us to move forward with making contact with the blue aliens at dawn instead of later in the morning.*

I'm moving First and Second Squads to join you at your location to assist in the operation, Captain Hopper continued. *Send some coordinates for where to position them so they can head there while in transit. I want you to detail off a fire team to head back to the Ospreys. They need to collect our first contact team and bring them to your position. Once the sun starts to come up and we've got a good visual of the area, then the ambassador will move forward and attempt to make contact. I need your squad ready to extract them if something goes wrong. Is that understood, Sergeant?*

Royce thought about that for a moment as a plan formed in his mind. *Yes, sir. We'll get the rest of the platoon sorted over here. I'll coordinate things with our diplomats when they arrive.*

Royce smiled, excited to put his plan into action. Using the neurolink, he plotted some positions on a topographical map of the area their drones had helped to create. He identified several places where he wanted First and Second Squads to set up. He still preferred the idea of snatching some of these guys and trying to make contact that way, but the higher-ups felt that'd give a bad first impression. Still, Royce didn't like the idea of the ambassador walking down to greet an unknown alien force without knowing how it was going to go.

The next couple of hours went by quickly as everyone moved into position. Sitting against one of the towering trees, Royce was finishing up some breakfast when Sergeant Wagner approached him with the first contact team.

"Master Sergeant Royce, this is Ambassador Nina Chapman and her assistant, Justin Ramseur."

Royce stood up and walked up to the ambassador. "Hello, ma'am. I'm Master Sergeant Brian Royce. You can call me Brian if you'd like. Would you like me to go over some aspects of your security and the path we'd like you to walk down and approach the aliens from?"

She smiled and shook his hand. "Hello, Brian. Yes, that'd be great," she replied, her British accent making her sound even more impressive to him. "We've been watching the videos your men have been collecting and listening to the AI translations. It's been fascinating to say the least."

He nodded. "It has been interesting, that's for sure. OK, so here's the skinny on the camp. It's actually a pretty large facility, but spread out. We believe there are roughly five hundred people inside. The camp itself seems to be broken down into a couple of functions: a group that heads out to the mine and brings raw ore back, and a second group that works what we believe are a couple of advanced smelters used to refine the ore."

Royce spent another twenty minutes going over some additional details of the camp. He wanted her to see some buildings and where they were located. If the initial greeting went well, then chances were she'd be invited into the camp. Next, one of Royce's men gave her a small surveillance kit. It consisted of a micro camera in the form of a contact lens and a two-way radio that would fit just inside her inner ear, transmitting everything she heard back to them. She already had a neurolink, so communicating directly with them wouldn't be a problem.

"So, what's the plan if things don't work out with them?" Nina asked. "Do we just run for it?"

Her assistant looked nervous but held his tongue.

"Hopefully, that won't happen," said Royce. "If it does, then our first course of action will be to show ourselves. If they see us and realize you have protection nearby, it may deter them from doing something rash. If that doesn't work and they do opt to fight—well, this is something we train for, ma'am." He spoke matter-of-factly, almost clinically, but the implications were not lost on her.

Nina sighed and nodded. "I guess we should get this rodeo going."

****

Captain Jayden Hopper looked at the disposition of his soldiers on the map; he felt good about their setup. Lieutenant Crocker had a squad positioned on the northwestern side of the enemy camp, putting them in a position to provide Ambassador Chapman with good cover should Master Sergeant Royce and his team need to extract her.

"Captain, we've got the M91 set up, along with both of our SAWs should things go south," one of the squad leaders announced.

Hopper nodded in approval. "Good job, Sergeant. Let's hope we won't need any of them, but I'm glad we have them."

The M91 or HB was the infantry's heavy blaster weapon. It was the equivalent of the twentieth- and twenty-first-century Browning M2 .50-caliber machine gun. The M91 was similar to the SAW but fired a much larger-caliber blaster. There was typically only one assigned to a company. They required a three-man crew to operate, but if they were going to be in a knock-down, drag-out fight, it was a nice weapon to have.

Hopper looked over at Royce as he gave some final instructions to the ambassador; he felt good about having Royce on this mission. While they were all Deltas, Special Forces, Royce had spent ten years with Joint Special Operations Command. The Unit, as they were called, were the elite of the elite. They were a small cadre of the best regular Army, and Special Forces soldiers in the military. There wasn't a lot known about them other than they did a lot of black ops work for the Agency and other types of jobs when the government couldn't be officially involved.

This whole first contact mission was something none of them were really ready for, but Hopper had a suspicion that this was right up Royce's alley. Hopper had been glad to let Royce run this part of the mission—he knew what he was doing, and the men in the platoon trusted him.

Sensing Royce was probably close to being done explaining things to Nina, he made his way over to them.

"Do you feel you're ready, Ambassador? Is there anything more we can do for you?" Hopper asked.

The ambassador turned to face him. "I think I'm about as ready as I'm going to be, Captain. I guess I should start heading down there now?"

Hopper nodded. "Yes, as soon as you're prepared, we can get started. We'll be ready to help you should you need it. Master Sergeant Royce here will be your guardian angel. We'll get you out of there, ma'am."

Nina nodded, then motioned for Justin to follow her, and the two of them crept out of the forested area and headed toward the worn trail the prisoners used.

****

Nina strode out of the tree line and covered position they had all been gathered in, walking through knee-high grass and underbrush until she was on the trail. She walked toward the unknown with such confidence and bravado, it caused the Special Forces soldiers to take notice. She had a swagger like this was just an ordinary day on the job.

The duo walked maybe a hundred meters down the path in the morning light until they came within thirty meters of what they suspected was the camp entrance, where the trail ended and entered the camp. Nearby was a guard shack of sorts, where two of the large blue aliens sat.

One of them spotted the two of them and immediately stood up. It said something unintelligible to its friend, who also stood up and reached for its weapon, which it had placed beside the guard shack.

Nina took that as her cue to say something. She had a small universal implant in one of her ears that had been updated with the best interpretation of the languages of the human-looking aliens and these big blue aliens. Knowing they didn't have such a device, she raised a small electronic device to her mouth and began to speak loudly into it so the audio would carry to them. Since they hadn't established a very good working understanding of the bluish aliens' language yet, she was going to rely on the human-looking aliens' variant of Chaldean.

Nina spoke confidently into the device. "Hello, my name is Ambassador Nina Chapman. We come in peace. We would like to speak to your leader."

The two blue aliens looked at each other, seemingly unsure what to make of what she had said or the clothes she was wearing. To them, she would have looked like the prisoners they kept watch over, but she wasn't dressed anything like them. They said something in their own language, and Nina's translator said it was something about how she looked like one of the prisoners that had somehow gotten out of the camp.

Nina quickly countered in a loud voice, "We are humans. We are from a different planet than here. We come as explorers. We wish to speak with your leader."

One of the aliens called out to them in his world's version of Chaldean, telling them not to come any closer. "We will summon our leader. Do not make any sudden moves."

One of the blue aliens then took off into the camp and disappeared while the other guard continued to stare at them. It kept the weapon in its hand pointed at the ground, clearly unsure if they posed a threat.

A few minutes went by before a group of seven aliens walked toward them. They all wore uniforms, and they were all armed.

Nina spoke again. "Hello, my name is Ambassador Nina Chapman. My friend and I are explorers. We come in peace and would like to talk with your leader."

The aliens looked at each other, then they talked amongst themselves, too softly for their translators to pick up. Eventually, one of them stepped forward.

"I am T'Tock. I am the leader of this camp. If you are not escaped prisoners, then how do you speak their language?" the large bluish alien asked. His words came across as harsh, unnatural, as if it was difficult for him to speak this language.

"We have observed you and the prisoners for several days," Nina replied. "Our computer was able to translate the prisoners' language so we could communicate with you."

Now the group of blue aliens looked nervous. They held their weapons a bit tighter.

"You have observed us for several days?" T'Tock asked, clearly concerned. "That means you have a starship in orbit of this planet. Where are you from?"

"Don't tell him specifics," hissed Justin, nudging Nina.

Ignoring him, Nina announced, "We are from a planet called Earth. It is very far from here. We have come to this planet as explorers. We have come in peace and would like to have further discussions with you if that is possible."

"In what star system is this planet Earth you speak of?" T'Tock asked in an accusatory tone. "We have not heard of it before."

"We can discuss that in more detail later on if you would like. May we approach you and continue to talk and get to know each other?" Nina asked calmly. She was cool as a cucumber, but she could see Justin's hand shaking through his suit.

"You may approach us," called out another one of the blue aliens.

The aliens had begun to spread themselves out a bit, holding their weapons low but ready should they feel they needed them.

"Follow me," Nina said, and Justin followed her toward the aliens.

When they had gotten within five meters of the blue aliens, the leader said, "You look, talk, and appear to be just like our prisoners. How do we know you are not just a group that escaped?"

Nina smiled. "If we were escaped prisoners, would we come back here to try and talk with you?"

The question caused a couple of the guards to look at each other as they waited for what their leader would say or do next.

T'Tock raised one of his four hands up and stroked his braided hair. Nina observed the beast's hand and saw what looked almost like talons in place of fingernails. It sent a shiver down her back, thinking about the damage this thing could probably do in a hand-to-hand fight.

"If you came here from this planet Earth, then you came here in a starship," T'Tock said. "How many people are in your starship? How many of your people are down here now, on Clovis with us?"

Nina's brow furrowed. "Clovis? Is that the name of this planet?"

With a wave of his hand, the beast brushed aside her question. "The name of this planet is irrelevant. Do you have a single starship in orbit? How many others are down here with you...Ambassador?" T'Tock seemed to have trouble pronouncing her title.

"Is Clovis your home world?" Nina asked, redirecting. "What are your species called? We are called humans." She was persistent.

T'Tock lowered the hand that had been rubbing his hair. "No, Clovis is not our home world. We are also from a system far from here. This planet is part of our empire. It is just one planet of hundreds that we control. You said your name is Ambassador Nina Chapman. What kind of name is this? What clan or tribe are you from?"

Nina tried to suppress a smile at the mention of a tribe or clan. The thought of a galactic empire still having clans felt very *Star Trek* or *Battlestar Galactica* to her. "My given name is Nina. My surname or family name is Chapman. The government of my planet has given me the title and job of ambassador. It means I have the authority to speak on behalf of our government and our people," she tried to explain.

The aliens stood there, listening very intently. Their interests were clearly up now; they wanted to know more.

"I am T'Tock of the clan D'Shawni. I am from the planet Shawni, one of our core worlds. Our people"—he waved two of his arms around—"are called Zodarks. If you have traveled to this planet, then you must have traveled here on a starship. How many starships are in the orbit of Clovis? How many of your people are down here on the planet?"

"When we first discovered this planet, we did not know it had anyone living on it," Nina calmly replied. "We sent several ships to this planet. Our intent was to establish a colony here."

"You have come here to claim this planet? This is a Zodark planet! It is part of *our* empire. How many ships have you brought? How many soldiers do you have on the surface already?" T'Tock roared angrily at Nina. The guards behind him scanned the area, looking for possible threats.

She held a hand up to try and calm the alien beast. "No, T'Tock. We have not come here to conquer this place. We have come here in peace. We just want to talk."

T'Tock cut her off. "Then answer my question. How many starships are in orbit? How many soldiers have you already landed on the planet?"

Nina shook her head. "I can't answer that right now."

T'Tock cut her off with a wave of his hand. He then looked up, as if he was trying to spot their starship in orbit, before he returned his gaze to her. "You are not answering my questions. Perhaps you do not want to talk like you say."

T'Tock then said something to the guards around him. The group began to spread themselves out until they had formed a U shape around Nina and Justin.

Sensing the change in the aliens' mood, Nina offered, "T'Tock, perhaps we can agree to speak again later today. Maybe when the sun is at its zenith?"

The large alien looked at her, and then he laughed. "No, I do not think so. I think you will come with us, and you will tell us more about your starship and the system your people are from."

Then the aliens finished closing the circle around them as they moved in.

Without taking her eyes off the leader, Nina said over her com link to Captain Hopper, "Captain, now might be a good time for you to get us out of here."

****

Royce, have your squad show yourselves, but do not engage. See if your presence will get them to back down so we can get the ambassador out of there, Captain Hopper said over the NL.

On it! was Royce's quick reply.

Seconds later, the twelve soldiers of Third Squad emerged from the trees and underbrush not more than sixty meters from the Zodarks. Several of the aliens turned, surprised by the sudden appearance of what were surely soldiers. One of them said something in an urgent voice that didn't sound friendly. Then T'Tock roared something as one of his arms lunged at Justin, Nina's aide. Grabbing the man by the neck with one of his large hands, he lifted him off the ground and turned to head into the camp at a quick trot.

In the blink of an eye, another Zodark grabbed Nina before she knew what was happening and turned to follow T'Tock into the camp.

The remaining Zodarks raised their weapons and proceeded to fire their blasters at the twelve exposed soldiers before they could react to what was happening.

Diving for cover, Royce landed behind a clump of underbrush just as several blaster bolts slammed into the ground and trees where he had just been standing.

Rolling to his right, he came up in a kneeling position with his rifle scanning for targets to shoot. At this point, the ten Zodarks were steadily retreating into the camp while they continued to lay down an onslaught of blaster fire at them.

Royce took aim at one of them with the help of the targeting AI built into his HUD and pulled the trigger. His rifle sent a single blaster bolt right at the large blue alien before him, hitting it squarely in the chest. He was already traversing his rifle to find the next target when he heard the most horrifying noise of his life.

Charging toward their positions from the right flank were fourteen additional Zodarks, firing their blasters into their position. Leaves, branches, and underbrush all started kicking up all about the human soldiers.

"Second Squad, shift fire to meet that threat on our right flank. Get that SAW on them now! First Squad, open up with those heavy guns and take 'em out!" Lieutenant Crocket yelled over the platoon net.

The soldiers manning the M91 HBs let loose a torrent of blaster fire that cut down half a dozen of the attackers in the first couple of seconds. The four other soldiers with SAWs joined the fray, adding their own volume of fire into the charging enemy soldiers.

Turning to look to his right, Royce saw one of his guys get hit by a couple of blaster shots and go down. Another one of his guys yelled out in pain when his left leg was ripped off by a blaster. Cries for a medic began to echo as blaster fire and shouting filled the morning air.

"Frag out!" yelled one soldier as an object flew out toward a couple of Zodark soldiers trying to flank their heavy weapons.

Crump.

The fragmentation grenade landed near a cluster of them before going off, throwing several of the Zodarks through the air like rag dolls.

A sudden whirring sound emanated from inside the camp, and then a pair of drones, two meters in size, emerged. One of the drones turned right toward Royce's squad and opened up with a rapid-firing blaster. Before Royce could even yell a warning, three of his guys got cut down by the flying killing machine.

Aiming at the drone, Royce flipped his selector switch from blaster to magrail and fired a short burst of 5.56mm slugs at the drone. The magrail slugs ripped the drone apart, and it fell to the ground in a heap.

The other drone started taking evasive maneuvers now that it had detected a threat to its existence. It fired a torrent of blaster fire into Second Squad's position as they continued to fire on the charging Zodarks. A couple more of his soldiers went down before they could react to the new threat.

Royce brought his rifle to bear on the second drone and started firing short burst after short burst at the drone, to no avail. It just kept ducking and dodging, all the while firing on his soldiers.

Then a couple of small explosions happened near the drone. One of his soldiers had fired his 20mm smart munition at it. The killer drone took a few hits, which slowed its movement just enough for Royce and a few others to slam it with a few dozen magrail slugs, destroying it.

As the ruins of the drone fell from the sky, another roar came from the camp entrance as close to thirty of these blue aliens charged forward, heading right for Royce's depleted squad. The AI in his helmet told him he had only moments until the big beasts would be on top of them at their current speed.

"Fall back to rally point Charlie!" came the urgent voice of Captain Hopper over the platoon net.

Royce flicked his M85 back to the blaster and let loose a string of shots at the charging Zodarks. He hit three of them outright before they dove for cover.

Royce jumped to his feet and ran over to where a medic was treating one of his wounded troopers. "We need to go!"

The medic looked up at him and nodded. He grabbed his aid pack and rifle and took off for the rally point, leaving the soldier lying on the ground. Royce glanced down as they ran away and saw that the guy had bled out from whatever had hit him.

Grabbing a grenade from his vest, Royce pulled the pin and threw it at a cluster of Zodarks that had just resumed their charge toward him. Flickers of light from their blasters were zipping all around him, hitting trees and other underbrush as he retreated into the woods.

Royce heard the explosion of the grenade moments later and hoped it might slow their pursuers down a bit. As he raced past several trees, Royce saw two of his guys leaned up against a pair of tree trunks, raising their rifles. They cut loose a string of blaster fire at whoever might still be pursuing them. When they had fired off thirty or so shots each, the two of them fell back until they came across a couple of Deltas who had two of their SAWs ready to cut loose as soon as they got out of the way.

As the two Deltas ran past him, the group with the SAWs opened up. It sounded like a buzz saw as their heavy blasters tore through the entire area, spitting out more than a thousand bolts a minute, shredding trees, underbrush, and the handful of Zodarks who had continued to pursue them into the woods.

Looking around him, Royce saw the rest of the platoon was still falling back to rally point Charlie while the SAW gunners laid down covering fire. They had another two hundred meters to go.

Royce scanned the area in the direction of the camp and fired all six rounds of his 20mm smart munition into the general area those aliens were charging from. He wasn't sure if he'd hit anything, but at this point, he just wanted to slow them down or hopefully get them to withdraw.

Once it looked like the enemy had stopped chasing them, Royce ordered everyone back to the rally point. When they arrived there, the remnants of Second and Third Squad had a wide perimeter set up, giving them close to a hundred-meter circle to work with. Fourth Squad, which had been watching the shuttles, broke up and sent one of their fire teams to join them. These Zodarks might have caught them off guard and taken a few of them out, but the Deltas weren't ready to give up just yet.

Captain Hopper was already on the radio to the *Voyager*, requesting the Quick Reaction Force or QRF to deploy to where their Ospreys were. The fire team still guarding the site would work on clearing out some trees to create a bigger landing zone. Hopper had also recalled the three other platoons of the company. In a couple of hours, they had nearly a hundred additional Deltas ready to go back and recover the ambassador and take that alien camp out.

Lieutenant Crocker walked up to Sergeant Royce. "Detail off a few guys to get our wounded back to the Ospreys. I want to get them taken up to the *Voyager* for some proper treatment. We can also have the Osprey ferry down some regular Army soldiers to help us out. I have a feeling this next engagement with these bastards is going to be a bit tougher of a fight. They know we're here."

"That's a good call, sir. I'll have the guys from Third Squad handle it. They need a short break from the action after this last attack," Royce replied.

Royce then walked over to where the platoon's medics were treating the wounded. They had a total of six guys injured and another twelve KIA. When they went back to attack the enemy camp, they'd recover their bodies. The fighting had evolved so fast they hadn't had the time to grab the dead before they had to get out of there.

Looking down at the wounded, Royce almost winced at their injuries. A few of them had blaster wounds, but many more had deep gashes across their arms, chests, or faces from the aliens' talon-like fingernails. There was only so much their medics could do down here with their limited kits and training. They needed to get them to the higher-level trauma treatment center on the *Voyager*.

The area around their perimeter continued to stay quiet. Lieutenant Crocker had their remaining surveillance drones launched to aid in monitoring the perimeter. In a couple of hours, they'd have plenty of reinforcements, more than enough to take the alien camp and liberate the prisoners. Then they'd recover the ambassador and her assistant, assuming they were both still alive, and try to piece together who these aliens were.

****

As the sounds of battle outside the camp continued to fade as it moved further into the trees, T'Tock turned to one of his commanders. "Send a message to the other camps that we just encountered a new race of humans. Also, send a message to Ka'Cha, letting them know there are enemy ships in orbit above the planet and that we are requesting immediate assistance."

"By your command," came the reply from his subordinate as he trotted off to their communications building.

Returning his gaze to the man and woman his guards had tied to a chair, T'Tock walked up to the man first. "Where are you from?"

The man looked nervous and scared. He glanced over to the woman, almost asking with his eyes if he should answer the question.

T'Tock held one of his hands out in front of the man and extended his talons.

"Like we said, we're from Earth," the human blurted out, obviously terrified. "It's a planet many light years from here."

"See? That wasn't so hard," T'Tock said in the Chaldean variant. He pulled out a tablet that had 3-D maps of the known universe. "Now, why don't you show me where your star system is located?"

"Don't tell him anything, Justin!" Nina yelled.

T'Tock turned his head to face Nina and backhanded her across the face with one of his four hands. The blow caused her nose to start bleeding and cracked her lip open.

Walking over to her, T'Tock said, "Since you appear to be the one in charge, here is what we're going to do, Nina. I'm going to ask you a question, and each time you don't answer it, I'm going to hurt your friend."

Nina looked up at the large blue alien with hate burning in her eyes. "My people will come back for me, and they will kill you all!" She then spat some blood in his face, which only further infuriated him. The beast punched her hard in the gut, causing her to gasp for air.

T'Tock walked back over to Justin. Then while glaring at Nina, he asked, "Where is this star system where Earth is located?"

When she didn't answer, T'Tock used one of his taloned fingernails to rip the man's shirt open. With his chest and belly now exposed, T'Tock used his talons to cut Justin's stomach. He didn't rip it wide open—it was about a six-centimeter cut, just large and deep enough to expose a small piece of intestines. Justin screamed in agony and pain as the wound began to bleed.

"I'm sorry, Justin," was the only thing Nina could say.

Looking at Nina again, T'Tock repeated the question. When she lifted her head and didn't say anything, T'Tock used one of his talons to catch part of Justin's small intestine and pull some of it out of him. Justin howled and cried out in pain. His face became ashen and he was sweating profusely. His body was going into shock.

"Nina, I could do this all day to poor Justin, but that wouldn't be fair or very nice. Why don't you just tell me what I want to know, and we'll patch Justin up? You both can live. What star system is your home world in?" T'Tock asked once again.

Just as T'Tock was about to pull more of Justin's intestines out, Nina finally relented. "Give me the tablet!" she cried. When he handed it to her, she pointed and explained, "Earth is in the Indus system."

****

Nina's answer was false, but she was hoping the Zodarks wouldn't know that. She needed to buy the Deltas some time to rescue them, and she hoped if she fed him some bad information, that just might work.

"You say Earth is here, in what you call the Indus system?" he asked skeptically. "That is a long way from here. Have your people developed faster-than-light-speed travel?"

Nina looked at Justin. He had practically passed out from the pain, and his stomach was still bleeding. Returning her gaze to the beast standing in front of her, she stated, "Yes, we have. We can cover many light-years with our technology. Now, I've answered several of your questions. I want you to give my friend some medical attention if we are to continue talking."

The giant blue beast raised one of his hands and played with his braided locks. "All right, Nina," he said. "Here is what we will do. I will have my medical people patch your friend up, but if you stop answering my questions, then we will start right back up. I assure you, Justin here may die, but we have the ability to bring him back from the dead and kill him many times over. Don't do that to your friend, Nina. Just answer my questions."

****

Several hours later, the three other Delta platoons, along with a company of Republic Army soldiers, had gotten themselves into position to attack the enemy camp and recover their people. The RASs had brought two of their 3.5-meter-tall Mechs with them for added firepower. The heavily built-up forested area was not conducive to bringing some of their heavily armored tanks, so the Mechs would have to do.

Captain Hopper kneeled next to a tree with his four lieutenants and senior NCOs. The RA battalion commander, Major Jenkins, and Captain a, his company commander, also joined him as they looked at the layout of the prison camp.

The camp was roughly three kilometers long and two kilometers wide. Much of it was taken up by what they suspected were industrial processing machines, along with a sizable stockpile of refined ore near the rear entrance. Based on their best intelligence, the door led down a path two hundred meters long, which opened into a large field that looked like it had been used by some sort of heavy transport aircraft.

Spaced out along the wall were some guard towers, which did not appear to be manned. Rather, they were likely autonomous towers, each fitted with a pair of blasters for weapons. The walls of the structures were four meters high. What they were made of, no one knew just yet.

Captain Hopper was going over the plan of attack when he got a coded message from the *Voyager*. Telling the others he needed to walk away for a moment, Hopper got up and accepted the video link.

"Admiral, we're outlining our attack now. What can I do for you?"

Admiral Halsey's face appeared on his HUD. "We've detected multiple messages from the camp you're about to attack; they were sent to at least six other locations on the planet. I'm not sure if those are other mining camps like this, or if there's an alien garrison on the planet. What concerns me more right now is that we've also detected several messages being sent outside the Rhea system. We believe these are distress calls."

Hopper shook his head in frustration; he knew they probably didn't have a whole lot of time left if this was the case. Either those other camps would send reinforcements, or a starship or two might appear near their own ships.

"I understand. You need us to hit this place fast and hard before help can show up," Hopper replied.

"Exactly. The *Rook* has broken orbit and will stand by to engage any ships that arrive in the system. But I need you to recover our people and liberate that camp. See if any of those prisoners want to come back with us, or if they want to stay and wait for their guards to return. Oh, and before I forget, our science team is telling me to make sure you guys grab whatever it is they're mining. They want you to bring back all those refined blocks of whatever that mineral is so they can study it. It's clearly crucial enough that these aliens have multiple camps mining it, and if it's important to them, then it's important to us. How copy?"

Hopper tried to maintain his composure. His job was to get their people back and liberate prisoners. *Now the science team wants my people to scoop up these refined minerals?*

The admiral clearly saw his look of frustration through the video feed. "Captain, just focus on getting our people back and liberating the camp. If there's time to grab those refined blocks, then do so, but once an enemy warship appears in the system, we need to evacuate as quickly as we can. We have no idea what their ships are capable of."

He nodded. "That's a good copy, Admiral. We'll launch our attack in the next twenty minutes. In the meantime, can you prepare a couple of our utility drop ships? If these prisoners want to come with us, we're going to need more ships to get them up to the *Voyager*."

"Will do, Captain. Now go get our people back. Halsey out."

****

Hopper kneeled down in his old position and laid out the order of attack and how he wanted it to go down. From what their microdrones had been able to tell them, the prisoners were all being held in a couple of large barracks. Their microdrones had also spotted about fifty reinforcements that appeared to have arrived from another camp. Hopper's drone guy had tried to use some of their specialized drones to get a better view of what was going on in the camp, but the guard towers' sensors had detected them and taken them out. So far, the towers hadn't spotted the microdrones, which were only the size of a fifty-cent piece, so their stealth had been valuable. However, they were also far less capable than Hopper would have liked for an attack like this.

Major Jenkins interjected. "Captain Hopper, now that this is a combat operation and we're intertwining Delta and RA forces, I'm designating new call signs. All Delta units are now Ghost elements. You are Ghost Actual. My call sign is Hammer Actual. Captain Foster's is Anvil Actual. I think you and I both got the same message from the admiral. Why don't you finish briefing the mission? I know we don't have much time."

Hopper nodded at the RA major, glad he wasn't the only person making decisions down here on the ground. "Captain Foster, I want your entire company and your two Mechs to attack the camp here, at the southwest corner," he directed. "It's close to the rear entrance of the camp, and that trail that leads to an open field. Have your Mechs destroy the wall if they can. If not, use some of your smart missiles to do it. I need you guys to create some holes in their lines and attract their attention. Send me a message when you believe they're fully engaging you. That's when we'll launch our other attacks."

Hopper now turned to his lieutenant in charge of First Platoon. "Lieutenant Able, you are now Ghost One. When I give you the word, I need your platoon to blow a hole in the wall section along the northern side of the wall, right here in the middle of the camp, near the industrial equipment. Don't try to breach the wall once you've broken through. Let the enemy come to you and do your best to keep them busy."

Hopper now turned to Lieutenant Crocker and Lieutenant Hales. "When the enemy is sufficiently busy with those other two attacks, Second and Third Platoons are going to charge into the front entrance. You guys are Ghosts Two and Three. Once you launch your attacks, breach the camp quickly and then start moving down through it, eliminating threats as you encounter them. Fourth Platoon, you're Ghost Four and are going to be my ready reserve. You're also responsible for taking those guard towers out with your anti-armor smart missiles. As the battle progresses, stand by to get sent to the side that looks like it needs the most help."

Before he wrapped up their briefing, Hopper added, "If we're able to take a few of these blue aliens prisoner, then let's try. I'm sure there's a lot we can learn from them. Now, let's go get our people back and take this camp out."

"Hooah" was the only reply they gave before they all headed back to their sections and got ready. In twenty minutes, it was showtime.

****

Major Jenkins and Captain Hopper positioned themselves near the tree line as the various units got into position. The longer this took, the more anxious Hopper was becoming. He knew the aliens in the camp had sounded the alarm to the other camps in the area and the star system. It was only a matter of time before additional forces showed up.

"Anvil and Ghost Actuals, we're starting our attack now," Captain Foster said over their secured coms.

The quiet of the late morning was broken by the sound of heavy-caliber blasters being fired and half a dozen smart missiles launched from the two Mechs. This was quickly followed by more than one hundred Republic Army soldiers opening fire.

Intermixed with the sound of blaster fire and explosions, the Earthers heard a loud guttural screeching noise emanating from within the camp. Not knowing what was making the noise was really unsettling.

Just as the RA had initiated the attack, the special weapons squad fired off their anti-armor smart missiles at the guard towers. Some of the missiles were blown up before they could hit the towers, but many others scored hits. The remaining towers would be taken offline in a few more minutes.

As the structures went down, Captain Hopper ordered their surveillance drones to head back over the enemy camp. They needed better eyes and ears on what was going on inside the camp than what the microdrones were giving them.

Hopper's radio came to life just as the drones passed over the walls. "Ghost Actual, Hammer Actual. The enemy is fully converging on my position."

"Good copy," the major immediately replied.

Hopper keyed his radio to start the next part of the attack. "Ghost One, Ghost Actual. Initiate your assault. Hit 'em hard."

A new set of explosions now rippled along the next section of the alien camp. More blaster fire could be heard, and so could those loud animalistic screams from the blue brutes.

Looking at the drone feeds, Major Jenkins pointed to something. Hopper saw it as well. The enemy had now split their force to attack the two breaches in their wall. The attack was unfolding just as they had planned it.

Hopper keyed his mic. "Ghost Two and Three, initiate your assault now."

Major Jenkins nodded when Hopper issued the order. Looking at the drone feeds of the battle unfolding, it was crazy to see a full-blown battle with laser bolts and magrail weapons. Aside from live-fire training, none of the human soldiers had been in a large battle like this with advanced weapons. The last major war fought between humans had been back in the 2040s.

As he watched the enemy soldiers, the first thing Hopper noticed was how fearless these blue brutes were. They charged right for the RA soldiers, firing their blasters the entire time. The four-armed beasts were terrifying to watch in action. One group of three of them managed to get right in close to a group of human soldiers and used their talon-like nails to slash the soldiers apart. One of the aliens actually took the time to stab his hand into one of the RAS's chest, pulling his heart out and eating it like a savage animal. The alien let out a bloodthirsty howl as he downed it in a single bite, bright red blood running down its face.

"Ghost Four, move to assist Hammer. Shore up their position *now*!" barked Hopper. He could tell the RA unit was about to get overrun, even if Major Jenkins hadn't spotted it just yet. He needed to make sure the enemy was focused on these two positions so his other two platoons could blow past the front entrance of the camp and sweep through it, shooting the aliens in the back if possible.

Boom…boom…boom…

A series of explosions rippled across the front section of the camp as Second and Third Platoon launched their assault. The handful of alien guards hunkering down behind some defenses were blown apart. Seconds later, the single guard tower providing overwatch to the base was destroyed.

Hopper and Jenkins watched as the first ten Deltas blew right past the camp entrance, blasters blazing, double-tapping the few enemy guards they ran across. The next batch of Deltas followed in as the two groups spread out. As the entrance was secured, the bulk of the two platoons moved in and broke down into smaller teams, moving methodically and rapidly through the camp.

By now, Ghost Four had arrived in Hammer's sector, and just in time. The enemy had nearly broken through their lines. Both Mechs had been taken out. The aliens had swarmed them and all but destroyed their ability to defend themselves.

Looking at the blue-force tracker, Captain Hopper saw Hammer unit had lost a little more than half their numbers. He almost had to do a double take to make sure the number of KIAs was correct. He didn't think they had taken that many hits, but apparently, they had. Ghost Four was now on the scene and speedily shoring up their position.

Suddenly, the enemy became aware that the front gate was under attack. They shifted their positions and pulled back from Hammer's sector into the base. As this happened, Ghost Four began to press their own attack and pursued the now-retreating enemy.

"Captain Hopper, I've got Sledgehammer deploying right now in that open field not far from the camp. We'll have another two hundred and twelve soldiers and four additional Mechs ready in ten mikes," Major Jenkins announced with confidence in his voice.

Hopper had practically forgotten he was standing next to Jenkins. "That's a good call, sir," he responded. "I think we've nearly whipped them, but I have no idea if more of them are on the way. Plus, we need to start evacuating our wounded."

"My thoughts exactly," Jenkins replied before directing the new units on their way to the surface.

The fighting lasted another ten minutes before it petered out. Patching into Lieutenant Crocker's coms, Hopper asked, "What's the status inside the camp? We're not showing any major fighting anymore."

A second later, Crocker replied, "We've cornered maybe a dozen of them in a building. Other than that, they're either dead, dying or wounded."

"We should get inside that camp, Captain—see if we can't round up some prisoners and start talking to them," Major Jenkins said.

Hopper nodded in agreement. "Lieutenant, the major and I are headed in. See if we can find some prisoners to take, and let's figure out what to do with those holdouts. Maybe we can get them to give up."

****

As Major Jenkins and Captain Hopper walked into the camp, Hopper was astounded by the amount of damage their forces had been able to inflict in such a short period. This was the first real combat action any of them had seen, and the first time nearly any of their equipment and weapons had been used in the heat of anger.

The camp was strewn with both dead Earthers and Zodarks. Small fires burned, and many of the buildings were pretty shot up. Some of the Deltas and the newly arrived RA soldiers were coming to the aid of their wounded comrades, patching them up and helping them out of the camp and to the open field not too far away, where additional medical personnel were standing by to treat the wounded. Some of the new arrivals were also tasked with collecting their dead and any human equipment nearby as well. They didn't want to leave anything behind.

One of the Delta soldiers came out of a small building holding Ambassador Nina Chapman. He called out to Hopper and Jenkins for them to come toward him.

"Is she all right?" asked Jenkins as he approached, concern written on his face.

Nina was looking pale, her skin sweaty like she was going into shock.

"I think she will be. I'm going to carry her back to the transports so we can get her sent up in the first wave. But you need to see inside there, sirs. What they did to her assistant..." The soldier's voice trailed off. Then, before either of them could ask him anything further, he started walking toward the transports.

Now that the fighting had all but ended, some of the human-looking prisoners were starting to poke their heads out of the two buildings they had been held up in.

Major Jenkins walked up behind Hopper. "Captain, why don't you go ahead and take the lead on talking with them while I focus on things out here? I was just informed that Professor Audrey Lancaster is on her way over to meet up with us. She came down with the last transport. I'll head inside that building and document what took place when the lead master at arms gets down here from the *Voyager*."

Hopper stood there for a moment, looking at the captives. Finally, he turned to face the major. "Copy that, sir. I'll do my best to get us some answers while I'm at it. I still want to know who the hell these aliens are and why they violently attacked us. If you need any other help from my Ghost element, Lieutenant Crocker, my XO can assist you."

With nothing more to be said, the major walked toward the far side of the camp, where some of the humanlike prisoners had holed up. Judging by some antennas on top of the building, it was probably their coms rooms. As he walked toward the captives, they all ducked their heads back in their windows and doors and did their best to disappear.

Making his way up to the front door of one of the large buildings, Hopper turned the external audio speakers on his helmet up and made sure his AI translator had the Chaldean variant loaded.

Clearing his throat to speak, he said, "Hello, my name is Captain Jayden Hopper of the Republic Army. My soldiers came here in peace. We mean you no harm. Earlier today, our ambassador attempted to speak with an alien by the name of T'Tock. His group attacked our people; this is why we attacked this camp—to recover our ambassador, and to speak with you. Who among you is your leader?"

Hopper had no idea if he had said the right thing. He hadn't anticipated speaking to them. That was the ambassador's job, not his. Just then, Professor Audrey Lancaster walked up next to him.

She leaned in slightly. "That was a good start, Captain."

"Thanks, Professor. I'm glad you're able to join us."

Hopper's initial question was met with silence. However, after another moment, a lone figure emerged from the darkness within the building. He walked up to one of the windows.

The man, who looked to be in his midfifties, sheepishly said in reply, "You speak our language?"

Looking up at the man who was speaking to them from a second-floor window, Hopper just nodded. "With the help of a translator, yes. My name is Captain Jayden Hopper, and this is Professor Audrey Lancaster. Are you the leader of this group?"

The man nodded sheepishly. "I am. My name is Hadad," he replied as he turned and waved his hand in the direction of his building and the one next to it. "And these are my fellow countrymen."

Captain Hopper motioned for the man to come forward so they could speak as he took his helmet off. All of the Earthers had their helmets on with the exception of Professor Lancaster.

Hadad made his way down to the front door and to them. As he approached them, Hopper pulled out a small box with a pair of earbuds in it.

When Hadad reached him, Hopper handed him the box. "Do you know what these are?" he asked as the man took the small box from him.

Hadad smiled as he saw the contents of the box. "I believe these are listening devices of some sort I should place in my ears? Am I correct?"

"Yes. We call them earbuds. If you insert them in your ears, you'll understand our native language, just as all my men understand yours," Hopper explained.

"Do you have many more of them?" Hadad asked, looking back at his fellow prisoners.

Hopper shook his head. "Not here with us. But on our ship, where we came from, we have more. Let's take a walk away from the others. I'd like to talk privately with you. As a matter of fact, we have some people from our ship who would like to talk with you and learn more about you and your people—but also how you came to this planet and who these blue aliens are."

As the captain, the professor, and Hadad walked toward the other building, the Republic Army soldiers started passing out some of their meals ready to eat or MREs to the prisoners, who looked skeptically at the packages. Once a couple of the soldiers opened them up and started eating the contents, the others did likewise. Soon, smiles spread across the group as they tasted food from a completely different culture and world for the first time.

A few minutes later, Hadad, Hopper, and Lancaster walked into one of the buildings in the camp that hadn't been shot to hell. There were two other civilians getting a table ready and some other equipment. As the trio walked toward the table, Hopper motioned for Audrey to take the lead.

****

Audrey couldn't believe what the camp and the entire area looked like when she was led into it. Trees had been shot to pieces, parts of the camp walls were missing, huge chunks of buildings were blown out, and nearly all the guard towers were smoldering ruins. She'd never been to a warzone before, but now she knew what one looked like. This place had been heavily fought over. There were dead bodies everywhere. Some human, a lot alien.

As the three of them sat down, Audrey took the seat closest to the human-looking prisoner. The first thing she noticed now that they had had a chance to sit down was how dirty and disheveled the man named Hadad was. She wasn't sure what to make of him.

Just as she was about to say something, one of the soldiers brought in some bottles of water and opened a couple of MRE packets and placed them on the table for the three of them. Hadad looked at the bottle of water and food with the look of a man who hadn't eaten a lot recently. Noticing his gaze, Audrey signaled that he should eat and drink.

Hadad unscrewed one of the water bottles and drank most of it down. The prisoner then tasted some of the food cautiously until he felt sure it was OK to eat. Once he thought it safe, he dug in.

While Hadad was eating, Audrey began her visual observations of him. The first thing she noticed was that he knew exactly what a bottle was and how to open it. That meant he'd probably seen something similar before, or his people had the same concept. Then she watched him as he ate. He didn't devour the food like an uncivilized person, cramming as much as he could in his mouth. He took purposeful bites and chewed, taking sips of water as he did. He ate with a careful deliberateness that suggested he had been used to eating quality prepared food at some point in his life. He also knew how to eat it without sounding like an animal chewing its cud. His teeth and mouth looked just like any other human's she had seen. Audrey didn't need some machine to sequence the alien's DNA. Hadad was human. She just didn't understand how that was possible.

"Hadad—you said your name is Hadad, correct?" Audrey asked cautiously.

The man nodded but didn't say anything, eying her and examining Captain Hopper's face and equipment.

"Now that you've had a chance to eat some food, I'd like to know if we can have a more substantive discussion." Audrey looked him in the eyes as she waited for his response.

Nodding as he used his sleeve to wipe the side of his mouth, he said, "Yes, Professor. That would be appreciated. I have many questions I'd like to ask you as well. Mainly, who are you and where did you come from?"

Taking a breath before she replied, she said, "We are from another system. A planet called Earth."

Not missing a beat, Hadad quickly replied, "Then that would explain why we have never seen your people before. Your soldiers' equipment looks very different from our own. What are you doing here?"

"We are explorers. We discovered this planet many years ago. We finally sent an expedition here to see if there was life on it," Audrey explained.

Lifting his head, he countered, "You shouldn't have come here. This isn't your world."

Audrey wrinkled her brow. "Is this your home world? Whose is it?"

The strange man laughed at the question. "No, Clovis is a mining colony. My people are from a planet called Sumara. It's a long way from this place. As to who owns this planet? This place belongs to someone else."

"The Zodarks?" she asked, head cocked to the side. "What are you doing here if this is not your home?"

Hadad reached for the second bottle of water and took a couple of drinks from it before he responded. "This is a prison colony. This is where the Zodarks and those in our government send people they feel are a threat to them, to work their mines and eventually die."

Hadad paused for a second as he shook his head in disgust. "This is a place of misery and death, Professor. Not a place any of us Sumerians ever want to visit."

"So, this planet is called Clovis?" she clarified.

Hadad nodded. "Yes, the mountains here are rich in resources called Trimar and Morean. We mine the raw ore from the mountains, then use those machines out there to refine it into blocks that are eventually picked up and shipped back to the Zodarks' core worlds."

Captain Hopper interjected, "This T'Tock our ambassador talked with—he's your taskmaster, then?"

Hadad turned to look at the soldier clad in armor. "Yes, T'Tock is the leader of this camp. A brutal slave master if you ask me. We heard some commotion at the front of the camp this morning, but we had no idea what it was or what was happening. Then we saw him and one of his guards carrying two people we'd never seen before into one of their buildings, and we knew there was going to be trouble. The Zodarks ordered us to stay in the compound. Then, a handful of hours later, you people started attacking the camp."

"What else can you tell us about these Zodarks?" Captain Hopper asked.

Audrey turned to him with an annoyed look; she was supposed to be the lead in this conversation.

Hadad smiled at the exchange. "I can tell you are the researcher and he the ever-present warrior. Our planet used to have warriors. I suppose we still do in some fashion, just not like we used to."

Audrey blushed but pressed on with her own question. "What can you tell us about these Zodarks?"

"Unfortunately, a lot. They are a brutish species, as you can tell. Aggressive and challenging to deal with. For hundreds of years, our two races have had a delicate relationship that has allowed us to coexist. In exchange for providing a yearly tribute, they largely allowed us to develop and grow on our own. We were even allowed to develop some spacefaring ships to explore our own star system, but nothing compared to what the Zodarks have. They didn't want us to become too powerful and challenge them."

Captain Hopper interrupted to ask, "Are there any more Zodarks on this planet or nearby?"

Hadad shrugged. "I couldn't say for sure. I've never been anywhere on this planet other than here where the mines are."

"What can you tell us about their spacefaring ability?" Hopper asked next.

Hadad leaned forward. "When we first started to explore space, it appeared the Zodarks might allow us to join them as a spacefaring people. They shared with us a type of power plant that ran on the refined Trimar mineral we mine from these mountains. It generates enormous amounts of clean power, unlike other fuel sources we used to use. Then, one day, using this enormous power source, our researchers discovered a way to travel from one solar system to another by folding space. It was an incredible discovery as it meant our people would be able to travel beyond our solar system just like the Zodarks are able to.

"However, within days of our breakthrough in space travel, the Zodarks invaded our planet with their armies and seized the technology from us. That was probably close to two hundred years ago," Hadad explained.

He went on in greater detail, describing more of the history between his people and the Zodarks. Audrey, Captain Hopper, and the other two civilians sat hanging on his every word for several hours as Hadad told them about his people, his planet, and the Zodarks. The small video-recording drones hovered at different angles, making sure to capture the entire exchange from different vantage points.

Before they dove into talking more technical mumbo-jumbo about this new means of space travel, Captain Hopper circled back to something Hadad had mentioned earlier.

"Hadad, when our ambassador attempted to speak with T'Tock, why did he attack her and the rest of us? We had come here in peace, hoping to talk, not fight each other."

Hadad sighed and shook his head slightly. "You cannot reason or negotiate with a Zodark," he countered. "Not unless you are coming at them from a position of immense strength. They probably saw your ambassador as weak and figured they could get her to answer their questions without having to give her any information in exchange. It's just the way the Zodarks are. They are a brutal species, Captain. You will see in time, now that you've met them."

Audrey asked, "Hadad, you said the Zodarks asked you to pay a tribute to them. What was the tribute they asked you to pay?"

Hadad turned and looked out one of the windows, afraid or ashamed to say what it was. Returning his gaze to the soldier sitting opposite him, he said, "Once a year, at the end of our winter solstice, the Zodarks came down to our planet with large transport ships and collected five percent of the people above the age of fifty. Then they took one in ten of our children under the age of three. What they did with them…none of us truly know. Some speculated that they ate them. Some said they were used to populate slave colonies or other slave worlds they control. Unfortunately, once a person or child was selected, they were never heard from again. I personally believe they may eat them. You saw how they dismembered and ate your soldiers they had just killed. They are barbaric monsters."

Audrey moved a hand to her mouth and gasped. She did her best to fight back the shock, horror, and anger she felt in that moment.

Captain Hopper didn't mince words as he uttered several curse words before muttering, "Damn animals."

Hadad shook his head angrily. "No, Captain. We…we are their animals! We are their cattle. That's how it's been for as long as our people can remember."

Hopper opted to change the subject. "Hadad, we know of at least five more camps. Are there more camps on this planet or other Zodark bases we need to be aware of?"

The man shrugged. "I am not sure. It would appear you know more than I do. What I'm frankly surprised at, Captain, is that the Zodarks hadn't detected your presence in orbit or once you landed on the planet. How long have you been observing us?"

"We've been in orbit now for five days. To be honest, we hadn't initially detected a lot of electronic transmissions emanating from the planet or anywhere else in the system until we did a more detailed spectral analysis."

Hadad wrinkled his eyebrows at the mention of electronic emissions. "What do you mean by that term, electronics? And what is this word emissions? It doesn't translate properly into our language."

The Earthers explained what the terms meant and how their technology could detect that kind of thing. Hadad told them the Zodarks operated their communication systems on a very different type of microburst transmission technology that allowed them to send large amounts of data over long distances with little in the way of an electronic signature. He asked one of the soldiers to bring some of the Zodark equipment over to him, saying he'd show them how some of it worked and what type of frequency it operated on.

Hopper held up a hand. "We can do that in time, Hadad. Right now, a small group of Zodarks has locked themselves inside what we think is their communications room. We're working on getting them to surrender right now."

Hadad suddenly looked very concerned. "If T'Tock and his people have locked themselves inside the communications building, then you need to take them out *now*. They have most likely been calling for help from the other camps, or worse, for a nearby starship to come to assist them."

"We're working on that, Hadad, and we know they've already sent a few messages outside the system. We're going to have to leave this star system soon, now that we have freed you and your people. Would you like to come back with us to our world, or would you rather we leave you here?" Hopper asked, hoping they'd agree to come with him voluntarily.

Hadad nodded. "Everyone in this camp would welcome the chance to come with you. To escape this place is something we all talk about, but until you arrived, it was nothing more than a dream. Yes, we will go with you."

"Excellent. Then let's head back out, and I'll let you explain things to your people. We have transports heading down now as we speak to start ferrying you back to our ships."

Reaching his hand across the table to touch Hopper's, Hadad added, "I would recommend taking as much of the refined Trimar and

Morean with you as possible. There is much we can help you with, but some of it will require these two materials."

Hopper smiled and nodded in agreement.

****

RNS *Voyager*

Admiral Abigail Halsey didn't know where to start. This newfound excitement about finding a habitable planet, a new home world for humanity, was suddenly turning into dread. While they had known there was the possibility of life on the planet, she was still in shock that one of the species there was apparently a group of humans. What really blew her mind was thinking about how this group could be speaking a variant of ancient Chaldean.

She snapped herself back to the present as her chief scientific officer, Dr. Jonathan Milton, stepped forward to the podium, the monitor behind him populating with data—or at least the information they knew up to this point.

Clearing his throat, he began to speak, his thick British accent further playing into the pompous demeanor he seemed to display whenever he was asked to speak in front of a group.

"Admiral," he said, pronouncing each syllable like he was talking down to a student who didn't understand his lecture, "I'd like to take just a moment to summarize what we know up to this point. I think it's good for us to establish some fundamental facts and then build on that knowledge base as we expand it further." He paused for a moment as he lowered his chin, almost looking down on her and the other crewmen present.

Jonathan Milton was a pompous bastard, having spent his entire career as a researcher working for the UK Astronomy Technology Centre. He was also a department chair at Cambridge. He was arguably one of the smartest people on the expedition, and he'd had the forethought to bring with him a leading anthropologist from the University of California–Berkeley and a sociolinguistics specialist from Harvard. The three of them, along with their lead data scientist and programmer from Carnegie Mellon University, Professor Ekhard, had deciphered the language of the humanlike aliens within twenty-four hours.

Halsey groaned softly to herself but nodded for him to continue, so he did. "As everyone is aware, a few days after settling in orbit around New Eden, we began to land geological and survey teams along with reconnaissance teams at various points of interest around the planet. One of those teams was a Delta platoon sent to investigate the possible signs of intelligent life."

The doctor paused for a moment before continuing, enjoying every moment of leading this monumental discussion. "What they found was nothing short of astounding." Behind him were several images of the large bluish aliens. "But what *else* they found is what I would like to discuss with you now." Pictures of the human-looking prisoners popped up next.

"While we weren't sure what to make of these prisoners, our soldiers on the ground were able to use their parabolic microphones to capture their communications with each other for nearly a day. Likewise, they were able to do the same with the large blue aliens. After nearly twenty straight hours of collecting both video and audio interactions between the two species, our quantum computer, using a sophisticated AI algorithm Professor Ekhard had created, was eventually able to sequence their languages. With the help of Professor Audrey Lancaster, we were able to decipher the language of the humans in its entirety. We've got a working understanding now of the blue aliens' language as well."

Dr. Milton held his chin up a bit as if he had somehow made this discovery and not the team standing there with him.

"As it turns out, the human-looking creatures are speaking a variant of an ancient version of Chaldean—we estimate their language to be related to Chaldean as spoken on Earth five thousand years ago. This dialect has origins that date back to the Sumerian civilization of Mesopotamia and of ancient Elam. That civilization dates back to roughly 4050 BC."

A few audible gasps and chattering started up by the people involved in the briefing. Halsey let it go on for a moment longer before she raised her hand to silence them. Most of her leadership team was only just now learning of this discovery.

"Dr. Milton, this is an incredible breakthrough, and congratulations to your staff for having achieved it. But how is it in the vastness of space, we managed to discover a group of humans on a planet twelve light-years from Earth, that just so happens to speak a variant of the Chaldean language that relates to a civilization from six thousand years ago?" asked Admiral Halsey, deflating the intellectual high that the doctor was currently riding.

Professor Audrey Lancaster, who had just returned from the surface, jumped in before the doctor had a chance to reply. "We're still trying to figure that piece out, Admiral."

Dr. Milton gave her a slight smile as if thanking her for the quick help he didn't need.

Leaning in, Halsey prodded, "What are these people calling themselves, and where are they saying they're from?"

Audrey stood taller; she was the only person to have spent a few hours with these new humans, so she eagerly took the question. "The leader of the group of prisoners says his name is Hadad. He said they are from a planet called Sumer, which would make sense if they came from an ancient Chaldean-speaking group on Earth, given their ancient Sumerian-Akkadian history.

"He said they call this planet we're in orbit of Clovis. It apparently belongs to the Zodarks, the large bluish aliens we just fought to recover Ambassador Chapman from."

"Excuse me, Admiral," Jonathan interjected briskly, "as much as I'm sure Professor Lancaster would like to talk about the history of the Sumerian people and how they came to be, I believe we should focus our attention on the threat this other species poses, and this so-called Zodark Empire."

Halsey nodded. "You're right, Dr. Milton. Professor Lancaster, we'll discuss the Sumerians at a later date. In the meantime, continue to learn as much as you can about them. Right now, I think we need to focus on this other immediate threat. Doctor, please continue."

Smiling now that he had control of the briefing again, Dr. Milton went on to explain, "The Sumerians told us this other species is called the Zodarks. As you can see, they are large brutish creatures who have apparently been a spacefaring race for many hundreds or even thousands of years. What little we know of them thus far is that they are an advanced apex predator species that have yet to run into a race of sentient beings they haven't been able to either subdue or eliminate."

Admiral Halsey noticed a few of her military officers becoming a bit uneasy by that proclamation. Captain Hunt, who was participating via holograph, didn't appear fazed, though.

Of course he's not intimidated—he's commanding our most powerful warship, Halsey thought jealously.

"The Sumerians have been able to provide us some data on the Zodarks' ships, but not much. While the Sumerians have been a spacefaring people for a few hundred years, their technological advancements have been greatly limited by the Zodarks. They've been largely confined to some interplanetary activity in their own solar system."

One of the officers in the room let out a soft whistle. "Nearly two hundred years? It sounds like these new humans we've discovered are pretty advanced if they discovered space travel more than two hundred years ago. Heck, we've only developed the ability to leave our own solar system in the last twenty."

Dr. Milton bobbed his head up and down before continuing. "That is true—a good point, Commander. I am hopeful that during our debrief of them, we'll be able to ascertain exactly how advanced their people truly are. Now, back to the Zodark ships. The Sumerians have been able to give us some information about them. For instance, their weapon systems are largely based on pulse beam technologies. In a way, that's a good thing because we're experienced in that field of research. Space Command's current and future warships also feature a modulated armor, developed to defeat pulse beam weapons. What we're unsure of is how strong the Zodark weapons are, and their effective ranges.

"We also know they have an advanced form of space travel," Dr. Milton continued. "The Sumerians said the Zodarks seized what we believe was some sort of wormhole technology, but they're not aware if the Zodarks were able to understand how it worked or implement it. Right now, the Sumerian leader said their current home world is two months' travel via a Zodark ship. Since we have no idea of how fast a Zodark ship can travel, we aren't sure how far that is. What we do know is it takes us two weeks to travel one light-year."

Interrupting the discussion, Captain Hunt began to speak via his holographic image. "If I may, Doctor, Admiral, why don't we show the Sumerians some star maps and see if they can point out their system or region? From there, we'll be able to figure out how far away their home planet is, and potentially where these Zodark core systems are. Right now, not knowing leaves us, and thereby Earth, pretty vulnerable to a species that now knows we exist. I think it would be prudent to compile as much information as possible and begin to transmit it back to Sol. We need to inform them of what we've found and warn them of this Zodark threat. We're going to need a united Sol to defend against them if they ever discover where we came from, Admiral."

"I agree, Captain. Doctor, I need you to compile everything we've learned up to this point and dispatch a com drone immediately," Admiral Halsey directed. "Next, your people need to keep unraveling everything you can learn about this threat from the Sumerians and send a daily com drone back home until we leave the systems. Make sure Dr. Johnson is brought into the loop on this. We need DARPA and NRO's brainpower working on this as well."

Halsey shifted in her seat to face Major Jenkins, who had recently arrived from the surface; Captain Hopper had been left to maintain a small contingent down there while they finished sanitizing the camp and collecting all the refined minerals the Sumerians had told them to bring.

"Major, tell us about the raid on the camp and the Zodarks we were able to capture."

Jenkins nodded and stood to speak. "As we just learned, the Zodarks are a fierce and brutal species. When our first contact team attempted to speak with them, they appeared interested. That changed rapidly when Ambassador Chapman wouldn't tell them which star system Earth is located in. When our Special Forces soldiers made their presence known, the Zodarks went completely berserk. They kidnapped the ambassador and attacked our soldiers. We were completely caught off guard by how fast and vicious their attack was and lost a number of good people right off the bat."

Major Jenkins continued, "Additional forces were brought down to the surface, and a plan was put into place to retrieve the ambassador and liberate the camp. We'll have some videos and our after-action reports drawn up soon to illustrate what happened. Suffice it to say, it was a real ballbuster of a fight. My battalion sustained fifty-three killed and another forty-eight wounded. Captain Hopper's unit sustained twenty-nine killed and eighteen wounded. We also lost three of our Mech units, which were torn to shreds by the electrified short swords the Zodarks use when they get up close to you. In the end, we were able to capture twelve of them, to include their leader, T'Tock. In all, we killed one hundred and fifty-two of them. Captain Hopper's remaining soldiers are working with some of our synthetics to get the bodies buried and sanitize the camp of anything that might lead them back to Earth."

Halsey took a deep breath. "I assume we have these Zodarks under lock and key right now?"

Jenkins nodded. "They're being kept in the brig. We have a contingent of soldiers assisting the master at arms in guarding them as well."

"I assume they were able to transmit a distress call before we subdued them?" she asked next.

Grimacing at the question, Jenkins explained, "They likely did that as soon as they abducted the ambassador. But, yes, when we launched our attack on the base, they probably sent another message out of the system. We can also be sure the other Zodark camps on the planet likely know of our presence and capabilities."

The admiral turned to look at Captain Hunt's holographic image next. "Captain, you're the tactical fleet commander. What is your suggestion for what we do next? How should we go about protecting the *Voyager* and the *Gables*?"

A short pause ensued as Hunt thought about his response. He finally replied, "We've detected an asteroid belt about two AUs from the planet. We can hide in the belt and wait for a ship to arrive and then leave the system or stay and fight—test our ships against them."

The admiral considered the options. On the one hand, the smarter thing to do would be to get out of Dodge and head back to Sol with what they knew. On the other hand, any intelligence they could gain on the enemy ships and their capabilities could prove invaluable, especially if they ended up having to fight them.

Halsey looked at Jenkins. "How long until our ground contingent is done collecting those materials and sanitizing the place?"

Jenkins leaned forward in his chair. "I'd estimate another twelve hours."

Halsey sat back in her chair and steepled her fingers. Turning to face Hunt again, she announced, "Here's what we're going to do. When the ground team finishes on the surface, we're going to send the *Gables* back with everything we've collected and as many of the wounded and the Sumerians as we can. The *Rook* and *Voyager* will stay here and wait to see what kind of starship shows up. When they do arrive, we'll look to engage them."

Chapter Fourteen
New Leadership

Earth—Sol
Space Command

Vice Admiral Chester Bailey looked over the reports from the two orbital shipyards. On the one hand, he felt he should be satisfied with their progress; they were clearly ahead of schedule on a couple of ships. On the other hand, they were also falling behind schedule on some of the larger transport ships. Those vessels were critical to the outward expansion of the Republic if they were to have any hope of keeping pace with the GEU and Asian Alliance's expansion into the stars.

There was a soft knock on his office door, and Admiral Jose Sanchez stuck his head in. "Mind if I come in, Chester?" He had a look on his face that said he had something important to say, and a mysterious small bag in his hand.

Unsure of what his boss wanted, Vice Admiral Bailey waved Admiral Sanchez in. He took a moment to close up what he was working on as the other admiral took a seat at the far side of his office, on one of a pair of couches angled to look out the window at the sea. One of the benefits of Space Command being headquartered at the Kennedy Space Center was the view: palm trees, white sandy beaches, and the Atlantic Ocean.

Once Bailey had joined him, Sanchez pulled a couple of glasses and an unopened bottle of Gran Patrón out of his bag. "I'm sure you're wondering why I'm here, Chester," he said. He opened the bottle of fine tequila and proceeded to pour a healthy amount into both glasses, handing Bailey one. "My wife bought this for me on her last trip to Mexico City. She's finalizing the purchase of our new home there, a big beautiful place right on the ocean in Cabo. It's a lot closer to where the rest of the kids and grandkids live these days."

Bailey's brow furrowed at the comment. "Being close to family is a good thing. Are you going to commute between here and there?" he asked.

Sanchez let out a soft laugh. He looked out the window for a second before he returned his gaze to Bailey. "This may come as a bit of a surprise, but I'm retiring, Chester. I've officially tendered my resignation letter to the Secretary of Defense and the President as of two hours ago. My final day on the job will be Friday, two days from now."

Bailey tried to keep his jaw from hitting the floor; he didn't even know how to respond, at least not right away. "I, I thought you were going to stay on a few more years—at least long enough to know how the Rhea expedition went."

Sanchez shrugged off the comment. "No, I'm getting up there in age, and so is my wife. Even with these medical nanobots coursing through my bloodstream, I'm still getting old up here," he said as he pointed to his head. "My wife and I want to spend more time together. I've spent sixty-eight years in Space Command. It's time to hang it up and let someone else take the reins."

Bailey felt a slight tinge of concern. This abrupt retirement had definitely caught him by surprise. He hadn't heard about the old man looking to throw in the towel yet, so he had no idea who might be coming in to take his place.

Clearly seeing the look of confusion on Bailey's face, Sanchez interceded. "Chester, I brought this fine tequila to your office to tell you that I'm ending my military career, but also to inform you that I have recommended that you take over as the new head of Space Command. As you know, Chester, I don't have the final say in who is selected for this position—it's politically appointed. If you *are* selected and confirmed by the Senate, you'll hold the post for seven years, at which point you'll need to be reconfirmed. If you aren't reconfirmed, you'll be retired. There's no rule limiting how many terms you can serve, but know this, Chester—it's all political."

The older man paused for a moment, sizing him up. "I'm not going to lie to you. You're young enough that you could conceivably serve another twenty or thirty years in your current position or even as a fleet admiral in charge of ships beyond Sol. Hell, with the continued advancements in nanotechnology, you could live well into your mid- or even high hundreds, which means you could serve fifty or even seventy years longer than me. However, if you leave your current post as head of space operations, your stint as the head of Space Command could end your time in the military if you aren't selected for subsequent terms. If you end up on the wrong side of things, you could find yourself a one-term commander. Think about that for a few days, OK? I personally think you're the right man to lead Space Command going into this new frontier of discovery, but I'd hate for you to have your space career cut short if you crossed the wrong senator or president."

Vice Admiral Bailey knew he had a bit of a temper at times—he'd been known to ruffle some feathers on occasion. He sat back in his chair and took a long pull of the tequila, feeling the smooth liquid race down his throat. To take over as the leader of Space Command had always been his dream, but the warning Sanchez had just given him gave him pause. He hadn't considered that he could end up serving only one term. *Then again, if we grow New Eden, they're going to need a governor and fleet commander out there. I could use my position as head of Space Command to create my own empire in the Rhea system...*

Bailey finished his drink and locked eyes with Sanchez. "You didn't have to tell me about the consequences of the terms. Why did you?"

Sanchez smiled at the younger man who had been gunning for his position for years. "Because despite our differences, Chester, I think you're the right man for the job. You've got a strategic eye for things, and that's what Space Command needs right now. You were right about the transport fleet. I should have seen that, but I didn't. Now we're paying for the decision."

He sighed as he refilled his drink again and held it in his hand. "We're entering a new race with the GEU and the Asians. We're going to need a younger, stronger man at the helm to lead us through this period. We won't get that from the politicians; we need that to come from Space Command. I believe you're the man to get that done and to really cement the head of Space Command's status as the strongest and most powerful person in the country. I can guide you with the politics, introduce you to the right benefactors, but you'll need to make your own way at some point. That is, if you still want my job...I'd understand if I scared you off. You're in the second most powerful position in the military right now, so I wouldn't fault you if you wanted to stay put where you are."

Bailey shook his head. "I'll do it," he declared. "If you're willing to help me learn the political ropes, I'll cement this position as you envisioned it to be."

Now it was Sanchez's turn to smile. "I knew I could count on you. Now, as one of your first acts as fleet admiral, you're going to need to know how to handle this."

Sanchez pulled out a small holographic disk from his pocket. He placed it on the table between them and hit play. A moment later, an image of a man appeared along with some documents lined up next to his image.

"What's this?" asked Bailey, concern in his voice.

"When President Roberts and the Senate opted not to renew the Space Exploration Treaty, the GEU, African Union, and the Asian Alliance did. Not only have they renewed the treaty, but they're also moving to establish a new joint governing body that'll fold all of their economies, technologies, and peoples together to pursue with one effort the further exploration and colonization of the Centaurus constellation and all its moons and planets.

"Our spy within their space program was able to obtain a copy of their findings on Alpha Centauri and the rest of the constellation they've explored up to this point. It's simply incredible, Chester. The planet is rich in resources, and so are the moons and other planets in the system."

The admiral paused for a moment before adding, "You were right, Chester. I was wrong, gravely wrong, to have gone along with abandoning that mission. We never should have backed out of that expedition or the SET. Our worst fears are now coming to fruition because I didn't stand up to President Roberts when I should have. Now we're going to have a united world government with multiple habitable planets they can call their own."

Bailey shook his head. The alcohol and the realization of how tough a position they were in both suddenly hit him. He understood now why the old goat was retiring. He didn't want to deal with what was coming down the pike or the consequences of his decisions. It'd be months before they received a probe with any news or details of how the Rhea expedition had fared or what they had found. Right now, all they had to go on was the news of the incredible find the other nations had made in the Centaurus constellation.

Shaking his head again, Bailey replied, "Perhaps it was good that you overrode me and had us build up warships first. We may end up needing them."

Sanchez placed his hand on Bailey's shoulder. "You need to speed up the production of those transports you're building and order many more. The Rhea expedition may yet prove to be a bigger find for humanity than the Centaurus constellation. You need to have our people ready to exploit that opportunity when it comes."

The two men talked for a little while longer as they drank more of the smooth tequila. The coming weeks and months would prove to be a challenging time for Space Command.
****

Musk Industries
John Glenn Orbital Station

Andrew Barry sat at his desk, studying the newly appointed Fleet Admiral Chester Bailey skeptically. Narrowing his eyes a bit as he leaned forward in his chair, he eyed the admiral for a moment. "This is a tall order, Admiral," he finally said.

Not one to mince words, Admiral Bailey quickly countered, "If you're not able to handle it, I can see if BlueOrigin can pick up your slack."

Andrew snorted at the mention of his chief rival. "I didn't say we couldn't handle it," he countered. "You're just asking an awful lot from us in a very short period of time." He swiveled in his chair to look out the floor-to-ceiling windows of his office on the orbital station. "As you can see, we're hard at work completing the original request for the *Ark*-class ships. We're still at least two years away from completing that second battlecruiser, the *Queen Mary*. Now you're asking me not only to design and build a fleet of sixty transport ships but also to compete for a contract to build not just a new battleship but a space carrier? We haven't even invented the technology for what you want these ships to do, Admiral."

Andrew turned around to look at Bailey and caught the man looking out the window. He was probably envious of such a view. Down at the lower portion of the orbital station, they could see the two vast shipyards on either end of them. Further off toward the African continent, they could see the other orbital station and a similar smattering of shipyards, no doubt just as busy as the Republic ones.

In a hushed tone, Bailey said, "Andrew, as a country, we're in a precarious situation right now. I need the help of your company to even the score—to be as prepared as possible for the future."

Andrew lifted his chin. "I understand the situation we're in, Admiral. That buffoon President of ours and the Senate have placed us all in a precarious situation. Without the SET, the other shipyards are now actively building warships of their own. Not only do they have two new planets to colonize, they're also building a navy that will overtake our own in the next two decades. I'm not sure even BlueOrigin or Musk Industries will be able to keep up with their combined capabilities."

The admiral looked a bit defeated at the news. "What about the Mars station? The yards out there have been building up in size, haven't they?"

Andrew nodded. "They have. Even now, we have four frigates under construction. We'll begin construction of four more once they leave the yard. Our capabilities on Mars are still growing. Most of the transports we're building will be used to take needed supplies to Mars and the Belt. I hate to say this, Admiral, but we're still at least one or two decades away from Mars being a fully self-sufficient colony and industrial center."

Bailey sighed. "Andrew, do you have a stiff drink around?" he asked.

Pulling a bottle of Kentucky bourbon out of the bottom drawer of his desk, Andrew poured them both a healthy glass and passed one to the admiral.

"Andrew, I think Musk Industries and BlueOrigin have done a good job with the shipyards you guys have. But as we move forward into the colonization of space and the building of a real honest-to-goodness space navy, we're going to need a much larger and more capable shipyard. Right now, there's only so much that can be done with the yards connected to the John Glenn. I think it's time we start looking to build an independent yard—one that has space to grow and can become a massive structure to support and build the type of warships we're going to need for the future."

Andrew's left eyebrow rose. "That's a big proposition," he replied. "Where would you want to build such a yard?"

"That's a question I have for you. Do you think we should build a yard in high orbit over Earth, the moon, or somewhere in between?"

Andrew took a sip of his bourbon and contemplated. "If we're going to build a long-term military shipyard," he said at last, "we need to make sure it has enough room to grow and expand. We also need to make sure it'll be able to build the monstrous ships we'll begin to build at some point. We're already running into problems trying to build the Arks at our current facilities because of their size. I think we should probably place this new facility just beyond the moon. It's close enough to Earth so workers can travel there, but far enough away to give us room to work. The bigger challenge we're going to face is resources. We're already stretched thin with the ships you've asked us to build."

Bailey nodded. "I've thought about that as well, and I've got a plan. The shipyard itself is going to be owned by Space Command, but we'll probably have it managed by shipbuilders like yourself and BlueOrigin. As to the resources to build it, I'm standing up a new naval fleet. We're going to field hundreds of mining barges to hit the Belt to acquire the resources needed to build this yard. This will make sure we don't interrupt the supply chain for your own projects."

Andrew let out a sigh of relief. "I'm glad you said that, Chester. Supplies are already hard enough to come by for all these ships. If we had to compete with you guys for the resources to build this new yard of yours, I was going to tell you to expect a big delay in finishing these ships."

"I agree, Andrew. That's why we're going to try and run this through the military. I need you guys focused on building these new ships. Speaking of which, how soon until the *Ark* ships are complete?"

"At least three years," Andrew replied matter-of-factly. "I might be able to cut that down by six months, but that would require me to purchase at least another thirty thousand synthetics. I also won't be able to start work on this new battleship until well after they're done. Aside from the manpower for the Arks, they're chewing through more resources than you can possibly imagine."

The admiral let out a defeated sigh. "I understand, Andrew. But I need a preliminary design on the battleship in six months. Once Space Command's had a couple of months to pick them apart, we'll ask both you and BlueOrigin some technical questions about them before we determine who wins the contract. Don't chintz on this, Andrew. This is going to be a contract for ten ships with an option to build ten more. We're talking about a twelve-trillion-dollar contract."

Andrew smiled, his eyes narrowing a bit. That was a lot of money. It would double the value of his company. "I'm confident Space Command will like the design we have in mind," he said, voice calculated. He paused for a second before adding, "Our engineers believe we've found a way to double the speed of the FTL drive. I wasn't going to mention it right away—we still have to test it—but if it works, Admiral, then I'd like to recommend we add this new capability to all the ships we currently have under construction."

Bailey smiled at the news, and then his look soured a bit. "Let me guess—this is going to be a costly addition for Space Command?"

Andrew shrugged. "Research and development is expensive, Admiral. I have shareholders I'm responsible for. I'm sure we can come around to an acceptable price."

The admiral snickered. Then he leaned forward, closing the distance between the two of them. "If this proves to be true, and it happened to be worked into the current ships under construction, and you could retrofit the *Rook* and *Voyager* when they return, I think I might be able to sole-source the bid for this new battleship."

Andrew had always liked Admiral Chester Bailey. The man knew how to drive a hard bargain. Bailey had fed enough Space Command contracts to make sure Musk Industries stayed competitive against BlueOrigin. A sole-source contract for the fleet's new battleships, though—now that kind of cash and long-term construction project could push Musk Industries ahead of any of their competitors for decades to come.

Extending his hand, Andrew replied, "I think something could certainly be worked out, Admiral. Come, join me for dinner. You've never had a dining experience like this. I had our engineers build it for me. It's a complete floor-to-ceiling glass box with a table and a set of four chairs essentially floating in space. Only my special guests get to dine in this thing. It's as if you're eating a fine meal directly in space."

Chapter Fifteen
First Contact

Rhea System
RNS *Rook*

Captain Miles Hunt lay naked under the bedsheets in his cabin, the door locked. There were two hours until he was due on the bridge. He had just placed this holographic visor on his head and turned the device on. Instantly, he was transported to Earth, remembering a wild romp with his wife.

For weeks before Miles had left for this deployment, Lilly and he had worn a pair of VR cameras during their private interludes together. His wife had reasoned that if they were going to be separated for two years, then they should create a couple of these holograph videos of themselves. She wanted to make sure her man wasn't tempted during his deployment, and she wanted a visual memory of him for her own pleasure.

Miles had been dead set against it for fear that it could somehow be stolen, but Lilly had eventually talked him into it. Now, having been gone from his wife for coming up on seven months, he was glad she'd talked him into it; these VR sims had given him something to look forward to in the little off time he had.

Besides the bedroom encounters, they had also recorded themselves having dozens of different conversations. Some were of them having breakfast together, others were walks along the Florida beach. His personal favorite was the one of them just sitting on the couch together watching a movie. The stress of these last few days had been building, and he needed an escape that didn't involve the usual vices people often turned to on Earth, like alcohol or drugs.

He missed his wife. Lilly was everything to him, his true partner in crime. They'd known each other since their senior year at the Space Force Academy. They had gotten married just after graduation and served together for two years until she had become pregnant with their eldest son. She'd then transferred to the reserves to finish her military commitment. That was thirty-two years ago. They had been stationed at the Neil Armstrong Base on the moon for several years, then they'd spent a ten-year stint on Mars before he'd done a couple of tours on two different military space ships before he spent six years as the chief of staff to Admiral Bailey, Head of Fleet Operations.

Now as the *Rook* hid behind an asteroid twelve light-years from Earth, Captain Hunt felt lonely. He desperately missed his wife. As his mind fooled his body into making love to her right now, he wished she was actually here with him on the *Rook*—sharing in the experiences of exploring a new planet and seeing some of the most incredible star formations and nebulas he'd ever seen. Even after his wife had left Space Command, she'd continued working in the field of astrophysics. She loved studying the stars and was immensely jealous of his assignment to the *Rook* and his new mission.

The months on end of nothing but blackness grated on a person's psyche. Sure, they had seen some incredible sights during some of their stops to recharge their FTL drive, but they didn't replace the warmth of a sun's rays on your skin, or the senseless banter of people talking in a restaurant or coffee shop. The ability to share these incredible sights with the one you loved left him longing more and more for home and Lilly's embrace than he thought he could bear. In the depths of space, all anyone had was the people and stuff they brought with them.

He laid his head back on his pillow, his mind reaching a state of ecstasy. Suddenly, the speaker in his room yelled, "Captain to the bridge!" Then the general quarters klaxon started.

Sorry to disturb you, Captain. Long-range sensors have just detected a ship entering the system, Commander Longman, his XO, said over the neurolink.

Thank you, XO. Stand down the GQ alarm but have everyone continue to man their battle stations. It sounds like that ship is a long way off. I'll be up there in ten minutes.

Placing his VR headset in the drawer next to his bed, Miles got up and jumped in the shower. He needed a cold one to clear his head. They'd been floating in the Belt for nearly five days waiting for this ship to arrive. Now it had.

The timing could have been better, he thought with a chuckle.

A few minutes later, Hunt walked onto the bridge in a freshly pressed uniform and took a seat in his captain's chair. "OK, people. What do we have?"

Commander Longman, who had been on duty at the time of detection, led off first. "Sir, we just detected a ship entering the system approximately one AU from New Eden. Since arriving in the system, it's been moving toward the planet at a pretty good clip."

Hunt held a hand up. "XO, let's not use 'a pretty good clip' when talking about the ship's speed. Give me specifics. How fast or slow is it in comparison to us?"

Blushing a bit, Longman replied, "At impulse speeds, it's traveling twenty-five percent faster than our MPD drive can at full speed. We're still not sure how fast they can actually travel, though. As to its propulsion system, we're still analyzing it. It looks to be using some sort of plasma drive similar to ours, but we're not one hundred percent sure just yet—we're still analyzing the data returns from our sensors."

Hunt nodded. "OK, has anyone confirmed with *Voyager* that we have a visitor? Also, I want no electronic emissions, if possible. The only ship that's going to run any electronics for the time being is us."

Lieutenant Arnold, the Ops officer, chimed in, "Yes, Captain. As soon as we detected the new contact, we made sure the *Voyager* knew we had a visitor. They've gone dark. No more sensor activity or communications activity."

Halsey had already sent the *Gables*, their transport ship, back to Earth three days ago while they waited to see what kind of Zodark ship showed up.

"Tactical, what're the specs on the ship? Do we have any information on them yet?" Hunt asked next.

"I'm starting to get some information now. One of the passive satellites we left in orbit over the moon 3AF is giving us some detailed images of the ship now," Commander Fran McKee said as he put the image up on one of the screens.

"Move that over to the main screen, let's start looking it over. Also, send this down to the CIC. I want them to start doing a deep analysis of the ship," Hunt directed now that he'd gotten his first glance of an alien ship.

The vessel reminded him of a Klingon warship in reruns of *Star Trek* he had seen. Toward the rear appeared to be two engines. They were glowing, which meant the ship was probably using a similar plasma propulsion system to their own, only more powerful. Upon further examination, it didn't look like the ship had the standard bridge that protruded above the superstructure of the vessel like most Earth ships.

"Nav, any idea of when the ship will be in orbit over Eden?" Commander Longman asked.

"At present speed, it should arrive in orbit in nine hours," Lieutenant Hightower replied, her fingers dancing across her keyboard as she continued to run calculations. Seconds later, their image of the ship winked out.

Hunt turned to his coms officer. "Did we lose the signal to the satellite?"

Lieutenant Branson turned her head. "It looks like they just blew it up."

No one said anything for a moment as they waited to see what would happen next.

Lieutenant Commander Robinson, the ship's electronics warfare officer or EWO, yelped, "We've just been detected! Captain, that ship is attempting to scan us."

Several of the bridge personnel turned to look at Hunt to see what he'd do next. This was an entirely new experience for everyone.

Hunt knew the fate of humanity might be decided by his choices right now. He needed to be steadfast and trust his instincts and training if they were going to get through this.

Hunt looked at his tactical officer, Commander Fran McKee. "What is the enemy ship doing now?"

Without taking her eyes off her screen, she replied, "They look to still be heading toward the planet."

Hunt nodded. "Coms, go ahead and send them our message in their own language, Sumerian, and English. Let's see if it's still possible to have a dialogue with them."

While they had been waiting in the Belt for whatever incoming ship was coming, the scientific crew on the *Voyager* had already developed a first contact message to be sent to the Zodark ship when it eventually showed up. They had crafted a message as best they could in all three languages, hoping that a dialogue could be achieved.

Minutes turned to hours as the crew waited for a response from the Zodark ship. Meanwhile, it continued to approach the planet. As it got closer, it found and destroyed the remaining satellites the *Voyager* had left in place around the planet.

Damn, thought Hunt. The satellites had provided them with a good amount of information. They'd identified the other Zodark mining camps and what appeared to be a small military outpost of sorts.

"Captain, we're receiving a message from the Zodark ship," called out Lieutenant Branson.

"Go ahead and play it," Hunt ordered.

The message showed a fearsome-looking Zodark standing on what it appeared was the bridge of their ship. It was dark, with red lights illuminating most of the Zodark's features and its surroundings. The message was short and terse. It boiled down to them demanding the Earthers submit themselves to Zodark rule and immediately comply with their orders.

"Well, that was pretty direct," commented Commander Longman, Hunt's XO.

Hunt snorted. "Yeah, not exactly what I was hoping for. Lieutenant Branson, send a message over to the *Voyager* advising the admiral on what the Zodarks said. Ask her for her response."

A minute later, the admiral sent her reply. She'd ordered Hunt and his crew to go ahead and prepare their ships to leave the system. There wasn't going to be any talking with the Zodarks.

"Helm, plot us a course out of the Belt and begin aligning us for FTL jump to our next waypoint back home while we still can," Hunt ordered.

****

RNS *Voyager*
Flight Deck

Admiral Halsey looked at the cleaned-up Sumerian sitting in the back of the Osprey. Since they didn't have a lot of room on the *Voyager*, she'd sent more than half of the Sumerians back to Earth on the transport. But one of her intelligence officers had wisely suggested interviewing some of the liberated prisoners in the rear compartments of the Ospreys for privacy. Halsey certainly had a lot of questions she was hoping to get some answers to.

As she studied the man in the back of the spacecraft, Halsey had to admit, he looked like any other human on Earth. The genetic tests the medical personnel performed had confirmed as much. They shared the same DNA as the Earthers.

The admiral turned to her right and saw Professor Audrey Lancaster was ready to join her—more than ready. She looked eager to talk with the man named Hadad, the apparent leader of this group of Sumerians.

Halsey nodded to Audrey and led them into the Osprey.

When she approached the prisoner, the two guards snapped to attention. The Sumerian might not have understood their protocols, but he was smart enough to know that whoever she was, she was important, so he stood out of respect.

Leveraging the universal translator device, Halsey introduced herself. "Hello, Hadad. My name is Admiral Abigail Halsey. I am the person in charge of this ship and the soldiers that liberated you."

In seconds, her statement had been translated into his language. He nodded and then thanked her for rescuing him and his fellow prisoners from the Zodarks.

"Hadad, I appreciate all the information your people have shared with us so far about the Zodarks," she began. "Incidentally, you were right—when we sent a message to the Zodark ship that arrived in the system, they wouldn't even entertain a dialogue with us. They simply demanded that we submit to their authority and stand down our ships."

"What did you do when they sent that message to you?" Hadad cut in.

Not put off in the least by his interruption, Halsey replied, "We left the system and are now heading back to our home system."

Hadad looked relieved by the news. His shoulders slumped back as he let out an audible sigh. "That was a good move, Admiral. I fear if you had stayed in the system, they would have attacked your ship."

Halsey leaned forward. "If the Zodarks were able to find out where our home system was, do you believe they would launch an attack on us?"

Hadad was silent for a moment before finally looking up. "That is hard to say. I do not have a lot of experience with the Zodark military or how they work. If they don't know where your home system is, they may not go looking for it."

He shifted in his seat. "There is another prisoner you should talk with. His name is Hosni. I can't say for certain if his information is accurate, but what I can say is he was not born or raised on our home world. He says he was born on a Zodark core world and was a slave to what the Zodarks call a NOS. It's an admiral or senior military leader. He may be able to give you more insight into their inner workings, but again, I cannot verify anything he says or if it's true. I've never met a person like him before."

Halsey nodded. "OK, that sounds good. I'll make sure we talk with him. In the meantime, let's get back to you, Hadad. Please, tell me more about you, and how you came to be on Clovis."

The Sumerian looked deep in thought for a moment, perhaps thinking back to a happier time. Finally, he replied, "Admiral, that is a difficult question. Before the Zodarks imprisoned me, I was a researcher at one of our universities. My area of study was applied physics. When it was discovered by a fellow researcher that I was looking into technology that could be used to create advanced weapons to challenge the Zodarks, the governing body in charge of my city turned me over to the Zodarks for violating the agreement not to research weapon technology—"

"Excuse me, they turned you in?" Halsey interrupted. "Why would they do that to you, Hadad?"

He looked downward, dejected. "It's a long story, Admiral. Suffice it to say, when the Zodarks occupied our planet two hundred years ago, one of the laws they imposed on us concerned what we could and could not research. Weapon technology and further advancements in space travel were chief among them. You see, for the Zodarks, maintaining their hegemony and power over us is paramount. We are nothing more than cattle to them. They want us to keep breeding, and they are more than willing to ensure we never want for food or medical assistance, but their entire vision for us is to cultivate the population growth of our planet, so they can continue to harvest us as needed."

Halsey still had a hard time accepting this as the official account of what was going on, but she held her tongue for the moment.

Professor Lancaster, however, seemed unable to accept this allegation. "That is so repugnant, Hadad. I cannot believe that it is even tolerated. Are you sure this is what's actually happening? We've talked with other prisoners that believe this may just be a myth."

Hadad shrugged. "Professor, there are many rumors about what the Zodarks do with those they collect from the tribute. Some say they simply feast upon us. That's what I believe. But others believe they are culling our population to grow other planets with humans on them for the same purpose, to breed us like cattle to be feasted on. Yet there are other rumors that perhaps they are growing our populations to use us as slaves for their various mining colonies, or maybe something else. To be honest, none of us really know what they are doing. We just know many of our people are taken each year during the tribute, never to be seen again."

Halsey leaned forward. "You said you were working on weapon technology before you got turned in. Would you be able to work with our weapon experts and scientists to help us defeat the Zodarks if necessary?" she asked pointedly.

For the first time since meeting Hadad, a devilish grin curled at the corners of his lips. "I've been waiting and hoping you'd ask me that question, Admiral. There is a great deal I can help you with." He paused for a second. "How do you currently power your ships?" he inquired.

Halsey lifted an eyebrow as she sat back in her seat. "I'm a little hesitant to answer that as we just met you, but given the current situation, I'm going to make an exception." She paused for a second. "As a matter of fact, why don't you follow me down to Engineering and I'll show you?"

The admiral told the guards to follow them but keep a little distance. She also sent a heads-up down to Engineering that she was bringing one of the Sumerians with her, wanting her chief engineering officer waiting for them when she got there.

The group walked out of the hangar bay and into the rest of the ship, with Hadad marveling at the internal design. Every space in the vessel was used, yet the hallways that honeycombed through it were clean, bright, and refreshing to look at. Every so many meters was a bulkhead with a hatch. When she saw Hadad pause to examine one, Halsey explained, "These are here to seal the ship up should we experience a hull breach."

Along the walls of the hallways was a series of color-coded lines that led in different directions from a junction point. "These lines help the crew and anyone else aboard know where the various sections in the ship are located," she clarified.

"How have your people solved the artificial gravity problem?" he asked.

"It was actually one of our alliance partners, a group known as the Asian Alliance, that discovered it," she replied. "Honestly, I don't understand the technical aspects of how it all works, but it revolves around the ship's ability to create an artificial gravity well that encompasses the ship. Most of the ships my people have built don't have this feature yet, but the larger starships do."

As they neared the elevator that would lead them up to the engineering deck, Hadad cleared his throat. "Admiral, if you don't mind me asking, is this a warship? I see a lot of people wearing uniforms and very few people dressed like Professor Lancaster."

Audrey held her tongue as she waited to see how the admiral would respond.

Halsey walked up to the elevator door and depressed the button, then turned to look at Hadad while they waited. "This ship is called the Republic Navy Starship *Voyager*," she explained. "It was designed to carry out several functions. Its primary function, however, is deep space exploration. I guess you could also consider us a warship. We have a contingent of soldiers that accompany us, but we also have a large research lab and facility on the ship. I'd like to think our weapons are pretty potent, and so is our armor, but having learned of the Zodarks, I'm not so sure anymore."

The door to the elevator opened, and the five of them got in. When one of the guards depressed the button to take them to Engineering, the elevator took off. Moments later, the door opened, and they were on a new deck of the ship. The group got off and headed toward the engineering room.

When they entered Engineering, most of the people working there stopped what they were doing momentarily to acknowledge Halsey's presence and stared at Hadad. The rumor mill had clearly gotten out that they had found humans on the planet, but now that they were all seeing one of them live and in person, they seemed unable to resist the urge to gawk. Halsey forgave their reaction—she agreed that it was certainly strange, eerie, to think there were humans on planets other than Earth.

Commander Aimes Morgan walked up to them, "Afternoon, Admiral. Hello, Mr. Hadad," the chief engineering officer said, a bit skeptical of the newcomer to his section.

"Hello," Hadad replied.

"Commander, let's walk over to your office," Halsey directed. "Mr. Hadad here would like to talk with you about some of the technology the Sumerians use and ask us some questions about our own." She motioned for them to talk in a private place, away from prying ears and eyes.

When the group entered the commander's office, they made their way over to a small briefing table and took a seat.

"Hadad, this is Commander Aimes Morgan. He's our chief engineer. I'd like you to talk with him about some of your own technology in comparison to ours. Perhaps there's something we can learn from your people that might help us in our dealings with the Zodarks," the admiral said.

Nodding at the go-ahead, Hadad looked at the engineering chief. "Um, how should I address you? Are you Aimes, Morgan, or should I address you by your rank?"

Audrey suddenly realized Hadad probably didn't understand their naming convention or ranks. "Sorry, Hadad. In our culture, we have a given name, then a surname or family name. His given name is Aimes, his family or surname is Morgan, and his rank is commander."

Commander Morgan quickly added, "If we're in my private office or talking informally, you can address me by my first name, Aimes, Hadad. However, in front of my subordinates or outside my office, Commander Morgan would be best."

Hadad nodded. "OK, that makes sense, Aimes. When I was talking with the admiral, I was asking how your ship is powered. On my own home world, I worked as a researcher in the field of applied physics. I may be able to help you in some areas unless you are more advanced than us."

"That would be greatly appreciated," Commander Morgan replied, still obviously a bit skeptical. "I think before we talk in-depth, perhaps I should give you a table that provides you with some basic information on what kind of reactors we use, what their power sources are, and what their power outputs are. This will give you a reference for us to use."

Aimes reached for his tablet and pulled up some information. He beamed part of it to his computer monitor on his desk and then turned it so Hadad could see. He then handed Hadad the tablet with some other data and proceeded to spend the next ten minutes or so going over how their ship was powered, how they measured units of power, what their ships were fueled with, and how they measured speed, time, and distance so they'd have a framework to work within.

Once some of these basic facts had been presented, Aimes continued, "As you can see, Hadad, for interplanetary travel, we use an MPD drive that runs on lithium pellets for fuel while our fusion reactors provide us with overall power. Now, so you aren't confused, MPD stands for magnetoplasmadynamic thruster. Do you know what that is?"

Hadad looked back at the schematics Morgan had shared with him and replied, "Yes, we are familiar with the MPD drive system. When our people first became spacefaring, we used the same type of thrusters. They're incredibly efficient."

He paused for a moment as he fingered something on the chart Morgan had shown him. "Looking at your information, I can see we use compatible units of measurement as well. This is good, it'll make it easier for me to explain things. One major difference in our approach to power plants is we don't use fusion anymore. We moved away from that form of power generation more than three hundred years ago. We've found a much cleaner-burning fuel that also produces substantially more power. For instance, our interplanetary thrusters are able to generate a thrust of up to four hundred newtons with an exhaust velocity of two hundred and fifty kilometers per second—"

"Whoa, hold up there, Hadad. How are you able to generate that level of thrust power and velocity?" Morgan demanded.

Hadad wrinkled his brow at the question. "Aren't you?"

Morgan shook his head. "No way, our thrust and velocity speeds are significantly lower. Right now, we're constrained by the amount of power we're able to generate."

"We use what's called a Trimarian reactor. It's run using the mineral we were mining down on the surface. We mine the ore, then process it into small blocks that are then used as fuel for the reactors we use on our ships. The Zodarks use the same type of fuel source. It's an incredibly powerful material—it's what allows the Zodarks to travel the galaxy with ease and how they've been able to maintain control over so many planets and systems," Hadad explained.

Chiming in, the admiral asked, "Is that why you had us collect some before we left the planet?"

Hadad turned to look at her. "I wasn't sure what type of reactor you used, so I wanted to make sure you had the fuel. We also had you collect the other mineral we refine, which is key in building the reactors."

Halsey nodded. "Well, I think you and Hadad have plenty to talk about, Commander. Why don't you guys continue your conversations and see if there's anything useful we can implement? In the meantime, I'll leave the guards here with you. They can escort Hadad back to the shuttle bay when you guys are done."

Turning to look at the professor, she said, "Audrey, I think you should continue to interview the rest of the Sumerians. Find out what their previous occupations were, and what more we can learn from them about the Zodarks and their own history and home world. We'll all reconvene and talk again at a later time. Right now, I need to check in on someone."

****

Leaving Engineering, Halsey made her way over to the medical bay to check in on Ambassador Chapman. Nina had been through a lot.

As she entered the medical bay, Halsey spotted Dr. Hani Gupta, her chief medical officer.

Hani smiled as he approached her. "Abby, you look tired. You need to get more sleep."

Hani was a civilian doctor, a brilliant physician from Chicago, which just happened to be where Halsey grew up. Hani and Halsey had made it a habit to spend one hour together twice a week, discussing anything from the crew to life back on Earth. It was a way for Halsey to keep tabs on the crew and get to know someone from her hometown. As a spacer, she seldom spent much time on Earth. Most of her career had been spent among the stars, discovering and exploring their own solar system.

Halsey smiled and chuckled. "Hi, Hani. I get my five hours of sleep. That's all a person needs, you know."

They embraced. He kissed her softly on both cheeks, which seemed to be his thing.

Turning serious, Hani asked, "I suppose you are here to see Nina?"

Abby nodded. "I am. How is she doing, Hani?"

Halsey was genuinely concerned. Since they had recovered her from the Zodark camp, she'd practically been in a catatonic state. She'd been held by them for less than six hours, but they had done something awful to her in that short time. It was as if her mind was lost somewhere in her head, and it wouldn't come out. She wasn't responsive to questions, and she wouldn't eat or drink. She'd just stay curled up in a blanket on her bed, eyes wide open but completely vacant.

Hani sighed as he guided the two of them over to his private office. They walked in and took a seat. He looked up at Halsey with those big brown eyes of his. They were warm and compassionate as he began to explain. "Nina has suffered an emotional trauma none of us can even begin to imagine, Abby. She's hardly said a word since she was rescued from the Zodarks. I'm not entirely sure what they did to her, but it was something unimaginable."

Abby grimaced. "Did they give her any drugs or do anything to her physically beyond what we already know?"

"You mean besides raping her? Yes, we ran a full spectral analysis of her blood when she was brought in. It showed traces of unknown substances. I've never seen anything like it. We ran some brain scans and a full-body MRI as well. Her brain scan shows all the signs of someone who was violently and psychologically assaulted for a very long time. Right now, it would appear that her mind has retreated deep inside itself as a defensive mechanism. I've been hesitant to try using any drugs or other stimuli to bring her back, but I think we may eventually need to."

Abby slumped back in her chair at the prognosis. They really needed to talk with her. What the Zodarks had done to her was horrific. What it appeared they had done to her assistant, Justin, was even worse. What she was concerned with right now was that they had no idea what either of them had told the Zodarks. For all they knew, the Zodarks now knew what star system Earth was in. She needed to speak with Nina.

Lifting her head as she steeled her resolve, she said, "Hani, I need you to try and bring her back. We've got to talk with her. It's been too long."

"Abby…she needs time. If we rush this process, she may never fully recover," Hani said.

"I know, Hani. Believe me, I'd love nothing more than to give her more time. But we've got to know what she told the Zodarks. Earth could be in danger. This is a lot bigger than her."

Hani nodded solemnly, acknowledging that she was right. "OK, Abby, I'll try to bring her out of whatever state her mind is currently in."

Before he got up and they left his office, he asked, "Have you seen the video of what they did to her assistant?"

Abby grimaced at the mention of the video; it had been brutal. The Zodarks had disemboweled Justin before they had cut off his genitals. They had accomplished a surprising amount of torture of Justin and Nina in the five hours they'd had them before Major Jenkins's ground force was able to recover them.

"I have, Hani. But that doesn't change from the fact that we still need to talk to her. We need to know what happened. We need to know if either of them told the Zodarks where Earth is."

"Haven't we been able to recover anything from the audio device from her ear or the AI translator?" Hani asked, almost pleading. "Surely one of those devices was able to give us an audio archive of what went on. I mean, we were able to capture the video from her contact lens."

Abby sighed. "We got some audio, mostly the first hour of what went on. But they shocked her body with an electrical device. The contact lens continued to record, but it fried the audio recorder in her ear. As to the AI translator, those things don't record—at least not the version she had. We need to talk with her. She told them Earth was in the Indus system, and maybe they'll believe that, but we need confirmation. If they know where Earth is, then we need to prepare Sol."

Chapter Sixteen
Unexpected Surprises

Florida
Kennedy Space Center
Space Command HQ

As he ran along the sandy shoreline, Admiral Chester Bailey pushed his body hard on the final stretch of his run. His feet splashed with every step, the constant waves from the surf adding their own twist to the morning routine. With every step, he felt the stress of the job leaving his body as the endorphins being released helped to clear his mind. The sudden burst of energy as the endpoint came in sight gave him an almost euphoric feeling, like the high you get from a drug, only this was natural.

Bailey breathed hard and his heart raced. His feet pounded the sand as his eyes caught sight of the sun finally cresting above the water. The predawn light was giving way to the sun as it began to claw its way into the sky, its warm rays now starting to be felt on his skin.

Twenty more meters...almost there...

He ran past his official endpoint, then slowed down until he was in a gentle walk. Turning, Bailey moved a little deeper into the water until he was walking at knee depth. The waves crashed occasionally against his waist, splashing cold water on his belly and chest, a welcome relief after a hard run.

He knew he shouldn't shock his system too hard with the cold water, but it felt so good right now. He moved a little deeper and dove into a wave as it barreled toward the shore. As he submerged into the ice-cold water, his skin and muscles were jolted. When his face broke out of the water, he gasped for air and immediately felt like a new man. He then made his way back to the shore and headed up to the parking lot, where his Jeep was waiting for him.

When he reached his vehicle, Bailey turned his neurolink back on and synced it with the vehicle's Wi-Fi system. He was immediately bombarded with a flurry of messages: some urgent, some mundane. He mostly let his neurolink's PA handle the less urgent messages and tended to focus on the critical matters and delegate the others to his staff. One message, however, caught his eye: a message from the DARPA facility on Mars marked URGENT.

Bailey dried himself off, climbed into his Jeep and headed to the office. He'd grab a shower to wash the saltwater off before putting his uniform on. Then he'd open the message from DARPA and find out what was so urgent.

****

As he walked into his outer office, Bailey's aide, an up-and-coming captain, greeted him. "Good morning, Admiral. There's a message from Senator Walhoon. He says it's urgent. There's also a message from Musk Industries for you."

"Hold my calls, Captain. I have another message that's a bit more pressing I have to attend to. Oh, and Captain, I'm turning the SCIF on in my office for this message, so no disturbances, OK?" Admiral Bailey instructed as he opened the door to his office and walked in.

Once he got himself situated at his desk, he turned on the specialized electronic equipment that would sanitize and secure his room. It would ensure no listening or recording devices were either present in the office or able to hear or record what was about to play. Spycraft had come a long way over the years, but so had the electronic means to disable it.

Bailey placed the holographic display unit on his desk and synced it to his neurolink. For the next ten minutes, he sat listening as Dr. Johnson recounted the data from the latest communication drone they'd just received from Admiral Halsey and her fleet. The previous drone message had indicated that they had arrived in the system and everything was going well—that was three days ago. They hadn't expected to receive another one for at least a week. In a way, it was ironic that it took a ship fifteen days to travel one light-year, but it took a com drone a single day to cover that same distance.

The more he heard from Space Command's lead scientist and R&D director, the more his stomach churned. When he read the report about finding humans on the planet, he thought there must have been a mistake. But then he saw the video of them, and there was no doubt. Worse, he saw the video of the first alien creature he'd ever seen. It was apparently called a Zodark. He wasn't sure what to make of it when he saw it, but one thing was unmistakable. It was close to twice the size of a human, standing at nearly three meters in height.

Next, he read the synopsis of the first ground battle that had taken place between a contingent of Deltas and RA soldiers and a Zodark camp of sorts. At first, he was furious that their first interaction with an unknown sentient alien race had been to kill it. Then the report talked about how the Zodarks had actually kidnapped the ambassador and her assistant and fired on them. Admiral Halsey, the commander on the scene, had then made the decision to liberate the prisoners and recover the ambassador.

What boggled his mind, and had stumped Dr. Johnson and her researchers, was how humans could be found on planets other than Earth. More to the point, how was it that this set of humans was speaking a variant of an Earth language?

As if all this wasn't enough of a shock, the information they had gleaned about the Zodarks from these newly liberated prisoners was chilling. This race was clearly an apex predatory species. One report claimed these humans were actually being groomed and cared for like cattle. The prisoner accounts of what was happening on their home world were grisly, to say the least.

When the message ended, nearly two hours later, Bailey had a lot to digest. He sat there for a moment, trying to think of how to respond to Dr. Johnson's message. He finally composed a short note telling her this needed to stay strictly "need to know" and to keep analyzing it. He also told her to be ready to travel to Space Command in a couple of days. They wanted to wait until they received another com drone from the *Voyager* before they called everyone back to Earth to discuss this most unsettling account.

Bailey needed a few days for himself to figure out how to break this information to the civilian leadership here on Earth. It was going to cause a stir. Potentially, there could be a real problem with the newly formed Tri-Parte Alliance or TPA, as they were calling themselves, the result of a new treaty that had seen the Asian Alliance merge with the Greater European Union and the African Union after the Republic had opted not to renew the Space Exploration Treaty. This new political, economic, and military union now encompassed nearly three-quarters of Earth. The only countries not part of it were those that comprised the Republic, which now consisted of Canada, Mexico, Central America, the

United Kingdom, and soon South America, once the details were ironed out. The TPA for their part had been all-in on colonizing Alpha Centauri and the Centaurus system. They had said publicly and privately that they did not want a clash with the Republic but hoped to maintain an amicable relationship, if possible, and peace so all parties could focus on what they all wanted: to colonize other planets beyond Earth.

He turned the SCIF equipment off, and the lights in his office changed. The electronic shades blocking his windows retracted, letting more natural light flood into the room. A moment later, his aide, Captain Tippins, walked in.

"Sir, I've held your calls, but I think you need to take this one from Senator Walhoon. He's been pretty insistent that he speak with you."

"The good senator can be that way when he wants something, that's for sure. All right, let me talk to the man," Bailey relented.

A moment later, Senator Chuck Walhoon's holographic image appeared in front of Admiral Bailey's desk. The senator smiled. "Ah, Admiral. It's good to see you. Sorry for bugging you first thing in the morning. I'm sure you're a busy man, but I needed to talk with you about this latest appropriations request you made. Is there a chance we can talk in person? I really hate doing business over these holographic machines and all."

Senator Chuck Walhoon was the senior senator from the great state of Texas—the largest, most industrious state in the country at this point. He was also the chairman of the Senate Armed Services Committee, which meant he controlled Bailey's budget. Every time the three-year budget would come up for discussion, Bailey would find himself having to cajole and coax every dollar out of the committee. Given that this was also part of his previous position in charge of fleet operations, it was something he was pretty familiar with and reasonably good at.

Smiling at the request that wasn't really a request, Bailey countered, "As a matter of fact, Senator, I was about to give you a call to invite you over here to discuss a matter of great urgency. I was wondering, would you be able to come here in three days?"

"If this is an urgent matter, Admiral, why don't we meet tomorrow and discuss it?" Senator Walhoon pressed.

"Senator, we just received a second com drone from the Rhea expedition today. We're still unpacking and analyzing the data Admiral Halsey sent, so I'd like to have a couple more days to make sure we understand everything that was sent to us," Bailey deflected, doing his best not to raise any red flags.

"Hmmm...OK, Admiral. Let's meet on Friday. That'll give you four days instead of three to have everything ready. Should I bring the rest of the committee with me?" the Texan asked.

Bailey shook his head as he looked at the holographic display. "No, not yet, sir. I think this would be best kept between us for the time being. Then we can craft a message on how to handle it."

Now the senator was curious. "Is everything OK? Should I be worried, Admiral?" Walhoon looked concerned. A lot was riding on the success of the Rhea expedition.

Bailey shook his head. "Nothing has gone wrong, Senator, but there are some things we'll need to discuss."

The senator seemed appeased by his answer. He didn't press it further. "OK, then. We'll talk on Friday. I look forward to seeing you then, Admiral."

The call disconnected.

Captain Tippins immediately jumped in. "How do you want to handle this, sir?"

Bailey drummed his fingers on his desk for a moment before turning to look at the young captain, another loyal officer Bailey was grooming to take command of a ship and eventually move through the ranks to become an admiral. Steadily, Bailey was building his cadre of loyal officers who rose through the ranks on his coattails—officers who would be helpful to him as he phased out Admiral Sanchez's people and replaced them with his own.

"Send a message to Dr. Johnson that her presence is going to be required here on Friday," Bailey instructed. "Also, tell Admiral Laughton he'll need to be here as well. Oh, before I forget, inform General Pilsner I need a meeting with him tomorrow—tell him to bring his Special Operations commander with him. We're going to need to start looping the ground pounders into this situation."

Once that schedule had been handled, Bailey got to the message from Musk Industries: it was the final proposal for the new class of warships Space Command had asked for. What he saw was not just a battleship—it was a true dreadnought and a brute of a ship. If half of what he'd just heard about these Zodarks was true, they'd need more than just a few battlecruisers.

Admiral Bailey's staff had been going back and forth with Musk Industries and BlueOrigin on the designs: what features they wanted, what functions the ship had to have, and what kind of defensive capability had to be built into it. It was a long list of requirements, and hundreds of staffers had been assigned to work on it. Thinking back to the video images he had seen of those Zodarks, he felt glad that he had begun the process of getting the ships designed. Now they'd have to decide which track to move down and determine which shipyard would get the contract.

****

Mars Facility
DARPA

Looking down at her wrist, Katherine saw she still had forty-two minutes of oxygen left on her tank. She bent down and picked up the rock on the ground, examining it closely, looking at the little divots and dimples on it. It was a hard material, not easily broken by her grip. She eventually placed it back on the surface and looked around at the rest of the area.

Off in the distance, she saw a towering dust storm heading toward the military base. The cloud had nearly reached the civilian habitats, towering biospheres and skyscrapers, which would soon be covered in the wall of sand and dirt as it made its way toward the military outpost and the mountains.

"Dr. Johnson, we should head back in. We're running low on oxygen, and that storm is approaching," one of her staffers said hesitantly.

Not everyone on her staff enjoyed accompanying her on these outings. The man meant well, but he was clueless when it came to understanding her reasoning behind these long walks on the surface of Mars in EVA suits. These ventures outside the biospheres were therapeutic to her. They helped remind her that she was on an alien planet, in a hostile environment that could quickly kill her if she wasn't careful.

Sighing to herself, she complied and made her way over to the rover. She climbed in and attached the oxygen cable to one of the ports on her suit. A second later, she was breathing from the vehicle's system while it refilled her tank. The two of them drove in silence back to the docking bay.

There's still so much to this planet we haven't even explored yet. So much I still want to learn about this place...

Katherine had now lived on the Martian surface for thirty-two years. She was among a very small group of people who had lived on Mars this long. With her children grown and living on Earth, she and her husband had chosen to make Mars their home. Her husband was a geologist, and while he didn't work for the government like she did, he did work for a university back on Earth. She envied him; he had the job of exploring the various aspects of Mars, looking for signs of a past civilization or other unique and interesting things about the red planet.

Katherine and her assistant drove for a few minutes back to the military outpost until they reached one of the entry control points. She entered her code and swiped her security card, unlocking the armored entrance. Once it had retracted, they drove in and continued their short drive until they reached the entrance to one of the docking bays that would connect them to the internal part of the facility.

They waited for one of the vehicle ports to depressurize so they could enter. It took a couple of minutes, but then the outer door opened up, and they drove into the docking bay. Once they were inside, the exterior door closed, and the room repressurized itself to match the internal docking bay. A moment later, another vehicle door opened, and they were able to drive inside the facility.

As they entered, Katherine immediately saw Commander Niles standing there with his hands on his hips, waiting for them.

"Enjoy your ride on the frontier, Doctor?"

"It was restorative, as always, Commander. Thank you for allowing me to venture outside the lab. It helps me think more clearly," she replied as she gave him a mischievous wink.

He didn't need to give her permission to go outside the base, but she liked to make him believe he did. She liked Commander Niles—he was a good man, a smart man. He probably wouldn't take command of a starship as Captain Hunt had, but he was a much better scientist than Hunt. Hunt was destined to be a ship commander, probably an admiral someday if she thought about it.

"Are we ready to present the *Voyager*'s findings to Admiral Bailey and Senator Walhoon?" she asked as the two of them began the process of gaining entry into the research lab and SCIF part of the facility.

"That's what I came out here to talk to you about."

She turned her head slightly as they continued to walk. "Something wrong?" She hoped there wasn't anything urgent she'd missed. The two of them were supposed to leave on a shuttle in a handful of hours to meet up with a destroyer that would ferry them back to Earth. Granted, the ride only took a matter of eight hours, but they were still going to be transported via a warship given the gravity of the information they were carrying.

As they walked, Niles stopped for a moment. Katherine stopped too and looked at him. "What is it, Commander?"

"We received another com drone an hour ago from the *Voyager*. We just completed the download when I came out to get you. We...have a problem."

****

Eight hours later, Commander Niles, Dr. Johnson, and six of their best analysts were camped out in the briefing room of the destroyer, going over the latest data dump they'd received from the Rhea system. There was a lot of information. They had images of what this new race's warships looked like as well as intel on their propulsion systems, armaments, power generation, and FTL capabilities. It was concerning, to say the least.

Of all the information being thrown at her team, the thing she found most interesting was the two minerals that were apparently in abundance on the planet, called Trimar and Morean. They had a chemical composition unlike any she had ever seen. What she found most helpful about this new data was some analysis from the *Voyager*'s science team, which had gone to great lengths to provide as much information about the minerals as possible. They had attached over a dozen different reports detailing what the minerals were, how the Zodarks were using them, how this new race of humans called the Sumerians had used them, how they mined and refined them, and other ways the minerals were used in their daily lives.

From what Dr. Johnson could discern, these minerals were to the Zodarks what petroleum or uranium was to Earth: a raw material that, when refined, produced an incredible amount of energy. When she came across an interview about how the Zodarks' reactors—which were apparently the same type of reactors the Sumerians used for their own energy needs—worked, her eyes went wide as saucers. The amount of power these reactors were putting out was beyond what she could comprehend with their current technology.

Looking at the notes about the Trimar and Morean minerals again, she realized these minerals were the key to it all. For whatever reason, these two materials were critical to making this reactor work.

The eight-hour transit from Earth to Mars gave Dr. Johnson and her team the needed time to synthesize the information they'd received and break it down into manageable chunks. For once, she was glad she was traveling on one of the older, slower Space Command vessels and not one of the newer FTL-equipped ones. She needed the extra time to digest and understand this information. A lot of important decisions were going to be made based on the information her team was about to brief later today. It was vital not to drown the decision-makers with information they couldn't understand. They weren't scientists or researchers. They were senior military leaders and politicians—a dangerous group if you gave them the wrong information.

Once their ship arrived in Earth orbit, her team boarded a shuttle that would take them directly to Kennedy Space Center. As their shuttle left their ship and began its descent, Dr. Johnson caught a glimpse of the ships being built in the yards surrounding the orbital station. Most of the vessels under construction right now were transport ships, most likely being constructed to aid in the colonization of New Eden. She wondered how many more transports would be built after today's briefing. She doubted there would be many.

****

Florida
Kennedy Space Center
Space Command HQ

Senator Chuck Walhoon reached for the glass of water in front of him, his hand trembling slightly as he wrapped his fingers around it. Lifting it off the table, he brought it to his lips and took a couple of gulps to push down the bile that was building up in the back of his throat.

Seeing the footage one of the Deltas had taken of the room in which Ambassador Chapman and her assistant, Justin, had been held was more than most of them could stomach. When they watched the video from the ambassador's contact lens, Chuck nearly lost it. He wanted to vomit. Not since his younger years, when he was a soldier in the last Great War, had he seen something so gruesome, so repulsive as this.

"Are you all right, Senator?" Admiral Bailey asked, concern evident on his face.

Putting the glass down, Walhoon replied, "I—I'm…just not used to seeing such barbarism. It…brought back some rather unpleasant memories I had suppressed of the last war."

The military men in the room all nodded. They shared some of those same memories. The others in the room also clearly felt uneasy at what they had just seen.

"Admiral, I know this is a formal briefing and all, but do you happen to have something strong to drink around here? I think I need a little something to calm my nerves a bit after having seen that," Senator Walhoon said sheepishly. The poor man looked pale as a ghost.

Admiral Bailey stood and walked out of the room, presumably to go scrounge up something for the senator.

Dr. Johnson straightened her jacket before apologizing to the senator for showing him that particular video. A minute later, the admiral walked back in with one of his aides in tow. They had two bottles of Kentucky bourbon and some glasses.

"I'm not condoning drinking while in uniform or on the job, but I understand if anyone needs a stiff drink to calm their nerves. As the senator said, these are some unsettling images we've seen," Bailey announced as he placed the bottles on the table. He prepared a glass for the senator himself and handed it to him. The man nodded gratefully as he accepted it.

Only one other officer, one of the Republic Army commanders, and the senator took Bailey up on the drink. The others chose to abstain while in uniform.

Once the senator had downed half a glass of bourbon, he looked at Dr. Johnson and said, "Tell me there is some good news to all of this—some reason why you've shown us that video." He was practically begging.

She nodded slightly. "There is, Senator. And again, I'm sorry for showing you those disturbing images, but I believe it was important for everyone to keep in mind exactly how vicious this alien race is. We sent a peace delegation to speak with them, to introduce ourselves to them. This was how they responded. As one of the liberated Sumerians said, these Zodarks view our species as little more than cattle and slaves."

Chuck felt the alcohol starting to kick in a bit. "Dr. Johnson, do you believe we can negotiate with these Zodarks if we try again?" he asked.

Dr. Johnson shook her head. "I would like to think we could. However, when their ship came into the system, we made contact with them again—we tried to speak with them. The response we received from them was not receptive. As you can see from the transcript, there is only one thing they will accept from us."

The others looked a bit unnerved by her proclamation. It was clear many of them had hoped that maybe if they tried a second time to communicate, this could all be cleared up. Clearly, that was not going to happen.

The senator thumbed through some of the reports in front of him before returning his attention to her. "Doctor, do we know if Ambassador Chapman or her assistant spilled the beans to these Zodarks about where Earth is?"

She sighed. "Senator, that is a good question. As you can see from the medical report from the ship's doctor, Ambassador Chapman has endured a lot. They may have been able to get her to open up and talk, but as of the time this com drone was sent, she was still in a catatonic state."

The senator shook his head in frustration. "We need to know if the Zodarks know where Earth is. If they do, this could be disastrous for us."

Admiral Bailey interjected, "We'll hopefully know more when we receive the next com drone from the fleet. Right now, I think we need to bring the rest of the civilian leadership into the loop. This is too big for us to keep under wraps. We're also going to need to brief the TPA."

The senator nodded in agreement. He wanted more information, but he also knew they couldn't just sit on this while they waited.

Senator Walhoon changed subjects. "Doctor, the next section of your report talks about a new resource we discovered on the planet. You also said this new resource was a game-changer for our space program. Can you please explain that a bit further? Is there a new technology that runs on this mineral that we may be able to employ to help protect Earth and our ships?"

For the next hour, Dr. Johnson and her team members went over how Trimar ran their reactors and how Morean was a crucial component in their actual construction. Her team showed them the power outputs of these reactors and how they allowed the Zodark ships to travel at unfathomable FTL speeds—one light-year a day, fifteen times faster than Earth's current technology.

By the end of the meeting, the senator and Admiral Bailey had agreed on the need to brief the President and the Senate. It was time to start getting them and the TPA ready for the news the *Voyager* and her fleet were sending back.

Chapter Seventeen
Surprises

John Glenn Orbital Station
1st Fleet HQ

Admiral Chester Bailey stood in front of the crowd of people—politicians, fellow officers, and those who lived and worked daily on the orbital station—and looked at the two drone cameras that hovered nearby. He knew that his image, and soon, his words, would echo across the rest of the world and probably the system.

He paused for a moment before speaking, collecting his final thoughts and willing them to be expressed. "My fellow Earthers, today marks the first day in a new chapter in our history. I use the term Earthers and not Republic citizens because today we are one people—not a conglomeration of nations competing against each other, but one unified planet in this new endeavor. Today, the space forces of the Tri-Parte Alliance and the Republic will form an allied fleet to stand up against this newly discovered threat to our species.

"Over the last thirty days, we have received multiple communication drones from the Republic-led fleet in the Rhea system detailing to us a new and grave threat to our very existence and way of life. They've also made what is perhaps one of the most profound discoveries of our time: not only is there intelligent life beyond our system, there also appear to be other races of humans on faraway planets. While we still do not know how these humans came to be on these planets, what we do know is that they are enslaved."

He paused for a moment to let that last sentence sink in before continuing. "For better or worse, humanity has now discovered an insidious race known as the Zodarks—a fearsome breed of aliens that have conquered many planets and subjugated our fellow humans on these other planets as nothing more than slaves to serve their growing empire."

Bailey knew that as he was speaking, the videos of the Zodarks were being played across the TV to emphasize his point.

"We are fortunate, however. We learned of this threat before they could pounce on us and devour our planet like they had so many others before. We are also lucky to have such brave men and women willing to serve in our armed forces to defend our way of life. Today, the people of Earth are forming up the 1st Combined Fleet, which will marshal together in defense of our planet. Starting this week, Republic and TPA naval forces will begin to provide joint combat patrols of Sol and our current colonies within the system. When the Rhea expedition returns, we will work with Admiral Halsey to put together a second, much larger fleet to return to the Rhea system and claim it as ours. This new system will act as a buffer zone and forward-positioned base to defend Sol against the Zodark threat.

"Today, we also announce the construction of a fleet of new warships that will protect Sol and ensure our people do not fall prey to these vicious and evil aliens that would doom our species to a life of slavery. I humbly request that you consider joining the armed forces to help protect our planet and our way of life. We are going to raise an army and build a fleet that will make sure our planet is never subjected to this kind of barbarism. With that, I hand the rest of this announcement over to President Luca. Madam President," Bailey said as he took a step back for her to take the podium.

President Alice Luca had been sworn in as the new president a few months back. She'd been doing her best to handle everything thrown at her. The previous president had really left her in a bad spot after pulling out of the SET and the Centaurus mission, only to discover the Zodarks instead.

The leader of the TPA also stepped forward to the second podium that had just been brought up. The two of them would now give a joint statement more or less reaffirming everything Admiral Bailey had just said, only in political double-speak and niceties.

It took nearly an hour for the two of them to finish their prepared speeches and then take some questions. Afterward, they left together to answer more reporter questions in another room set up for private interviews. It was quite the dog and pony show, one Bailey was glad he didn't have to participate in.

Admiral Bailey made a beeline to get out of the room before a reporter could corner him. The CEO of Musk Industries held a side door open and motioned for him to head in his direction. Bailey smiled at the gesture. The man knew exactly what he was trying to do, and he was helping him out. Several reporters saw him making a break for it but were unable to stop him before he ducked out of the room and away from their ability to hurl questions at him.

"Thanks for that, Andy. I owe you one," Bailey said as the door closed in the face of a particularly nosy reporter.

"No worries, Admiral. I could see the vultures circling for you the moment the President was done with her speech. If you don't mind, why don't we come back to my office? Actually, I have a better idea. Follow me if you will," Andrew said secretively.

Bailey's left brow rose, but he didn't say anything as the two of them walked briskly through one of the unknown corridors of the station. They walked through a couple of long hallways until they made their way onto the Musk Industries side of the station. Once there, Andrew led him up to the glass room where they had had dinner a while back. Bailey had to admit, it had been the most fantastic dining experience of his life: sitting at a table in a glass cube floating above the station and Earth below while sipping on an expensive scotch and eating a Kobe steak. He doubted he'd ever top that.

When they climbed into the cube, the CEOs of BlueOrigin and the two largest Tri-Parte Alliance shipyards were there sitting at that same table, each with a scotch in hand. They rose as he entered the room and offered a quick greeting.

"I have a feeling this meeting has been in the works for some time," Bailey said quizzically as he approached one of the empty chairs. A glass of the brown gold awaited him.

Shrugging, Andrew simply replied, "The politicians had their meeting. We felt it was time to have ours. Our other guest should be here momentarily."

A second later, Admiral Bailey's counterpart in the TPA showed up, looking just as surprised as Bailey. The two shook hands before they took their seats next to each other.

Sensing the unease in the two military men, Andrew started the discussion off first. "Admirals, we apologize for arranging this meeting in the way we have. We felt it better for this discussion to take place away from the prying eyes of the press and politicians. I hope you don't mind."

Andrew had already turned on the electronic countermeasures in the cube, which blocked anyone outside from seeing in or listening to anything going on inside.

The two military men looked at each other and shrugged. They had about as much use for the press as these titans of industry did. Bailey used the media when he had to, but otherwise, he kept them at a distance.

"Admiral Bailey, that was a great speech you gave. But we've all been reviewing the footage and information Dr. Johnson has provided, and we must say, it is rather alarming. I fear our political leaders may not understand the gravity of the situation," Andrew said, concern and a little bit of bitterness in his voice.

"How do you mean?" asked the Chinese admiral, Zheng Lee. He leaned forward but looked a bit skeptical at the proclamation.

Andrew looked at the four other shipbuilders before he replied, "These ships, the ones the Zodarks have, do not look to be small ships. When we examined the power outputs on the reactors they're using, we quickly came to the conclusion that these ships are putting out nearly a thousand times more power than our current technology can. While we have no reason to doubt the accuracy of the information Admiral Halsey's team has provided, we're pretty confident there is no possible way our current ships will hold up against one of their lasers. We're also working under the assumption that, if this is their true power output, their armor systems are also going to be shielded to handle a hit from similar ships and weapons. If that's the case, we're in a lot more trouble than has just been publicly expressed."

Admiral Bailey stepped in. "So what are you saying, Andy? We're about to start the largest buildup of warships in human history."

"He's trying to say, Admiral, that we don't believe it's going to matter if we're using our current technology against theirs," the European shipbuilder said flatly.

No one said anything for a moment. The Chinese admiral looked at Bailey, concern in his eyes. Bailey returned his gaze to the men whose responsibility it was to build them the tools of war to fight and win this coming conflict.

"We can't accept defeat, gentlemen. Not before we've even fought the Zodarks. So, with the information you have available, what do you suggest we do?" Bailey asked. He eyed each of them as he sought to convey a sense of urgency and optimism.

"When Admiral Halsey returns, she's bringing with her more than a thousand of these liberated Sumerians. We'd like to work with them on recreating this Trimar reactor system the Sumerians and the Zodarks use," one of the Chinese shipbuilders announced. "We believe if we can generate the same level of power, we can engineer a set of weapon platforms around them that will allow us to defeat the Zodarks. We have several things going in our favor. Chiefly, they probably haven't fought an adversary like us. But we need to test our armor against a laser as powerful as theirs. If we know the strength of their pulse beams, we can engineer a countermeasure to deal with it."

Bailey let out a sigh, more from exhaustion and stress than anything else. "Gentlemen, I appreciate that you want to integrate as much of this new technology into our ships as possible, and we will. But right now, time may not be on our side. What if you were to start laying the hulls for these new ships, and we held off on the reactors and engineering sections until we can integrate this new technology? Would that work?"

Shaking his head, the CEO for BlueOrigin countered, "Yes and no. You see, until we can build the reactor and then determine from the Sumerians how strong the Zodarks' lasers are, we don't know how thick to make the hulls or what type of armor we'll need to build them with. Right now, we're building with a layer of modulated armor to counter a pulse beam laser. It's a technical problem, Admiral. Suffice it to say, we don't know how thick the modulated armor needs to be to stand up against one of their pulse beams, so if we go ahead and build the ships now, we could be building them with armor that's too thin."

Now that he was on a roll, he continued going over the technical challenges. "The other issue we have is this—until we know to what extent we can recreate the Zodark reactors, we can't say precisely how thick or insulated the power cabling throughout the ship will need to be or how we even structure the engineering room or decks. When we build a ship, Admiral, we build it around several key functions: the reactor and engineering room, the weapon systems, and the armor. Right now, we don't have a good read on what those three variables will be, and we can't build a ship to win this fight until we do."

Admiral Bailey slumped back in his chair. He understood the problem now. More importantly, he understood their apprehension and why they were asking, in so many words, to hold off the construction of the new fleet until the *Voyager* returned from Rhea.

"I hear your concerns, and they are duly noted. But we can't sit on our hands for two months while we wait for Admiral Halsey to return," Bailey insisted. "They sent that information ahead of them to give us time to develop a plan. We just spent an entire month going through all the political hoopla to come to an agreement to create first and second fleets. What do you propose we do?"

If these CEOs think we're going to do nothing until the fleet returns, they're crazy.

The European shipbuilder chimed in. "We don't want to sit idly by—we want to rapidly build up our transport fleets. We wish to begin evacuation efforts to the Centaurus system and begin relocating some of our shipyards there, away from Earth. When a fight between us and the Zodarks happens, we could win, or we could lose. If we lose, we want to make sure humanity has a fighting chance. That means we need to start moving people, equipment, and capability to Alpha Centauri immediately."

The CEO of BlueOrigin added, "Don't think of this as giving up or retreating, Admiral. Think of it as dispersing our forces. If we can get the Centaurus region built up quickly, we can have more shipyards producing the tools of war, and we give ourselves a backup base in case Sol is invaded and we are unable to stop them."

"That is a political question, not a military one," the Chinese admiral said. "Only the Supreme Leader can make that decision. However, I do happen to agree with you. We need to have a backup plan. If Admiral Bailey concurs, then I will make the case to the Supreme Leader myself that we should do this."

Everyone turned to look at Bailey to see what he'd say next. He thought for a moment before replying. During the negotiations concerning this new fleet, the TPA had agreed to allow the Republic to set up a colony on one of the four continents of the planet in Alpha Centauri in exchange for sharing the technology acquired from the Sumerians. The deal was immediately agreed upon as it offered the Republic a fallback in case Earth was attacked. That way, the Republic would have the ability to evacuate at least some of its people.

"I...can see your point. Let me do this—let me brief this to the President and get her OK on it. I'll recommend that we put all of our resources into the completion of the *Ark* transports that are already under construction along with the other freighters and transports currently being built. However, in exchange, you all are not to build any new ships. As these current ones are completed, you spend your time and efforts stockpiling the supplies and resources you'll need to rapidly begin construction of the new warships we'll be building with the Sumerian and Zodark technology once the *Voyager* arrives in the system. Is that understood?" Admiral Bailey directed. While neither alliance had nationalized the private shipyards yet, Bailey wanted to make sure they were ready to fulfill the government contracts that were about to be thrown at them.

"Admiral Bailey, I have a question," said Admiral Zheng. "I know you have started construction on a purely military shipyard just beyond the moon. How long until that new facility is completed? Can it begin construction of new warships?"

Normally, Bailey wouldn't answer a question like that, but seeing they were all suddenly in this thing together, he didn't see the harm. "As it stands, at least two more years before we'll have the first three slips ready. We're looking at completing six slips a year, once the primary facilities and fabricators have been completed. The shipyard is still close to two years away from being able to produce the kinds of ships we need."

Zheng nodded. "This is good. By the time it is ready to start building, we should know how to integrate this new technology into our warships. It'll give us one more large facility to build the ships necessary to defend Sol."

Chapter Eighteen
Reverse Engineering

RNS *Voyager*
Science Deck

Dr. Jonathan Milton looked at the crude drawing the woman sitting across from him had scribbled. It didn't make sense to him. No matter how many times she tried to explain it to him, he just couldn't square it with the laws of physics he'd known his entire life. It shouldn't work…yet somehow, it apparently did.

The Sumerian, a woman named Satet, looked about as frustrated as Jonathan felt. She'd been doing her best to try and describe their version of theoretical physics, but it wasn't going very well.

"Jonathan, it doesn't have to make sense to you. It just works—that is all you need to know," she said, exasperated.

Jonathan bit his lower lip and shook his head. "According to our knowledge of physics, this shouldn't be possible," he insisted.

Tilting her head slightly, she countered, "Have you ever considered that your people may not know everything there is to know about physics? From what you have told me, your planet has only been exploring space now for one hundred and fifty years. We first went into space some two hundred and fifty years ago. The Zodarks have been a spacefaring race for thousands of years. There is much your people still need to learn about the universe."

Jonathan felt his cheeks redden as she calmly informed him he was not as smart as he had led everyone to believe. He had to admit, he was really starting to feel attracted to her. It wasn't just that she was a stunningly gorgeous woman when she had cleaned up—it was her intellect that attracted him to her. She was incredibly brilliant—he couldn't fathom how she'd been selected as a tribute to the Zodarks. On her home world, she had been a university professor, just like him. To imagine a society willingly giving up people with her intellect was dumbfounding to him. Yet if they hadn't, their paths never would have crossed.

Shaking his head in frustration, he finally gave up on understanding what she was telling him for the time being. "With the technology and materials that we currently have available to us on my home world, is it possible to build one of these Trimarian reactors?" he inquired.

She politely smiled. "Yes, it is possible, but only because you were smart enough to grab several tons of refined Morean as Hadad told you to. It's a specialized mineral we mix with some other materials to make the containment system for the reactor and would not have been possible to recreate."

Jonathan wiped his brow in relief.

"How long will these reactors take to construct once we get back to my home world?" Jonathan asked.

"That will depend on the sophistication of your industrial capabilities. If they are on par with what we have on my own home world, then I think it could be done in weeks. Judging by the construction of your ship and the fact that you have achieved faster-than-light travel, I believe your industries should be more than capable," she explained.

"With the materials we have on board, how many reactors do you believe we'll be able to build and adequately fuel?" he asked.

She smiled. "You want to know how many ships you'll be able to make?"

Jonathan blushed. "Now that we know what a threat the Zodarks represent, we want to be prepared to take them on."

She crinkled her brow. "You really believe you can take them on and defeat them?"

Jonathan shrugged. He was British, not American, so he wasn't as militaristic or aggressive as his American counterparts. Britain had joined the Republic to become a smattering of one hundred new member states following the end of the last war. They had made the alliance more out of spite against the old guard in Europe than anything else. As fate would have it, it turned out to be one of the best moves for the UK; Europe was swiftly overpowered by Russia and Germany, who now made up the bulk of the military and economic power on the continent.

"I don't know, Satet," he finally responded. "I am a scientist, a researcher. If I can help protect our people and our way of life through the use of my brain and not my brawn, then that's what I will do."

She smiled warmly at him before changing the subject. "You know, Jonathan, the tribute isn't so bad. In a way, it allows us Sumerians to live even fuller lives than we otherwise would. We all know we're guaranteed forty years, so we maximize that time we have. Any time beyond that is a gift to be celebrated."

Jonathan shook his head in disgust. "But how can you accept that, Satet?" he pressed. "In our society, through the advancements in modern medicine and nanotechnology, we can extend a person's life well into their mid one hundreds. Forty years is so short." The very idea of such a short life span was appalling to him.

Reaching across the table, she placed her hand on his as she looked him in the eyes and held his gaze for a moment. "Jonathan, it's not the amount of time you have in this life that matters. It's about what you do with the time you have. How you lived your life. How you loved those around you. I've lived more in forty-two years than I'm guessing most of the people on your home world have in that same time. I've made peace with the fact that I was given forty years of life and nothing more. Everything beyond that is a gift."

Jonathan looked at her warm smile, those deep brown eyes, and he knew she was right. He was fifty-six years old, unmarried and, more often than not, unhappy. He'd try to flirt with women, but he knew he was no looker. He was a scientist, and he embodied every bit the stereotype of a university scientist or researcher. The only action of the female persuasion he got was through the exchange of money or grades. It ultimately left him feeling used, dirty, and worthless. She was right—she had probably lived a much happier and fuller life than he ever had, and deep down, he wished he had lived the same way.

He went to open his mouth but closed it when he realized he didn't have anything to say. Satet got up and walked around the table and sat down next to him. She looked him in the eyes and smiled. "Jonathan, you are an incredibly brilliant man. But you need to learn that there is more to life than smarts, wealth, or accolades. There is *life*, and there is happiness; there is a sense of fulfillment that far outweighs all of that." She leaned over and gave him a gentle, warm kiss on the lips before getting up and leaving him in stunned silence.

****

Troop Deck—RNS *Voyager*

Captain Hopper looked at the Sumerian before him, Hosni. He was dressed in a Republic Army uniform with his name stenciled above his right chest pocket, and the word “Sumerian” stenciled where the words “Space Command” usually were.

“So, this weapon the Zodark guards were using was not their standard military weapon?” Hopper asked again.

“No, this is a weapon the guards carry,” Hosni explained. “The Zodark soldiers, which, I might add, are fearsome warriors—much tougher than the guards you encountered at the camp—carry a much different weapon, better in many cases. The weapons their soldiers use have a shorter barrel than this, plus it has another section located here that can launch an energy burst at buildings or clusters of enemy soldiers.”

“Hosni, have you seen one of their weapons actually used?” interjected Master Sergeant Royce, thoroughly intrigued at this point.

Turning to look at him, Hosni nodded. “I am Sumerian, but I did not grow up on our home world of Sumer. I grew up on the planet Zincondria. This is the Zodarks’ capital planet, their original home world, if you will. To answer your question, I have seen these weapons used many times by my master and his soldiers.”

Lifting an eyebrow, Captain Hopper clarified, “You lived on their capital planet? What more can you tell us about this place, Hosni? Better yet, who was your master, and what can you tell us about him?”

Sergeant Royce leaned in, waiting to hear what this Sumerian had to say next. So did Lieutenant Crocker.

Hosni stood straighter. “My master was a NOS. What you would consider an admiral or general in your military,” he explained with pride.

“And what was your job? What did you do for him?” asked Captain Hopper, assessing the Sumerian’s access.

“I…was a slave, like all Sumerians who live on the Zodark home world. More precisely, I was his slave. My mother was a house slave to his wife, so when I was born, I was allowed to live in their home. When I was old enough, the master started taking me with him everywhere he went as his errand boy. Eventually, he started taking me with him on his ships or when he would go into battle. I was there to do whatever he wanted done, from cleaning his clothes to shining his boots, to any other need he had.”

“It sounds like your master found you useful, Hosni. What happened?” asked Lieutenant Crocker.

Hosni shook his head softly. "Have you ever lost your temper, Lieutenant? I did. I said something I shouldn't have under my breath about one of his superiors who had slighted him. This superior heard my comment. He was irate and demanded my master punish me for my insolence. My master, out of consideration of many years of service, had me sent to a mining colony where I could live out the rest of my days. It may sound cruel, but I assure you, it was much kinder than what could have been handed down to me."

Captain Hopper leaned forward. "Hosni, one of the other Sumerians, Hadad—he mentioned that each year, the Zodarks would demand tribute from the Sumerians. Hadad believes the Zodarks took those tributes and ate them. All the other Sumerians we've talked with have the same belief. Is there any truth to that?"

Hosni didn't speak right away. He looked like he was trying to figure out how he should respond. "I don't mean to contradict what Hadad has told you, but my experience with the Zodarks is that it's not true. I believe that is a myth they perpetuate with my people, but I have not personally seen that happen. That is not to say it doesn't, but I have not seen it."

"Then what do you believe is done with the tributes?" Hopper inquired.

"I cannot say for certain. I have also heard that there are other worlds the Zodarks control that are populated by Sumerians who are not slaves—people who actually fight alongside the Zodarks. I never asked my master about this, so I cannot say for sure if that is true or, again, another myth they allow to circulate."

It was evident by the way the Sumerian talked about his master that he had a positive emotional connection to him, even if he had been his slave. Despite further probing, Hosni wouldn't speak ill of his former master; instead, it came across like he might have had a good relationship with him.

Captain Hopper caught on to the Sumerian's demeanor. *Stockholm syndrome*, he thought.

Hopper decided to change the subject. "Tell you what, Hosni—I'd like to have you work with one of our programmers and help us visually program in what a Zodark military rifle looks like, how it works, and what it sounds like when it's fired. We'll try and build this into our virtual reality simulators and iterate the process with your help until we can recreate its likeness. Then I'd like you to help us understand how their soldiers fight, what tactics they use, things like that. I'm sure the spacers, the fleet sailors who operate our warships, will ask you for similar help with understanding their ship's weapons and defensive capabilities."

Captain Hopper reached over and took the Sumerian's hands in his own. Looking the young man in the eyes, he added, "You're with us now, Hosni. If you want, we'll make you a soldier, just like us, and you can help us protect our home world from the Zodarks—and if we're lucky, we may be able to one day liberate your own home world of Sumer."

The young man, no older than late twenties, beamed with pride. Tears formed in his eyes. "I'd love nothing more than to help you, Captain. I cannot wait to see a world without Zodarks. To live free of slavery is something I never thought possible. To know there is an entire planet full of free people…it's almost more than I can imagine."

The rest of the journey back to Sol was spent creating a realistic representation of the Zodark military, from their ground force to their space force. The soldiers and sailors interviewed and worked with the Sumerians to recreate as best as possible the type of enemy they would soon be fighting.

The small intelligence unit on the *Voyager* spent the trip questioning and interrogating the ten Zodarks relentlessly. The questioning started out easy. Then it got tougher as the prisoners realized they were being transported to a system outside their race's control. Hunger also became a problem. Being flesh-eaters, they did not take well to the dietary restrictions that were suddenly placed on them.

****

RNS *Voyager*—Brig

Halsey stood in front of the reinforced plexiglass wall separating her from the Zodark inside. T'Tock's legs and arms were shackled to the floor, limiting his ability to move about the room. When he had become violent and started pounding on the see-through wall and attempted to attack the guards, they'd had to restrain him.

T'Tock walked as far as the restraints would let him as he approached her. "My people are going to find your planet, and then we are going to destroy it," he growled, his hot breath momentarily fogging the window separating the two of them.

Halsey looked at him. "Your people will never find Earth, and one day, we're going to liberate the Sumerian people from you."

T'Tock let out a guttural howling scream of frustration. He fought with all his strength against the constraints holding him back. His muscles flexed with tension as he tried to break free before giving in to the reality of his own bondage.

"It doesn't feel good to be a prisoner—a slave to someone else, does it?" Halsey said, almost taunting him.

T'Tock looked at her with fire in his eyes as he raged again against his restraints.

Walking up behind her, one of the masters-at-arms said, "I'm not sure it's such a good idea to get him so worked up. At some point, we have to feed him."

Halsey turned to see the head of security standing next to her. She blushed briefly, realizing he was right, of course.

"Sorry about that, Chief. I sometimes think about what they did to Ambassador Chapman and her assistant. I guess I like to rub it in a bit that he is now our prisoner and not the other way around."

The chief smiled. "I'm not saying it's not fun to toy with them, Admiral. I think we all like to do that a bit. There's just so much we don't know about them. I wish they weren't so violent toward us."

Just then, one of the scientists who had been studying the Zodarks came in. He signaled for her to join him.

"What do you have for me, Khalid?" she asked as she approached him.

Khalid and two other researchers had been studying the Zodarks' psychology and biology, trying to gain a better understanding of the Zodark bodies and how their minds might think based on social interactions.

"Admiral, wouldn't it be better to talk in the lab instead of here?"

Khalid was visibly nervous around the Zodarks. He'd spent most of his time examining some of the dead ones they had brought back with them and virtual scans of the live ones.

"They're locked up, Khalid. Nothing to be afraid of. Tell me what more you've unraveled about our guests." Halsey walked over to one of the guard stations and took a seat.

Sighing in frustration, Khalid took a seat next to her. "Admiral, as you know, we've been examining the anatomy of the Zodark body and their physical aspects to try and gain a better understanding of them. What we've discovered when looking at their brain is fascinating. Aside from their frontal cortex being extremely large, it's also very active. We believe this has led them to be an incredibly intelligent species. It also means that they require significantly less sleep than a human being."

Nodding as she took in the information, Halsey went on to ask, "Is there something we can use against them? Something that can give us a competitive edge, maybe?"

Khalid paused for a moment. "That is a tough question, Admiral. Their lung structure is unique and allows them to live in a variety of atmospheres. They have a third lung that acts like a filtering machine. Air is breathed in, and then their body appears to change its composition to meet whatever their true oxygen requirement is before the air is drawn into the next pair of lungs."

Halsey held a hand up. "Whoa, they have three lungs? How is that even possible?"

Khalid shrugged. "There is much we do not understand about their physical structures, Admiral. It's not like we have a Zodark doctor to help explain it to us. Pretend the atmosphere on New Eden had a higher percentage of carbon than it did. In order for us to breathe it, we'd need to wear a mask that helped to filter out the carbon. This additional lung they have essentially performs that function organically."

Halsey thought about that for a moment before moving on. "So, what experiment are you looking to run today?" she asked.

Khalid smiled. "Today, we're going to introduce contrast dye into T'Tock's water and food. We want to see how it circulates through his body. This will aid us in determining what pathogens they might be susceptible to based on their digestive systems and circulatory systems."

"Are you guys looking into designing a bioweapon to use on them?" Halsey inquired, concerned.

He shook his head. "Not exactly. Right now, we're looking to learn more about how their bodies work. In this case, it'll help us identify how they break down proteins and circulate them throughout the body. I'm not a virologist, but this would be the first step in developing a biological or nerve weapon we could use against them if we were ever asked to create one."

Just then, one of Khalid's assistants walked into the brig carrying a tray of food. He brought it over to their station. "Hello, Admiral, Khalid. I've got the stuff. We're ready to begin if you are."

One of the guards walked over to them. "Is this the special food you said you wanted us to feed him?"

Khalid turned to the guard. "It is—just take it to him like you would any other meal."

The guard nodded. He turned and called out to a couple of his fellow comrades to come over.

"OK, guys. This is the stuff. We're going to rock, paper, scissor it to see who gets to take it in."

The other two guards grumbled but didn't disagree. No one liked going into the room to bring the Zodarks their meals. Most of the time, they could slide it under the trap at the bottom of the door, but only if the Zodark wasn't in restraints. If it was, then it couldn't reach the trap to get its food. Then someone was required to go into the room and place it within reach.

To the chagrin of the admiral, she watched as the three masters-at-arms each held a hand out and went through the process of determining who would end up taking T'Tock his meal.

"Ah, man. I had to do it last time," complained the guard who'd been beaten.

"Sorry, man, scissors beats paper every time," one of his comrades chided.

"Whatever, just give me the damn food," the guard shot back.

"Come on, Dave. It's not so bad, we got your six," the chief said as he walked over with a wide smile on his face.

"Don't mind us, Admiral. We try to make it equitable with who has to go in and feed them. So far, none of them have lashed out or attacked any of my guys. They're just scary-looking," the chief petty officer said reassuringly.

Halsey laughed at the scene unfolding before her. "It's OK, Chief. I actually enjoy the banter. It's nice to see. I'm just going to stand over here with Khalid and try to stay out of everyone's way."

Looking at the room containing T'Tock, Halsey saw he had calmed down a bit. He had repositioned himself on the far side of the room and looked almost like he was in a meditative state.

The MA walked up to the door as one of his comrades unlocked it and held it open for him. "Go on, Dave. You'll be fine. We're right here if you need us," his friend offered encouragingly.

Dave cautiously crept his way into the room holding T'Tock, trying not to say anything or make any noise if at all possible. He obviously just wanted to take the tray in and get out of there.

T'Tock continued sitting against the wall on the far side of the room. He had just enough slack to stand if he chose, but in that moment, he was frozen, his third eye open while his other two remained shut.

Is he paying attention or zoned out? Halsey wondered. She had an eerie feeling he was just waiting to pounce.

Dave never took his eyes off T'Tock. He was practically trembling with fear just being in the same room as this monster, the leader of the captured Zodarks. When he was about three meters away from T'Tock, Dave bent down to place the tray on the floor.

T'Tock suddenly opened his two other eyes and looked at Admiral Halsey through the plexiglass wall. Then he let out a guttural howl and lunged at Dave with a lightning speed no one had expected from such a large creature.

Before anyone could react, T'Tock had sprung like a coiled snake. The restraints holding his feet and the zip ties on his hands snapped like they weren't even there. His long arms lashed out at Dave, knocking him to the floor. In the flash of an eye, two of his four hands had dug their talon-like fingernails into Dave's legs and yanked his body toward him.

T'Tock swiftly straddled Dave, plunging his teeth into his neck and upper chest. His rows of pointy canines sank deep into the soft human flesh, slicing through bone and muscle like a knife through a plate of pâté. Blood gushed and sprayed the wall, and then it began to pool on the floor around Dave. The guard desperately tried to scream for help before he fell silent moments after the violent attack.

A handful of guards rushed into the cell, attempting to taser T'Tock into submission and rescue their friend. They hit the brute with multiple darts.

T'Tock howled in rage and flicked the electrodes off his body like they were nothing more than annoying horseflies. He then dove for the remaining guards. His arms flayed about as he pounded, punched, and smashed the guards' bodies relentlessly.

One of T'Tock's hands slashed at one of the guard's chests, his talons slicing right through the man's ribs as he sought to grab at something. When T'Tock retracted his hand from the man's chest, he held the guard's still-beating heart, covered in blood.

T'Tock backhanded several of the guards who had charged him, throwing their bodies against the wall. He turned his head and looked at Admiral Halsey, anger burning in his eyes as the hand that held the human heart moved closer to his blood-covered face. T'Tock devoured the organ in a single bite and then returned his attention to the remaining humans in the room, looking for more to kill and eat.

The chief in charge of the guard force hit the emergency button on the side of the wall, sounding an alarm. Seconds later, Halsey ordered the general quarters alarm and called out for more help to the brig.

The chief grabbed for his extendable baton he carried when in the brig. Then he rushed forward fearlessly and attacked T'Tock with it. He whacked him across the side of his head with a hard thwack that drew bluish blood.

T'Tock stumbled briefly from the hit. One of his hands moved up to block the chief from hitting him again. Bluish liquid continued to run down the side of T'Tock's head and face from where the chief had hit him. One of T'Tock's other free hands reached out at the guard and managed to grab the man's arm in midswing, breaking the bones with an audible snap before tossing him across the room into the wall. The chief screamed out in agony.

Then T'Tock looked at the door leading out of the room and ran right for it.

Admiral Halsey was in absolute disbelief. The attack had happened so fast. T'Tock was going through the guards like they didn't even matter. She had barely been able to respond, but when she saw him rush toward the now-unguarded door, she knew she had to get out of there before she was also torn to shreds.

She grabbed Khalid by the arm and pushed him out the door of the brig with her. "Run, Khalid, we need to get out of there!" she blurted out, panic in her voice.

Racing down the hallway, she used her neurolink to alert the security detachment on the ship to the prison break. *A Zodark is about to be roaming the deck!* she warned.

The flashing GQ lights and the blaring warning klaxon only added to the surreal scene that was unfolding around them as they ran down the corridor for their very lives. Halsey turned to look behind her when she heard a noise. Suddenly, the door to the brig violently burst open and clattered across the floor as it was ripped off its hinges. T'Tock let out a primordial scream that echoed down the hall as he raced after them or anyone else that might be in his path.

"I'm coming for you, Admiral!" T'Tock roared, feet pounding on the floor after her.

Oh God, don't let me get eaten by that beast, she thought selfishly as she ran ahead of Khalid.

Rounding the next corner as quickly as she could, she saw several Republic Army soldiers moving toward her, their rifles at the low ready. She saw the look of uncertainty and fear written on their faces as the Zodark beast let out another of his guttural howls, his feet pounding on the floor as he sought to close the distance between them.

"Set your blasters to kill! It's right behind us," she managed to say through ragged scared breaths as she raced past them. She stopped maybe four and a half meters behind them as she turned around to watch her soldiers kill that psychotic animal.

One of the soldiers turned his head slightly to look at her. "We got this, Admiral," he said confidently.

Emerging around the corner moments later, the nearly three-meter-tall four-armed bluish beast named T'Tock saw them and let out another screeching animal shriek as he charged right at them. In seconds, he was practically on top of them.

The first soldier, the one who'd told Halsey they had this, opened fire with his blaster, hitting one of the left arms of the Zodark as he tried to dodge the incoming fire from the guards. The blaster sheared the arm right off the beast, severing it from his body, and the limb fell to the floor with a sickening thud.

Bluish liquid sprayed the nearby wall as T'Tock let out another ear-piercing scream before his body bulldozed into the soldier who had just shot him. Two of his three remaining arms grabbed the soldier who had managed to hit him and ripped the man's head clean off his body. His third arm thrashed at the other soldier, clawing the man's face and torso with his talons before the soldier could fire his blaster.

The soldier fell to the floor as his blaster was ripped from his hands by the sheer force of the hit. T'Tock reached down for the soldier's blaster and attempted to figure out how to use one of his captors' weapons against them.

Admiral Abigail Halsey fell backward, tripping over one of the bulkheads as she backed up in horror. She landed squarely on her duff, then looked up in horror at T'Tock as he steadily moved toward her. Hate, anger, and pain filled his eyes as his pupils narrowed at her. Blood dripped from around his mouth and from his talon-like fingers.

As he approached her, T'Tock must have seen that she had no discernable weapon, because a sardonic smile spread across his lips. "This is only the beginning, Admiral. My people are going to devour your pathetic species."

T'Tock laughed in satisfaction as he approached her, towering over her shaking body. Looking down at her as she lay there helpless, he said, "I am going to enjoy eating your heart and sucking your brains out through your eye sockets, Admiral."

In that very instant, Halsey realized she was dead—dead because she'd failed to adequately protect her crew and the mission from this beast. Then T'Tock was hit by a barrage of blaster shots from several soldiers who'd arrived just in time to save her and Khalid.

****

Thirty minutes later, as she sat on an examination table in sickbay, Admiral Halsey looked down at her hand and saw a slight tremble. She balled her hand into a fist so no one else would see it. Although that horrid beast was dead, she was still frightened. What she'd just lived through was by far the most terrifying thing she'd ever experienced. Never had she been as scared as when she had seen T'Tock unfurling himself in front of her, looking at her with those eyes that saw her as nothing more than food.

A nurse walked up to her with a small pneumatic injector. "This will help calm your nerves, Admiral. It's normal to feel the way you do."

Halsey nodded, not saying anything. She was trying to stay strong and stoic, but she knew she needed some help if she was to carry on.

"Thank you for this. I…I need to stay strong in front of the crew."

The female nurse smiled briefly as she nodded. "It's OK, Admiral, and you have this."

The nurse then turned to head over to treat one of the other injured people from the attack.

A few seconds later, Halsey felt a lot better. Her nerves were calmed down, and she didn't feel like it was the end of the world. She made her way to a couple of the injured crew members and talked with them for a few minutes.

Captain Hopper walked into sickbay. He spotted Halsey and made his way over to her. He was kitted out in his exoskeleton combat suit and weapon, ready to wage war on the decks of her ship if he needed to.

"Admiral, I've got a squad of my Deltas on watch over the remaining Zodark prisoners. I've taken the liberty of establishing a full twenty-four-hour guard rotation to make sure something like this doesn't happen again," he announced in a commanding, authoritative voice.

She only nodded at the warrior standing before her. The Deltas stood a full three inches taller when wearing their exosuits, which encased large swaths of their body in protective armor. The suits seemed to fit smoothly over their chiseled bodies and allowed them a great deal of mobility.

"Thank you, Captain, for seeing to this. I think it's important that we reassure everyone that these dangerous beasts are firmly locked up and secured. We still have a couple of weeks until we arrive in Sol, and I don't want the crew any more distracted than they already are," Halsey said evenly.

The two of them talked for a few minutes more before they left. Hopper was about to lead her back to the brig—the place T'Tock had broken out of—to walk her through his security plan when she stopped.

Halsey turned suddenly. "I trust you to handle it," she said, and then she left to head back to the bridge. She couldn't bring herself to see the carnage T'Tock had left in his wake just yet. It was all still too fresh in her mind.

No, I'm going to need some time to recover from this one, she realized.

A few hours later, in addition to the Deltas on guard rotation in the brig, she had the Republic Army soldiers posting sentries on every deck and maintaining a lockdown of the crew. For the remainder of the trip, she wanted to keep everyone safe until they were able to hand over the nine remaining Zodarks to Space Command.

Chapter Nineteen
Colonization Highway

John Glenn Orbital Station
Earth, Sol

Admiral Bailey looked at the colossal transport as it docked at the station. It had just completed its five-day shakedown cruise with resounding success. BlueOrigin and Musk Industries had paused nearly all other construction projects to create the first several *Ark*-class transports. They had finished building three of them in record time. The other three were still a ways from completion.

The three *Ark* transports that were ready would start the process of ferrying tens of thousands of Republic citizens off Earth to Alpha Centauri and getting the new colony going while the military went into overdrive, preparing to defend Sol against a potential alien invasion.

As Admiral Bailey watched one of the new ships and saw all the people there to look on at the impressive structure, Bailey remembered that the *Voyager* and the *Rook* were due in Sol sometime in the next couple of days. The *Gables* had already arrived and caused quite the stir. Right now, there was a lot of anticipation for the remainder of the fleet. They were bringing back with them proof of alien life—ten of these Zodark creatures. It was thrilling, but also terrifying.

Then there were the Sumerians. Humans from another system and planet but who might have some connection to Earth, based on their language. The thought that there were other planets in the galaxy with humans wreaked havoc on the religions of the world, causing many to ask whether a deity had created life on Earth or if humans had also been created on other planets. Then, of course, there was the theory of intelligent design. Some postulated that an alien race was genetically engineering humans like cattle or crops and then planting them on various planets to grow and thrive, only to be culled at a later date and time.

The whole idea of humans being domesticated for food sent a shiver down Bailey's back. He looked at the gigantic transport outside the station and realized the lucky passengers boarding it would be spared whatever was potentially heading toward Sol. Then again, he wasn't sure if they really were the lucky ones. They'd be leaving behind all they had known for a new and strange planet that no one knew for sure would be better than Earth. It was a gamble either way.

"She's a beauty, isn't she?" Andrew Berry said as he walked up to Bailey. The two of them looked out the window at the mammoth creation.

"It's a big ship. I still can't believe we were able to construct something so massive," Bailey said, waving his hand at the thing.

"Let's put it this way—it wasn't easy. We had to place multiple FTL drive systems along the sides of the hull just to make sure we could create a warp bubble large enough to encompass the entire ship. Frankly, it's an incredible engineering accomplishment."

Bailey nodded. "I'll bet. How do you even slow something that large down once it gets moving?"

"That, Admiral, was a hundred-billion-dollar problem," Andrew replied with a wink. "On a normal warship, we'd route a second set of MPD thrusters to the forward section of the ship to slow it down. With a ship the size of the *Ark*, that's not possible. We'd lose too much power from the plasma drive system. We had to build a second engineering room at the front of the ship to handle the load."

Admiral Bailey grunted. "Admiral Halsey's fleet will arrive in Sol in a few days. Are your construction crews ready to begin work on the new warships once they arrive in the system and have some additional data to work with?" he asked. His own masters in the Senate were anxious to get the new fleet under construction. They were practically in a panic at the idea that Earth could become a food colony for some horrible alien race. It was every science fiction nightmare come true.

"We have an army of engineers standing by to receive whatever data the *Voyager* can provide on the Zodark ships, weapon systems, power generation, and propulsion systems. We've also stocked up enough supplies to build at least four of those original battleships we had planned to build. We're about as ready to start production as we can be at this point," Andrew assured him. "Musk Industries has even placed an emergency order for four thousand additional synthetic humanoid workers to help with the workload."

Turning to face Bailey, but keeping his voice low so no one else could hear, Andrew asked, "Are the rumors true about building a Synth army?"

The admiral glanced over his shoulder to make sure no one else was nearby. "That's highly classified information you're asking about," he responded in a hushed tone.

Lifting an eyebrow at the cryptic response, Andrew whispered, "So it's true, then? I thought they were illegal—against the Laws of Armed Conflict."

The LOAC governed what types of military equipment each nation was allowed to build. It had been put in place to prevent the kind of bloodshed that had taken place during the last Great War.

Bailey shrugged. "Rules change when you're facing a threat that can extinguish your race, Andy."

Andrew shook his head in dismay. "I think you're playing with fire, Admiral. We saw what could happen when humanoid AI drones go rogue. It was a bloodbath that nearly wiped out humanity last time."

"I know what happened," Bailey snapped hotly. "I've been assured safeguards have been put in place, and something like that can never happen again," he continued. "Besides, I'm not even sure we'll end up needing them. We're just making sure that *if* they are needed, we can crank them out and have them ready if the time comes." He held Andrew's eyes for a moment, forcing the man to look away.

People hadn't forgotten about the last year of the Great War of the 2040s. The war had changed until it was no longer a war both sides fought against each other but one fought by the machines both sides had unleashed on each other. When it had appeared the United States was going to lose the war to China, they had let loose new AI-equipped surrogate fighting drones on the Chinese. The drones had something close to consciousness and had the ability to learn, adapt, and overcome the enemy they were fighting. For several months, the marauding machines were all but miraculous as they turned the tide of the war in the Republic's favor.

The drones themselves operated somewhat autonomously in that they could restock themselves with ammo from resupply drones. They could power down to recharge their battery using a combat solar panel or attach themselves to a fossil fuel generator. They needed very little in the way of maintenance or support once they had been deployed. That was what made them so effective. Then a Chinese hacker got inside the code and tried to disable them.

Instead of disabling the drones, the hacker accidentally disabled the safeguards, and the drones went rogue. They went on a killing spree of Biblical proportions, attacking and killing all human life. The only thing that stopped them was a concerted effort by the remaining Chinese and American forces to defeat them. It was in that gravest hour of possible species extinction that the warring parties saw what they had done and put an end to the fighting. They had coalesced together to defeat this unintended threat and save humanity.

The one saving grace the humans had during the war was that the rogue drones had not captured any drone production facilities or been able to get themselves organized into a coherent fighting force. They were small bands of sheer terror bots, running roughshod on anything they encountered until they were overwhelmed and destroyed.

From then on, the only humanoids allowed to operate were civilian synthetics, with extreme safety protocols in place. The world's militaries had agreed to a moratorium on such tools of war. That moratorium, however, appeared to be coming to an end with the discovery of an even more deadly threat: the Zodarks.

Chapter Twenty
Homecoming

RNS *Voyager*
Sol

"We're coming out of warp now, Admiral," called out the helmsman.

Seconds later, the warp bubble around the ship collapsed, and the blackness of space returned. The light of the ever-present stars winked into existence seconds later, and then the visuals of the planets known in Sol. It was a welcome sight after all they had gone through. It was home.

Admiral Halsey looked at her helmsman. "Secure FTL. Prepare the ship for MPD thrusters and bring us up to three-quarter speed. Set a course for the John Glenn Station. Coms, send a message to Space Command that we've arrived safely in the system and are making our way to the John Glenn."

"Yes, ma'am," several of her crew members replied as they went to work executing her orders.

Looking at the radar display, Halsey saw the *Rook* had arrived safely and was following her lead to the orbital station. While they were returning home early, they had still been gone for nearly fourteen months. A lot had happened during their absence.

Lieutenant Adam George, her coms officer, announced, "Admiral, we're receiving a message from Space Command. They're welcoming us home from a successful mission. They've also asked that we relay all information we've been able to collect from our mission to the Mars DARPA facility for analysis and dissemination."

Halsey nodded. "Very well. Send everything via enhanced encryption. Let them know it's going to be a lot of data," Halsey replied. She was happy to finally have someone to share the information with.

During the six-month trip back to Sol, her people had had a lot of time to debrief the Sumerians and the nine remaining Zodarks. They had collected tens of thousands of audio interviews of the two factions, learning every aspect and facet of their cultures, planets, people, economy, technology, and anything else they thought might be of value. Everything was fed into the quantum computer, and the sophisticated AI crunched the data and identified additional questions the interviewers should ask or areas they should explore. The AI had built an incredibly detailed summary of what they knew of the Sumerians and Zodarks up to this point.

Admiral Halsey had even had several Sumerians review and listen to what their AI had created so they could help edit it and fill in any gaps. The Sumerians, for their part, were astonished and amazed at how quickly the Earthers were able to develop these profiles of their people and the Zodarks.

Some of the critical pieces of information they had been able to glean revolved around the technology used by both the Sumerians and the Zodarks—particularly around propulsion, energy generation, and space travel. What still baffled Admiral Halsey was how the Zodarks had been able to transit such a vast, sprawling empire. Only a handful of the Sumerians they had liberated had ever been off their home planet besides their tenure as prisoners on Clovis, so their knowledge of how the Zodarks traveled hundreds of light-years was limited. They were only able to share rumors—and until those rumors could be validated, she wasn't sure how much stock she'd put in them.

Hosni, one of the Sumerians whose master was apparently some sort of admiral, had said the Zodarks leveraged some transwarp-like technology. It acted like a portal or miniature wormhole that could be created, connecting one system to another. Then they'd use their FTL systems to travel between these so-called gates. She wasn't sure what to make of that concept or how such a thing was even possible. Hadad had said when their people developed a technology that could essentially open a wormhole and travel between points without the use of these stargates, that was when the Zodarks had come down hard on them and locked them out of future space travel.

Hosni also gave them a piece of information that completely contradicted what the other Sumerian prisoners had said. While the Sumerians insisted the Zodarks were culling their world as part of their food source, Hosni had said that was a myth perpetrated by the Zodarks. He'd told them there were other colonies populated by Sumerians who had been culled. These worlds were being used to condition and train Sumerians into fighting in the Zodark Empire and expanding their reach as they fought other species.

Halsey didn't know what to make of that claim. No one could confirm it, and no one else really believed it, but Hosni was insistent that this was all part of how the Zodarks used and manipulated other species. In the final report about this piece of information, she annotated that it needed further analysis and shouldn't be outright dismissed. Something just didn't add up, but she wasn't sure what it was.

Another piece of technology the Zodarks had mastered that Halsey was sure they'd move to integrate rapidly was their version of artificial gravity. While the Earther ships had to rely on an enormous energy-consuming artificial gravity well to create a one-g atmosphere on a large vessel or orbital station, the Zodarks had found a much more efficient way to accomplish this. Next to the information about the Trimarian reactor, the artificial gravity system, or AGS as they were now calling it, was probably the most significant technological discovery.

Of course, the discovery of human life on other planets and the Zodarks trumped the technological innovations, and they had also opened Pandora's box for the Earthers. Naively, Admiral Halsey had to admit, humans had thought they were the only intelligent life in space. Perhaps that was because they hadn't found evidence to support or disprove that theory, but they had now. What they'd discovered was so profound from an anthropological standpoint, it was going to upend centuries of doctrines and religious beliefs.

"Admiral, there's a private message coming in for you from Space Command. Would you like me to route it to your office?" asked her coms officer.

Halsey smiled as she stood. "Yes, please do. XO, you have the bridge," she announced before walking over to her office.

A minute later, she was seated at her desk and logged in to her computer terminal. She opened the communication application and waited. Seconds later, an image of Fleet Admiral Chester Bailey popped up. She lifted an eyebrow as a smile spread across her face. "Admiral Bailey, I wasn't aware Admiral Sanchez had retired. Congratulations on your promotion," she said.

Admiral Bailey had pushed for her to be the commander of this mission; she owed him for that. Admiral Sanchez had an old friend he had wanted to lead the first Republic expedition outside of Sol, but Bailey had pushed back, insisting that such a mission should go to a younger admiral, one who would be around to share that experience for generations to come, not retire shortly after returning to bask in the glory and accolades that would surely follow.

"Thank you, Admiral," Bailey replied. "A lot has happened while you've been gone. And congratulations on a successful mission. I briefly heard about the Zodark incident on your own ship. I'm glad you're OK. It would have been a great loss had you been killed."

Halsey grimaced at the memory of that fateful day. She still wasn't entirely over it. Her heart raced each time she thought of what had transpired.

Bailey continued, "I know the loss of any crew member is tough. I just wanted to say you did a good job of minimizing casualties and protecting your fleet. Your ploy to hide in a nearby asteroid belt was genius. A lesser admiral would have either turned tail and run or charged in there and attacked that Zodark ship when it came into the system. In either case, we would have lost out on the immense amount of intelligence and data you've been able to collect for us. I dare say you may have saved not just our nation but the world with what you've done on this mission, Abigail."

She blushed at the gushing praise from her mentor and the head of Space Command. "I did what you and many other leaders have taught me to do. To be fair, though, it was Captain Hunt who suggested we hide in the asteroid belt. He was a big help during this mission."

She drummed her fingers on the desk. "When our ship reaches the station, what would you like us to do next, sir?"

Bailey smiled at her bluntness. "All business—I like that about you, Abigail. OK, so first things first. Any of your folks who did not go planetside are to be debriefed for forty-eight hours on what transpired during the mission. Then they'll be given a couple of weeks of R&R before reporting back to the ship to resume their daily duties. Next, the individuals who went down to Rhea Ab or have interacted extensively with the Zodarks or the Sumerians are going to have a five-day debrief before they can go on R&R. We need to collect as much information as possible from them."

She nodded.

Bailey continued, "We're going to hold the Sumerians on the John Glenn for the time being until we can get them medically cleared to be on Earth. We don't want them to suddenly get sick because they're exposed to something on our planet they have no natural immunity to. Then they'll be brought planetside and split up. Half of them are going to the Republic; the other half are going to the Tri-Parte Alliance, where they will be further debriefed. If you have any Sumerians you want us to keep, you need to identify them to Space Command before they end their quarantine period."

"Um. Tri-Parte Alliance? What happened while we were gone?" Halsey asked, confused.

Smiling, Admiral Bailey simply replied, "Abigail, we have a lot to catch up on. When you arrive at the station, delegate your responsibilities to your XO and head to Space Command HQ immediately. You and I have a lot to discuss."

They spent another twenty minutes going over some other issues before the call ended. Halsey looked at the nav chart and saw she had about eight hours before her ship would be fully docked at the orbital station and her crew would be ready to disembark. She planned on spending a few hours of that time going through the intelligence summaries she'd just received from Space Command and getting caught up on everything that had gone on while she was away.

****

John Glenn Orbital Station
Docking Berth 5

Walking off the docking tube, Captain Miles Hunt smiled when he saw his wife waiting for him at the other end. She was standing there with a homemade welcome home sign, wearing a formfitting dress that was driving him wild. After not seeing his wife in person now for fourteen months, he was more than ready to get reacquainted.

"Hey, sailor…you looking for a fun time?" Lilly joked as she tossed the sign aside and wrapped her arms around him tightly. They shared a long passionate kiss.

Holding her tight felt great. All the stress of the last fourteen months washed away, and he felt safe at that moment. Pulling away from her, he grabbed his small bag and guided them toward the temporary quarters he'd be staying in for the next couple of days. He still had about five days' worth of work and reports that needed to be taken care of before he could start his own leave.

The two of them walked and talked for a bit. He regaled her with the stories of what they had discovered, at least what he could share. He promised to show her some images and videos they'd taken on their many stopovers to recharge the FTL drive.

When they reached his quarters, they quickly locked the doors and got down to the immediate business at hand. One hour later, Miles was lying in bed next to Lilly as he shared with her many of the pictures and videos the ship had taken along the way to the Rhea system. She was thrilled to see them, and he was excited to finally be able to share these incredible moments with her. She was an astronomy nerd herself—it was one of many reasons why she'd joined Space Command. She wanted to explore the stars with him; it just hadn't happened yet.

When they had finished looking through his videos and pictures, they got dressed and headed out for dinner. There was a fantastic restaurant down on the promenade that had seats with window views overlooking the Earth below. When they walked in, the place was packed. With all the passengers starting to show up to board the *Arks* and the return of Admiral Halsey's fleet, there was a long line to get a table.

One of Hunt's officers spotted him and his wife as they stood in line. A moment later, the officer was talking with the maître d'. He must have mentioned who Hunt was, because twenty minutes later, he and Lilly had one of the coveted tables right in front of the windows.

After placing their orders and getting a glass of wine, Hunt asked, "So what's the mood of things going on back home? I've been gone a while, and it looks like a lot has happened in that time."

"Um, yeah. Like everything has changed in your absence, honey," she said, sounding like one of their kids.

"No, be serious. What's going on? Everything seems different."

Shrugging, she reached for her glass of wine. "Space Command has been putting out some of the information you guys sent back—information about you guys finding humans on other planets and this terrible new alien race, the Zo-something-or-another. Then there was the announcement of this new treaty with the Tri-Parte Alliance, and suddenly we're all best friends. No more talk of possible hostilities, just best buddies. They're even letting us set up a colony on Alpha Centauri." She finished her glass of wine in a couple of gulps before she added, "It's as if they're hiding some terrible news from us. Do you know what it is?"

Miles wasn't sure what he could tell her yet, so he feigned ignorance for the time being. "I don't know, Lilly. I just got back in Sol.

I'm still trying to play catch-up right now. I'll probably be able to tell you more in a few days or weeks. For right now, let's not worry about what might be wrong. Let's focus on the here and now and having ourselves a perfect dinner with a spectacular view of Earth."

The rest of the dinner was spent talking about their two kids and what they were up to. Both of them were at the Space Academy right now. They wanted to be spacers like their dad and mom.

****

Space Command HQ
Kennedy Space Center

Captain Miles Hunt sat at the table with Admiral Halsey as the senior leadership of both Space Command and the Tri-Parte Alliance questioned them for the third straight day about the Zodark ships. It had been four weeks since they had returned from the Rhea system—more than enough time for the data they had collected to be analyzed and gone over by both groups, AI computers, and thousands of analysts. They had looked at every speck of electronic information, imagery, interview notes from the Sumerians, you name it, to try and understand the threat.

"Captain Hunt," said one of the TPA admirals, "if your ship had fought the Zodarks with your current capabilities, do you believe you would have won?"

It was a question Hunt had asked himself a million times—and one he didn't have the answer to. Looking at the foreign admiral, he simply replied, "I would like to think so, but I honestly can't say. During our transit back to Sol, I had some time to study the energy output of those ships. I have to imagine their pulse beam lasers are pretty strong, given the power outputs. I don't know if our current armor would have held up against it. Not knowing the exact power of their lasers, they could have sniped at us from a great distance while we tried to close the distance for our own weapons."

Many of the military leaders around the table nodded at that assessment. They couldn't fault him for his logic, but that didn't mean they wouldn't try if they thought they could.

"Admiral, if you were unsure of the enemy's military capabilities, why didn't you try and engage them, or at least test your weapons?" asked another military leader, again from the TPA.

Admiral Halsey leaned forward in her chair as she answered, "I was responsible for more than just my own ship. I had the *Rook*. Our initial intelligence of the system indicated that this system and planet were not populated. We saw signs of possible life, but no cities, no electronic activity in orbit, in the system, or on the planet. As such, we didn't arrive with a fleet of warships to do battle. I couldn't risk our ships being destroyed and not bringing back to Earth the information we had just discovered."

"You didn't hesitate to attack one of the mining colonies and liberate a few hundred of these Sumerians. You killed more than a hundred Zodark guards in the process," snapped a TPA general, pouncing.

He looked Russian if Halsey had to guess. *Yeah, he's Russian...*

"General, when the Zodarks abducted our ambassador and her assistant, it didn't leave us much choice. We couldn't just leave them," she said with as neutral a face as she could.

Admiral Bailey then cleared his throat. "Admiral Halsey, do you believe the Zodarks would be open to a dialogue with us if we tried to speak with them again?"

"No," Halsey replied, perhaps too quickly. "I believe the Zodarks have viewed our race as slaves or even food for hundreds, maybe even thousands of years. They are not going to take us seriously until we make them take us seriously."

Several of the generals and admirals broke out in conversations amongst themselves before Admiral Bailey brought the room back to order. "Admiral, if that's how you feel, then how do you propose we make them take us seriously?"

All eyes turned to her. She calmly looked everyone in the eye before she spoke. "We punch them in the face. We go back to the Rhea system and take New Eden from them. We turn the system into a fortress. That's how we make them take us seriously."

One of the TPA generals—the same Russian from earlier—snorted at the blunt approach. "And if that doesn't work, Admiral, then what do you propose?" he asked snarkily.

"If that doesn't work, General, then we take the fight to them. We make a move to liberate Sumer, the Sumerian home world. They're an advanced race and, if brought into our fold, would be an incredible ally," Halsey countered.

Holding a hand out to keep everyone from bursting out in chatter again, Admiral Bailey said, "While I appreciate your aggressiveness, Admiral, I do not believe we are in a position to do that right now."

Halsey blurted out, "Then we conduct a rapid buildup using the new technology and information we've learned from the Sumerians, and we hit them with it. I believe this race has become lulled into a sense of false security. From the nearly one hundred hours I've spent talking with the Zodark prisoners and Sumerians, I am confident we would catch them completely by surprise. Their only interaction with humans has been as slaves. The moment the humans they controlled looked like they might become dangerous, they knocked them down. They've never fought against a human foe that knows how to fight. If there's one thing we Earthers know how to do and do well, it's kill each other. We can bring that same skill to bear on the Zodarks."

****

Four Hours Later

"That was a hell of a suggestion you made in that meeting," Admiral Bailey said, eying Halsey.

She shrugged. "You asked what I would do if I was in charge. That's what I would do."

Bailey liked Halsey. She was cool as a cucumber under pressure, and blunt and direct when needed. He needed military commanders like that. He also required commanders who understood that sometimes, the better part of valor is knowing when not to kick a hornet's nest—something he'd had to learn over the years.

Sitting back in his chair, he blew out some air through his lips. "I don't disagree with your assessment, Abigail. But things have been changing a lot in your absence. The discovery of the Zodarks and the Sumerians may have actually prevented another war. We all suddenly realized there are bigger threats in this galaxy than each other."

Bailey watched her analyze what he said but didn't add anything to it. She waited silently for him to make the next move.

"Level with me, Abigail. If we were to pursue your punch-in-the-face approach, how large a force do you believe we should bring, and more importantly, is our current technology able to win?" he asked pointedly. "The Rhea system is a long way from Earth."

Abigail nodded. "I believe our magrails should be more than powerful enough to hurt them," she replied optimistically. "I'm not so confident about our pulse beams, though. Not with our current power outputs. However, if we convert our ships' fusion reactors to these new Trimarian reactors, I think the increase in power to the pulse beams might have a chance. We'll also be able to reduce our travel time to the system considerably."

She paused for a moment before adding, "Admiral, I think our ace in the hole against the Zodarks is going to be our magrail systems. We're going to punch holes right through their ships."

Bailey lifted an eyebrow at that. "Really? You believe our magrails would blow through their ships' armor?" He was curious why she had come to that conclusion and the analyst up to this point hadn't.

Abigail smiled coyly. "When I was speaking with one of the Sumerians, he said he was a slave to what the Zodarks call a NOS. It's their version of an admiral. He told me he was on board his master's ship during a battle with another alien race and that the aliens' lasers couldn't hurt the Zodark ships because they weren't strong enough to make it through their ships' armor.

"So I asked him about the armor, what it was made of. He said the armor was coated in some organic mixture that could absorb a large amount of energy from a laser burst. He wasn't sure how the technology worked, and I frankly don't understand how it could work either, but that got me thinking. If they've put all their stock in either deflecting or absorbing an enemy's laser energy, then chances are they aren't going to be prepared to handle a direct kinetic hit like our magrails will be able to provide."

Bailey nodded as he bit his lower lip, deep in thought. "That's a decent theory, Abby. But we don't know that for sure. Plus, we don't know the effective range of their lasers—they could end up sniping at us before our magrail slugs ever hit their ship. And then, you'd have to fire a lot of shells at them to compensate for any adjustments in their trajectory."

"I agree, but with our fabricators, producing enough slugs to keep firing at them isn't going to be a problem. Our gun systems can maintain a pretty high rate of fire," Halsey explained. "What we need to do, Admiral, is send a ship back and attempt to test this theory. If it pans out, then we can configure our fleet operations appropriately. If it fails, then we know to try a new approach before we take a fleet back there and risk everything."

Bailey snorted at the proposal. "That's a big risk, Abby. We'd first need to reconfigure one of our ships with this Trimarian reactor. Then we'd need to reconfigure the weapon systems for the new power source. Then we'd need to be willing to lose the ship to test your theory. I don't suppose you have a ship and crew you'd be willing to risk?"

Lifting her chin up, she said, "I could take the *Voyager* back, minus our troop contingent, of course."

Shaking his head, Bailey waved the suggestion off. "Not a chance. You're my most experienced fleet commander at this point. I couldn't risk you, Abigail, not for a test like that."

"The *Rook*, then. They could test the Zodarks. Attempt to make contact with them first, and then engage them if that doesn't work. I could use the *Voyager* to watch from a distance and monitor the battle and then report back what we learned," she offered as a compromise.

"Did Captain Hunt do something to piss you off on the trip?"

She blushed briefly, realizing she had just offered up her former XO and friend—Bailey's former chief of staff as well. "No, sir, I think the *Rook* is probably the best ship for the job, and he just so happens to be the captain of her."

Taking a deep breath in and holding it for a moment, he finally let it out as he nodded. "OK, Abby, here's what we're going to do. We're going to prioritize getting the *Rook* and the *Voyager* fitted out with this new reactor and upgrading their weapon systems. Your two ships will head back and attempt your test. *If* it fails, you have to return and report back what happened. That information will be vital to our survival and success in defending Sol. Is that understood?"

She nodded. "Yes, sir. You can count on me."

Chapter Twenty-One
Fire in the Hole

Sol
Jupiter Test Range

Captain Miles Hunt watched the asteroid some five hundred kilometers away with bated breath, as was everyone else on the bridge, as they test-fired their new, enhanced pulse beam laser.

The nine months since they'd returned from Rhea had been busy. His ship, the *Rook*, had been nearly taken apart in the shipyard as they'd gutted her engineering, propulsion, and weapon sections to upgrade them with the new Sumerian and Zodark technology.

Hunt hadn't thought it was possible to take the ship apart as they had, gut out what needed to be gutted, replace it with new alien technology, and put it all back together in nine months. But somehow, someway, they had. It did help that they'd had a drydock prepared and an army of both human and Synth workers ready to go.

Now, two months later, they were at the Jupiter test range, doing a final check of the weapon systems. They'd already checked the FTL and propulsion systems. They all worked—better than their old systems. They could now move inside the system four hundred percent faster with their MPD drive, and the FTL drive could propel them at speeds of up to one light-year per day, fifteen times faster than their old system.

Breaking into his thoughts, the weapons officer, Lieutenant Cory LaFine, anxiously announced, "Pulse beam capacitors are now at full power. Ready to fire, sir."

The young lieutenant and the engineers standing near him were visibly nervous about the test. It was an enormous amount of energy they were going to transfer through the power junctions to the forward laser banks. They were all hoping it wouldn't blow up or melt something as the power traveled to the front of the ship.

Looking at his crew, Hunt could feel the excitement, the tension building. This was a dangerous piece of alien technology they were testing. He knew he should probably say something to calm their nerves. *But what…?*

"OK, people, we've tested everything up to this point, and it's worked. Our Sumerian guests and engineers have been top-notch so far.

Let's not doubt them now. Let's acquire one of those asteroids and give it a try. Weps, find us a target and engage," Hunt ordered nonchalantly like this was an everyday occurrence, doing his best to convey a calm demeanor for his crew—the image of a smooth, stoic captain, confident in his weapons and his people's capability.

"Firing!" announced the weapons officer loudly, almost causing everyone to jump.

A second later, a pulse beam shot out and hit the asteroid they had been aiming at. Everyone on the bridge saw it bore a hole right into the rock before the entire thing exploded into a million smaller pieces.

Hunt snorted. *Well, I'll be damned. It worked...*

"Target destroyed," Lieutenant LaFine said excitedly. Others on the bridge let out an audible sigh of relief that the test had worked and they hadn't blown themselves up in the process.

"Excellent job, Lieutenant. Did you engineers get the data you needed?" asked Hunt. The weapons engineers had been analyzing the amount of power each pulse used, how fast the capacity bank could be recharged, and how soon the laser could fire again—all pertinent information they'd need to know in the heat of a battle.

"We got our initial set of information, Captain. We now need to test the system under a sustained stress test. Can we begin that test now?" asked one of the engineers.

"Weps, please find us a few more targets and continue testing the weapons as the engineers requested," Hunt ordered. He then pinged his engineering chief. "Commander Lyons, how are things holding up down there?"

A few seconds later, his chief engineering officer, Commander Jacob Lyons, responded, "It appears to be going well. One of my guys reported that the starboard power relay spiked to above normal levels when we fired, but it didn't cause any problems."

Hunt pushed his lower lip out in a semi-pout. "Lieutenant LaFine, check fire on the test. There's an issue in the power relay on the starboard side I want to be checked out first."

Several of the engineers perked their heads up at the news. One of them walked over to him. "Captain, can you tell us what section? We'll send a team over there now to check on it. We may need to beef up the system if it's spiking beyond tolerable levels," the man replied.

Nodding, Hunt gave him the relay junction location, and a group of them headed off to inspect the section. This was one of the things that concerned Hunt about adding all this new technology. His ship hadn't been built initially with the needed tolerances or systems to use the alien tech, so everything they were doing was being thrown together in hopes that it would work.

Four hours later, they determined what the problem was and found a solution. It took the engineers a full day to correct the problem. The next step was to test the laser banks again and see if it had worked.

Hunt had them run through several test fires of the laser, each shot increasing in power until they reached their maximum. The engineers monitored the relay junctions throughout the ship with each pulse burst, checking to see if the cables were holding up and the relay boxes were functioning the way they needed to. After three more days of tests, they were able to certify that the ship was ready for combat—the first human ship fully equipped with the new Zodark and Sumerian technology.

Chapter Twenty-Two
Punch in the Face

Rhea System
RNS *Rook*

"We're coming out of warp in ten seconds," called out the helmsman, Lieutenant Donaldson. He'd been with Captain Hunt since their first visit to this system.

"OK, people, this is it. When we land, I want a full system-wide scan. Go active with everything we have. Understood?" Hunt ordered as he looked at his tactical officer, Commander Fran McKee. It would be her responsibility to coordinate with the CIC and the other sections on the bridge to generate the tactical picture of the system. This information was vital in determining what they'd do next. Tactical was a big department on the ship, and thus, Fran McKee was third in line for command.

McKee nodded, a serious look on her face. "Yes, sir, we're standing by." She'd been drilling her section hard, making sure everyone knew exactly what they had to do the moment the ship dropped out of FTL drive in any system, not just a potentially hostile one.

The *Rook* had been in transit now for twelve days, a much shorter trip than the six and a half months it had taken them last time. What they were unsure of was what would be waiting for them when they arrived. Prior to leaving the system the previous time, they had liberated a mining colony and wiped out the Zodark guards manning it. Hunt was eager to see if the Zodarks had noticed and, if they did, what they planned on doing about it.

Before Hunt's mind could go any further down this rabbit hole, the ship came out of warp and stopped one AU from the planet New Eden, or Clovis to the Sumerians and Zodarks.

"Helmsman, transition us out of FTL and over to the MPD drive. I want us moving at one-quarter propulsion toward New Eden," Hunt directed as his crew went to work.

Looking over at Fran, Hunt saw she had her folks getting things spun up, just like she had drilled them many times before. The various electronic detection antennas were being extended, radar domes raised out of their armor sheathing and brought online. Her department was gearing up the ship's multiple targeting systems and electronic detection equipment. Their radar and lidar systems would blast the system with a full spectrum of radio waves. In short order, her team in the combat information center or CIC room behind the bridge would start analyzing the data returns and begin alerting them to what was in the area that posed a threat to the ship.

A few minutes went by with nothing significant happening. Visually, they couldn't see anything yet. They'd have to wait until they started to get some electronic returns from their various scans to know what was in the system. Depending on how far away a Zodark ship was, it could take them a little while to get a picture of the system and who all was in it. In the meantime, they'd start heading toward New Eden and see what they could find planetside.

I hope the Voyager was able to slip in undetected, Hunt thought as he patiently waited for his tactical officer to start receiving some signal returns. He knew that it was an incredibly dangerous plan Space Command had thrown together, but he also knew that it needed to happen before they sent a more significant force to New Eden.

Two hours later, they started getting their first picture of the system. Sure enough, a Zodark ship was in high orbit over New Eden. It appeared like it had detected their presence and was in the process of breaking orbit.

"Tactical, how long until we're in weapons range of the Zodark ship?" Commander Asher Johnson asked. Hunt's XO was just as eager as he was to get things going with the Zodarks.

McKee calmly replied in her usual measured voice, "Commander, it would appear they are still in the process of breaking orbit. I'll have a better answer once I know how fast their propulsion system is. However, at their current speed, they'll be in weapons range in six hours."

Hunt turned to Lieutenant Commander Robinson, his EWO or electronic warfare officer. "Start monitoring the enemy ship for electronic signatures. I want to know what type of targeting sensors they're using. Once you figure that out, get with the guys in CIC and figure out if we can jam them or degrade their effectiveness."

"Roger that, Captain. We'll get right on it," Robinson quickly replied.

Electronic warfare was an art form and a significant component of warfare on Earth. Space Command was hoping it would be just as useful

in space combat as it was in the air, on the ground, and at sea with conventional forces. Space Command had been testing this capability in Sol with great success. Jamming an opponent's target systems could render them inoperable when they needed them most. It might give the Republic ships just the time they needed to deliver a fatal blow.
****

Several hours went by as the Earthers moved steadily toward the Zodark ship.

"Coms, hail the Zodarks on all known frequencies. Use our preprogrammed message in their language and let's see if we can open a dialogue with them before we get in weapons range," Hunt ordered.

He crossed his fingers. *Maybe, just maybe, they'll want to talk this time*, he hoped. Their last attempt hadn't gone very well.

Twenty minutes went by with no response. Hunt had to keep telling himself there was a lot of distance between the *Rook* and this Zodark ship. He needed to stay patient and wait. In the meantime, he had the CIC analyzing what they knew of the enemy ship in comparison to the ship that had been in the system the last time they were here.

What they knew thus far was that this ship was larger than the last one—about twice the size of the previous ship they had encountered and fifty percent larger than their own ship. This Zodark ship also appeared to be a straight-up warship, given the appearance of several laser pulse batteries on the vessel. Looking back on it, Hunt wasn't sure if the other ship they had encountered their last time in the system had perhaps been a transport. What *was* clear was that these two ships had very different purposes.

After thirty minutes, Lieutenant Molly Branson, his coms officer, announced, "Captain, we're not getting a response from the ship."

Before Hunt could say anything, Commander McKee jumped in. "Captain, we're detecting a targeting radar or sensor attempting to paint our ship."

Hunt turned to his EWO officer. "Commander, see if you can jam that signal. No reason to let them get a perfectly good lock on us if we can avoid it," Hunt directed. He then brought the ship to general quarters. This would lead the crew to begin sealing the vessel up and rouse everyone out of their beds to man their battle stations.

"We're jamming their signal. It looks like they're unable to maintain a lock," called out the EWO officer excitedly.

Hunt smiled at the news. One of their critical tests against the Zodark ships was successfully completed.

"Captain, the enemy ship is picking up speed. They're heading toward us at a much faster pace now," announced Commander McKee, her voice moving up an octave with excitement.

This was precisely what they had thought would happen. Once the enemy realized their targeting radar was being jammed or degraded, they'd close the distance between their ships and try to break through the jamming.

"How long until they're in weapons range?" Hunt asked, trying to do some quick calculations in his head. The tension on the bridge picked up noticeably as the realization that they would be in combat in a few minutes began to sink in.

"At current speed, five minutes. They're still close to four hundred megameters[1] out," replied Lieutenant Cory LaFine, his weapons officer. He looked at Hunt, anxious about what to do next when they reached their weapons envelope.

"Weps, if that Zodark ship fires its lasers on us, I need you to deploy the SWs. Don't ask for permission, just do it. We won't have much time if they attack. Understood?" Hunt ordered.

Lieutenant LaFine nodded.

The SW missiles were a combination of sand and water packed into a little high-speed missile that would explode between them and the enemy ship, creating a cloud of sand and water crystals. The belief was that this cloud would dampen the force of the enemy laser before it hit them. It was a completely untested theory, though.

Turning to look at his coms officer, Hunt asked, "Are we continuing to hail them?"

"We are, sir. They're still not replying."

He shook his head. *Well, if they want a fight, we'll give 'em a fight.*

"Helm, bring us up to full speed. Prepare to swing us to their starboard side so we can get a good broadside with our magrails. Weps, prepare missiles one through six to fire. Power up our forward pulse

---

[1] A megameter is one thousand kilometers, so four hundred megameters is 400,000 kilometers

beam batteries and let's get our magrails ready to go," Hunt ordered as a flurry of activity started to take place on the bridge.

While the ship had a large magazine of ship-to-ship missiles and four pulse beam laser batteries, two on each side of the ship, the *Rook*'s primary ship-to-ship weapon was her three magrail turrets. Like the dreadnought ships of a few hundred years ago, the *Rook* had three forward gun turrets. Each turret had two twenty-four-inch magrails that would fire a five-thousand-pound projectile at speeds approaching thirty megameters[2] per hour. The armored tip of the penetrator was designed to punch through up to six meters of advanced composite armor before detonating a two-thousand-pound high-explosive warhead inside the guts of an enemy vessel.

"One minute till we're in range of our missiles," called out Lieutenant LaFine as he prepared to fire their first weapon system at the charging enemy ship.

"The Zodark ship is starting to reacquire us with their targeting radar. They're burning through our jamming," Commander Robinson announced urgently.

Hunt anxiously shouted, "Increase power to our jammers. Keep trying to jam their systems!" He wanted to keep them from getting a solid lock on his ship for as long as possible—he had no idea how powerful their weapons were or what kind of range they had.

"Enemy ship is slowing. They're starting to position themselves to come across our starboard side," called out the tactical officer. Sweat was now beading on her forehead and running down the side of her face.

"The Zodark ship is now one hundred and eighty megameters and closing quick. He's got a lock on us…they're firing!" Commander McKee blared moments later.

"Launching countermeasures!" Lieutenant LaFine announced.

A pair of SW missiles shot out ahead of them to create an antilaser barrier between them.

Fractions of a second later, the automated warning alarm blared "Brace for impact!" throughout the ship.

The high-energy pulse beam hit the sandy-watery cloud, dissipating some of its energy before it slammed into the forward section of the ship.

---

[2] Thirty megameters per hour is 30,000 kilometers per hour

The *Rook* shook violently from the hit as alarms sounded on the bridge, letting them know they had sustained some damage.

"Hull breach in section one bravo. Sending damage control teams there now," called out Lieutenant Arnold, Hunt's operations officer.

"Fire missiles one through six. Engage them with our laser batteries!" Hunt yelled over the alarms. "Someone turn those damn things off," he added for good measure.

"Firing weapons now!" shouted Lieutenant LaFine. "Missiles away. Firing lasers now." The thundering sound of the ship-to-ship missiles caused their pods to shudder, letting everyone know they had left for their targets. Moments later, the two starboard pulse beam batteries fired a three-second burst. The two lasers hit the side of the enemy ship, ripping a couple of holes in the armor but failing to penetrate deeper into the hull.

"Firing countermeasures!" someone shouted as they continued to throw more objects to defray the enemy laser's potency.

"Brace for impact!"

The *Rook* shook violently again as it was hit with a second laser, ripping another gash in its armor. More warning alarms went off, letting them know a couple of sections of the hull had been breached.

"Helm, rotate the ship and engage maneuvering thrusters!" yelled the XO as he tried to get the enemy laser off the *Rook*'s armor.

Lieutenant Arnold yelled out, "We've got a hull breach in section three delta. We're venting oxygen in deck two. There's also a fire in section six."

"Fire the main guns!" Hunt roared angrily, frustrated at the damage his ship was taking. He knew he'd lost people—he just didn't know how many yet.

The ship shook as the hefty projectiles of the main guns started firing at the enemy vessel. The three front turrets fired their twenty-four-inch magrails, sending the massive armor-piercing slugs at the Zodark vessel. The turrets would continue to fire until their magazines were depleted.

Hunt ordered the main guns to keep firing. He wanted them to blanket the path of the enemy ship with slugs, hoping the AI targeting computer would be able to plot a thick enough smattering to ensure a good number of them hit the ship. It would take roughly six minutes for their slugs to reach the enemy ship.

The *Rook* shook hard again as they took another hit from the enemy's pulse beam. Each time they took a hit, the helmsman would execute an emergency course change to get the enemy laser beam off their armor.

As the ship continued a series of twisting turns and dips to throw the enemy lasers off, Hunt watched as the first set of armor-piercing shells tore right into the Zodark ship. The initial volley punched right through its armor. The slugs penetrated deep into its hull, and then the two thousand pounds of high explosives went off. Jets of flame shot out the six holes the *Rook* had caused. Then a series of secondary explosions rocked the Zodark vessel further.

"They're maneuvering to dodge our incoming slugs," called out one of the targeting officers.

Seeing their initial success, Hunt roared with rage and excitement, "Keep firing the magrails—pump 'em full of holes!"

"Enemy vessel is attempting to turn away and put some more distance between them and us," called out Commander McKee from tactical.

"Missiles should impact in five seconds," called out Lieutenant LaFine gleefully.

The continued thundering booms of the magrail turrets were music to their ears. The steady stream of slugs being thrown at the enemy vessel scored hit after hit. The enemy vessel became consumed with more and more fires and explosions as the slugs continued to find pay dirt. When the Zodark ship made a sharp maneuvering turn, a string of thirty slugs completely missed.

The gunners on the *Rook* adjusted to the course change and started leading the enemy vessel with their guns. Between the three turrets, they were able to blanket several possible locations the enemy vessel could maneuver into and still score some hits, especially now that the two ships had closed to less than thirty megameters.

Then the six Hammerhead missiles impacted, their dual-stage warheads punching right through the ship's armor before the second stage of the warhead erupted inside the hull, spewing more flames and incendiary nastiness inside the vessel.

"Brace for impact!" called out the warning as another light beam arced out from the Zodark ship for them. It drilled into the *Rook* near the midsection of the ship for three seconds before the helmsman was able to get them out of the way.

A violent explosion shook the *Rook*. The lights and computer screens flickered off. When the power returned, the systems had to reboot themselves.

"What the hell happened?" demanded Hunt as he righted himself in his chair. Had he not been strapped in, he feared he would have been tossed about the room.

"Captain, Engineering, that last hit blew our power capacitors. We've got a three-meter hole on deck four, section eight," Commander Lyons said over Hunt's communicator.

"Damn it, Lyons, I need power. We need those magrails to stay operational. We need maneuvering thrusts!" barked Hunt angrily to his chief engineer.

"We're on it, Captain. I've got a couple dozen Synths en route to the damaged areas now. Give us twenty minutes, sir, and we'll be fully operational."

"Some systems are coming back online," called out one of the bridge crew members.

The main monitor flickered on, and they were starting to get an image of what was going on outside the ship again. Despite the damage they'd just sustained, the Zodark ship appeared to be in far worse shape. The steady stream of slugs the *Rook* had been firing continued to pummel them. They were still attempting to turn away and flee from the battle and put some distance between themselves and the *Rook*'s magrail guns.

Twenty painful minutes went by as they watched the distance that had been closing between their two ships start to grow as the enemy tried to limp away. Then the bridge lighting switched from their backup power to the primary power system.

Hunt's communicator chirped. "Captain, we've got the relay switches back online. We had to reroute power through our auxiliary network. I've got things held together with duct tape and superglue right now. You can use the magrails, but the lasers are out of the question," Commander Lyons explained.

"Great job, Commander. See what you can do to get us some power to the MPD thrusters. The enemy is trying to get away, and I'm not about to let them," Hunt roared with excitement.

"Resuming fire with the magrails," Lieutenant LaFine announced as the three turrets opened up. It was the only offensive weapon they had for the time being.

They watched as the magrail turrets sent a slew of projectiles at the Zodark vessel. The enemy ship was trying its best to evade some of the slugs, but it was clear the ship was in trouble. A handful of slugs tore into one of its engines and ripped it apart with a series of secondary explosions. Then the other engines winked out as the ship either lost power or lost propulsion. In either case, it was dead in the water.

Hunt unstrapped himself from his seat. As he stood, he looked at his weapons officer. "Tell the main guns to fire the remainder of their magazine and then cease fire. I think she's had it, but I want to make sure."

Moments later, part of the Zodark ship erupted as a series of secondary explosions and geysers of flame enveloped the front half of the ship. Then a series of smaller crafts began to disembark from the larger vessel—it looked like these were probably the escape pods.

The enemy was abandoning the ship.

It took another five minutes of fires spewing out the various holes in the ship before they finally went dark as the atmosphere feeding them was gone. The vessel exploded moments later, breaking apart in multiple chunks. Many of the life vessels appeared to have gotten outside the blast radius.

Looking at the debris and chunks of the destroyed ship before them, Hunt could barely believe what he was looking at. They had somehow survived Earth's first significant space battle.

Suddenly, Hunt remembered they still had alarms going off on the bridge. He'd been so focused on taking the enemy out, he had forgotten all about the damage they had taken themselves.

"Ops, damage report," barked Hunt. He felt his cheeks flush a bit as he realized he should have been checking on that throughout the battle. He'd allowed his focus to be solely on the enemy ship and not on the care of his own. That couldn't happen again.

"We're showing damage to the starboard forward and midsections of the ship. Decks one and two in sections alpha and bravo are venting oxygen and on fire. Damage control teams have the area sealed off, and we're going to depressurize it to put the fires out," Lieutenant Arnold said. "We also took some damage to section kilo on deck six. It doesn't look like it penetrated the armor, but it damaged the starboard MPD thruster."

"What about that hit we took to the midsection of the ship?" asked the XO.

Lieutenant Arnold pulled up a schematic of the ship. Multiple areas were showing yellow, and a few were showing red. "That hit to our midsection was actually pretty severe, sir—by far the worst damage we sustained. It looks like Engineering is still conducting a damage assessment, but as it stands, we have a three-meter gash in our midsection. It penetrated nearly halfway through the ship, some forty-eight meters deep." He paused for a moment before adding, "I think if they'd held that laser for two or three more seconds, they might have cut completely through us."

Blowing some air out his lips, Hunt realized they had really dodged a bullet. They had nearly been cut in half, or at least had a hole right through them. "What kind of hull damage are we looking at?"

Arnold shrugged. "That'd be a question for Commander Lyons."

"How many casualties?" Hunt's XO asked next.

"Right now, the medbay is reporting forty-two injured. Some of the sections and department chiefs are reporting in their numbers as well. It looks like sixty-three killed," Lieutenant Arnold explained.

Hunt grimaced at the news. He'd known they had probably lost a few dozen folks, but sixty-three, plus another forty-two injured—he wasn't ready to hear that a quarter of his crew had just been injured or killed.

"Thank you, Lieutenant Arnold. Are the damage control parties able to seal up the sections of the ship that have been hit?" asked his XO, Commander Johnson. "Make sure medical teams are getting the injured back to sickbay. Captain, if it's OK with you, I'll handle the damage control parties for you so you can finish handling the Zodarks."

Hunt nodded, letting his XO take charge of those duties so he could focus on the task at hand. Turning to his Ops lieutenant, he ordered, "Arnold, tell the shuttle bay to get our shuttles spun up. I want them to go out there and collect up the life pods. We'll bring them back to the ship. Tell the Deltas to be on standby to receive them. Also, send a message to the *Voyager* and ask them if they can help us collect some remnants of this Zodark ship. I think it'd be worth bringing some of it back with us for further study by DARPA."

The next six hours were pretty busy. The damage to the *Rook* had been partially repaired, at least enough to carry on with operations while the damage control parties worked on the more critical sections of the ship. They could still run at full thrusters for the time being. The FTL drive was down, not that they could make a jump anyway until they got the gaping holes in the ship repaired.

The *Voyager* and the *Rook* managed to scoop up one hundred and thirty-two Zodarks from the pods. They were going to be locked up in a holding facility on the *Voyager* for the time being.

The two ships had also brought aboard several broken-up chunks of the Zodark ship in hopes that their R&D departments could analyze the structure and composition of the hulls and the armor. The more they understood about the enemy ship's design and its flaws, the better off they'd be in a future engagement.

****

Ten hours later, the damage control teams were still working on getting the ship repaired enough so they could engage their FTL system. The hole the Zodark ship had bored through their midsection had damaged part of the structural integrity of the ship. The more they examined the problem, the more they realized how close a call it was that they hadn't been blown in half. The issue now was getting the ship repaired enough so they could get out of the system before another Zodark ship showed up. They were in no shape to fight.

As Hunt made his way down to inspect some of the damage, he had to take an alternate route to get there. Along the center spine of the ship was a transport system that allowed a person to traverse the ship pretty quickly. The system, however, had been heavily damaged by the laser blast.

When he got to the first sealed section, he saw two damage control workers explaining something to a handful of Synths, going over whatever they needed them to work on in the exposed section of the ship.

Just then, Commander Lyons came around the corner. "Oh, Captain. I was hoping I'd find you. The bridge said you were headed my way."

Hunt grimly asked, "How bad is it, Jake?"

Lyons turned serious. "It's bad, but it could have been worse."

"Are we going to be able to jump soon? I'd really like to get out of the system in case another Zodark ship shows up."

Lyons shrugged. "Right now, not a chance. I mean, we could, but I couldn't guarantee the ship wouldn't crumble under the pressure of the jump. We need a few hours to reinforce the superstructure and get a few more of the support areas shored up. We can't put the entire stress of the ship on a key section that's been damaged. We've got to get some of these other support sections repaired and sealed up. The Synths will get it done, and this is a repair we can make—but it's going to take us some time. Probably at least the rest of the day, maybe two to make sure we're OK."

Hunt shook his head in frustration. He had to keep reminding himself they had just survived a major space battle. They were lucky to be alive and dealing with these problems.

"Do what you can, Jake," he responded. "Just keep in mind if a Zodark ship arrives in the system, we may need to make an emergency FTL jump out. We won't survive another engagement in our current shape."

Commander Lyons nodded in agreement. "We'll do our best, Captain. You can count on that."

Two anxious days went by as they got the ship repaired enough to jump back to Earth. Finally, they felt confident enough in the repairs to use the FTL system. Now they'd travel back to Sol and hope the sacrifice they had just made was worth the sixty-two souls lost to test a weapon system and a few theories.

Chapter Twenty-Three
Terminators

Alamogordo, New Mexico
Walburg Industries

"I'm not comfortable with this, Admiral," Dr. Alan Walburg said, reiterating his concern about this program.

Admiral Bailey sighed audibly as he turned to look at the richest man in the world, who also happened to have a conscience. "Doctor, you've been shown a classified video of these Zodarks—what they are capable of doing and, more importantly, how they view us humans. You saw what a lone Zodark did on the *Voyager* when it broke out of the brig—and *that* wasn't even one of their soldiers. Can you imagine what they would do if they invaded Earth? This is a lot bigger than you or me."

Admiral Bailey had been growing impatient with the man's handwringing over what they were asking him to build. He kept going on and on about what had happened in the last war and not wanting it to happen again.

"I understand the threat this new alien species poses, Admiral. I'm just not sure if this is the best solution. It will take us years of development to even come close to training a combat Synth to have the same agility, alertness, and fighting capability as their human peers. Due to the legal and treaty restrictions on such weapons research, we've never looked into this. This isn't something that we can rapidly produce, Admiral."

"Doctor, I need you to understand something. If we have to attack the Zodarks with Republic Army soldiers, we're going to lose a lot of people. You've seen how they fight. Their size alone makes them incredibly hard to handle, and the fact that they have four arms that apparently their brain can effectively independently control makes them even more challenging. I'm not asking your company to replace human soldiers. I'm asking your company to help augment our guys on the ground and give us a better chance of winning," Bailey explained, trying to take a different approach to this impasse.

The doctor shook his head in frustration. "Admiral, I understand the problem, and I'm sympathetic. We can start the programming and training process now. But I need to set some expectations with you. It's going to take the better part of twelve months before the first combat Synths will even be ready to start their test trials.

"First, we need to figure out the type of body and shell we're going to give them. Then we need to test that shell for durability in combat. While that's taking place, we have to program its AI to think, act, and perform as a real human soldier would. What I would caution you on, Admiral, is allowing the programming to become intuitive and self-learning. If we go down that route, we could end up creating a machine that will become a smarter and more cunning fighter than our own people. I do not want to see a repeat of the last war. Please let us at least control how far we let the AI develop."

Bailey turned and looked out the office window at the factory floor for a moment. He hated to admit it, but Walburg had a point. The thought of being able to unleash a small army of super AI combat-trained synthetics on some Zodark worlds was appealing, but a repeat of the Synths going rogue—that was a risk not worth taking. It had nearly destroyed humanity the last time around. Technology and weapons had improved a lot since then. He didn't need an army of Synths suddenly deciding they didn't want to fight for humanity anymore and forming their own society.

Turning back to the doctor, Admiral Bailey nodded. "OK, Dr. Walburg, you've convinced me on that last part. I'll detach a platoon of Deltas and a platoon of RASs to work here at your facility. You can use them to run as many virtual and real-world simulations as you want to help train the AI. You need to get this program ramped up rapidly, though. I have no idea how big the Zodarks systems are or how many planets they control, but I can tell you this—we're going to do our best to liberate the human worlds and put an end to their barbaric rule and threat to humanity."

****

John Glenn Orbital Station
1st Fleet HQ

This feels like déjà vu all over again, Captain Hunt thought as he sat at the large conference table with half a dozen military and civilian officers on the other end.

"Captain, can you please tell us what happened to the enemy ship when you fired your pulse beam weapons?" asked one of the TPA admirals. He leaned forward as he waited to hear Hunt's response.

Hunt tried to maintain a neutral expression. "Admiral, as you'll see from the reports and the videos of the engagement, our pulse beams were not powerful enough to cut through the Zodarks' armor. I can't say for sure how thick their armor is or the composition of it to fully know why. From the videos, you can see our laser never made it through."

The admiral appeared simultaneously pleased with the reply and alarmed by what it meant. He jotted a few notes down. Another admiral, this time from Space Command, asked, "Why did you engage the enemy ship with your missiles first, then the pulse beams, and then the magrails? What were you hoping to achieve by engaging them in this particular sequence?"

Hunt tried to hide his frustration at the question. He had to remember, none of these men had ever been involved in space combat. No one had. Despite all these weapon systems having been built into their shiny toys over the decades, they'd never actually had to use them against another ship. So no one had any idea how to really fight in their starships.

Captain Hunt sat forward in his chair to give the appearance of someone trying to convey something personal to them. "Admiral, this decision about which weapons to use and when was largely based on the effective distances of the enemy in comparison to our ship more than any tactical choice or decision on my part. The missiles are perhaps our slowest weapon, so we fired them first so they could maneuver into position."

He continued, "We fired our pulse beams next. As you know, a laser weapon is almost instantaneous. When we fired, the enemy ship was roughly one hundred and ten megameters away. As you can see, the lasers had a minimal effect when they hit.

"We then started firing the magrails, but at these distances and speeds, it was going to take close to six minutes for them to hit. So we had the batteries do their best to spread their slugs where we thought the enemy ship would be in six to eight minutes. While all of this was happening, we fired a series of SW missiles to try and interfere with their laser shots. By and large, they had little effect. That could be because we don't fully understand how to use them correctly, or because they were just not creating a thick enough debris field between us and the enemy ship to really dampen the laser."

Hunt tried to be patient. He knew they had all read the reports and seen the videos, but nothing beat a firsthand account of what had transpired. Before anyone else could ask him another question, Hunt added, "If I may, Admirals, I'd like to explain why I think our ship survived this engagement and why we succeeded in ultimately destroying the Zodark vessel."

The group collectively nodded for him to proceed, ready to hear what he had to say. He proceeded to regale them with a detailed play-by-play of the encounter, starting from the beginning. They hung breathlessly on every word.

By the time Hunt finished giving them a summary of the battle, the admirals and engineers in the room looked pleased at the outcome but also nervous about the results. He'd outlined what had worked but also identified some significant shortcomings in both Earth's current ship designs and weapon systems.

The enemy's ability to detect their ships from further out was certainly an issue. The pulse beam batteries were supposed to be the primary weapons on warships because lasers almost instantaneously hit their target when fired, but they had been completely ineffective against the Zodarks. The missiles, while useful, were the slowest weapon in the inventory. The magrails, while tried and proven, had limits because it took them time to cross the distance between ships, and if the enemy ship moved, they missed—it would require a huge number of slugs in an almost shotgun effect in hopes that a few of them would score some hits.

The one advantage the Earthers now had was that they had beaten a Zodark ship and lived to tell about it. They could incorporate what had worked and build on the success of it while they looked to overcome the deficiencies in their current tech.

The meeting lasted another hour as the admirals turned their attention to Admiral Halsey, whose ship had mainly observed the battle from a distance. They wanted to know what data she had been able to collect from the sidelines and what she believed could be done differently. When the admirals had completed their lines of questioning, the meeting was finally ended.

Hunt couldn't have been happier when he was finally released from that room. He was tired of having to relive that event and even more sick of having to recount his failures as a commander. They had won the battle, but the loss of a quarter of his crew still stung. That wasn't a feeling that went away with a couple of days' sleep or a few bottles of bourbon. It would take time, and time wasn't something they had—and he knew it.

"Captain Hunt!" called out Admiral Bailey before he could slip away.

Hunt saw the admiral waving for him to come over and talk to him and Admiral Halsey. He knew he couldn't duck whatever was coming, so he did his best to put on a happy face and meandered over.

"Sir, how can I be of assistance?" he said with a smile that belied how he truly felt inside. Last night he had finally written the last next-of-kin letter. It was all he could do not to drown himself in a bottle and hide under a rock. He'd spent thirty minutes in the shower this morning, just trying to sober himself up for this meeting.

As Hunt approached, Admiral Bailey looked at him for a moment. Hunt knew he probably could tell he was having a hard time. He didn't say anything to him about it—at least not publicly. But he'd probably hear about it in private.

As the other brass left the room, Bailey explained, "Miles, that was a very informative brief you gave us. We're going to have to make a lot of adjustments to our ship construction. Speaking of which, I'm hosting a meeting after lunch with Musk Industries and BlueOrigin to discuss the revised specs for the new battleships and destroyers we're going to start building. I'd like you and Admiral Halsey to attend. If we're going to tackle this Zodark threat, we need firsthand information on how best to design our new warships to meet this challenge."

Captain Hunt leaned in toward the admiral. "Sir, have our analysts had any further luck deciphering the captured enemy material yet?" he inquired.

When the *Rook* and *Voyager* had picked up the survivors from the doomed Zodark ship, they'd captured a fair bit of material on them and amongst the wreckage. Hunt was hoping there might have been some useful information uncovered.

Bailey nodded. "As a matter of fact, yes. The Sumerian team has been incredibly helpful. I'm not sure how you guys did it, but apparently, one of the chunks of the blown-up ship you brought back happened to house part of the ship's data cores. One of the Sumerians insists we've got a functional copy of the ship's star map. If that's so, then it means we have a working knowledge of their entire empire and where the other occupied human worlds are."

Hunt's eyes went wide as saucers. "If that's true, Admiral, then this is a remarkable piece of intelligence, one I would love to exploit," Hunt said with a smile. He was itching for some payback for the crew members he had lost.

"I agree, Captain," Bailey said with a nod. "Let's meet back up at my office ten minutes prior to fourteen hundred hours. The two shipbuilders are going to present their initial ship concepts to us. I'd like your take on their designs before we move forward with one of them. Once we finalize the plans, we'll begin full production."

With that, Admiral Bailey concluded their little sidebar. He left to head off to his next appointment, leaving Hunt and Halsey to themselves for a few hours.

They looked at each other. "Want to grab some lunch, Miles?" Halsey asked.

"Yeah, that sounds good, Abby. I need a break," Hunt said with a nod.

Halsey smiled. "Despite hundreds of years of military evolution, death by PowerPoint continues to persist," she said with a chuckle.

****

After a meal, Captain Hunt found himself sitting in a room listening to a briefer from BlueOrigin discuss the new ship designs. "As you can see, the *Ryan*-class battleship has four pulse beam laser batteries: two located in the fore section of the ship, and two in the rear, giving the ship the ability to engage multiple targets from several different vantage points. The ship is also equipped with twenty-four ship-to-ship missiles for long-range engagements. These are our newest generation of Havoc missiles with four booster phases of guidable range. They can be fitted with either a ten-thousand-pound warhead or a variable-yield nuclear warhead, depending on the target."

As he spoke, they watched several 3-D renderings of the ship, followed by a cinematic video they'd created of it in action. The briefer was obviously proud of the design and the ship's capabilities.

"What's the armor belt of the ship like?" asked one of the naval captains as he flipped through a few pages of notes looking for something.

"The ship is double-hulled," the briefer quickly replied. "The most critical functions of the ship are located in the inner hull, which has a two-meter belt of armor separating it from the outer hull of the ship. The outer hull has a four-meter armor belt with both modulated and reactive armor to handle both kinetic and energy-based weapon impacts."

"What about magrails? I didn't see any listed," commented one of the other officers at the table.

The briefer nodded. "The ship has ten 40mm magrail batteries. These are more for intercepting smaller craft and kinetic projectiles fired at the ship."

Admiral Halsey and Captain Hunt exchanged skeptical glances at each other. This looked like it'd be a great ship if they were fighting the Tri-Parte Alliance, but they didn't look like they'd fare well against a Zodark ship, not with that level of armor and no heavy magrails.

The BlueOrigin briefer must have seen their interplay, because he directed his next question to them. "Uh, excuse me, Captain Hunt, you've fought the Zodarks. If you'd had the *Ryan*-class battleship at the time of the fight, how well do you believe it would have fared?"

Hunt looked at Admiral Bailey as if asking for permission to be blunt. Bailey nodded but smiled ever so softly.

Hunt let out a deep breath before he answered the man's question. "If I had been commanding this vessel during the battle, chances are I wouldn't be here. The outer armor belt isn't thick enough. When we got hit with the Zodarks' pulse beam, it cut through the *Rook*'s armor like a hot knife through butter. Our own pulse beam battery wasn't able to cut through their armor and get into their hull. We had to rely on the magrails to do that, and sadly, your ship isn't equipped with anything large enough to get the job done," Hunt explained. He continued to go over the different aspects of the ship and how they would have held up against the Zodark vessel they had encountered.

By the time Hunt and Halsey had picked apart the BlueOrigin ship, the poor fellow looked like he wanted nothing more than to sulk back to where he had come from.

Musk Industries was next on deck, and sadly their design featured a lot of the same flaws. Both companies had proposals for a new battleship based on their assumptions about how the first Zodark ship looked and what they thought its weapons were capable of. In light of the recent engagement Hunt and Halsey had just experienced, it had quickly become apparent that the current crop of ship designs wasn't going to cut it.

When the meeting was over, Hunt asked if the two briefers could stick around for a few minutes. With Admiral Bailey's blessing, he had the two men bring up a clean design of a ship—no armaments, just a shell. Hunt then used a stylus and elongated the ship, stretching it to forty-five hundred meters in length, five hundred meters in height and five hundred meters in width. He then flattened the ship a bit with a slight rise in the center and bottom of the ship, where he proposed the electronic suite of equipment would be located. The bridge and the CIC would be located in the center of the ship, where it was most heavily protected. Across the entire top and bottom of the ship, he drew a line of six squat turrets on the top of the port side of the vessel, and another six on the bottom. Then he matched them with another twelve on the starboard ship, covering the top and the bottom of the ship. It was similar to how a twentieth-century battleship might have looked, only this ship had weapons on both sides.

On the turrets, he placed three thirty-six-inch magrails, giving the ship a total of forty-eight port and starboard main guns on the top of the ship, and the same number on the bottom. Intermixed between the primary turrets, Hunt drew a total of eight pulse beam laser turrets on either side of the battleship. This would give the ship sixteen pulse beam lasers. Below the primary line of guns, he drew in twelve smaller turrets on either side of the ship. These were the secondary magrail turrets, which would fire dual twenty-four-inch slugs.

Between the primary and secondary magrail turrets, the ship would be able to unload an enormous barrage of slugs at an adversary. This was critical because at a hundred megameters, a ship could move, and dozens, even hundreds of slugs could miss. It was important to be able to throw a huge barrage of projectiles at various positions the enemy ship could move to and hope one or more of the firing patterns would score some hits. The primary and secondary turrets could also be used to hit targets on a planet during an orbital bombardment—something the shipbuilders hadn't even considered in their original designs.

Along the sides of the ship, below the turrets and near the centerline of the vessel, Hunt drew a series of missile launch tubes. He counted them out, listing thirty-six on each side of the battleship. This would give them some long-range punching power with the new variant of ship-to-ship missiles being produced.

For close-in protection, Hunt added one hundred seven-barreled twenty-millimeter gun batteries. They were placed in various positions around the ship so they'd be able to provide numerous overlapping fields of fire to support each other. Unlike the other projectile-driven weapons, this platform was going to make use of standard liquid propellant rather than railguns. This would ensure the guns could maintain a very high cyclic rate of fire for self-defense actions.

Just when the engineers thought Hunt was done, he drew an extendable flight deck on the bottom of the ship. He left that section a bit more vague for the designers to come up with something, but he made sure they knew it should either be retractable into the lower section of the ship during ship-to-ship combat or heavily armored and able to sustain a lot of hits. He also annotated that they'd need to see if his proposal to include weapons on the belly of the ship would still be possible. Ideally, they'd want to have some weapons down there, even if they couldn't have the full gambit. Space combat was fought in three dimensions; it wasn't linear.

Interrupting him, one of the engineers asked, "This flight deck you've mentioned—do you intend it to handle flight operations for some sort of starfighter, or is this kind of like the orbital assault ships?"

Hunt paused for a moment to think. "If we build a warship like this, we have to keep in mind that this ship is probably going to last for at least a hundred years if it isn't destroyed—meaning we need to anticipate how technology is going to change and make sure we're designing a ship that can keep up with that change. As you've previously noted, we currently do not have starfighters. But that won't always be the case.

"Initially, I think the flight deck will primarily be used to support either Special Forces or Republic Army soldiers, probably at least a battalion-level unit, though if we could, fitting at least two battalions and their equipment on the ship would give it an incredible amount of versatility. In reality, this ship is large enough that you could probably design at least two separate flight bays. Perhaps one could be dedicated to handling fighters while the other handles the ground forces. The point is, this ship needs to handle a multitude of taskings and missions, gentlemen."

Another engineer asked, "How thick of an armor belt do you believe this thing should be wrapped in?"

"Based on the strength of the Zodark pulse beam and the damage it inflicted on my own ship, I recommend we wrap the ship in twelve meters of armor around the critical functions and weapon platforms while the rest of the ship is encased in eight meters. This'll allow us to protect the most vital parts of the ship to keep it in the fight while reducing the volume of armor on some of the lesser critical portions," Hunt explained as he drew a few notes on the side of the tablet.

"Now, I'm not sure how you guys can make this better, but we need to find a way to improve those SW antilaser weapons and integrate them across the ship. We need some type of defense against their lasers, particularly when we encounter multiple enemy ships at the same time. I'd also recommend adding dozens of maneuvering thrusters to aid in turning and shifting the ship when it starts to take a hit. We can't allow the enemy lasers to stay fixed on a single spot on the armor, or they'll burn their way through it."

Once Hunt had gone over the outer weapon systems, he broke down the internal guts of what they absolutely had to have. Mainly, he wanted two Trimarian reactors, not just one. This would increase the power to the pulse beams, but more than that, he explained his idea for improving the ship's ability to jam the enemy's sensors and communications. He reiterated the importance of forcing the Zodark ships to get within knife range to engage them. That was when their magrails would be able to tear them apart.

When Hunt had finished explaining what he thought would make an exceptional warship, one of the shipbuilders finally blurted out, maybe in frustration, that something this complicated and broad would take years to design and build. He proposed that they build a fleet of smaller ships that could be more easily produced; they could be used in a swarm rather than relying on a couple of large juggernauts.

"I don't disagree with your suggestion," Hunt replied. "Creating a few squadrons of capable destroyers is certainly a viable option. Right now, we don't know if the Zodark ship we fought was a standard-size ship or if they have larger, more capable warships. The destroyer idea you proposed is not bad, but it'd take more than one of them to take out a Zodark ship, and its armor wouldn't be nearly as thick as even the *Rook*'s was when we went toe-to-toe with this one. If we were to build a handful of battleships like I drew up and then fielded them with a handful of these destroyers, I think we could create a very formidable fleet to take them on."

One of the other admirals jumped in to add his own point. "I think you're both right. We need to move down a track of building out as many of these destroyers as we can while also beginning work on these battleships that'll eventually anchor the fleet. Right now, I'm concerned that we don't have a proper fleet to defend Sol, let alone take the fight to the enemy. We need to secure our home system first, and then we can look to expand outwards."

"We *need* to capture and hold New Eden," Admiral Halsey interjected. "Whether we like it or not, we need the Trimar and Morean mineral deposits. The planet has several extensive deposits of the mineral, and we'll need it for future ship construction, or none of this will matter."

They had a sudden realization, which was that they'd been talking about building this massive fleet without considering that they'd need to capture New Eden first—with that realization, their grandiose plans came to a halt. They needed New Eden, no two ways about it. Now, the question was how best to capture it with the resources they had on hand.

Chapter Twenty-Four
The Belt

Asteroid Belt—Sol
Gaelic Trading Outpost

As Captain Liam Patrick approached the immense asteroid, he could see more than two dozen ships of various sizes all docked at the different docking arms connecting them to the man-made port carved into the giant floating piece of rock.

Fifteen years we've been slaving away at this—it's finally going to happen, Captain Liam Patrick thought as his shuttle approached the station.

"I can't wait for you to see the final touches we've made to the station while you've been gone," Sara Alma said as she squeezed him excitedly.

Looking around the shuttle, Liam felt an energy and excitement he hadn't felt in a very long time. Turning a massive asteroid, practically a planetoid, into a habitable station was no easy feat. It had taken them the better part of fifteen years working in secrecy. Liam wasn't proud of what he'd done to make this dream a reality—the piracy, stealing, and killing.

Liam's shuttle connected to the docking arm, making a few mechanical clunks and noises. A couple of minutes later, the hatch sealed. One of the shuttle crewmen unlocked the connecting doors and opened them up to the station.

"Come on, Liam. You have to see this," Sara beckoned as she grabbed his hand and pulled him along. She was like a giddy little girl dragging her parents into the toy store the day after Thanksgiving to start buying Christmas presents.

Walking off the shuttle, Liam followed Sara as she dragged him through the hangar where the ships would dock to the station and they would offload cargo. The terminal of sorts was immediately connected with the local warehouses and storage facilities. This would facilitate the various trade functions that would take place at the station.

Moving past this section of the docking port, the two of them followed the other passengers as they made their way through the corridor toward the vast promenade that lay beyond. This part of the station had some digital signs providing newcomers some necessary information about the station as well as the rules they'd need to abide by.

Next, there was an entry control point all new arrivals had to pass through. Here, they'd have to register with the station. They'd be given some information about where they could stay, job openings, and other residency and permits they might need to acquire. They also had to pay a visa fee—all part of monetizing the station and paying for the services it'd be providing its residences and visitors.

As they made their way through the long hallway that connected the outer part of the station with its inner works, Liam started to hear a lot of people talking excitedly and laughing. As they got closer to the noise, it suddenly began to calm until it was practically gone.

Liam smiled when he realized what was going on. Sara had arranged some sort of surprise or welcome home party for him.

When they exited the corridor, he saw a massive crowd of people waiting there for him with bright smiles on their faces, holding up handheld signs. Kids sat on their parents' shoulders, and a loud, raucous cheer erupted.

"Surprise!" they yelled in unison.

Liam felt his face redden at all the attention. His heart skipped a beat when he saw that all these people had come to welcome him—the man who had fought so hard and risked everything to build this oasis in the stars.

Well-wishers came forward and shook his hand. Others wanted to get their picture taken with him. Many just wanted to say thank you for creating a welcoming place and a new home—a home away from the central governments and politics of Earth, a place where people could start over.

A short while later, Sara pried him away from all the people and began to take him on a private tour of their new refuge in the stars.

Craning his head up to look at the expansiveness of the station, he couldn't believe they had finally gotten this place livable. It had taken them nearly ten years to carve out the center of this enormous floating rock. Once they had, they started turning the inside of it into a functional living facility. The ground floor of the asteroid was approximately three kilometers by two and a half kilometers. In height, it was twelve hundred meters tall. It was a giant cavern they had turned into apartments, businesses, shops, a school, hospital, research centers, and agricultural and farming facilities. In terms of food, they were completely self-sufficient.

Along the sides of the stone walls hung intricate flowery vines and other plants. Interspersed throughout the station were small sections with large bamboo trees and other trees and shrubs that would act as carbon sinks to help keep the air clean and fresh. They had a state-of-the-art water reclamation and treatment facility and their own artificial gravity generator to make it all work. What they needed now was people—that was the reason for Liam's recent absence.

"Come this way," Sara said with a mischievous look. She led him over to the foyer entrance to the largest building in the facility. They walked over to an elevator bank and climbed into the first one that arrived.

Moments later, they were getting off on the top floor. The one-hundred-and-eightieth level to be precise. Sara coyly led him over to a large double oak door. The hallway itself was ornately decorated with beautiful marble floors that had been specially delivered from Italy. The top floor of this building was truly marvelous. Sara waved her hand near a small electronic pad, and the doors hissed softly as they unlocked. Smiling, she led him into the penthouse suite.

As she walked into what was perhaps the most elegant living space Liam had ever seen, Sara waved her arms about. "These, love, are our new quarters. No more living on a cramped ship. No more having to share our living arrangements with dozens of workers. We have this two-hundred-square-meter flat to ourselves. The new residents of Gaelic insisted on turning this place into a bona fide palace in the stars for us."

Sara gave him a quick tour of the place, making sure he saw everything. Then she walked toward the largest room in the suite, the grand living room. It was adorned with some famous paintings, a bookshelf with actual books on it, and several framed pictures of the two of them over the years.

While all that was great, the view of the outpost below was incredible. The suite had floor-to-ceiling windows overlooking what they had spent more than fifteen years building.

Turning to look at him, Sara beamed with pride. "The view from this living room is unrivaled in the station. You can see just about anything you want from this vantage point while also knowing that no one can see inside. Our suite is also completely sealed from the outside.

So if, God forbid, there was ever a containment breach and the facility was compromised, we could survive in this suite for months until help arrived."

Shaking his head at what Sara had accomplished during his absence, Liam sauntered toward her. His eyes clearly fixated on the most beautiful woman he'd ever known, the one and only true love of his life.

Sara smiled coyly. Reaching her right hand up to her shoulder-length curly blond hair, she twirled it briefly as she turned her body to look out the window. Liam made his way up behind her, pulling his body tight against hers as he wrapped his arms around her. Brushing the hair away from the left side of her head, he leaned in, his lips brushing against her ear.

"You truly are amazing, Sara," he whispered softly.

Sara squirmed a bit in his embrace, turning around so she could look him in the eyes. "I couldn't have done any of this without you, Liam. I love you."

She leaned in and kissed him on the lips with the fire and passion of a woman who hadn't seen her man for a long time. The two continued to kiss, and in barely any time at all, they were tearing each other's clothes off and passionately making love.

Several hours later, lying in their new bed together, Sara turned to look at him. "For a little while there, I wasn't sure if you were going to return."

Smiling softly as his hand brushed away some hair on her face, Liam gently replied, "I was starting to think the same thing at one point, Sara. I told the authorities at the MOS that our corporation would pony up half a billion dollars to be paid to the families of the piracy victims. I didn't have to admit my own role in it, just that employees in our company had been involved, and they had been dealt with."

Sara wrinkled her brow at him. "And they bought it? They didn't suspect that you were either involved or the leader of the pirate force?"

Liam chuckled. "Oh, I suspect they thought that. They probably would have done something about it too, if they weren't in such a frenzy over other matters. But I think their attention and focus is purely on the threat that new alien race poses and not some past acts of piracy.

"You should have seen the shipyard, Sara. That place is humming with activity. I've never seen so many warships being built. And not small ones either. Space Command is even building its own colossal shipyard. I've never seen anything like it. It has to be bigger than the entire MOS or even the John Glenn Station. It's enormous."

Turning over on her back, Sara sat up. "Really? How many of these warships did you see?"

Feeling himself starting to recover from their earlier romps, Liam didn't really want to talk about warships. He wanted to go for another round with the love of his life.

Seeing him looking at her like he wanted something, she quickly snapped him out of it. "Hey, Liam, this is important. We can have more sex later. How many warships did you see them building?"

A little annoyed, Liam let out a sigh as he lay back on the bed to look up at the ceiling. "I saw the hulls being laid for three new destroyers. They had also started construction on four other ships. I'm not sure what they are, but they look huge—probably two or three kilometers long. Probably a new battleship or something. Why are you suddenly so interested in what they're building? We've brokered an incredible deal with the Republic and the TPA. They're going to leave us alone here in the Belt to build our own little community. It's what we've always wanted."

Shaking her head in disagreement, Sara explained, "They're leaving us alone, Liam, because this new threat is serious. I know you haven't paid much attention to what's been going on, but the Republic apparently discovered some hideous new alien species that actually cultivates humans like cattle to feed their population. It's horrendous, Liam."

Liam snorted. "I've heard a few rumors about this new species. Some say they eat humans; others say humans are just slaves. I don't really know what's true, but right now, my only concern is making sure our people have food in their bellies, a place to sleep, and if at all possible, some money in their pockets."

"We *need* to start paying attention to this, Liam," Sara insisted. "We have a station to manage now—our own little world that's depending on us to do more than give them a job or a place to stay. We have to protect them. I think we need to start looking at creating our own self-defense force."

Liam almost laughed. "Our piracy days are over, love. The Republic and TPA now have frigates patrolling the Belt and the trade routes between everything these days. The shipyards aren't going to sell us warships when they're busy trying to build a fleet of them for the major powers."

Sara tilted her head to the right. "Then we build our own," she countered. "We're nearly done with our own shipyard. We can build our own ships, train our own people how to use them, and defend our outpost."

Liam shook his head. "No, we'd be better off turning the station into a well-defended fortress. We may have an endless supply of raw materials out here, but we lack a lot of essential technology and equipment we'd need to create real warships. I think we should look at creating our own pulse beam and magrail sentries we can anchor near the station or on some of the asteroids around us. We have the resources and money to do that, but not to build our own warships like you're proposing, at least not right away."

Sara pouted. She turned away for a moment before she finally sighed and turned back around. "OK, Liam, I concede your point. Sometimes my mind just races. I saw some images of those Zodark things and got scared. They're really evil creatures, Liam—terrifying. I just hope the Republic and this new alliance they're working on can take them out."

Smiling, Liam pulled her close to him. He softly whispered, "I'm sure they'll do fine. Now, let's get back to celebrating the completion of this station."

Chapter Twenty-Five
Decision Point

Kennedy Space Center
US Space Command

"So it's been decided?" questioned Captain Hunt, unsure if he was happy about the decision.

Admiral Bailey looked at him and Rear Admiral Halsey. "It has. You two will lead the assault force to capture New Eden and the Rhea system. Once we've secured a foothold, we'll look to turn the place into a fortress."

Admiral Halsey as she nodded at the news. "OK, are we going to wait until a few more of the ships are complete before we ship out?" she asked.

Once it had been decided that New Eden had to be captured, the shipbuilders had done a quick inventory of the Trimar and Morean they had left to see how many new ships they could build. They could build one battleship or eight destroyers. The decision had been made to build the eight smaller warships and do what they could to beef up the *Voyager*'s and the *Rook*'s weapon systems a bit before the fleet would head out. But they could only build the ships so fast, even with the help of the Synths.

"We aren't going to have all eight destroyers ready for you," said Admiral Bailey. "I only want you to stick around until ship number four is complete, which won't take that long now."

They nodded grimly. It had been nearly a year since they'd left New Eden. Undoubtedly, the Zodarks would have reinforced the system—the question was by how much.

"What about transports for the ground force?" asked Halsey next. She was already trying to plan ahead, beyond the initial battle to secure the system.

"That's going to fall to us," Bailey responded. "The TPA doesn't have any orbital assault ships like we do. They'll be sending a squadron of eight heavy transports to carry additional soldiers, but they won't be able to assault the planet, not like we can. We're going to send everything we have.

"The *Voyager* will deliver a full battalion of Deltas. We've got three other orbital assaulters right now that can deliver three Republic Army battalions each, and their accompanying equipment. That'll give us seven battalions that can hit the planet at once. Beyond that, the heavy transports will be carrying another twenty-one battalions that'll have to be ferried to the orbital assaulters or wait until we get a space elevator constructed," Bailey explained. This was by far the largest troop deployment they'd ever attempted: twenty-four thousand soldiers across twelve light-years.

"Are we going to bring any combat Synth units with us?" asked Hunt, not sure if he should bring them up or not, as he'd only just been read on to the covert program a week ago.

Bailey sat back in his chair for a moment, eyeing Hunt and Halsey before he replied. "We thought about it. If it were my decision, we would. But I've been overruled for the time being. Let's see how things work out on New Eden with the RASs and Deltas. I'm confident our soldiers will be up to the task. The units that have been slated to deploy are currently being put through their paces, training against the Zodarks on a near-constant basis in the simulators. They'll be about as ready as we can get them for the real deal."

Hunt nodded. "OK, then when do we leave?"

Admiral Bailey chuckled. "We're still a few months out," he replied. "The *Rook* and *Voyager* are still having their main magrail turrets and loading systems swapped out for the larger-caliber thirty-six-inch shells. They're also being outfitted with the new Havoc missiles and given a complement of sixteen variable nuclear warheads per ship."

Captain Hunt grunted. For better or worse, the *Rook* and the *Voyager* were going to be the capital ships of this fleet. As such, they were being outfitted with the most firepower possible to ensure they won the day.

As the meeting ended, Bailey asked Hunt to stay behind for a minute. When Halsey and a couple of their staffers had left, Bailey motioned for Hunt to follow him over to his private study. It was a small room that connected with his main office.

Inside the room, several large bookshelves were built into the wall. There was also a fireplace, which seemed odd, considering they were in Florida. In front of the fireplace were a couple of overstuffed leather chairs and a table between them.

"Take a seat, Miles. I want to talk to you about something that's come to my attention," Bailey said as he motioned for Captain Hunt to sit.

Bailey turned on the electric fireplace and sat down. The two didn't say anything for a few minutes; they just watched the artificial flames dance. Bailey finally sighed. "Miles, what's going on with you?" he asked in a soft, almost fatherly voice. "Since you've returned from the Rhea system, you haven't been yourself."

Hunt was taken aback by the question; he immediately felt a little defensive. "I'm not sure I know what you mean, sir."

"Miles, it's just the two of us. No *sir*, no *Admiral*. When I promoted your XO, Commander Longman, to take over command of the destroyer squadron, he mentioned you had been going through a rough time. Are things OK with you and Lilly or the kids? Is there something I can do to help you?"

"After all I've done to help Asher," Hunt muttered hotly to himself.

"Hey, it's not his fault, Miles. He greatly respects you. He considers you a great friend and mentor. He's just concerned for you. What's going on? How can I help you, Miles?" Bailey countered in a calm, reassuring manner.

Hunt suddenly let his body fall deeper into the chair. He took in a breath and held it for a moment, trying to hold it together. The last thing he wanted to do was cry in front of the fleet admiral, even if he was a friend.

Bailey reached a hand out and touched Hunt's arm. "It's OK, Miles. You've been through a lot. You can talk to me—I won't judge. I'm here to help."

Hunt continued staring at the flames as he spoke. "During the battle with that Zodark ship, I had been so focused on the battle going on…I wasn't staying on top of the damage the ship was taking. I was more interested in destroying that enemy vessel than in protecting my own ship or staying abreast of the damage we were sustaining. I lost a quarter of my crew, Chester. Men and women who trusted me with their lives, families who lost a loved one because of my orders…I failed them, Chest. I failed to save more of them…"

"No, Miles, you didn't fail them, and you certainly didn't kill them," Bailey replied. "The Zodarks killed them. The Zodarks are responsible for their deaths, not you. You did what every ship captain must do, fight and win. You have a command staff. It's their responsibility to handle the damage control duties. It's your job to fight the ship and ensure you guys survive and win. Had you not done that, Miles, your entire crew may have been lost. You did what we've trained you to do, and I couldn't be prouder of you."

Captain Hunt wiped away a tear. "Thank you, Chester, I think I just needed to hear that."

"Look, Miles, we're sending you back into battle soon. You're going to lose more sailors and soldiers. We're about to fight a savage new species we still know very little about. As much as it pains me to say this, we're going to lose a lot of good people in the coming days. Unfortunately, this is part of the job of being in command, ordering people into positions and situations where you know many of them may not come back. It's unfortunate, but it's going to happen. With this new war we find ourselves in, it's going to happen a lot more."

He paused. "I can also tell you this, Miles. You aren't the only one who's going to struggle with this. I'm going to need you to be strong for your officers. They're going to be experiencing the same things you are. They're going to be looking to you for leadership and guidance. You need to stay strong, and you need to be there for them, just as I'm here for you, OK? Can you do that for me, Miles?"

Not saying anything for a minute, Hunt turned to look at his friend. "I can, and I will. Thank you, sir. Thank you for talking with me and giving me some perspective."

****

Mars Orbital Station
RNS *Rook*

The small shuttlecraft hovered a thousand meters from the bow of the *Rook*. Captain Hunt and a couple of inspectors peered out the windows at the forward starboard section of the ship. This was where the Zodarks' pulse beam had torn a gash in the *Rook*'s armor and hull. It had taken the engineers close to five months to rebuild this part of the ship. Using the searchlights to illuminate that section of the ship, they could see it looked good as new.

They continued to move along the starboard side of the ship as they inspected the next section of the hull. While they were completing the final outer hull inspection, the crews were working feverishly inside to complete the armament upgrades. A lot had changed in that department since their last foray into the Rhea system. They had more than a few nasty surprises in store for the Zodarks.

****

During the five months in the drydock, the *Rook* had been given a considerable boost in firepower. They'd swapped out the twenty-four-inch magrails for thirty-six-inch guns to give them more hitting power. The fifty percent increase in size allowed them to incorporate a revolutionary new design into the weapon.

One of the R&D engineers at BlueOrigin happened to be a bit of a historical weapons nut. One evening, while watching the History Channel, he had seen an episode about the first Gulf War, when a coalition of nations had joined forces against the government of Iraq to oust them from Kuwait. The episode talked about how the Americans had taken what were essentially unguided dumb bombs and attached a kit to them that turned them into guidable smart munitions.

The following day, the engineer had looked at the new thirty-six-inch shell they were adding to the *Rook* and the *Voyager*. Thinking about the episode from the previous night, the engineer tried to figure out how he could turn an unguided magrail projectile into a guidable high-explosive penetrator. Then it dawned on him: if he leveraged the same amount of explosives from the previous smaller shells, it'd give him just enough room inside the body of the shell to insert a small canister of compressed air.

Next, the engineer looked at the shell itself. If he carved some grooves into the rear section of the shell, he could create a means of steering the projectile once it was fired by using a small cannister of compressed air. Next, he had to develop a guidance system on the nose of the slug that could survive the high-powered magnet used to hurl the projectile down the barrel at incredible speeds. To compensate for this, he sheathed the tip in a steel core specially designed to peel off once it had been fired. This would allow the guidance system to receive a short microburst message from the ship, assigning it a target. As the projectile flew toward the enemy, it could make microadjustments to its trajectory with the compressed air to give it a better chance of hitting the target.

At first, no one had thought it would work, but once it had been tested a few times, they'd only had to make a couple of adjustments and it was done. They'd officially found a way to turn a dumb round into a guidable projectile.

****

The inspector flying in the shuttle with Hunt maneuvered them deftly around the huge ship to the next section. "I don't envy you, Captain, having to go fight the Zodarks and all. But these upgrades should allow you to give 'em hell." As he spoke, the Musk Industry inspector electronically signed off on his portion of the paperwork.

Nodding in agreement, Hunt took the tablet and added his signatures to the inspection. *Outer hull repairs are complete. Turret upgrades are complete. Just need to take on our new ordnance, replenish the ship and wait for the rest of the crew to arrive.*

"Here you go, Bob. I think everything looks good. Please tell your men we appreciate all the hard work on this. We brought you a beat-up ship, and you guys got her repaired and ready for battle in under thirteen months. Quite an accomplishment," Hunt said with satisfaction as he handed the inspector his tablet back. The electronic forms would be sent to their headquarters, where they'd be forwarded on to Space Command for final payment.

"Just keep those bastards away from us, Captain. We've all worked too hard these last fifty years to build a piece of heaven out here in the stars. I'd hate to see what we worked for all lost to some hostile alien race," the man said somberly.

The shuttle then returned to the *Rook* and docked. The pilot expertly guided them to the hangar bay. Once inside, the magnetic landing gear fastened to the floor of the landing bay, holding it in place while the outer doors were closed. Then the bay repressurized, and the shuttle pulled inside the main hangar of the ship with the others. It was a somewhat cumbersome process of transiting shuttles from the inner hangar to the outer launch bays and back. However, it was currently the only way they'd been able to devise to retrieve and launch ships aside from having them attached to the outer hull. The orbital assault ships used that method, but not the conventional warships like the *Rook*.

****

Two days later, a transport arrived from Earth, ferrying the last of the crew to the ship. The *Rook* was fully loaded down with their provisions, weapons, fuel, ammunition, and now the crew. They were ready.

Hunt sat in his office, going over the personnel files of the new officers and enlisted he'd been assigned. Unfortunately, a lot of his original officers had been either promoted or transferred off his ship to take up commands or senior positions on the eight new destroyers.

A total of four destroyers had been finished and would be traveling with the *Rook* and the *Voyager* to New Eden. The other four would be out of the shipyard within a month. Those ships would stay in Sol, along with the *Rook*'s sister ship, the RNS *Bishop*.

The *Bishop* was only the second battlecruiser to be built. Space Command had looked at building a small fleet of them, but given the Zodark threat, the Navy was now focusing on building battleships and frigates. Hunt hoped they'd keep building battlecruisers like the *Rook* and the *Bishop*; they needed a midsize warship to help fill the gaps, but he wasn't in charge of procurements or fleet operations, so those decisions were outside of his control.

The one saving grace Hunt had was that they had left him his tactical officer, Commander Fran McKee. Fleet HQ had wanted to promote her to take over as a captain of one of the new destroyers, but he had made the case that he needed at least one senior officer with experience from the last fight. Tactical was going to be the most critical function for this next mission, and it was a position he couldn't go without. At the same time, he didn't want to hurt her promotional opportunities in the future, so he finagled it so she'd be dual-hatted as his XO. He'd also made a secret deal with Admiral Bailey for her to take over as the CO for the *Rook* when he took command of one of the new ships being constructed.

Despite them not having all the raw materials to complete the new battleships, Musk Industries had already started construction on six of them, along with twenty additional destroyers. BlueOrigin had been contracted to build forty new orbital assault troopships along with coming up with the design for a new carrier. Both contracts were daunting jobs, but they had to be completed.

Knocking on the door frame to Hunt's office, Commander McKee asked, "Penny for your thoughts on the new crew members?" She walked up to his desk and then took a seat at one of the chairs in front of it. The two of them had now worked together for nearly three and a half years. They'd developed an excellent professional relationship.

Hunt shrugged at the question. "I miss our old crew, but I understand the need for the transfers. We need these other ships to have some experienced officers and enlisted as well."

"I'm more concerned with how it may affect our ability to fight the *Rook*," Commander McKee said, putting her own two cents in. "This isn't like the first time we traveled to New Eden, Captain. On our maiden voyage as a crew, we had six and a half months to run them through constant drills and keep them sharp. Now we'll be arriving in New Eden in eighteen days whether we're ready to fight or not."

Hunt smirked. "Well, then, XO, it'll be your job to whip them into shape, won't it?"

She smiled back. "I suppose it will be, sir. So, if you don't mind me asking, what do you think we'll encounter when we arrive in the system?"

Hunt thought about that for a moment. "That's a good question, Fran. We'll either arrive in the system and find they beefed it up, or we'll arrive and see they're just as unprepared as they were last time."

She bit her lower lip. "Well, I guess we'll see in three weeks, won't we?"

Hunt nodded. "All right, XO, I think it's time we got this ship underway, don't you? We need to head over to Earth and pick up the rest of our fleet. They want us to ship out in four days."

The two of them left his office and headed to the bridge. It took them another twenty minutes to get the ship ready to leave the station. They had to seal the vessel up and disconnect from their berth. Then they had to wait for a tug to help push them away from the station before they could light up their engines.

Two hours later, the *Rook* was finally a safe enough distance from the orbital station for them to initiate their MPD thrusters. Once they got the engines fired up and ready, they headed toward Earth. At maximum speed, it'd take them six hours to travel the distance. Not too long compared to what it had been even ten years ago. They could use the FTL and arrive in a single minute, but Hunt wanted the extra time for his crew to start gelling and getting a feel for their new home away from home.

As they approached Earth, the sight of the fleet almost took Hunt's breath away. Over the years, he'd seen the size and number of spacefaring ships continue to increase, but what he saw before him was incredible. The fleet was massive, unlike anything he had seen assembled before. There was the *Voyager*, the four new destroyer-class ships, three orbital assaulter troopships, and eight heavy transports, courtesy of the TPA. For their part, they were also sending two of their own warships, but these would mostly be held back to protect the heavy transports.

"That's a hell of a fleet," Commander McKee exclaimed as she sat at the tactical station.

"Fifteen ships in all—Earth's first-ever military fleet," Hunt said more to himself than anyone else. The others on the bridge were just as impressed as he was.

"We're receiving a message from the *Voyager*," announced Lieutenant Molly Branson, his new communications officer. "Admiral Halsey sends her regards and welcomes us to the fleet. She said we'll be leaving in twenty-four hours."

"Very well, send our regards. Tell them we'll be ready," Hunt replied nonchalantly. He was doing his best to remain calm and stoic. This was a critical moment in human history. They were about to embark upon a campaign to conquer a new planet and establish their first-ever forward military outpost on the outskirts of a galactic empire they knew very little about.

The rest of the day was spent getting the ship ready for their final departure. Crewmen sent out their final messages to their loved ones, checked over equipment one last time, and made sure the ship would be ready to depart when the order came.

The following day, the armada of fifteen ships lined up. They were going to collectively jump to New Eden. It would take them twelve days to reach the planet. Their new FTL system could now travel one light-year per day, a far cry from the time it used to take before their integration of the Sumerian technology.

"Captain, we're receiving a message from the *Voyager*. They're sending over a new time hack. We're to commence FTL travel in thirty minutes," announced Lieutenant Branson.

Nodding at the information, Hunt replied, "Very well, acknowledge receipt of the message and time hack. Navigation, plot us a course to

New Eden. Helm, shut down the MPD thrusters and begin preparations for FTL travel."

With his initial set of orders issued, it was now time to wait for what would be an incredible new chapter in human history: the order to invade and capture their first occupied system.

****

The Rhea System
RNS *Rook*

"We're coming out of FTL now, Captain," Lieutenant Donaldson, the helmsman, called out as the warp bubble around the ship collapsed.

Captain Miles Hunt stood up from his chair as he addressed his bridge crew. "OK, people, it's go time. Transfer full power to our active sensors. Ping the entire system for any signs of electronic activity. Pay special attention to New Eden and its moons. If there's a Zodark ship in this system, I want it found. Let's go Zodark hunting!"

Coms officer Molly Branson got his attention. "Captain, we're receiving a message from the *Voyager*," she said. "Admiral Halsey says they're moving toward New Eden now. She's requesting that we advance at maximum speed ahead of the assault fleet and pave the way for them."

Turning to her, Hunt replied, "Acknowledge the order, and let them know we're advancing to contact now." Hunt then turned to his helmsman. "Donaldson, bring us to full speed and head toward New Eden."

As the ship increased speed, the crew felt a slight vibration as the thrusters reacted to the increase in power. Earth's most powerful warship raced ahead of the assault force.

For the next thirty minutes, the crew could do little but wait for some of their sensor signals to start feeding them data. Their electronic sensor suite had been fully extended, allowing the ship to soak up as much information as possible from the myriad of electronic pings they were emanating as they approached the planet. If there was a ship or any electronic signatures in the system, they'd find it.

Commander Fran McKee asked the navigation officer a few workstations down from her, "How long until we're in orbit?"

"At present speed, we're two hours out," replied Lieutenant Hightower.

Tim Hightower was one of the original crew from their last venture into this system. He had an excellent working knowledge of where they were going, which was helpful, considering they were fully expecting a fight.

"Captain! We're getting our first signal returns," Commander McKee suddenly announced, concern in her voice. "It appears there are two Zodark ships in the system. One is breaking orbit from New Eden, and another was in orbit around one of her moons. They both appear to be heading toward us now."

The Earth fleet had only been in the system for sixty-eight minutes before the Zodarks had detected them. "Very well. Let the war begin," Captain Hunt said as he clenched his fists.

From the Authors

Miranda and I hope you've enjoyed this book as much as we have loved writing it. The series continues on with *Into the Battle*, which picks up right where this book ended. You can purchase or download the next book today.

In case you haven't found it yet, we have an exciting Facebook page for the series and a private reader group you can join where we regularly provide readers the opportunity to name characters, ships, and give early feedback on chapters for the coming books. You can follow the series page on Facebook, Friends of the Republic, or you can jump into the action by joining our series reader group, Members of the Republic.

We have really valued connecting with our readers via social media. We also have a general Facebook page, https://www.facebook.com/RosoneandWatson/. Sometimes we ask for help from our readers as we write future books—we love to draw upon all your different areas of expertise. We also have a group of beta readers who get to look at the books before they are officially published and help us fine-tune last-minute adjustments. If you would like to be a part of this team, please go to our author website, and send us a message through the "Contact" tab.

In addition to the military sci-fi series you are currently reading, we also have a gripping military technothriller series called the Monroe Doctrine. In this series, we explore what the future of modern warfare may look like as the use of autonomous and semi-autonomous drones, artificial intelligence, and machine learning shape the battlefields of the future. You can learn more about this series on Amazon.

If you would like to stay up to date on new releases and receive emails about any special pricing deals we may make available, please sign up for our email distribution list. Simply go to https://www.frontlinepublishinginc.com/ and sign up.

If you enjoy audiobooks, we have a great selection that has been created for your listening pleasure. Our entire Red Storm series and our Falling Empire series have been recorded, and several books in our Rise of the Republic series and our Monroe Doctrine series are now available. Please see below for a complete listing.

As independent authors, reviews are very important to us and make a huge difference to other prospective readers. If you enjoyed this book, we humbly ask you to write up a positive review on Amazon and Goodreads. We sincerely appreciate each person that takes the time to write one.

Nonfiction:

Iraq Memoir 2006–2007 Troop Surge
Interview with a Terrorist (link to audiobook here)

Fiction:

The Monroe Doctrine Series
Volume One (link to audiobook here)
Volume Two (link to audiobook here)
Volume Three (link to audiobook here)
Volume Four (link to audiobook here)
Volume Five (link to audiobook here)
Volume Six (available for preorder)
Volume Seven (available for preorder)

Rise of the Republic Series
Into the Stars (link to audiobook here)
Into the Battle (link to audiobook here)
Into the War (link to audiobook here)
Into the Chaos (link to audiobook here)
Into the Fire (link to audiobook here)
Into the Calm (audiobook still in production)
Into the Terror (available for preorder)

Apollo's Arrows Series (co-authored with T.C. Manning)
Cherubim's Call

Crisis in the Desert Series (co-authored with Matt Jackson)
Project 19 (link to audiobook here)
Desert Shield
Desert Storm

Falling Empires Series

Rigged (link to audiobook here)
Peacekeepers (link to audiobook here)
Invasion (link to audiobook here)
Vengeance (link to audiobook here)
Retribution (link to audiobook here)

Red Storm Series
Battlefield Ukraine (link to audiobook here)
Battlefield Korea (link to audiobook here)
Battlefield Taiwan (link to audiobook here)
Battlefield Pacific (link to audiobook here)
Battlefield Russia (link to audiobook here)
Battlefield China (link to audiobook here)

Michael Stone Series
Traitors Within (link to audiobook here)

World War III Series
Prelude to World War III: The Rise of the Islamic Republic and the Rebirth of America (link to audiobook here)
Operation Red Dragon and the Unthinkable (link to audiobook here)
Operation Red Dawn and the Siege of Europe (link to audiobook here)
Cyber Warfare and the New World Order (link to audiobook here)

Children's Books:
My Daddy has PTSD
My Mommy has PTSD

Abbreviation Key

AC	Alpha Centauri
AG	Antigravity
AGS	Artificial Gravity System
AI	Artificial Intelligence
CIC	Combat Information Center
CMS	Commercial Mining Ship
DARPA	Defense Advanced Research Projects Agency
DZ	Drop Zone
ELINT	Electronic Intelligence
EM	Electromagnetic
EMP	Electromagnetic Pulse
EVA	Extravehicular Activity (suits made for being outside a spaceship)
EWO	Electronics Warfare Officer
FRAGO	Fragmentation Order (change in orders)
FTL	Faster-than-light
GEU	Greater European Union
GQ	General Quarters
HUD	Heads-Up Display
JSOC	Joint Special Operations Command
KIA	Killed in Action
LOAC	Laws of Armed Conflict
MA	Master-at-Arms
MASINT	Measurement and Signature Intelligence (often includes radar, acoustic, nuclear and chemical and biological intelligence)
MOS	Mars Orbital Station
MPD	Magnetoplasmadynamic
MRE	Meals Ready to Eat
NASA	National Aeronautics and Space Administration
NL	Neurolink
NOS	Zodark admiral or senior military commander
NRO	National Reconnaissance Office
PA	Personal Assistant
PT	Physical Training
QRF	Quick Reaction Force

R & D	Research and Development
RA	Republic Army
RAS	Republic Army Soldier
RNS	Republic Navy Ship
SAW	Squad Automatic Weapon
SCIF	Secured Comparted Information Facility
SET	Space Exploration Treaty
SF	Special Forces
SW	Sand and Water (missiles)
TPA	Tri-Parte Alliance
UK	United Kingdom
VR	Virtual Reality
XO	Commanding Officer

Made in the USA
Coppell, TX
14 March 2024